"You spoil me too much, you magnificent man.
Mirella said. **"I think you may have**
ruined me. . . ."

They sat opposite each other in the hot water, made satiny smooth with oil of lily of the valley and orange blossoms. Looking into the mirror that the maid brought, Mirella was stunned. She could have been an odalisque, with her hair wrapped in a glamorous turban of gold lamé, her deep violet eyes aflame with a heat she could not disguise.

Her fair skin shone like flesh–colored marble from the bath oil. She held the mirror now in front of herself in one hand, while with the other she caressed her shoulders and fondled her heavy, glowing breasts. She was mesmerized by the woman she saw, by the beauty, the erotic being her lover tirelessly seemed able to realize in her. She loved this image that was his handiwork.

"You really would like to turn me into something as exotic and remarkable as your sexual slave, wouldn't you?" she asked.

"With the adventuring gift you have for the erotic, of course, I would like nothing better than to enslave you. I wonder if there is any erotic act to which you would not give yourself up completely, if you did love me. After every sexual encounter we have, I see you wanting to go further, wanting me to push you that much closer to submitting totally to eros in me. Only time will reveal which of us will break or try to run. . . ."

SOFT
WARM
RAIN

Roberta
Latow

BANTAM BOOKS
TORONTO · NEW YORK · LONDON · SYDNEY · AUCKLAND

SOFT WARM RAIN
A Bantam Book / March 1986

Grateful acknowledgment is made for permission to reprint the following:

"September 1903," from Edmund Keely and Philip Sherard, trans. C.P. Cavafy: Collected Poems, ed. George Savadis. Translation copyright © 1975 by Edmund Keely and Philip Sherard. Reprinted by permission of Princeton University Press in the U.S.A., the Philippines and Canada. Reprinted by permission of The Hogarth Press in the United Kingdom.

ISBN 0-553-25452-9

Published simultaneously in the United States and Canada

Bantam Books are published by Bantam Books, Inc. Its trademark, consisting of the words "Bantam Books" and the portrayal of a rooster, is Registered in U.S. Patent and Trademark Office and in other countries. Marca Registrada. Bantam Books, Inc., 666 Fifth Avenue, New York, New York 10103.

PRINTED IN THE UNITED STATES OF AMERICA

H   0 9 8 7 6 5 4 3 2 1

For
Yvry and Hamish
and
the man who took me to Turkey
Jason

To have been so close so many times
to those sensual eyes, those lips,
to that body I dreamed of, loved—
so close so many times.

—C. P. CAVAFY

Mirella Wingfield arrived at the reception alone. Mirella Wingfield usually arrived alone at weddings, funerals, cocktail parties, bar mitzvahs, fund-raising functions, and intimate dinner parties.

She was the perfect *single woman* guest. Men liked and admired her for her dazzlingly erotic beauty, brilliant mind, wit, charm, success, and independence. Women liked her because she dressed down her stunning good looks, never posed a threat to them, was wrapped up in her work, uninterested in man-hunting, was a Massachusetts Wingfield—a plus on anyone's guest list—and was always hard to get.

Mirella handed her engraved invitation to the steward, who discreetly announced her to her host, the secretary general of the United Nations. Javier Pérez de Cuéllar greeted her warmly, then introduced her to the king and queen. She curtsied, walked down the receiving line, and paused to talk with Kurt Waldheim, the former secretary general. Suddenly a flurry of sharply dressed, clean-shaven, good-looking men with short haircuts pushed their way through the entrance, and surrounded the reception committee. It was all very Secret Service, very Washington, very White House.

All the scene needed, Mirella thought, was Ed McMahon, delivering that old melodious announcement: "and here's"—not Johnny, as in the Johnny Carson show, but—"*Nancy.*" And it was.

Nancy Reagan stood at the beginning of the reception line, accompanied by her walker, Jerry Zipkin, and her girlfriend, Betsy Bloomingdale, and more Secret Service agents.

Dressed in an elegant Galanos gown, the First Lady looked like a fashionable, anorexic teenager in sixty-five-year-old skin. Mirella always thought Nancy Regan seemed rather like a coat hanger with a Barbie doll head and lots of changes of clothes. That image was belied, though, by one glimpse of Nancy's chin. If only the President had a chin as determined as his wife's! Yet there *was* something sweet and nice though voiceless that floated off her, easily accounting for her appeal to American women. After all, Mirella thought, she looked the way they strove to look. In addition, she had what so many of them believed they wanted: a figure, a man, clothes, money, position, power.

Obviously happy to be just a guest for a change, Nancy Reagan waved and smiled vaguely at everyone nearby before she and her friends started to greet the dignitaries in the receiving line. As the Reagan party moved, Mirella was discreetly but firmly pushed from the end of the line and out into the whirl of the party.

The party in the living room of the secretary general's penthouse was in honor of a Middle Eastern king and his American wife. The king was scheduled to address the General Assembly the next day, and because of his power as a potential peacemaker in his troubled region of the world, this was an especially select event.

Mirella moved through the crowded center of the room. The huge windows permitted magnificent views of Manhattan from this perch atop the slim, glass-walled United Nations building. There was the sparkling river to the east, the lights of the posh Upper East Side to the north and of the bustling sections of Manhattan to the west and south. The night was clear and the city lights and stars seemed to melt together, twinkling like massive diamonds on black velvet. There was nearly as much glitter within the huge apartment. It radiated from the guests and from the delicacies and decoration in the impressive rooms.

Gorgeous, full-blown white lilacs and huge pink and scarlet peonies were arranged with stalks of lime-green foliage in baroque silver cachepots, dozens of candles burned in branched candelabras. Three long tables swathed in crisp linen formed a U-shaped buffet with each of its side tables boasting an imposing swan, four feet high and carved from a block of crystal-clear ice. Within deep grooves fashioned like the feathers of their wings, the swans proffered pounds of the best black beluga caviar. Galantines of duck and stacks of tiny grilled quail teased the palate alongside pyramids of huge succulent shrimp and whole poached salmon swimming on lakes of *sauce verte*. Mirella smiled when she noted the absence of the hams and suckling pig dressed with fresh white daisies about its neck that had been featured at the last party the secretary general had given, for a Scandinavian diplomat. The menu for tonight's feast clearly had been planned to respect the religious dietary laws of both the honored guest and his avowed enemies. Ironic, Mirella thought, that Arab and Jew could agree only on this one fundamental thing in life.

As she shook her head, she caught a glimpse through a wide arch of the next room. There, silver-leafed ballroom chairs with kidskin seats encircled small round tables draped in snowy damask. The place settings of silver and crystal sparkled in the enchanting light of tall white candles in towering candelabras twined with ropes of delicate foliage, wild violets, and tiny mauve cyclamen. Tucked into a cut-glass cooler on each table was a magnum of chilled Roederer crystal champagne.

The assembled guests were as amazing as every other aspect of the party, and included some of the most powerful delegates to the United Nations.

Looking glum, dumpy, and square in double-breasted suits made of coarse brown wool, rows of large Kremlin medals plastered across their wide chests, the Russians salivated not over food, but over the delectable young women in the room. They stood in clumps mopping their moist, pudgy faces with large, rough white cotton handkerchiefs while belting back straight vodkas and mumbling *na zdorovye* to each other.

The American delegates had all brought their wives, who stuck to them like Siamese twins. They were handsome, powerful-looking couples, well-dressed, well-pressed, and well-spoken. They could have passed as retired athletes who ate the great American low-cal breakfast, ran the marathon, and oozed sincerity along with belief in the Stars and Stripes forever . . . and nothing else.

The delegation from Japan was large. Both men and women were elegant, amiable, yet distant. The women were dressed by Balmain, Dior, and Lagerfeld, and carried Gucci handbags. Quiescent samurais of the 1980's, the men were handsome, in well-tailored dark silk suits. They mingled, almost tinkled, through the crowd.

The French women delegates all looked like intellectual versions of Jeanne Moreau. They wore Chanel evening suits with long skirts, and Cartier gold jewelry, while their dapper male colleagues were dressed in Armani suits and Sulka ties and hid their acutely sharp minds and greedy acquisitive natures behind handsome dark looks and roving bedroom eyes. They mixed well among the guests, gave a raised eyebrow of surprise and approval to the lavish elegance and quality of the buffet, and spoke nothing but French to everyone.

The Germans were very *Cherman*. One could see by their looks—just a little too Aryan—and by the cloak of superiority they wore as they clicked heels in time to the short, sharp, clipped drop of the head (the old Prussian bow), and kissed only the most beautiful ladies' hands that they had indeed forgotten the First *and* the Second World Wars.

But for the Israeli delegates the Second World War—rather, the Holocaust—could not, would not, be forgotten. Here in this setting, though, the Israelis seemed like well-dressed New Yorkers with Yiddish accents. They spoke several languages fluently, switching from one to the other with ease as they mingled with guests, talking in a friendly but somewhat socially aggressive manner . . . unlike the English, whose large delegation hardly spoke or moved at all.

The English men wore suits from Savile Row, and were handsome, courtly, and reserved. They had some of the most naturally beautiful women in the world on their arms: English beauties who, following their fashion-conscious future queen, were dressed in silk taffeta with puffed sleeves and a bow on the shoulder, the bosom, or the cuff. Like stately English swans they wore three-strand pearl chokers, the family gem set in a clasp at the front and center, on their long aristocratic necks.

There were black Africans from Nigeria, the Sudan, Kenya, Liberia, speaking the accented English of Oxford, Cambridge, or Sandhurst, and wearing their national dress, military dress, or old school ties with impeccable suits from their London tailors.

The Arab bloc represented every country in the Middle East and numbered as many as all the other guests put together. They were a dark, sultry group of men, ranging from handsome to ugly, and they reeked of power, heady perfume, money, and good Western educations. They brought few wives but many beautiful, long-legged, blonde, bejeweled mistresses dressed by Saint Laurent, Givenchy, and Pierre Cardin. All smiles, charm, and caution, they drank nothing but fresh orange juice.

In a smaller room being used as a bar, Peter Duchin was playing Cole Porter tunes on a white baby grand piano. The romantic, sophisticated music dampened the sound of chatter, the tinkling of silverware against crystal. It was hardly one of the United Nations budget public functions one expected and loathed, but attended out of respect for the organization, its aspirations, and its world-weary, hard-working delegates. It was more like a private affair because only the most senior delegates were invited, and more, because Wynn Taggart, a middle-aged Texas millionairess with aspirations to an embassy all her own, had organized the evening and would pick up the tab.

A devout Republican, girlfriend of Nancy Reagan—which accounted for the First Lady's presence—sponsor on a grand scale (said to be in the millions) of Ronald Reagan's presidential campaigns, Wynn was a social animal with sharp intelligence and a great deal of ambition. She added new dimensions to a United Nations party: money, opulence, young and pretty women dressed in American couture and Texas-sized jewels, fun, and a buzz.

And because of her quest nothing was too extravagant for Wynn Taggart, nor too small a detail for her to pay attention to. The waiters, for example. Not trusting the regular channels at the U.N. to secure the highly efficient, supremely deferential male waiters she considered requisite for one of her premier parties, she had even had Chicano men brought up from her ranch in Texas to serve. Dressed in black trousers, red cummerbunds, and short white jackets, they waited on the guests in just the manner Wynn Taggart thought they should. Now they were passing trays laden with delicate puff-pastry hors d'oeuvres or a selection of manhattans, martinis, margaritas, whiskies, bourbons, and, of course, straight vodkas for the Russians. Other waiters wandered about with jeroboams of pink champagne, refilling empty glasses. And still others offered fresh fruit juices, Malvern water, and Perrier for the nondrinkers.

Mirella had seen it all many times before—this passing parade of world diplomats at play—but never quite as it was tonight. American women like Mrs. Taggart—smart, chic, knowing all the right things and doing them to get a place in the international world of politics—were becoming a force. Throughout the room there were other ultraslim, almost frail, exquisitely dressed and bejeweled millionaire widows from Chicago, Cleveland, San Francisco, and Palm Beach, who loved being around power, and being part of the international political system. It was as if Nancy Reagan's girlfriends were taking over the world.

Because of her job, Mirella had become part of the U.N. social scene in the last few years, but she had never been comfortable with it. As a woman working an average of twelve hours a day in one of the most important jobs at the U.N., she found it difficult, nearly impossible, to accept that the social scene played a major role in world politics. But she knew it did.

Mirella said hello to a few colleagues, took a martini from one of the trays, and allowed Lord and Lady Beeley, old friends of hers, to usher her into a group that stood listening to Nancy Kissinger, Henry's wife, telling Jackie Onassis, Sheik Yamani, Abba Eban, and Lord Carrington her impressions of the present crisis in Central America.

She took a sip of the martini, and felt the bite of the gin in her mouth. She loved that first taste of ice-cold gin that warmed with its coldness and gave an immediate pick-up, a momentary surge of well-being. It worked as always and she suddenly felt relaxed and joyful.

Just as dinner was announced her eyes inadvertently met those of a handsome, black-haired diplomat standing in a group of people a few yards away from her. He was sending out waves of sexual confidence to her, unspoken whispers that thundered, "I can take you, conquer you, possess you, show you what a real man is." He had black, dreamy eyes that revealed his desire to practice bizarre sexual acts on her and act out lewd fantasies with her.

She gave him a look of complete disdain, not because he was interested in her but because he wasn't . . . except sexually. She sighed heavily, as she tried to remember the last time she had met a man on the make who cared anything for her beyond the size of her breasts, how accomplished she was at fellatio, and what job she held.

She bit the inside of her lip and lowered her eyes to avoid that gaze of his which stripped her naked. What a bore, she thought. They never changed, these high-ranking foreign diplomats. They were always trying to show their mettle in bed, so anxious were they to be known in discreet whispers as cock-of-the-walk in this international political arena overlooking the East River. She wondered if their conquests in bed made them feel more potent in the General Assembly Hall. What a charade!

She smiled to herself as she raised her eyes again, making sure not to look in the diplomat's direction. She wondered how many senior United Nations delegates she had managed to sidestep these past fifteen years while working her way up the ranks to her present position as assistant director of translations.

If she included the attachés who were sent forth to procure her, and who then made a pitch for her themselves, Mirella Wingfield figured she had rejected the entire international political world once, and representatives of France, the Middle East, and Africa at least twice. Some would say this was quite a sacrifice for not wanting to mix one's job with sex, but Mirella wouldn't.

The party was a great success. Not for one minute did the excitement flag. Protocol dictated that the guests remain until the king and queen left, which they did, long after midnight. Then people slowly started drifting home.

Donald Davies and Ahmed Sahid Whabi were just leaving when Donald saw Arthur Goldberg deep in conversation with Mirella Wingfield. At least he thought it was Mirella Wingfield. He paused and studied the woman with the silky shoulder-length raven-black hair worn in a well-cut bob. The hair was a perfect frame for her beautiful oval face. It accentuated the high cheekbones, the large seductive deep violet eyes, the straight elegant nose, the sculptured jaw line, and the voluptuous lips, which were played down with just a hint of natural-colored lip gloss.

She was dressed in a magnificent cream silk blouse with a low V neck and voluminous balloon sleeves buttoned tight at the wrists. It was tucked into a long wraparound mauve suede skirt that clung to her body and finished at the ankle to show a pair of rust-colored high-heeled calfskin shoes.

Around her slim neck she wore an ancient Mayan necklace. It was a ring of solid gold an inch thick, worn as a choker. From it hung a large flat golden frog that nestled on her bare skin just above her large breasts, made so appealing by the taut silk of her blouse. There was a coolness about her beauty, but an abundance of fertility about it too. She was tall, and she stood proud. There was a grandness about her and a certain presence. She was like fire and ice, and Donald was quite overwhelmed at seeing her again after so many years.

"Forget it, Don," Ahmed said. "I saw her first, spotted her hours ago and asked around about her. She doesn't play on her home ground, and this *is* her home ground. She works here as an executive in one of the departments. Too bad, because I had plans for her," he added with a lascivious glint in his eye.

Donald Davies broke his gaze and smiled at his friend. "You always did have a good eye, Ahmed, but you're wrong. I saw her first. About twenty years ago, in fact. Seeing her again, I'm flooded with all sorts of memories."

"Who is she, Don?"

"She *was* Mirella Wingfield. May still be for all I know. Remember Maxim Wesson Wingfield, who used to lecture on philosophy at Harvard? He was as brilliant as he was odd, and she's his daughter. I knew her when she was at Vassar and in love with a classmate of mine, Paul Prescott. She was terrific. I was besotted by her and her family. They were splendid, impoverished, eccentric Massachusetts aristocracy, living in an earthly paradise called Wingfield Park. I spent a long weekend there once, and never forgot it. It was a wonderful house set in a hundred and forty acres of overgrown gardens, wild woodlands, a lake, and rushing streams. It was an enchanting, mad, wonderful place, filled with family treasures her father inherited. Imagine a collection of Rembrandt drawings, a fine library of rare books, sixty-two vintage cars, ancient samurai armor, lots more . . . and no money."

"How can that be, no money?"

"I know it's hard for you to believe, Ahmed, but there are people who are rich without having any liquid assets. If you had seen the place, you would understand the Wingfields. It was run-down and almost shabby, overrun with Chinese red deer, ducks, geese, and occasionally eminent visitors, when they were allowed admittance. Guests usually ended up polishing a Bugatti, or cooking the dinner, or going shopping, because the Wingfields never thought about things like that."

"How did they manage to keep everything if they had no money? They must have had servants, advisors. How did they survive?" asked Ahmed, who found the idea of being rich without money too impossible to believe.

"Oh, they had helpers. A seventy-year-old English butler, a cook-housekeeper, a gardener, Dr. Wingfield's private-secretary-cum-archivist, a cleaner for the forty-one-room house. There were always people around who attended to all the mundane things of life, while the family pursued what interested them. For the father it was his work, his passion for beautiful women, his daughter, and his wife, in just that order. For the mother—I think Lili was her name, a great beauty of Turkish extraction, who seemed almost pathologically vain, selfish, and self-centered—it was becoming the world's most beautiful concert pianist. For the brother, Lawrence, it was to be a successful criminal lawyer, another Clarence Darrow. And for Mirella it always was to live the great adventure of life, and be able to speak to the world through herself."

Ahmed smiled broadly. "Ah, Don, when I first saw the woman, all I wanted was to fuck her. Here it is the end of the evening, I haven't even met her, never mind fucked her, and I can't wait to meet her family."

The two men laughed at themselves and then stood silent for a few minutes, watching Mirella and Arthur Goldberg, who was clearly enchanted by his conversation with her. He must have said something amusing because a smile slowly broke across her face and she tilted her head up as she laughed.

Donald Davies was besotted by her again. Still watching her, he said to Ahmed, "The Mirella Wingfield I was acquainted with all those years ago was truly her own woman. I think she was the only woman I ever knew who always chose freedom. She was determined to be the master of her fate and the captain of her soul. Way back then, she went beyond the women's libbers of today, without even trying, and without being destructive or aggressive. Oh, and by the way, Ahmed, she is the only really sexually 'liberated' woman I've ever met."

"I guessed that under her cool and arrogant façade beat the heart of a libertine," said Ahmed, clearly self-satisfied at his perceptiveness.

Mirella shook hands with Arthur Goldberg, took her leave of him, and started toward the exit. As Donald realized she was leaving the party, he turned to Ahmed and said, "Look, you go on, I'll meet up with you later at your place, but I must have a word with her at the very least."

"All right, introduce me to her and I promise to leave at once," Ahmed said. Donald agreed and the two men weaved through the thinning crowd to meet her.

Mirella recognized the Arab diplomat as the man who flirted with her earlier in the evening. She was about to give him a withering look and walk past him, when she saw Donald. She stopped, surprised and somewhat confused, because all at once the years rolled backward, memories rushed in, and she recognized him.

She tucked her Loewe rust-colored leather envelope handbag under her arm, stretched out her arms, and placed her hands in his. They looked into each other's eyes and remained silent for what seemed to be an awkward length of time. Ahmed broke the spell by clearing his throat.

"Mirella, how wonderful to see you again," said Donald.

"And you, Donald," she answered.

"Won't you introduce me, Don?" Ahmed asked.

"Oh, I'm so sorry. Mirella, I'd like you to meet an old friend of mine, Prince Ahmed Sahid Whabi, who's one of the Saudi Arabian delegates here at the U.N. Ahmed, I would like you to meet Mirella . . ." He hesitated, not knowing what her last name might be.

"Wingfield," she said. "I'm still Mirella Wingfield."

"I am delighted to meet you, Miss Wingfield. Don is staying with me while he is here in New York. I hope he will bring you to me," said Ahmed, picking her hand up and kissing her fingers.

The kiss sent a shudder of excitement through her. Mirella's gaze met Ahmed's for the second time that evening. A slow lascivious smile crossed his lips and the sensuous eyes grew hard and mean. Mirella felt a momentary surge of pure lust, but then went cold with fear because of what she saw in those eyes. Very slowly she withdrew her hand from his and gave him a knowing smile that told him she would never be his.

"I must go, it's very late," she said, looking now at Donald.

"Mirella, do please let me take you home," Donald insisted.

She nodded her approval and they swiftly parted from Ahmed.

There was an awkward silence between Mirella and Donald as they rode the elevator down to the ground floor. So much so that they both found it embarrassing. He slipped the handsome mauve, pink, and rust suede and knitted-wool jacket he retrieved from the cloakroom for her over her shoulders, remarking, "Who said reunions were easy and fun?"

"Not me," she said. "I've always loathed the idea of a class reunion and now I know why. It's the time-lapse and the different paths you and your old friends have taken, and the fact that all the things you once had in common have changed or disappeared."

"And all the things you want to ask, which seem so relevant when you first meet an old friend, seem irrelevant by the time you get them out of your mouth," he continued.

"And suddenly the element of fear comes into it, and you're not quite sure what the fear is and why you have it, except that you suspect it might have something to do with disappointment," she added.

"And you don't know whose disappointment: yours in yourself and what you have to tell of the years in between your last meeting, or being disappointed by your friend. Or maybe it's just fear of revealing as unfulfilled the dreams you once shared." He smiled wryly as the elevator doors opened. "Yes. Some fun, reunions!"

He slipped his arm through Mirella's and they looked at each other and laughed heartily. They walked quickly through the lobby and through the glass doors of the Secretariat building. Outside, he pulled up short and turned her around to face him.

"Well, fuck it!" he said. "We're too special to let a reunion happen to us. So, for my part—hello, Mirella Wingfield, my name is Donald Davies. I've been a widower for three years. I have six children, a two-thousand-acre ranch in Texas, and twenty-two oil wells, pumping. I spend my life having a good time with naughty friends like Ahmed, when I am not playing father to my children or hustling for aid to the needy in the Third World. I find you very sexy and want to spend the night making wild, passionate love to you. Now you can tell me who you are, where you live, and what you want. But not here. In the taxi."

With that, Donald hurried her from the entrance across the plaza to the sidewalk, where he stood looking up First Avenue for a taxi. The air was warm but the breeze coming off the East River had a chill to it. Traffic was light at that hour and the sound of the city was muffled behind the tall buildings opposite the U.N.

There was something terribly raunchy about the huge dark skyscrapers, the lonely black asphalt of the streets, broken by large potholes and swirling puffs of steam rising from the bowels of the city. A long dark shiny car with a couple in it rushed past, and the silence seemed even deeper when it disappeared. The regiment of street lamps, aiming volleys of eerie blue-white light onto the pavement, made the night scene even more raunchy. It was mysterious, almost surrealistic.

Donald stepped off the curb and hailed a taxi. The driver ignored him. Another sped by, then another, then an empty one, a few hundred yards later. Donald turned back to look at Mirella. He stepped up to her, put his arms under her jacket and around her, and kissed her. His hands caressed her breasts and he kissed her again. He felt her lips tremble and open ever so slightly, the tip of her tongue on his lower lip. Her nipples became erect.

Much as he tried to block out the past, he couldn't, because he had never been sexually sated by a woman since the last time he had had Mirella Wingfield.

He stepped away from her abruptly and into the street. He caught sight of a taxi discharging a fare a long way down the avenue, let out a shrill whistle, and raised his arm. The taxi blinked its headlights, signaling Donald that the car was his. The traffic lights flashed green all the way up the street as far as he could see, and the taxi shot toward them.

Donald put an arm around Mirella's waist and walked her out into the street where the driver stopped for them. He helped her into the backseat, then settled in next to her, picked her hand up in his, and they looked at each other and smiled.

"Where do we go from here?" he asked.

Mirella did not miss the double entendre. She leaned forward, tapped the window dividing them from the taxi driver, and spoke into the grill.

"Good evening," she said pleasantly and gave her address on East Sixty-fifth Street.

"Ya mean good morning, don'tcha? Well, no matter, morning, evening, afternoon, rain or shine, whatever, I'll get ya there," answered the driver, chomping on a huge, smelly cigar. The meter started ticking and off they shot through the littered city.

Mirella leaned back, rolled down the window, and turned to Donald. "Hello, Donald Davies," she said. "My name is Mirella Wingfield. I have never married; I have no children; I live here in New York; I am the assistant director of translations at the United Nations, and I speak French, Turkish, Arabic, and Greek fluently. I am contentedly immersed in the comfortable life I have created for myself. This includes my father, mother, brother, a part-time lover I have had for fifteen years, a few good friends, and the occasional sexual adventure. And the greatest lesson I have learned in life is, *I don't always get what I want.*"

Donald merely smiled then, and these two old friends who were pretending to have just met in order to spare themselves the embarrassment of "reunion" remained silent during the short ride. Still holding her hand, Donald looked at her while she looked out the window as they whizzed by the buildings.

East Sixty-fifth Street was deserted except for the parked cars on both sides of the street. Donald got out first, then helped Mirella out. They stood together beside the open taxi door, still holding hands.

"I am going to ask you once more, Mirella. Where do we go from here?"

And he knew her answer from the kiss she gave him.

2

What woman can ever forget the physical fun, the passion of copulation rooted in real tenderness and warmth that comes from the gut? The scent of a man's naked body entwined with her own, covering her like a second skin? The sheer weight of sensual lust pressing down on her? Exquisite kisses where two mouths become one, where the phallus can vanquish the vagina and there is no victory, only orgasms, powerful and rich, that pour forth immeasurable ecstasy?

No woman.

What *is* forgettable is anything less.

With the tip of his tongue Paul tenderly licked away the froth of his seed from Mirella's lips. He stroked her hair, kissed her eyes, then her mouth. He looked into the deep violet of her eyes and felt himself drowning in her soul. So he ran his fingers through her hair and took a fistful of the black silky strands, pulled tightly and slid on top of her, as if to save his life.

He bruised Mirella's lips with his kisses. That touch of sweet violence that can accompany acute sexual excitement replaced tenderness as he sucked on her nipples and dug his teeth into her breasts. When she called out in a frenzy of passion and pain, he stopped and caressed her, whispering, "I love you, oh, how I wish I didn't love you," as he slid slowly down her body, kissing her everywhere, sucking deeply on mouthfuls of her sweet flesh. He ran his open lips over the soft, silky patch of black pubic hair, pressed his face into it, and became intoxicated with her vaginal scent—more beautiful and erotic for him than any other perfume in the world.

He replaced his mouth with his hands and ran his fingers lightly, teasingly, along her voluptuous closed lips. He toyed with them, at times opening them just wide enough to fondle the soft, moist, deep pink inner lips.

Mirella felt herself giving way, sliding slowly into ecstasy, bliss. Though she remained silent, her body called out for more. It was as if the vaginal mouth he played with had a voice of its own that begged to be opened and heard.

With his thumbs he pulled back the fleshy outer lips, sucked and nibbled on the luscious inner ones, so warm, exotic, and mysterious that he felt himself descending into chasms of desire and lust. He wanted to devour this part of her, eat away her erotic lips, plunge his tongue deeper and deeper, until he could lick the very tip of her womb. Her orgasms filled his mouth until he tasted more of her than he did of himself.

Then, in an instant, she was aware of the change in Paul. Roughly, he pushed her legs farther apart, raised them high above him and pulled her across the mattress to the edge of the bed where he charged into her, rampant, with raging and extravagant sexual lust. Their intercourse became more like a rout, a wild, unlawful act of fucking.

Mirella gasped and whimpered. She could scarcely catch her breath because of the utterly thrilling physical reaction of being flayed raw, made sensitive to the extreme, filled completely by a man's penis, and the seemingly endless release of her own orgasms. Paul, holding her down by the waist, watched her every reaction to him as he drove into her again and again. Then, coming in a crescendo of passion, he called out, like some conquering sexual hero, "To the death."

Sex, for Paul, was death, immortality, assurance of reincarnation, because he rose yet again and again. It was not the great physical fun, the ecstasy like no other for him that it was for her, Mirella thought as she lay pinned under Paul's weight. She could feel his heart racing, pounding on top of her own. Hearts beating, almost but not quite in unison . . . and soon growing calm.

Paul raised himself up over her body, looked down at her, and smiled. He gave her a kiss devoid of the gut-tenderness and warmth she occasionally felt with him, then eased off her body onto his stomach and lay next to her, his head turned away from her. He reached for a cigarette from the pack of

Camels on the table next to the bed, then lit it with his brown enameled Dunhill lighter.

Mirella watched the cigarette smoke rise and curl above his head. She ran her finger lightly down his spine. At the small of his back, she drew a circle with the tip of her long red-lacquered fingernail. Impulsively, she bent down and placed a kiss on the spot, then lay back, covering them both with the fine cream-colored linen sheet.

It was Mirella who broke the silence that separated them. "Sometimes you make me feel like a whore, Paul. Especially at times like this. We've fucked with such passion that I feel we've dissolved into one being, and then you give me a kiss that feels more like a handshake. Why do you look away from me? Are you afraid we might learn more than we want to know about our real feelings for each other?"

Paul remained quite still and silent. Too silent.

"Well, maybe not quite a whore," she added. "More the unkept kept woman, the 1980's version of the mistress. And you, what have you become—my part-time lover-protector, my stud? It makes me wonder what's happening to our feelings for each other."

Paul continued to smoke in silence. Then, with his face still turned away from her, he asked, "What are you trying to say, Mirella? That I don't love you? You know that's not true, and I also know you love me. That we should leave each other? That's foolish; we tried it once and it didn't work. That you don't like sharing me with my wife and family? That is a tedious female rationalization, and, as it happens, a lie. You love your independence, your aloneness when I'm not with you. So, what are you trying to say?"

"I don't even know."

"No, I guess you don't."

Paul took a long pull on his cigarette before stubbing it out in the Lalique ashtray. Slowly he exhaled and turned around onto his side, facing Mirella. He pulled the sheet that covered them away and gathered her in his arms. She leaned against him, and he ran his palm slowly over her breast, along her hip, and moving his hand between the inside of her thighs, he massaged her pussy, warm and wet with their orgasms. But he never looked into her eyes. Paul raised the palm of his hand, covered with the result of their lust, for her to see. He grazed her lips with it.

"Everything," he said, "is illusion, except what you can

see, feel, and touch, grasp in your hand like this." He closed his fingers over his palm. "Even this, when washed away by one of your scented soaps or your emotional thinking process, becomes illusion. Don't think about us, Mirella, or you'll lose me. We are erotic lovers involved in your false belief that love has to be shared, that lovers interchange themselves to their very souls, that a deep and true love can change lives. All illusion.

"You never cease to amaze me, Mirella. For years we can go on, happy in the life we have made with each other, and then you slip, and try to turn us into something banal and bourgeois, fiction."

Paul, still holding Mirella tightly to him, felt her stiffen, grow cold in his arms. He reached down and pulled the sheet over them and, at last looked into her eyes.

He was annoyed with her, but touched, as he always was, by her exquisite natural erotic beauty, and those eyes, which he called the violet mirrors of her soul. Paul Prescott loved Mirella Wingfield for those two things and those two things only. And he hated her because she gave them to him joyfully, willingly, without reservation . . . and held him prisoner by her gifts.

Mirella sighed. It was a sad sigh, one of resignation. She hoped he would say no more. She was sorry he had said as much as he had, but not nearly as sorry as she was for the emptiness she saw in his eyes, and the coldness he carried in his heart.

Only his arms, and the way he cradled her in them, and his hands, and the way they stroked her long lovely raven-black hair, and his fingers tracing the outline of her sensuous, pouting lower lip told her that he would always want to possess her.

She couldn't smile at him, nor could she be angry with him. She could think only that, for better, for worse, he was the man in her life. Then she rationalized in just the way he called "typically female" and that he despised. She reminded herself that she was a free woman and, when the relationship no longer worked, she would leave him. She had been doing that for the last ten years.

Mirella took the hand he was stroking her cheek with by its wrist, turned it over, raised it to her lips, and kissed it. Then she looked him coolly in the eyes and said, "You still have the gift to spellbind with the tongue."

His eyebrow rose and he smiled. "Only the tongue?" he asked.

"No," she said. "There was a time, years ago in college, when it was the tongue, the heart, and sex that kept me spellbound. Now, you're even more clever and generous with your tongue and in sex, but you're very stingy with anything that comes from the heart. There's a real deep streak of parsimony that runs through you, Paul, like the dark, rich vein that runs through white marble."

"Oh, I see. I have a marble heart, do, I?"

"Yes, you do, because you're selfish and mean, real mean, and getting meaner all the time. How odd that I've never seen it quite as clearly as I do right now. I wonder just how much your selfishness and meanness of heart has damaged my life, if at all. How am I to tell? Who knows, being spellbound by you for so long, maybe I've become just like you in order to survive."

He tipped his head back and gave one of his deep, rich laughs. A twinkle came into his eye, and he took her so firmly by the shoulders that she winced. He half lifted her up from the pillows and said, with a smile still lingering on his lips, "You're really mad now, aren't you? You're really spoiling for a fight, aren't you? Well, you can't have one because I won't give you one. You don't even have a good basis for a fight.

"Can you honestly say that you're not content, even happy, with your life? That you don't revel in being a self-made woman, holding a top job at the U.N., being beautiful, intelligent, sought-after? That you don't take pride in being financially independent, and in love with a man who fits into *your* life because he satisfies you sexually and emotionally? Come on, Mirella, tell me you haven't created a perfect life for yourself."

He pressed his thumbs deeper into her naked flesh, hurting her right to the shoulder blades. She bit the inside of her lips, as if to seal them closed, not wanting to answer him. Her eyes watered with the pain he was causing her. He attempted to shake her, goad her on.

"Come on, answer me," he ordered. "I dare you to answer me. You can't, can you?"

That did it. Mirella gathered up her strength and broke free from his hold. She went on her knees facing him, and with both hands roughly pushed him down against the bed pillows and went for him with clenched fists. He laughed at her and grabbed her by both wrists, pulling himself up onto his knees. There they sat facing each other.

"I love you when you're like this," he said. "I adore it when you lose control and you have no defense against me. I adore seeing the fire and fight you still have in you, and hide so very well. But, most of all, I relish being the only man you allow yourself to submit to completely."

"Oh—oh, one day I will—"

"Will what?" he laughingly interrupted. "Mirella, your life is set. You and I have a history together and an ongoing relationship that has continuity to it, and you are a thirty-nine-year-old woman who likes continuity. You no longer like change, and don't take chances anymore. Our relationship is set. You will *never* leave me because you have a good life that gives you all you want and you're too smart to walk away from that."

Paul released her wrists. He kissed her on the tip of her nose, as if he were dotting an i or placing a period at the end of a sentence. He was putting her in the place where he wanted her to be, with a male confidence that women really never understand.

"Selfish! Mean! Well, not all that mean," he said, getting up from the bed.

Naked, he walked across the beautiful, rare Isfahan carpet on the dark polished floorboards. At the chaise longue, covered in huge, soft mustard-yellow silk cushions, he paused and picked up Mirella's pearl silk dressing gown, which he draped over his arm. From the inside pocket of his navy-blue pinstripe suit jacket, lying neatly over the back of the chaise, he took a long, slim, folded document.

Mirella was mesmerized by Paul, astonished by his summary of her life, and overwhelmed by his ego. It came somewhat as a surprise to her that it had been a very long time since she had really had a good look at her lover, the first and only great love of her life, the man she had been engaged to, who jilted her and then wooed her back.

She did a quick assessment of him as she watched his every move. At forty-five, he was still the virile, clever man he had always been. His athlete's body was still magnificent, but he had lost some of his good looks, some of his hair, most of the softness of heart and poetry of soul he once joyously shared with her. His vanity and success had taken their toll.

Only undressed, in bed, in the throes of pure lust, did she

know him. Otherwise, she realized much to her amazement that her lover was nothing more than just another rich, successful stockbroker, who lived in a big house in Scarsdale, with a society wife and three children.

Paul returned to Mirella, who was still sitting on her haunches in the middle of her large canopied bed. He sat next to her and placed the document on the sheet between them, then helped her on with her dressing gown. He was very gentle, almost tender in the way he covered her nakedness and tied the sash. He kissed the tip of her nose again, and she sighed that same deep sigh of resignation.

Some sort of uneasy peace emerged between them. Paul reached for his platinum Patek Philippe watch lying on the table next to the bed and strapped it on his wrist. He checked the time.

"I'll go run your bath for you," he said. "We have only an hour and a half until curtain time for *La Bohème*. I've booked a table for a late dinner at the Palm, but I can't stay the night. I'm expected home. Is the Palm all right, or would you rather go somewhere closer to the Met?"

"No," she said pleasantly, "the Palm will do nicely. It sounds like a good evening."

"Great!" He leaned forward and rested his cheek against hers, leaving it there for a few seconds. Mirella put her hand on his shoulder, and then at the same time they moved away from each other.

"Not always selfish and mean," he said with a tease in his voice.

"Here, this is a little present for you," and he handed her the document he had removed from his jacket.

Mirella read the bold black letters, LEASE, and was surprised and somewhat embarrassed. This was a strange gift for Paul to give her and a gesture that was totally out of character for him.

"It's a wonderful beach house," he said quickly, before she could speak. "You're going to love it. I've leased it for you for a year. It's marvelous—on Dune Road in Southampton, right on the water. The Atlantic Ocean practically rolls up into the living room, and it's completely and beautifully furnished.

"I know you've accumulated a great deal of vacation time and are planning to take it over the next few months. I thought this would be a perfect place for you to go as it's only a few miles away from Gin Lane where my new summer house is. I'll be close by and we will be able to spend a great deal of time together. Aren't you pleased?"

Mirella scrambled off the bed and walked to her dressing table to put her hair up, leaving the lease on the bed.

"Yes, of course I'm pleased to have a house on the beach for a year. And it certainly spares me the bother of having to think about what to do for a summer holiday that I don't want to take anyway." She paused and took a deep breath. "It's quite a gift, Paul, and I do thank you. I suppose you would be offended if I refused it on the grounds that I find it embarrassing to be brought that close to your family setup. It's just a little too Fannie Hurst for me. You know, the 'back-street wife' syndrome, and all that."

Mirella watched Paul in the mirror as he picked up the lease and walked up behind her. He did look offended. He bent forward to surround her with his arms and dropped the document on the dressing table.

"Don't be stupid, darling," he said to her reflection in the mirror. "Of course I won't allow you to reject my gift. The house is yours for a year. Do with it what you like. Invite your friends, your parents, your lovers, stay there by yourself, have me there when you want me, leave it empty, I don't care what you do with it. I rented it to please, not to offend. And just forget that *Fannie Hurst* drivel. You're a free woman. Now, I'll go run your bath."

He kissed the top of Mirella's head and paused for a moment. Their gazes met in the mirror and slowly they smiled at each other.

"Thanks, Paul, I've never had a beach house before."

"Ah," he said, "I knew you would be pleased." He went to draw her bath.

3

Mirella stood in front of the full-length mirror in her bedroom, buttoning her white flannel jacket. She slipped the last large mother-of-pearl button through its hole and gave a gentle tug at the overlap to make sure the jacket hung evenly.

She had always liked this suit. How concerned she had been

when she bought it! She could still remember worrying about her decision. Was it foolish to buy a two-colored suit? A black skirt? Wouldn't that get too shiny? A white flannel jacket? Wasn't that madly impractical? Wouldn't the cleaning bills alone make it extravagant? She wasn't neurotic about money, just careful. The fact of the matter was that she and her family had never had very much money. They were a family rich in possessions and ideals, with no real understanding of the monetary world and how it worked.

She had never regretted buying the suit. Now, she adjusted the floppy black silk bow tie of the blouse that peeped out from under the crisp cut of the lapels, and in doing so noticed that the edges of the cuff were showing signs of wear. She felt a twinge of sadness at the realization that the suit was wearing out. It represented the time when Paul courted and won her for the second time. She smiled sadly as she smoothed out the jacket where it nipped in tightly at the waist.

She slipped into a pair of black patent-leather cuban-heeled shoes and walked away from the mirror to one of the pair of armoires in the bedroom, opening the doors and taking out a large soft black cashmere beret. She returned to the mirror and put the hat on at a jaunty angle.

From the Empire chaise she picked up a huge black patent-leather half-moon-shaped handbag, slung the short straps over her shoulder, and left the yellow-and-white bedroom, which took up most of the third floor of the house.

Down on the second floor the sun was pouring in on the magnificent living room, highlighting the eighteenth-century pine paneling, the faded tangerine velvet draperies, and a pair of priceless Chippendale settees, placed on either side of the *fleur de pêche* marble fireplace. The settees were covered in sheets and stacked high with books.

A fine collection of Japanese prints in their gold-leaf frames were stacked one behind the other against the walls. And boxes and crates half opened, with straw and objects spilling onto the Oriental carpets, were only part of the organized chaos of the room.

Mirella sighed and made a mental note to do something about it soon, the same mental note she had been making since she moved in three years before. That's when she thought of Paul again and how he would give her a lecture for the hundredth time about the room, the house, and her lack of imagination about what to do with such a marvelous place.

She would have to bear yet another of his speeches on "the inverted snobbery of those who don't hire an interior decorator to do the job they are incapable of handling." As usual he would probably end his dissertation by saying: "Well, let's go to bed. At least you've managed to get the bedroom together."

For the last few days the bedroom had seemed to loom large in Mirella's thoughts. On Thursday night there had been the erotic encounter with Donald Davies. She hadn't realized quite how much Donald had aroused her until after he had left her at the front door, and she had walked into the silent, empty house.

She had stood in the dark with her back against the door hoping that the passion welling up within would subside, and questioning why she hadn't accepted Donald. He would have quelled her sexual frustration. She had imagined the strong, thrilling flow of orgasms they both knew he was capable of bringing her to, and her heart pounded. Contracting her vagina, she had squeezed hard and released slowly, feeling the delight as if someone were massaging her womb, and then she had come. She had wanted to come again and again, but flushed with embarrassment at her own sexuality, she had finally reached out and switched on the hall lamp in the hope that the light would extinguish her desire.

It hadn't. All it had done was shine a light on reality, making her see what she already knew, that she didn't want a one-night stand with Donald Davies. She had wanted Paul that night, and he hadn't been there.

It was Paul who knew how to satisfy her erotic needs and fantasies. It was Paul who had taught her how to come when she was alone, and to come with giant orgasms that left her exhausted and sated. He had taught her to masturbate, had watched her, and they both reveled in her joy and release. It never occurred to Mirella that he had taught her so well that, except on very rare occasions, it had become a substitute for any other man.

They shared a sexual lust that bound them together, there was no doubt about that. But, on the Friday night when he *was* there, Mirella gave in to some niggling questions that had been in the back of her mind of late. Had Paul finally killed the love she felt for him? Did their relationship really still work? They fitted into each other's lives conveniently. They loved and trusted each other. Wasn't that enough? What more did she want from Paul Prescott?

On Saturday she managed to put the questions out of her mind. She spent Sunday with her best friend, Deena Weaver, and was relieved that all her friend could talk about was herself and how she would like to change her life. There was one odd thing, though. Just as Deena was leaving, she said, "You know, Mirella, life is so perverse—I'm the one who wants a new life, and probably you're the one who is going to get one."

"Thanks a lot, Deena, but no thanks," she had said. "It would take a bomb to make me change my way of life. I have everything going just as I want it to go. I like my life."

Now it was Monday morning . . . and everything was *not* as she wanted it. She was upset about Paul. She sighed, annoyed for wasting precious time on things she knew would never change. She went to her desk, rummaged through some papers and books on the top, selected several oak tag files, and shoved them into her handbag.

On the first floor, she left a hurried note on the kitchen table for Moses, her housekeeper. Taking a green banana and a ripe mango from the fruit bowl, she dropped them into the handbag as well and left the house.

A glorious spring morning greeted her. She took a deep breath of fresh air as she shut her front door. The air was still crisp but had a hint of warmth to it and the faint scent of flowers coming from primroses, hyacinths, and tulips planted underneath the two bay trees in the large bronze tubs that stood like sentinels on either side of the handsome front door.

The morning had not yet been polluted by the day's dose of carbon monoxide from cars. It was six A.M., the hour for joggers, walkers, workaholics, not traffic.

Mirella picked up the *Times* from the doorstep, unrolled the paper, and quickly read the headlines of each article on the front page. Folding it in half, she opened her shoulder bag again and slid the newspaper in between the files. She stood on the step for a few minutes, as she did every morning, and looked up and down the tree-lined block.

For those few minutes she saw the street as her village, her small town, her Elm Street, Anywhere, U.S.A. She saw it as a haven of private life plunk in the middle of the greatest city in the world. Every building on both sides of the street was a brownstone, as were so many of the buildings on the Upper

East Side, east of Park Avenue. Built around 1900, of the soft, porous, and perishable brown sandstone from the Connecticut River Valley or along the Hackensack River, the houses were unique on this block because of their preservation. Not one chic, esthetically perfect contemporary architectural conversion by Edward Durell Stone, or Philip Johnson, or Skidmore, Owings, and Merrill had slipped in.

More than half of the buildings were single private dwellings, a few were divided into duplexes, and the remainder apartments. Mirella knew this not because she was familiar with her neighbors but because of a quarterly street association newsletter. Its members were determined to keep the street perfect.

It was, in fact, street and house pride that had given Mirella the opportunity to buy this treasure on East Sixty-fifth Street. Her father's uncle, Hiram Wingfield, an eccentric, reclusive, ninety-four-year-old bachelor, faced with only a few months left to live, had wanted a Wingfield to buy his family house. He offered it to Mirella after her father passed up the offer. The terms had been that the sale be immediate, that he be allowed to live his life out there, that she must live in it for a minimum of five years before selling it, that it could never be sold as anything but a one-family dwelling, and that she never sublet it or change the exterior of the building. Under those conditions, he—old tightwad that he was—was prepared to accept all her savings, less ten thousand dollars, plus money from the largest mortgage she could raise, and proof of her income to make sure she could keep the house in good condition.

At the time, Mirella had found the whole thing a burden she could quite happily have done without. She was content in her one-room apartment, even though it was impossibly cramped. Many times she had considered buying a larger apartment, but somehow her life had always been too full of other things to carry through on.

When she went to meet her great-uncle Hiram, she was unsure of everything. By the time she left the house she had bought it on his terms. Uncle Hiram, apparently content with his last deal and happy in the knowledge that a Wingfield still owned the house, died in his sleep forty-eight hours after the sale had been completed.

As part of the deal, Mirella had agreed to keep on Moses, the housekeeper-cum-chauffeur, with the condition that after three months if either wanted to sever the arrangement they could do so, giving a month's notice. After three weeks they were devoted to one another and Mirella wondered how she had ever done without Moses.

Two joggers waved and called good morning to her as she went down the front steps and started walking east toward First Avenue. Every day, rain or shine, she always walked the nineteen blocks to her office in the Secretariat building at the United Nations headquarters at a brisk pace, stopping for black coffee and a pumpernickel bagel with cream cheese and grape jelly at the H and O Snack Bar.

Mirella always smiled as she approached the H and O. Snack bar, indeed! A snack was meant to be a light meal, a bite to eat. Not so at the H and O. Everything, but everything, went into the stomach like a lead balloon: even the orange juice was the heaviest she had ever drunk. She often wondered how the owners, Hymie and Ossario, managed to achieve that.

She liked to think of the H and O as her neighborhood café, her greasy spoon, her morning pub. For fifteen minutes every morning she had a taste of real New York at Ho's, her nickname for the white formica palace of ethnic fast food.

She pushed open the steamed-up glass door and called good morning to Hymie, who was at the far end of the long narrow shop, swishing a wet rag mop in wide arcs across the spotless white ceramic tile floor. She climbed up onto the red plastic counter stool near the door. This was her favorite seat because it offered the perfect vantage point for seeing it all happen, inside . . . and outside as well, when the steam dripped away in long rivulets down the glass window.

"Hi!" Two voices rang out simultaneously as Ossario popped up from under the service counter. In one hand he held a tray of chopped liver in a mound the size of a football. In the other he carried a worn white plate with a great slab of pastrami crowned with a thick layer of yellow fat.

Hymie and Ossario were one of New York's oddest of odd couples. Hymie Levine, the original owner of the snack bar, was a seventy-three-year-old Orthodox Jew, while Ossario Buenavita Diaz Sientese, his partner of five years, was a thirty-two-year-old Puerto Rican and a Roman Catholic. Despite their extraordinary differences, theirs was a great partnership.

The smell of freshly ground coffee dripping into the Cona

maker mixed with the scent of cinnamon, almond, and vanilla rising from the warm mountains of Danish pastry piled high on the bakery's wooden delivery trays, and mingled with the slightly sour but pleasant aroma of rye, caraway seeds, and yeast escaping from the huge shiny loaves of Jewish rye bread. The perfume of hot corned beef and pastrami hadn't taken over yet because Ossario was only just putting them into the steamer in the window.

"The usual?" shouted Hymie down the length of the luncheonette, as he stepped backward through the swinging doors to the kitchen, pulling his bucket and mop. As he did so he almost collided with Hester, the formidable bleached-blonde waitress, who pushed past him crushing to her bosom two large glass jars filled with half-sour pickles.

"Of course she'll have the usual," said Hester as she trundled menacingly toward Mirella and the window. "Every morning she comes in and she has the usual. And every morning *he* still asks 'The usual?' like he's not so sure she won't change her mind. I ask you, has she ever said, 'No, today I'll have bacon and eggs or a toasted English muffin, hold the butter?' Never."

"Who knows?" shouted Hymie as he came through the swinging doors wiping his hands on a clean dish towel. "So maybe she'll change her mind. She has a right; this is a democracy. And what business is it of yours, anyway?"

The front door opened and two policemen came in and sat a few stools away from Mirella. Hester handed Ossario her cargo and walked behind the counter brushing imaginary specks off her breasts and smoothing out nonexistent wrinkles on her short, tight red cotton uniform.

She walked up to Mirella, just as Hymie arrived from the left and Ossario from the right.

"A beautiful morning, eh?" said Ossario, palms up, nodding his head, as if giving thanks to God, and added, ". . . for a beautiful lady." He was the Latin lover of the trio.

"So, vat it'll be for Miss Vingfield on this beautiful day?" asked Hymie.

Hester frowned at them both. "I'm the waitress around here," she snapped, "so I'll take care of Miss Wingfield. Hymie, you can have New York's finest." She pointed with her pencil at the two policemen. Turning to Ossario she said, "That guy who makes the chili called. He says he's going to be late but not to worry, he's bringing today's tacos with him."

Ossario came out with a few *caramba*'s over the late chili maker that were echoed by a couple of *oi vey*'s from Hymie. Hester looked happy.

"The usual, honey?" she barked at Mirella.

Mirella smiled.

"Good morning, Hester. Yes, please, the usual."

The "usual" had originally been decided by a process of elimination. In the final analysis, it was all that Mirella found palatable at Ho's. The "odd couple" and Hester hadn't made it easy for her either. She had been put through an agonizing tasting period. It had taken far more diplomacy than she had ever used at the U.N. to reject without offense. But finally, the trio gave birth to "the usual." (Hymie's suggestion had been the pumpernickel bagel, Hester's the cream cheese, Ossario's the grape jelly, and Mirella's had always been the black coffee.)

Mirella lifted the cup to her lips, and quickly replaced it in the saucer. It was hot to the boiling point. She struggled with the cellophane lid on her prepacked tub of grape jelly and had it snatched from her hands by Hester, who was just passing in back of the counter. She ripped off the lid and slammed it back on the side of Mirella's bagel-covered plate without even stopping.

Two old men, impeccably dressed in Lacoste sportswear, came in.

"Hello, all," one of them said in a slight Yiddish accent.

The other went directly up to Mirella. "Good morning, my dear," he said in a soft, supposedly sexy voice, and then gave a shout over her shoulder, "Hello, Hymie, you old dog, come and have breakfast with us. Hester, we'll have the usual."

Mirella's eardrums vibrated, but she smiled and greeted Mr. Cohen.

Hester let out a tirade about Cohen and Shlamowitz never changing their order, just as she had about Mirella. The two took a tiny table against the wall, and in walked two pretty, flashy hookers, who sat at the end of the counter near the wall telephone and the kitchen doors.

Hester slammed down on the counter two deep dishes filled with puffy prunes, covered with dark rich juice, two cups of milky coffee, and a plate of dry all-bran crisp-bread.

"You may work at the U.N.," she said, none too softly, "but just listen and you will hear the geriatric prune brigade solve the problems of the world in half an hour."

The two policemen laughed and smiled at Mirella.

Hymie walked around to the front of the counter, frowned at Mirella, raised his eyebrows, and shrugged his shoulders. He picked up the order for his friends.

"She has *some* mouth," he said, in an apologetic whisper. "A *little* common, a *little* rude, but underneath, a heart of gold."

Mirella was just able to sip her coffee. She scraped some of the inch-thick cream cheese off the bagel and onto the plate, spread the grape jelly over it, and began her breakfast. She looked out the window and watched the cars going by, the garbage men hoisting the bins up and emptying them into the mouth of the monster van that devoured everything it was fed. And she listened.

Ossario was giving a lecture on nutrition to the two hookers. Cigarettes and black coffee were not enough. Pills and God knew what else they swallowed was not going to give them flesh on their bones. At least a good breakfast would give them something to work on. He was quick to point out that they must keep their looks—their only form of advertising. He talked one of them into bacon and eggs; the other into a stack of pancakes smothered in butter and dripping with Log Cabin maple syrup.

The two policemen were talking shop: the Mafia, promotion, the murder squad, the drug squad, prostitution, the Police Athletic League, pension plans, retirement plans, police benefits, drug pushers, police informants, private policing, and back to the Mafia again.

Cohen and Shlamowitz were trying to convince Hymie to share a house with them for the winter in Sarasota, Florida. They tried everything: his age, the cold weather, the pressure of work for a man who should be retired, the rich widows at the country club. His children, and how unhappy and worried they were about him, was the final straw. Hymie lost his temper.

"Oh, so that's it," he shouted. "One of my children called you to try to make me see reason. Who was it, my Rachel? Her idea of my seeing reason is that I sell out. Not just the H and O, but this building, and go live near her in California in one of those retirement homes, so she can call me once a day and see me once a month. Oh yeah, my Rachel with her Hollywood nose and her swimming pool and her 'Pa, why do you want to work in that dump when you are sitting on a gold mine and all you have to do is sell to the highest bidder?'

"Or was it my David, the doctor, who changed his name from Levine to Le Vine? Levine was too Jewish for a Johns Hopkins *surgeon* with a St. Louis wife and blond children. No, it wouldn't have been David. He at least thinks I should do what I want, even if he doesn't agree with it."

"It was Rachel. She was always a little buttinsky, always sticking her nose in," said Shlamowitz. "Too bad, though. We would have liked to have had you with us. No pinochle game is the same without you. You're such a lousy loser."

The men laughed off his anger and Hymie said, "You never know. It's a free country and I have been known to change my mind. And on big issues too. Would you ever have believed that of me?"

Hymie pointed to the wall above the table where the men sat. There were pictures of all the Roosevelts; Jack, Bobby, and Teddy Kennedy; a large one of Harry Truman and a smaller one of Bess and Margaret. One of Adlai Stevenson and another of Wendell Willkie; and two of Ronald Reagan, one dressed as a cowboy and another as President.

Mirella was watching a traffic cop having a fight with a woman walking a large white poodle with a pink satin bow in its curly topknot, when she heard him say, "Me, Hymie Levine, voting Republican: I can hardly believe it myself. But, what can I do? I like the man, he makes me feel good, reminds me of my strength and how great my country is. Mind you, I am still a registered Democrat."

Mirella had finished her coffee, paid Hester, and was waiting for her change when she saw Old Minnie. She was toothless, dirty, and ragged, with two overcoats on, one over the other, and an extra pair of men's shoes tied together and hung around her neck. Over her filthy hair she had a battered fedora with an ostrich feather stuck in its band. Four huge shopping bags, two in each hand, were stuffed with her possessions, and she was beginning to unload them in front of the luncheonette.

Hester slapped Mirella's change on the counter in front of her and swiped the dishes away.

"Well, that's all I have to see to make my day—our own Lady Hobo, at this hour of the morning. Hymie, Ossario: Minnie is here."

More *caramba*'s and *oi vey*'s from the men. Ossario went into action in the kitchen, preparing ham and eggs and toast. Before Mirella had put her change away, one of the policemen had helped Hymie carry out a table and a chair, which they placed on the sidewalk in front of the luncheonette for Minnie. Hester had filled a huge mug with strong tea and went up and down behind the counter with a brown paper bag in her hand. The tyrant of the luncheonette was filling it with doughnuts and Danish, and rolls and bran muffins. Minnie was partial to bran muffins.

For Mirella, breakfast at Ho's was twenty minutes of escapism into a world she lived in but would never know. It was, for her, live soap opera, only with humor and without gloss. It was the poor people's "Dallas" and "Dynasty" all rolled into one, along with "Upstairs, Downstairs" and Archie Bunker and a full Sunday morning of religious programming. Mirella adored it. She was an outsider on the inside, a role she enjoyed and felt comfortable in. Of course, she felt as comfortable in her role at the U.N., but that was different. Her job brought out a sense of being stretched to use everything she had, everything she was. It had to do with power, achievement, success, and stamina. It had to do with life—and especially a New York life.

These were her thoughts as the 540-foot-high slab of the Secretariat—only seventy-two feet wide—loomed into view. It was the building that dominated the group of buildings at the United Nations Headquarters. She liked approaching it on the thinner end of the slab because it had alway been more sculpture than architecture for her. The team of architects had included Le Corbusier of France, Oscar Niemeyer of Brazil, and Sven Markelius of Sweden, and representatives of ten other countries. For Mirella it was the genius of those three men that dominated the whole scheme. The Barbara Hepworth sculpture standing in the pool in front of the Secretariat was an added bonus of beauty as far as she was concerned. The Secretariat building and the sculpture were for her monumentally powerful and sensual. No matter how many times she saw them, they gave her a thrill, moved her in an inward mysterious way that she never questioned or analyzed.

Adjusting the shoulder straps of her handbag, she approached Forty-eighth Street and doubled her pace. There were few people around at that hour, and she enjoyed the luxury of quiet and the symbolic impact of a united world that the complex of buildings was supposed to represent. She walked past the General Assembly building, past the fluttering flags of some of the one hundred fifty-nine member nations, around the Hepworth wading in its pool, and was about to enter the building when she suddenly stopped.

She turned around and took a long look at the United Nations Headquarters. Mirella was not one to wallow in her own accomplishments, but, for some unknown reason, on this morning she was filled with pride over her contribution to the organization during the last fifteen years. Running a department in which translating all documents into the six official languages of the Assembly—Arabic, Chinese, English, French, Russian, and Spanish—was just a small part of her work. There were more than one hundred fifty mother tongues represented there, and although English and French were languages used by staff members in their daily work, Mirella had rarely turned away an important request for translation into another language.

Just thinking about her life's work made her happy. She turned and, after showing her identification card to the guard, entered the Secretariat, enthusiastic as always to see what the day had to offer.

The building was empty except for cleaners, security guards, and the odd executive like Mirella; silent except for the occasional sound of a vacuum cleaner or a door slamming. Mirella took the elevator up through the building to her department.

Her large office faced the East River and gave her an extraordinary view far up and down the river as well as the whole of Queens and Brooklyn and whatever lay beyond.

Her high-back chair was placed behind a large and ordinary desk with three gray chairs facing her. On the desk was an IBM computer, three telephones, several stacks of papers, and a pile of foreign dictionaries.

Except for the one wall of glass, the others were lined from floor to ceiling with books on sagging metal shelves, and along the far wall was a long, narrow table with a microfilm viewer on it, and stacks of box files. A dark brown sofa stood in front of another wall, two deep comfortable soft chairs were placed in front of the window wall, and a high-powered telescope was aimed toward the heavens. High-tech tables and floor lamps were dotted around the room. In one corner was a nest of rosewood tables, one stacked over the other, ready for use whenever needed. The combined effect was efficient and indifferent.

The only personal touches were an English bone-china cup and saucer, an elegant silver thermos filled with hot black coffee made for her by the cleaner, and a small crystal fruit bowl at hand on her desk.

Opening her bag, she took out the fruit she had brought from home and put it in the bowl. Then she removed the files and laid them out in front of her. She poured herself a cup of coffee, switched on her computer, dropped her beret and handbag on the sofa, and returned to her desk. Opening the top file, she began to review "The Desert Rescue Mission," a report from the delegates to a special U.N. conference in Nairobi seven years before. Government representatives at that meeting had agreed to a twenty-eight-point plan of action to halt the process that created man-made deserts because of desperately poor people overgrazing, overcultivating, and deforesting the land. More than fifty million acres of land—an area twice that of Bangladesh—became useless each year, and the goal of the conferees was to reverse this trend by the year 2000. Little had been done, and even less action in the future seemed likely. The 1977 conference had been a failure.

Mirella had persuaded those in power to go along with her decision to publish this U.N. document in both hardback and paperback editions because of its importance and the demand for copies of it from the general public around the world as well as U.N. member countries.

She was pleased with the job her people had done in editing the report for publication but still felt the book would benefit from more illustrations. She wrote out her suggestions for more photographs of the 1968–1974 drought in the Sahel, a map of the Gobi Desert that showed its size in relation to the rest of China, and some photographs and rudimentary information on the tribes inhabiting the deserts of Ethiopia and the Sudan, who until recently had managed for centuries to survive and even flourish self-sufficiently.

The red telephone on her desk began to ring. She looked at her watch. Eight thirty-five. That would be Paul's morning call. Mirella screwed on tightly the top of her black Mont Blanc fountain pen, formed the papers she had been working on into a neat pile, and laid the pen on top of them. She swiveled her chair around to face the window, slowly tilted it back, and picked up the telephone.

Mirella and Paul spoke on the telephone at least once a day every day. Their conversations were always caring and erotic and culminated in an arrangement about three times a week to dine together or have a drink somewhere. Occasionally they went to a concert or a play, but whatever they did they always made time for a few sexual hours at her house, or in a suite at the Sherry Netherland. Last Friday night was just another ordinary night out together for them. At least it was supposed to have been. But it hadn't, because for once she had seen Paul clearly.

She put the telephone down after fifteen minutes, wondering when their conversations had changed from erotic to lewd, and why she hadn't noticed it before. There had been a hollow ring to their talk this morning. It had been superficial, more habitual than inspirational. All was not well with them and, she wondered, if he knew it, what—if anything—would he do about it?

She was more curious than worried because she had long ago come to terms with the fact that she could never love Paul as she once had. They loved each other, yes, but they loved each other now with reservations and compromises. As their sexual life grew stronger, wilder, and more thrilling, other emotions she had once felt for him withered.

Shortly before nine o'clock her secretary, Barbara Smythe, arrived with a list of her appointments for the day. Together they went for a meeting with the head of her department, Roland Culver, a brilliant linguist of seventy-two. He was twelve years over the mandatory retirement age, kept on by yearly appointments, and had been threatening for the last two years to retire for good and make her head of the department. At ten o'clock, with her assistant Bryan Palmer, Mirella went to a meeting with the interpreters working in the General Assembly Hall. At ten forty-five she was back in her office sitting in on the dismissal of a French translator by her other assistant, Edward Cole. At eleven o'clock she met a Greek delegate with a list of demands that he was not entitled to. It was a day like any other day, until her twelve o'clock appointment arrived.

4

Mirella was absorbed by the panoramic view through her window and, as always, because her office was so high up in the sky, she had the sensation that she was poised on the edge of the world. If she let her mind drift and imagined stepping through the glass and making the jump, she got a jolt of danger and excitement.

Her office was so silent that it hummed a tune of nothingness, and when a knock on the door disturbed the stillness, she flinched.

Barbara stepped into her office and announced Brindley Ribblesdale.

Mirella turned away from the window, rose, and took a few steps toward the tall, slim, well-dressed young man carrying a battered but highly polished leather briefcase.

There were a few awkward seconds of silence as her secretary left. The young man who stood facing her appeared to be mildly traumatized, but managed at last to shake her hand and tell her how pleased he was to meet her. The awkward silence returned. Mirella thought it best to take over.

"Mr. Ribblesdale, won't you sit down?" she asked, indicating the sofa.

"Yes, thank you, Miss Wingfield."

He waited for her to be seated, then sat down at the other end of the sofa.

"Now, what can I do for you? I understand you called early this morning and insisted that you had to see me as soon as possible. I believe you told my secretary that it was about a private and personal matter."

He was looking more composed. "Yes. I do beg your pardon, Miss Wingfield, for not being more forthcoming with your secretary, but I am indeed here on a very personal matter. Please let me introduce myself properly. I am Brindley Ribblesdale, a solicitor from the London firm of Rumbold, Grumthorp, and Ribblesdale. We have been family solicitors for over two hundred years, and pride ourselves on caring for our clients from the cradle to the grave. Our firm still acts on behalf of some estates that were once administered by the original members of the firm."

"Then you are here to see me about some legal matter, Mr. Ribblesdale?"

"Yes, I am," he said. He put his briefcase down on the floor, turned at an angle to face Mirella, and for the first time since he had walked into the room, smiled.

"Miss Wingfield, I have the agreeable duty to inform you, on behalf of Rumbold, Grumthorp, and Ribblesdale, that you have come into a legacy."

Mirella was astonished. "But who would leave me anything?"

"Your maternal great-grandmother. You have inherited her estate, Miss Wingfield."

"But that can't be! My mother's family was poor and lost all its money in Turkey by the time my grandmother was born."

"I'm afraid you've been misled. None of that is true. But to answer your first question: the legacy comes to you because your great-grandmother left instructions in her will that her estate be left to her eldest daughter's first female grandchild. And that, Miss Wingfield, is you."

They remained silent while the news sank in, the element of surprise started to subside, and a calm, joyful realization began to arise in Mirella of her fabulous luck.

"Are you sure I am the rightful heir?"

"Quite sure. You are the direct descendant of a beautiful and clever woman, the Kadin Roxelana Oujie, recognized concubine of a Turkish sultan. She was your great-grand-mother. We have substantial documentation; there are genealogical records to prove it."

Mirella's astonishment passed, and she was momentarily shocked by a series of emotions involving pride, loyalty, and family unity. She became aware of a certain sense of power that arose from continuity, and from being the one favored by the goddess Chance. She was moved that the legacy should have come down to her from a woman thrice removed who had passed it through another woman in the family. A wave of timelessness rolled toward Mirella. Then, in a split second, one ripple of consciousness after another rolled over her: her present one, and then others, as if from many different lives. She was left with a sense of posterity so strong that it frightened her and she had to blank it out.

"How extraordinary," she murmured. "You must appreciate that it's a great deal to take in all at once . . . this, this becoming an heiress, not to mention discovering an ancestor with such a history. What have I inherited? I do hope it's money. I would so like it to be a large amount of real hard cash, something we Wingfields have never had. Oh yes, lots of money to play with. How lovely that would be!"

Mirella saw a look of disappointment in Brindley Ribblesdale's face, and she thought, "Oh dear, there's not much money involved." She was embarrassed by how greedy she sounded. But then, how could this English solicitor understand that the last thing she wanted was to be enslaved by inherited objects as her father had been? She felt obliged to say something to cover her embarrassment, so she asked, "How did you discover this legacy and trace it to me?"

"The story of the legacy and finding you is long, and very interesting. I would like you to bear with me. It's a rather convoluted tale. The part that most directly involves you began about eight years ago when my father retired and passed on to me one of our firm's accounts, the administration of the estate of a man who died fifty or so years ago. His name was Oberon Winslow-Ward."

Mirella raised her hand, chuckling as she did so. "Fifty years ago! Indeed, it is a long story—and one that mandates a tea break, don't you think, Mr. Ribblesdale?" At his nod of agreement, she buzzed her secretary and made the request. Then she gestured to the solicitor to continue.

"My father drew up the last will and testament of Oberon Winslow-Ward, which he took away to consider one final time before signing it. But that same day he left a long and very detailed letter with the firm instructing it to act as custodian of his estate if something should happen to him before his will was returned. He died within a few days, and his will was never found. This left us as the custodians of the estate, and, as such, we have been following his instructions ever since."

"You make it sound like the beginning of a wonderful Victorian murder mystery," Mirella said.

"Oh, it gets better than that, much better," he said, clearly delighted by Mirella's enthusiasm.

"I had been administering the estate," he continued, "for a few years when three seemingly unrelated events occured. The first was the discovery and reading of Oberon Winslow-Ward's will, found in a secret drawer of a Louis Quinze *secrétaire,* on loan to the Paul Getty Museum in California. The second happened shortly afterward. I was asked to attend the official opening of a safe-deposit box that had been sealed eighty years earlier, at Coutts and Company. The bank held a letter of instruction that the box be opened in the presence of someone from our chambers, and that the contents be handed over to us, along with whatever moneys were left in the account of their client, Madame Ottoline Sinan.

"The officers at the bank were extremely enthusiastic about the event. And when we were all standing in the strong room in front of the deposit boxes, even I felt excitement over the box a woman had sealed eighty years before. I began to wonder why she had done it, what we would find, why she had chosen our firm to reveal her secrets.

"The box was a large one, the sort that usually held the family silver. I opened its lid, and the first thing I saw was a letter addressed to Rumbold, Grumthorp, and Ribblesdale written in lavender ink." Brindley was clearly relaxed now and allowed himself to grin at Mirella. "The penmanship was as exquisite as the color of the ink," he added. His expression changed abruptly from amusement to awe.

"The safe-deposit box was packed with objects, each wrapped in a piece of silver or gold brocade and tied with a brightly colored silk cord. There were about two dozen parcels in all. I began to transfer the contents into a carton the bank had furnished for me, and opened one or two of the packages out of sheer curiosity. The first packet contained a rock crystal casket with heavy gold mounts. I opened it and spilled out onto the dark blue baize-covered table a treasure of magnificent cut diamonds in all shapes and sizes. It was a staggering sight.

"Near the bottom of the box, I found a parcel containing a small oil portrait in a silver frame studded with pink diamonds. The painting was of a most hauntingly beautiful young woman. The chairman of Coutts pointed out that it was a Fabergé frame and that the portrait had been painted by the French painter Gérôme."

Tea arrived and Mirella silently directed Barbara to put it on one of the rosewood tables. She did so, then carried the table over to the sofa and placed it in front of Mirella, who, lost in Ribblesdale's tale, automatically poured the tea while he continued.

"I was captivated by Ottoline Sinan and her strong box. I

wanted to learn everything I could about Madame Sinan. The letter she left contained very few clues to her background, but held some interesting information about the life she had led and her last wish, which was to find the rightful heir to her treasures. I soon realized the contents of the box were more clues to follow up, if I were to honor her last wish, which I was determined to do. My firm was custodian of two mysterious estates then. I had been working on them for a considerable time when, to my utter amazement, I discovered something that linked them together.

"One of Madame Sinan's objects was a large ruby seal. It was set in a gold frame encrusted with diamonds, in such a way that the ruby was able to be spun around, showing either the seal, or the clean surface of the gem. The jewel hung on a chain of pavé diamond links. It held a special fascination for me, and one day I suddenly knew why. The seal was familiar. I had seen it before. Then I remembered where: it had been printed on the will, under the signature of Oberon Winslow-Ward.

"I examined the document, tested the Sinan seal: they were exactly the same. Oberon Winslow-Ward's things were brought from the firm's safe and examined. We found an exact replica of the Sinan ruby and diamond necklace, the only difference being that the Winslow-Ward seal was an emerald. In Winslow-Ward's archives we found a reference to the seal as having been his mother's, and a gift to him from her at his birth.

"Oberon Winslow-Ward and Ottoline Sinan had the same mother but different fathers, and they both left their estates to the first female grandchild of their elder sister. In other words, Oberon Winslow-Ward, Ottoline Sinan, and your grandmother were half sisters and brother, and their mother was the Kadin Roxelana Oujie, your great-grandmother."

Mirella let out a long sigh. "What a story! I am quite overwhelmed. But, quickly, do tell about the third event."

"An American archaeologist appeared at our offices with twenty-six hand-bound volumes containing a family's archives. He had discovered them in central Turkey—Anatolia, to be exact—in an ancient Hittite burial mound that had been plundered and resealed several times.

"My first question to Mr. Corey was why had he brought these papers to us? To my great surprise, he handed me an old document with the letterhead of Rumbold, Grumthorp, and

Ribblesdale written across the top—found, he said, in the fly-leaf of the first volume of the archives. The annals revealed a remarkable family history, and detailed a vast estate, rich in land, natural resources, and treasures assembled several centuries ago by an Eastern Jewish family.

"They were financial wizards serving ancient kings. Later they became powerful princes of the Ottoman Empire. To protect their personal possessions from confiscation because of their Jewish blood, they hid their estates behind responsible custodians, and bound themselves to the law through reputable solicitors. They further protected their heritage by making the rightful heir the first female grandchild of the eldest daughter. It has been that way for centuries.

"Here was the key to finding the heir to my two mysterious clients' estates, which were in fact part and parcel of one large estate, that of your great-grandmother."

Mr. Ribblesdale smiled again and leaned against the back of the sofa.

"Well, that's my story, Miss Wingfield, and it has taken me five years to put the puzzle together, and another three years to prove it and be able to come here and tell it to you."

Mirella, riveted by the exotic tale, sat quietly looking at the smiling young man who had told it. Suddenly she was struck by how profound his involvement was in this whole affair. Why, he had given years of energetic devotion to tracking the mystery, to tracking her. What on earth would he do now that his quest was coming to an end?

"That, Mr Ribblesdale," she finally said, "is an amazing saga, and fascinating. I hardly know what to say to you. It sounds like the sort of thing that dreams are made of, that romantic novels are written about. Not at all something that would happen to me, on a busy Monday in my office. I am moved by discovering this hitherto-unknown family, and the legacy itself, but I live a very organized, busy life and, although I speak Turkish, the country of Turkey is unknown to me . . . and very far away, I must add." She paused, but when Ribblesdale said nothing, she added, "What makes this legacy even more extraordinary is the fact that I am quite sure my mother knows nothing about it. My grandmother might have, but if she did she never said a word about it to us."

She lapsed into silence then, her thoughts turning to the extraordinarily beautiful, intelligent, romantic creature who was her grandmother. Family stories hinted at her unusual and exotic past, left behind in Turkey. She had been swept away from her patron, the last reigning sultan of Turkey, and her country by a dashing American diplomat much younger than herself, Mirella's grandfather. He had brought her to America and been forced to resign his position over the scandal they'd created. They had lived a somewhat reclusive life on the border between Bostonian high society and genteel poverty, and had subsidized themselves with a small income he inherited and the sale of her jewels. Like so many immigrants to America, her grandmother had done everything in her power to forget her past and the loss of her husband's career, ruined because of his love for her: they wiped Turkey out of their lives, so as not to be reminded of the price they had paid for love.

Ribblesdale's voice startled her. "I appreciate how much of a shock all this is to you, but I'm here to make everything as simple as possible for you. I have brought with me a great deal of the paperwork, and assembled it in such a way as to make it relatively easy for you to read before you come to London to settle the estate. If you would allow—"

"London?" Mirella interrupted. "Go to London? Surely that's not necessary?"

"Oh, but I assure you it is *absolutely* necessary. When you have read a fraction of the documents now available on the estate and the family archives, I think you might have a different opinion about visiting London and Turkey."

Mirella rose and walked to the window, looked out and then back at Ribblesdale. "Why, for heaven's sake? I agree I have an obligation to read some of the material you've brought with you, to put myself in the picture, so to speak. But, once that's done, I see no reason why I can't liquidate the estate through your London office, right here, from New York. You could remain here for a week or so and work with me."

The shocked look on Ribblesdale's face made her feel very uncomfortable. The angry stare embarrassed her. She recovered herself and shot him a determined look.

"Are you so sure you want to liquidate this estate? Forgive me, Miss Wingfield, but I believe that you are being rash, premature in making such a decision. Besides, it would be impossible to do without a great deal of work in London with your advisors and other members of my firm, who have acted as custodians for you for years. You have not begun to comprehend all that is involved. As I started to say before, if you will allow me to call on you at your home this evening and deliver some documents for you to read, we can make a start and accomplish a great deal before you leave for London. It is, I am afraid, the only way you will be able to expedite the settlement."

Mirella knew he was right, and though she was feeling an excitement about the magnificent legacy, she could not help but feel a tedious burden had been laid upon her. Grudgingly she went to her desk and wrote her address on a piece of paper and tore it from the pad.

"Brindley Ribblesdale, I do want you to know that not only am I impressed with the way your firm has handled this affair, but I am very impressed with you and your determination to see this thing through properly to the end. Now, fortunately, I've accumulated a great deal of vacation time that I'm compelled to take during the next few months. So, we will do it your way for the time being but I must remind you that I have a full life, which includes a job that is demanding and rewarding, right here, in a city I love. I doubt that there is room in my life for a complicated legacy, so I probably will dissolve the estate as soon as possible. It will take a great deal to change my mind about that. Here is my address. Will seven this evening be convenient?"

The young man looked very relieved, even pleased. For the moment all was well. He had found his heiress, and she had turned out to be beautiful, intelligent, and obviously a more than capable executive. *And* she was willing, for the moment, to be advised by him. He could have hoped for her to be a little less American and have a little more romantic a nature, such as he had read flowed through the lives of her ancestors. Maybe he had lived with those dead beauties too long, and expected too much. He smiled and answered, "Yes, thank you, Miss Wingfield. Until this evening then."

5

It was a rainy night, a night of heavy showers. Adam Corey liked rain. He found the music of rain and the sensation of it on his skin erotic. He greatly enjoyed making love in it. On a dark hot night under torrential rain, it could be mad, wild, thrilling. Under a soft warm rain, on a summer's afternoon, in a field or garden, it could be a fragile, sensitive poem transcending ecstasy. He stood with Brindley Ribblesdale in the rain before a house on East Sixty-fifth Street.

He was taken aback when Mirella Wingfield opened her front door. She was dressed in a pair of wide camel-hair trousers that clung to her hips and fell straight from there to the top of her flat white ostrich-skin shoes. The cashmere sweater she wore was the same color as her trousers and had dolman sleeves and a low V neckline. Around her throat, a tiny red and white polka-dot silk scarf was tied to one side in a minute bow. He had had no idea what to expect when Brindley Ribblesdale had rung the bell of this house, but it certainly was not meeting a woman he would like to fuck in the rain.

Mirella was surprised to see a big man with rugged good looks wearing a ten-year-old Burberry trench coat, its collar turned up against the weather, standing on her doorstep. He was a tall, broad-shouldered man, deeply tanned, with dark blond hair graying at the temples and streaked silvery white from the sun. He had dark blue eyes, with decadent creases at the sides that reflected both intelligence and sensitivity. And her first instinct told her that to be with him would be to conquer worlds she had yet to see.

Next to Adam Corey, Brindley Ribblesdale was trying to close an umbrella.

"Good evening, Miss Wingfield. This is Mr. Adam Corey. I hope you don't mind my bringing him along. We'll take only a few minutes of your time." He picked up his battered briefcase. "Just long enough to deliver these documents."

"Do come in out of the rain," said Mirella, noticing a dark gray Rolls double-parked in front of her house.

The two men stepped into the hall. Both were surprised to see a huge, handsome black man standing behind Mirella.

"May I take your coats, gentlemen?" Moses asked.

Adam Corey removed his coat, handed it to him, and ran his fingers through his damp hair. He was dressed in a J. Press tweed suit, a white button-down shirt, and a yellow handwoven wool tie.

Mirella thought he looked like a cross between a Princeton professor, the chairman of AT&T, and a great lover. She imagined that he came from sturdy pioneer stock, those men who trekked across America in covered wagons, and she was right. She also thought that he was about forty. He did look much younger than his forty-eight years, this millionaire who was an adventurer, explorer, big-game hunter, and archaeologist.

Adam Corey was a man who used his money to excavate lost wonders of the world. He was a man with a reputation as much for his exotic life-style and sexual prowess as for his accomplishments. When he was not on an adventure in some remote part of the world he lived in the style of the great sultans in a famed white marble palace on the Bosporus in Istanbul. But she knew none of this as they stood together for the first time in her front hall.

"Miss Wingfield," Ribblesdale said, "I am pleased I have this chance to introduce you to Mr. Corey. You see, he has a longtime interest in Turkey and knowledge about certain aspects of your legacy."

"And he is the man who found my long-lost family archives," she added. "For that I know I must be grateful to you, Mr. Corey. Forgive me, but I'm not sure that I am."

He smiled at her for the first time and his smile reached into her and warmed her in a way she had never been warmed before. It was madness but all she could feel was an incredible happiness. It was sexual and it was love.

"You will be. Oh, you will be, Miss Wingfield. You have no idea what is about to unfold for you," Adam said.

Mirella tried to compose herself. It was difficult because the sensation of happiness bubbling within her would not go away. It was as if she had been given a gift of love, for the first time in her life. She said, "I have the most dreadful feeling this is going to be much more trouble than I am prepared to take on." Then she quickly changed the subject by suggesting, "Why don't we go up to the living room. There's a lovely warm fire in the hearth there and Moses can fix us a drink while we go over these documents."

Adam watched her as she mounted the stairs. He was attentive to every curve of her body and the way she moved. The swing of the wide trousers from below the hip was outlandishly provocative. He was impressed by her, found her exquisitely erotic and beautiful. He sensed at once that she was her own mistress, and that here was a woman who kept a strict control over her passions. But this was no repressed lady: this was a free woman fully capable of exercising choice.

Halfway up the stairs she turned abruptly. "I simply cannot keep on calling you Mr. Ribblesdale. Please call me Mirella and then I can call you Brindley."

She turned her back on them again and walked quickly to the second floor.

Mirella's and Adam's gazes met for a moment while she was speaking on the staircase, and he knew he was in love, that they would, one day, be together and when that happened it would be for eternity. His imagination took flight: he saw her in his arms and turning into a white dove in his hands. He raised her up and, when ready, threw her up into the wind and set her free. His fanciful vision reminded him that he had fallen in love with a free spirit, one not unlike his own. He knew he must go cautiously with her.

Following Brindley into the living room, Adam was enchanted by it. The light from the fireplace flickered and played shadows across the white-sheeted settees in the center of the paneled room. Large and beautiful Ming, Tang, and Han pieces were bases for the lamps, whose handsome but worn and tatty ivory silk shades were not quite straight on their frames, in some cases even tilted dangerously to one side. They were dotted around the room, standing on a crate here, a table there, on the floor spotlighting a section of Oriental carpet, and on a lovely Boulle desk at the end of the room that overlooked the garden in the back.

There were Queen Anne wing chairs, covered in tattered and torn tapestry. Three of them were placed around an impressive French Directoire table, whose ormolu mounts were magnificent birds with their wings flung back. The tips of the wings held up a pale mauve marble top with a crack across it. It was a room that created great expectations, the more so for several large English eighteenth-century gilt mirrors on the floor, leaning against the walls reflecting the room yet again.

Mirella started unloading books from the settees. She put them in a pile in back of the sofas. As the two men began to help, she said, "I'm always pretending to myself that one day I'll get this room into shape. You see, I know how it should look, it's just that I have never found the time or had the inclination to follow through with it. And now I have grown used to the room in this state. Occasionally I put something in its proper place, hang a picture, move a mirror, rearrange it, as we are doing now, to suit the evening. It's sort of spontaneous stage setting, bad interior decoration, and frankly, I like it this way. Actually it's a throwback to the way I was brought up. Well, maybe not quite."

"I like your room," Adam said. "It's handsome, organized chaos. A very original period."

Mirella looked at Adam and gave him a winsome smile. With a twinkle in her eye she said, "Please take note that it is *clean* organized chaos, thanks to Moses. You know, I really think you mean it. You do like this room, don't you?"

He nodded in the affirmative before he bent down to pick up another load of books. Moses came into the room with a silver drinks tray and put it on the Directoire table, then lifted and placed it in between the settees in front of the fire. "Thank you, gentlemen," he said. "I can take over now." He gathered up the sheet, books and all, from one settee, then the other, and put the bundles behind a Japanese screen.

The three sat down, Brindley next to Mirella, Adam opposite them.

"Mirella," Brindley said while Moses was mixing drinks, "you have so many wonderful things."

"Exactly! That's why I'm determined not to be saddled with any more. I've been lucky to be surrounded by beautiful things all my life, yet to have had to work my way through Vassar and always earn my own living. I have always had to watch every penny I spent. Please don't think that's a complaint, it isn't. All I am saying is that for a change I would like to have a great deal of money so that I could restore some of what I and my family have. It would be nice to feel that these beautiful things weren't a burden. But, mind you, they are, without a proper income to maintain them. Remember, I am only an international civil servant, earning an executive paycheck."

While Mirella was speaking, Moses mixed and served the drinks. Mirella and Brindley had large dry martinis, in forty-year-old Lalique glasses, and Adam a malt whisky and soda in a handsome antique crystal tumbler engraved with scenes of rolling hills and flowers, and two lovers lying together under a spring rain.

He was amused as he turned the glass around in his hands, examining it. "Oh, yes," he thought, "one day, Mirella Wingfield, we will make love in the soft warm rain."

"So, Brindley, let's get on with it. What do you have there for me to read? You will excuse us for a minute, Mr. Corey?"

"Adam," he interrupted.

"Of course. Adam."

He stood up. "You carry on. Do you mind if I look around at some of your things?"

"No, please do," she answered.

Adam was relieved to wander alone around the room. He went to the window overlooking the street and saw his chauffeur with the car, still double-parked under the street-light, waiting in the rain. He wondered how this could have happened to him . . . this sudden falling in love. He could taste her name on his tongue. It made him feel young and foolish. He watched and listened to the rain: it made him feel carnal.

He turned around with his back to the window and watched her from a distance, listened to her voice. It was sweet but firm, and still carried the trace of a Massachusetts accent. He studied her lovely hands, the long slim fingers, and hoped she played the piano, and well. Her breasts were large, almost heavy, but firm and high, and as he examined the rest of her body he was lost in it, captivated by her lust. He had bedded enough women in his life to know a naturally lustful woman when he saw one, and he knew that she was a perfect match for him.

He heard her say, "Brindley, just one minute, stop right there. What are you trying to tell me? This afternoon in my office you led me to believe that the estate was more important historically than it was financially."

"Oh no, Mirella, I'm sorry. I said nothing to indicate that to you."

"Brindley, I promise to do my homework," she said, with just a hint of annoyance in her voice, and patted the stack of papers next to her. "But I want you to be straightforward with me. Just how big and how valuable is this estate? How much time is it going to take for me to settle it? It has already taken too much precious time out of my day, *and* I am getting confused.

"A stranger walks into my office and lays a fabulous family saga before me and tells me I am an heiress. I call home and my father coolly says, 'I wouldn't be surprised. After all, your grandmother was a remarkable woman.' But he knows nothing about it. I bother my brother with this story, and he laughs and says, 'God, not more things' and that he knows nothing about it. I call my mother, who says, 'I have never heard of such nonsense. Be very careful, they are hoaxers.' I call Marcus Weinbaum, my father's secretary and the family archivist, and he tells me, 'There are no records of your mother's family anywhere. But having known your grandmother, I would venture to say that whatever her mother might leave you, and from the manner in which the legacy has been set up, it will be important.' So, let's get down to basics, Brindley. What's involved? And none of your English understatement, please."

Adam went back and sat down across from her. They looked at each other, and she was aware of that incredibly warm feeling again. He was the most attractive man she had ever met. She knew he wanted her from the way he looked at her, and she hoped he had no idea how much she wanted him.

He placed his empty glass on the table and said, "Mirella, would you prefer me to leave? Although I know a great deal about your legacy, I don't know everything, and what Brindley has to tell you might be confidential."

She didn't want to let him go. "Adam, that's not necessary. All I want is a brief, clear picture, then Brindley and I can go into the details in private another day."

Brindley stood up and went to the fireplace, turned and faced her.

"Mirella," he said. "It is an enormous legacy, consisting of large land, oil, gas, and mineral rights in Turkey. There are houses and vineyards, stables and farms, businesses of all kinds, even banks, in England and France as well. There are works of art, and jewels. The list of assets is long. The income the estate receives annually is in the region of forty million dollars, and is nothing compared to the *value* of the estate. As you Americans say, that is 'the bottom line.' How could I tell you in your office this afternoon when all you were concerned about was liquidating what you assumed to be some little inheritance you knew nothing about?"

Mirella was faint. She thought she was going to be sick, and fought to take control of herself. Her face was chalk-white, and she felt cold and tried to raise her hand to her head. Adam reached her first. He sat down next to her, put his arm around her and steadied her. He reached out to the drinks tray and poured her a whisky in his glass and held it to her lips. She took it in both her trembling hands and drank it straight down.

"Steady on, Mirella," said Brindley, as he, too, went to her aid, taking the empty tumbler from her hands.

"Take a deep breath," said Adam. "Another and deeper, Mirella. That's it. Better? And another."

Adam was rubbing her hands now, and the color had come back to her face. He stroked her hair. It was like silk and gave him a sensual thrill. He removed some strands from her cheek. Her skin felt wonderful to him. He could feel the beginning of an erection and told himself to put *that* out of his mind. But it wasn't easy. He pulled the tail of the little polka-dot bow and slowly slid the scarf off her throat. She still had a problem breathing normally. He put his large strong hand against her throat and gently massaged up and down, up and down.

"More deep breaths, Mirella," he said.

She did what she was told and felt much better for it. But she was embarrassed at losing control. His hands were so strong and sensual, she wanted him never to stop touching her. She felt his hand slip lower on her neck, to her chest where he massaged harder, and when his fingers touched her cleavage she felt a rush of ecstasy. She looked at him and said, somewhat nervously, "I'm all right now, Adam."

He smiled at her and asked, "Sure?"

"Yes, sure."

And, without any awkwardness or embarrassment, Adam slowly removed his hand from her chest, stroked her hair again, and stood up. He went to the fireplace and asked Mirella if she minded if he smoked a cigar. She didn't, so he lit a large, thick Cuban cigar, rolling it between his fingers as he sucked. In between puffs he said, "You know, Brindley, I think you had better stick with the English understatement."

"Actually, I did, Adam," said Brindley, then, realizing what he had revealed, gave Mirella a nervous look of concern.

Mirella had recovered herself completely. She said, "Brindley, it's going to be wonderful to be rich, to have all the money in the world to play with, to be generous with, to be extravagant with. This is not the time or the place to talk about the legacy. In a few days we can meet and work out the plan of disposing of everything as soon as possible. I will go to London with you to expedite matters, but I have no time to go to Turkey. This inheritance is going to add to my life, but not change my life. So it's quite simple: whatever we do, that's your brief. And now I had better get on with my reading. I won't let you down on that."

She stood up, making it quite clear without saying anything that their visit was over. Adam had not moved from in front of the marble fireplace. He was shocked at her indifference toward the legacy, and her lack of interest in the country he loved. He was so profoundly disappointed in her, he couldn't look at her, so he dropped his eyes and concentrated on the cigar in his hand.

"Mirella," he said in a soft, hynotic tone, "I know part of your great-grandmother's estate. I have seen fields of poppies that go on for miles broken only by an ancient Greek temple, and Hittite burial mounds and excavated Hittite cities that are on your land. I have walked up Mount Ararat and found ancient treasures, sailed along the Mediterranean coast of Turkey and watched the waves wash over the ruins of an ancient white marble amphitheater on your property. I have for years met dubious men exploiting your land and seen bad management that could destroy part of the history of civilization. And that, too, was on your land. I have canoed down the Euphrates: whole sections of it are yours. I have saved caravansaries, for the sheer architectural and historical beauty of them: some are yours too. I have slept in the conical churches of magical Cappadocia, part of which belongs to you. I have stood where Paul of Tarsus preached, on stones trodden by your ancestors. All this and much more is yours, and you have no time to go to Turkey? You have no interest to see Turkey? How can you liquidate your heritage?"

His words wiped out her initial impression of how she felt about him. She resented his intrusion.

"Adam, the legacy is a private matter and has nothing whatsoever to do with you. I don't want to look back to a load of ancestors, any more than my mother did or my grandmother did. I don't like it."

"Why, Mirella? Is it because it gives you a sense of your own mortality, and you don't want to face that?"

She was furious with him, but maintained her control over the fury. She turned to Brindley and said, "If you call me at the office tomorrow, I'll check my calendar and we will be able to make a series of appointments to work this thing out, as well as a date for when I can leave for London."

Brindley closed his briefcase, and looked at Adam. He was sorry he had brought the man along. He hadn't wanted to, and he should have followed his instinct. Mirella started to leave the room. The men followed in silence.

In the downstairs hall, Moses helped them on with their coats. They were about to leave when Brindley realized he had left his fountain pen somewhere upstairs in the living room. He followed Moses up to find it. Mirella opened the front door for Adam. It was still raining. She stood back so he could leave. He didn't. Instead he quietly but firmly closed the front door. Disgusted that she was not prepared even to listen and learn with an open mind about her fabulous legacy, he turned to her and said in a low voice, "When you opened the door this evening I was surprised. I thought, 'She is too good to be true. This erotic beauty is going to be the mistress of some of the great wonders of the world. There is justice, God is good.' My heart went out to you. What a romantic dream! And what a disappointment to discover nothing but a beautiful, ignorant, and unimaginative philistine with no feeling for culture. I find you the pitiful descendant of a once-remarkable family." He turned his collar up and stepped into the rain.

Mirella was shocked by his words, shocked and distressed. She put her hand on his arm as if to stop him. He did stop. She wanted to say something to him, prevent him from leaving her. But his words of disapproval had cut too deep. Her hand and arm were getting wet. He gently removed her hand from his sleeve, and he said in a hard, cold voice, "Mirella, we *all* are guilty of writing at least one wrong scenario for our lives, and are so busy trying to make it work, we forget about life. You are going to have to start living again. Don't take it too hard."

He gave her a short sharp salute and was gone. In the back of the Rolls, he relit his cigar and waited for Brindley. He never looked back at Mirella: he couldn't be bothered. He opened the door for Brindley, who waved good-bye to Mirella who still stood in the lighted doorway. But Adam didn't see her: she didn't exist for him. He felt incredibly horny—the rain, he thought.

As the car pulled away from the curb, Adam said, "Brindley, my friend, we are going to have a night to remember. We are going to have dinner at a private club called Partouz. They serve the best food, wine, and sex New York has to offer. No scenarios for us: just *life* to be lived."

The first flowers arrived on Mirella's desk at three forty-five in the afternoon the next day. They were long-stemmed tea roses, three dozen of them.

6

Mirella picked up the tiny envelope, removed the white florist's card, and looked at the signature again, as she had half a dozen times since the roses had arrived. *Adam Corey*. That was all it said. Just *Adam Corey*. A handsome, bold signature, written in black ink that nearly filled the card.

An apology? Or was he making some sort of overture? she wondered. He had been incredibly rude. On the other hand she had seen a lustful look for her in his eyes. But there was that horrid farewell. She winced. She could still feel the pain of his words. They had indeed cut deep.

Mirella had had a day full of people waffling and being indifferent . . . until the flowers arrived. It had begun with Moses, who rambled on about the living room and was indifferent to the news that she had become an heiress. At the H and O, Mrs. Kravatz, a Lexington Avenue specialty dress shop owner, sat next to Mirella and went on and on about angry and aggressive New York City. She only made her own point when, on leaving Ho's, she pounded on the plate-glass door, screeching to the man trying to enter, "Push! Don't pull! What a shmuck!" Then she yanked the door open and tapped him on the chest with a rigid finger that was more like a truncheon, saying, "Learn to read, buster. Time is money."

Indifference to Mirella's news had definitely been Paul's reaction. During their morning telephone conversation, she had sensed a note of annoyance rather than interest, and had had to endure yet more prevarication when he had hemmed and hawed about whether he could or could not meet her that evening.

In the assembly room, where she had gone to meet the head of her department, a dense fog of boredom, created by speaker after speaker droning on over the same subject, settled like a slow-killing gas, leaving the smattering of an audience that remained physically and morally limp. She woke Roland Culver from the stupor he had drifted into, and they left together.

While walking through the reception hall, crowded with delegates each vigorously lobbying and bargaining for their own resolutions before they took their turn in the General Assembly Hall, Mirella had asked Roland what he was doing there.

"It's a valuable discipline for foreign representatives to have to plead their cases before a global delegation," he said. "It enables governments to measure their acceptability, or lack of it, and, one hopes, see how the wind of compromise is blowing. It is also a good discipline for me to note how articulately they plead their cases. Unfortunately it was scarcely a linguist's joy. It was, in fact, just boring."

She had smiled at him, knowing full well the real reason he had been there was that, after thirty-nine years, he still loved and believed in the U.N., no matter how boring, mundane, and ineffectual it could be at times. Roland was a master of languages, and the maelstrom of written and spoken words was never a waste of time as far as he was concerned. He felt that although the speeches and resolutions were quickly forgotten and the world's problems rolled on, the U.N. at least gave world leaders a unique meeting place. He was convinced that the world would be marginally worse and less manageable without the General Assembly and his department. Mirella was not sure she didn't agree.

In his office she had conferred with him on a few important problems. Roland had sidestepped the immediate issues, and had bumbled on and on about them. Mirella knew that was his way of making her take over. But he waffled too long, and suddenly something in her snapped: she had had enough.

She had interrupted him, excused herself for changing the subject, and told him that, if he agreed, she would rearrange her work load and start her leave as soon as possible. He seemed delighted that she was at last taking some time off: all he wanted was for her to use up the accumulated nine weeks before the third Tuesday of September when the fortieth annual session of the General Assembly opened after the summer recess.

Ah, yes, Mirella thought now. A day of waffling and indifference all around. She slipped the card into the little white envelope and, yet again, placed it squarely on her desk. She swiveled her chair to look at the mass of beautiful full-blown long-stemmed tea roses arranged in a crystal vase on one of the rosewood stack tables placed between the shabby chairs. No waffle there. The roses were a direct statement, and although she didn't know quite what that statement was, she knew it was a positive one.

Brindley Ribblesdale woke up in a strange double bed between a magnificent naked dusky-brown lady and an equally magnificent naked blond Norwegian, who looked more like a god than a man.

His first thought had been of Adam Corey, who had treated him to a night to remember. He had never had such a night, nor had he ever met a man like Adam. From the moment they entered the Club Partouz the man drank, dined, laughed, and womanized with an enthusiasm for life, sex, and the moment such as Brindley had never seen in any human being before. Then he had remembered the meeting between Adam and Mirella Wingfield: quite a different thing that was nearly as explosive. This big, handsome, generous, usually quiet American who had been so helpful to Rumbold, Grumthorp, and Ribblesdale was full of surprises.

For Brindley the wild and depraved night was over: not to be forgotten, but over. It was business as usual now. How very English, he thought, as he tried to figure a way to get out of bed without rousing his sexual playmates. He had turned back the white cashmere blanket and tried to slip over the sleeping Negress without waking her. It had been impossible. The moment his skin grazed hers, he had been aroused by its satin texture. He smiled to himself, thinking business as usual would have to wait another fifteen minutes, and he woke her without words.

It was a passionate, liquescent awakening, and after he withdrew, he lay on top of his magnificent black lady, regained his breath, then slipped off her and quit the bed. He placed his finger on his lips, as if to tell her, "Don't say a word," then put the palms of his hands together and to his cheek, tilted his head to one side, and closed his eyes, as if to say, "Go back to sleep." The Norwegian god never woke up and the thousand-dollar-a-night hooker, who was used to doing what she was told, turned onto her side and closed her eyes. Brindley had discovered yet another new sexual wonder: the wordless fuck.

Now he padded into the bathroom, where he found everything neatly laid out for him. He shaved, showered, dressed, then returned to the bedroom, where he took a last look at his sleeping bed partners. He had never had sexual slaves to command before, men and women to help release those sexual inhibitions that were the very foundation of an English gentleman of his class. Much of the evening was still hazy in his mind, thanks to the drink and the drugs, but what he did remember of his night of debauchery gave him great pleasure. He smiled, then left them.

In the hall he met a foreign man in a white jacket who looked like a wrestler, but was in fact a houseman carrying a breakfast tray. He asked the servant to direct him to a telephone. Turhan showed him into a huge elegant library, with a graceful wooden staircase winding up to a narrow gallery that circled the upper half of the book-lined walls. Until then Brindley had had no idea where he was. Immediately on entering the room, though, he knew he was in Adam Corey's apartment.

It was hard to tell what made the room so much a reflection of his new friend. The worn deep-tufted Edwardian tobacco-colored leather sofas? The springing stuffed cheetah, or any of the other half dozen trophies standing or mounted in between the books? The French Directoire reading tables? The large bronze Remington sculptures, all looking like John Wayne riding, charging, rearing up in the wind on his favorite horse? Or was it the massive Boulle desk with books and maps spread over it? The antique Oriental carpets? The exquisite feathered American Indian chief headdresses standing under huge glass domes? Perhaps it was the antique high-back chairs, covered in tapestry depicting hunting scenes in faded blues and greens, scattered around the room. It was probably all of those things, and the dozens of silver-framed photographs of Adam with family, friends, and famous faces in exotic places.

It was from this room that Brindley made his first call of the day to Mirella, who told him she had begun to read the mass of documents he had left her. She asked where he was, so that she might call him back later in the day when she would know better when they could meet, and might even be able to tell him when they could leave for England.

Since there had been no mention in their conversation of the night before or of Adam Corey, Brindley's instinct was not to tell her where he was. Instead he told her he was moving around the city and would call her back.

He had an excellent breakfast. Strawberries, and oranges, bacon, eggs, sausage, toast, and endless cups of delicious hot black coffee were served to him by Turhan on the vast terrace of Adam's flat, very high up over the city, in the sunshine, sheltered from the wind by large pine trees.

After breakfast Turhan led him back to the library, where he met Adam, who was staring thoughtfully through the window. He appeared to be miles away and only when he was made aware of Brindley's presence did he snap back to reality. He rose from his chair and greeted Brindley with a smile and a handshake. The only reference Adam made to the previous night was when he said, "Quite a night, Brindley; you're good company, fella," and then added, "If you need any help from me on the Oujie legacy, you know I'm available to you. I'll be leaving for Turkey in about a week and will remain there for the next few months. You have the address and the telephone numbers."

The only allusion Brindley made to the night before was when he said, "Thank you for your boundless hospitality, Adam," as Adam walked him to the elevator.

Mirella Wingfield's name came up when, as the elevator doors opened, Brindley said, "Adam, I hope one day I may be able to do you some kindness for all the help and friendship you've shown me."

"You have, Brindley. You introduced me to Mirella Wingfield."

The elevator doors closed and during its smooth descent through thirty-seven floors to the lobby, Brindley tried to figure that out. He couldn't.

It was not until he walked into and out of the lobby, and through the entrance onto Fifth Avenue, that he realized Adam lived in his own penthouse apartment at the Sherry Netherland Hotel. Brindley was not very far from his own hotel, the St. Regis. It was from his room there that he called Mirella for the second time and received a message to please call at four o'clock.

Now he phoned once more. Their conversation was short. She told him it was done: she had her schedule all worked out. And she asked him if he could stop by her office between then and six o'clock to discuss it. He could.

Things were moving fast for Mirella, faster than she would have liked, and she harbored some resentment that the legacy was doing just what she hadn't wanted it to do—interfere in the comfortable, safe, secure life-style she had created for herself.

She pressed her lips tightly together and bit the inside of them, turned her head from side to side, and sighed, while with an open hand she slapped the top of her desk. She sniffed and was amazed that the scent from the roses filled the room. It served to remind her of Adam Corey's harsh words about her, and she was not amused.

She called her executive staff into her office and told them of her plans to take a nine-week vacation, but that she would not take it all at once. She explained that the first part was to begin as soon as she had put her office in order and that she expected to be away for a week, possibly ten days.

She was mildly astonished at how easy it was for her to arrange her absence, and was surprised to hear her secretary and her two assistants express a degree of excitement about her going away. They made it quite clear they felt she needed a change. Mirella noticed how each of them kept stealing glances at the flowers.

"For Christ's sake, Barbara," she finally said, "what's the big deal? You'd think I never receive flowers. Why do you all keep sneaking glances at them? They are only a few damned roses."

"Sorry to correct you, Mirella," said Ed Cole, her senior assistant, "but those roses are not *just* flowers: they're really sumptuous roses with the longest stems, and the most hauntingly beautiful color I have ever seen. They are probably rare, and there are so many of them. They have taken over the room and changed it. I hope they have something to do with your vacation, because if they do you're going to have a great time."

Mirella had known and worked with her colleagues for ten years or more. They were friends, not intimate ones but still friends nevertheless. She looked at the roses again and grudgingly had to admit to herself that they were indeed fine specimens and certainly did make a glaring change in the room. She appreciated Ed's kind thought, and knew that not only he but the others wished her well. So she told them that the flowers were nothing but an apology from a man she met who had been very rude to her.

"Boy, if that's how he says 'I'm sorry,' can you imagine how he says 'I love you'?" Barbara remarked.

"Rude? My dear, there is rude and there is rude. If his expression of regret is anything like his rudeness, the guy must have dealt you a whopper of an offense," Bryan Palmer said.

"Stop fishing, Bryan. I'm not going to tell you about it."

"Who's fishing? I was wishing," shot back Bryan.

They all laughed and Ed said, "Men don't usually send roses to say they're sorry unless they are emotionally involved. Are you sure you're reading this guy right, Mirella? Maybe you've been in New York too long and can't tell the difference between a man who cares and an insult. Women tend to get things like that mixed up when they live in a smart-ass fag city."

That remark took Mirella aback, but she covered up beautifully by chuckling and said, "I had no idea I had a staff of hopeless romantics. You all look so disappointed. Cheer up. I do have something I *will* tell you. The reason I am taking leave now is that I've come into an inheritance, and I have to go to London to settle it."

She furnished them with no details except that it came to her from a great-grandmother. The news took the edge off speculation about the flowers, which was a great relief to Mirella. She allowed them a few minutes to wish her well in her good fortune and then asked them to get down to the business at hand, which was to go over the department's work load and rearrange things to allow for her absence.

In a short time her office was a hive of activity. She had her assistants bring in the files on their projects. She called for her department's agenda. Barbara brought in the office roster. Ed and Bryan were on and off her telephones, buzzing their secretaries for various bits of information, computer disks, microfilm, the "problems file."

Within the hour Mirella had such a good picture of things she needed no progress report, and was able to start delegating authority to her two assistants, who called in their secretaries to take notes on the conference.

There was a moment when she tilted her chair back and was

deciding to whom to hand over one of her pet projects. It was the translating and publishing in Chinese of all of the several thousand speeches that would be delivered from the seven main committees and the plenary of the U.N., and the several hundred resolutions adopted during the coming year. That was to be her department's contribution to the United Nations fortieth-anniversary celebrations. That made Mirella feel something close to anxiety.

Priorities were changing, everything was turned upside down, and so fast. And the worst was that she was the one doing it, against her own will, and, so far as she could see, for no good reason. Mirella had the grace to correct that thought because she had to admit that forty million dollars a year was a good reason, even if she didn't like the idea of the disruption in her life.

The private telephone rang. She answered.

"Hello."

"Hi, can you talk?"

It was Paul. Mirella turned her chair away from the hubbub of the office. She closed her eyes, and her heart skipped a beat. She was so relieved—nothing was really changing. His voice zapped her back to feeling safe and secure, and she realized what was upsetting her. it wasn't the legacy—she could handle that—but those lovely flowers. They were a lethal reminder of Adam Corey and what he thought of her. The realization, and accepting it, made her feel better. She could live with his disapproval. The flowers suddenly became magnificent to her, and that, so far as she was concerned, was the end of that.

"Briefly," she told Paul, "I have a room full of people here who are all busy with each other at the moment."

"About tonight . . ."

"Yes?"

"I can only manage to come between seven and nine. That's o'clock, not times, by the way." He chuckled and asked, "Does that suit you?"

"Do you mean the o'clock or the times?" she asked mischievously in a low voice.

"Oh, it's like that, is it? You sound to me as if you want to be ravished."

"*Loved* and ravished," she whispered, then in her normal voice added, "I'll be home by seven and I really look forward to seeing you. There are so many things I want to talk to you about."

"I hope you're just saying that for the benefit of your staff, because I don't want to talk. I want to fuck, and I mean fuck. I've been thinking about crucifying you with my cock all day." With that, he was gone.

The disconnected telephone whined in Mirella's ear. She removed it, held it in her hand, and looked at it, while the empty cry continued. She replaced the receiver on its cradle. There it was again, that ruthless, mean overtone in his voice. Oh yes, she would be sexually ravaged this night, but not loved and ravaged as she had suggested.

Slowly she swiveled her chair around to face the mayhem in her office. Her best friend Deena's words rang in her ears. "Shoot for a hundred, but if you get fifty percent of what you want, you're still winning. And always remember fifty-one percent would have been better."

Deena. Mirella made a mental note to call her that evening. There hadn't been time to call her about the legacy, and now there was even more to surprise her with: taking time off work, her trip to London. Deena Weaver, her friend for twenty-five years, who loved and adored her, but was very disapproving of Mirella's well-organized life, so very different from her own, would be overwhelmed by the news. Mirella smiled.

Paul was forgotten, and she and her executive staff worked on together for another hour until Brindley arrived.

He watched the flurry of people flow out through her office door, and overheard snatches of conversation.

. . . "team effort," "deserves it," "too much work ethic," "ten o'clock meeting," "never," "bombshell" . . .

Brindley was impressed by all the activity. He walked into the room expecting to see a harried Mirella Wingfield, inundated with work, buried knee-deep in papers. Instead, he saw her sitting on the edge of her desk, long luscious shapely legs encased in smoky-gray nylon stockings, crossed and showing just a hint of thigh where her narrow gray gabardine skirt rode up. She was peeling a banana. Her elegant but sensible Ferragamo gray calfskin shoes stood empty and neatly together on the floor beneath her. The desk was covered with tidy stacks of documents.

"Hello, Brindley, come in. I'm sorry I had to put you off until now, but I saw no sense in wasting your time or mine until I knew for sure how I could arrange things."

"I quite understand," he said.

She indicated a chair just opposite her. He placed his briefcase on the floor next to it and sat down.

"I must confess, Mirella, I have been quite concerned about you since our meeting last evening. I know what a shock, albeit a good shock, I dealt you. But please be assured I'll help you in any way I can."

"There is no question in my mind about that, Brindley. I began reading the information you left me and I want you to know I haven't changed my mind about liquidating as soon as possible. That's why I have arranged to take a long leave from the office. I want to be able to work flat-out with you to that end.

"I have several weeks off from this office. I plan to leave for London as soon as I have everything in order here: that should be in four or five days. I'll spend a week, ten days, even two weeks if it's necessary, working with you every day in your offices, then return here. I have a house at the beach and I will take the remainder of my vacation there, where I will set up an office specifically to handle the estate. And you will fly in when necessary to confer with me. That should about do it. Would you like a banana?"

Mirella turned to get the small crystal fruit bowl. Brindley looked at the top half of her body, with the same admiration he had for her legs. She was wearing a white silk long-sleeved shirt, with a fine rust-colored pinstripe in it. It was open at the neck and, as she stretched out to take the bowl, he could see clearly the swell of her breasts as they moved, the shadow of her nipples, the narrow waist under the silk.

Yesterday he had been thrilled because his long-sought-after heiress had turned out to be a rather beautiful, if a little too "American," lady executive. Last night in her home, she had revealed something of what was under that façade: An aristocratic, somewhat sensitive, attractive, very determined woman. And now he saw another Mirella Wingfield: a sensuous, sexy lady. Oh yes, the blood of her fabulous ancestors ran through *her* veins, only she didn't believe it or accept it . . . yet.

He had peeled a banana and taken a bite before he realized what he was doing. He began to chew; they ate in silence, looking at each other.

"I do rather detest bananas," he said as he stood up. "They make me think of nursery food. I forgot I don't like them."

"Sorry, Brindley; how about a pear?" she said as she slipped smoothly off the desk into her shoes and walked around it to fetch the wastebasket, which she offered him for the unwanted fruit. She sat down at her desk, and he sat back down in his chair.

"No, no pear, nothing, thank you, Mirella. It appears you have it all worked out."

"You seem surprised," she said with an engaging smile.

"Not so much surprised as filled with admiration for the swiftness with which you work. I am delighted we will be able to work together in London, and so soon. I think it would be advantageous for me to leave for England at once, in order to prepare for your arrival. I'd like to suggest that you read everything here and hold off with any questions until we meet in London. Of course, I will be available to you at all times by telephone."

Mirella agreed. She slipped into her suit jacket, a wide-shouldered, well-tailored double-breasted Armani in camel hair, took her handbag, and the two left the building together. They parted on First Avenue, going in very different directions, she going north, he going west, and both feeling a surge of excitement about their next meeting.

Mirella was exhausted, and hoped her hike home would revive her. She walked quickly, aware of the hustle and bustle of New York rushing into the cocktail hour, and was looking forward to her own chilled martini. By the time she hurried up the front stairs of her house, having mulled over her day all the way home, she was quite pleased with herself. In a few weeks she would be rich—very, very rich. In a few months she would have disposed of the estate, have had her vacation in the Long Island house Paul had rented for her, and this inconvenience to the order of her life would be over. She had it all worked out.

She fished in her handbag for her key, opened the front door, and called out, "Moses, I'm home."

There was no answer. She called again. "Moses."

The telephone light on the hall table was flickering. She went to it and picked it up.

"Hello, Moses, I'm all done in. Will you make me a lovely, large chilled martini and bring it up to my bedroom?"

"Of course, Miss Mirella. But may I suggest you come on down here into the kitchen and have a small one? Then I'll bring you a fresh one, to have in your bath."

"Okay, Moses," she said.

There was nothing unusual about Moses's suggestion. They often did it. It gave Mirella a chance to discuss her plans for dinner if they had not already worked them out, and to go over the events of the day.

In the kitchen she found Moses stirring her martini. She had learned to read him and what she saw this evening was an amused and mischievous Moses. She sat down.

"Why don't you have something, Moses?"

He took a beer from the refrigerator, sat down opposite her, and asked, "Are you in for dinner?"

"Yes, but can you make something you can leave in the oven? I'll come down around ten to eat it, and have it here in the kitchen. Oh, and can you do a crudité, with a nice lemon-and-tarragon mayonnaise and put that upstairs? Mr. Prescott is coming for an hour or so."

Moses made a mental note—bourbon and branch water. He sipped his beer.

"Well, what is it, Moses? What are you just dying to tell me? I know there's something because you look as if you are about to burst."

"Not tell you, Miss Mirella, show you. Come on."

He smiled and Mirella was amused. She drained her glass and felt much the better for it. She imagined it was one of his wondrous cakes on a pedestal dish in the dining room. They passed the dining room, there was no cake. They were about to go up the stairs, when she thought, Oh, how wonderful: the plumber had at long last come and fixed the dripping pipe in her bathroom. The doorbell rang. Moses had been leading the way and Mirella was closest to the door, so she said, "Never mind, Moses, stay where you are, I'll get it." She opened the door and was taken aback when she saw a man in a chauffeur's uniform holding a country basket with a lovely arched handle. It was brimming over with magnificent African violets.

"Miss Wingfield?" the man asked.

Mirella nodded.

"These are for you," he said and handed her the basket.

There was the same plain white florist's envelope tucked in among the blossoms. Mirella was speechless. Moses came to her aid, took the basket from her, thanked the man, and closed the door.

She knew they were from Adam Corey before she even opened the envelope. She was astonished for a moment because she had managed to wipe him out of her mind for the last two hours.

"Aren't you going to read the card?" asked Moses, as he reached into the basket and handed it to her.

"I don't have to," she answered. "I know who they're from. The same man who sent me roses today."

"You mean daisies and—"

Mirella interrupted. "Moses, I know the difference between a daisy and a rose, silly. I'll say one thing for him: he certainly has a good florist. Come on, let's put them in the living room, that room could use some flowers," and she started to walk up the stairs, Moses following, and she thinking maybe Ed Cole was right, the unopened envelope still clutched in her hand.

On the first floor landing Moses excused himself and passed in front of her.

"Let me go first," he said, "and put on some lights."

And before she could say anything he handed her back the basket. She followed close behind, saying, "Lights? Why do we need the lamps on when it's still light out?"

Her last words slipped into a gasp as she entered the room. For the second time, a broad-smiling Moses took the basket from her, and said, "I, too, know the difference between a daisy and a rose."

The room was exactly as it had been the night before, except for one thing: it was filled with flowers. Potted flowering shrubs. Umbrella-shaped greenery growing from three-, four-, and five-foot-high, three-inch-thick tree trunks. Pure white daisies with rich yolk-yellow centers. Magenta, red, and hot-pink azaleas everywhere. They turned the room into an eccentric, exotic conservatory without glass. Mirella was overawed by it all. She walked around the living room among her things and Adam's flowers, bending down to take in their scent, touching them.

She said almost in a whisper, "He must be mad."

"I don't know about mad," said Moses, "but I know about rich: that's what you have to be to send a lady flowers like this, very rich."

"How, _when_ did all this happen? Was there a note?"

"About half-past four. A large van arrived, with two men and a young girl: she was the florist. She handed me an envelope and a card. The envelope was addressed to me and the card to you. They waited outside until I read the note, then asked if they could make the delivery." From the inside pocket of Moses's jacket, he produced the two items.

Mirella felt an excitement she had not experienced for a very long time. It was akin to the warmth she felt when she first met the man. She opened the envelope and was surprised: all it said was "Adam Corey." She turned the card over: there was nothing there, and she thought that odd. It was exactly like the card that accompanied the roses. Then she took the note addressed to Moses. It read:

> Moses,
>
> I am the gentleman who accompanied Mr. Ribblesdale to Miss Wingfield's house last evening. I would like to surprise her with these flowers. These people will help you to place them. Thank you,
>
> Adam Corey

Moses was walking around the room turning on all the lamps. She watched him, went to one of the settees, sat down, and put her feet up.

"Well, what do you think?" Moses asked.

"I think it is absolutely wonderful," she answered.

"Do you think we will be wealthy enough, once you have your inheritance, to keep it going like this?" asked Moses, who was well aware of Mirella's finances and managed the household on a shoestring.

"Oh, I don't know about that," she said, then hesitated and added, "What's the matter with me? Yes, of course we will. I forgot, I'm going to be very, very wealthy. We can, Moses, but we will still have to be practical, you know, like have duplicate trees and alternate them. We can give them six-month rest periods in my dad's greenhouses at Wingfield Park. Oh God, just listen to me. I haven't signed a paper yet and I'm making plans to be extravagant. I can see we'll have to watch that sort of thing, Moses."

She looked at the signature on the card again. "Moses, do me a favor: bring me a drink. This is too wonderful to leave." She placed the small card on top of its envelope and tried to shove them into her jacket pocket. She withdrew them again, because something else was in her pocket: the card that had been tucked into the violets.

The violets. "Oh, Moses, while you're at it, the violets

don't seem to be right in here. They will look lovely up in my bedroom on my dressing table, don't you think?" He nodded his approval and left the room with them. Mirella opened the little sealed envelope expecting nothing but his signature. She was pleased to read more:

Have lunch with me, tomorrow, one o'clock, Mishimo's?

Adam

7

"Will you?"
"Yes."
"That's *wonderful*."
"The flowers you sent, Adam, *they're* wonderful."
"The flowers are a beginning."
"Adam . . ."
"Not now. At Mishimo's tomorrow."

In the back of the taxi, Mirella went over that short conversation, again and again. She remembered every word he said: the emotion she heard in his voice was registered with her forever. Nor would she ever forget her own emotional reaction to his call. She had cried, put the receiver down, covered her face with her hands, and wept again.

The cab was stuck in a traffic jam four blocks from the restaurant. It had been murderous traffic all the way across town, and she could not bear one more minute of the driver's complaints.

"We're going west, you're going to a place that's on a one-way street going east. You think this is bad, wait until we cross Fifth Avenue, and God knows when that will be at the rate we're going. Sit back, try to relax, that's all you can do. What else can you do? What a city! Gone to the dogs. The filth, the dirt, the potholes, not to mention the muggers. The joggers are another menace to the cabbie. You should've picked a restaurant on a street going west. Now I'll have to go two avenues over out of the way to make a right turn. Huh, that's if the street's not blocked off for *emergency repairs*. How can a man do a job like this in a crazy city like this, four feet in five minutes, that's about what we're averaging, a fucking—

excuse my language, lady—four feet in five minutes. I ask you, isn't that pathetic?"

"Yes, *pathetic*, I'm late, I'm getting out," Mirella said, as she opened the door.

"Frankly, I don't like that. Not exactly good passenger manners to leave a cabbie without a fare in the middle of a block. But I don't blame you. You should have walked in the first place."

Mirella paid the driver the fare and a fat tip, through the driver's window, while standing in a five-inch-deep pothole. When he looked at the bill in his hand and was satisfied, he bent his head out the window and called after her, "Have a good day," as a new victim opened his cab door and sat down.

Weaving between the people on the pavement, Mirella hurried through the streets. She was late and wished that she wasn't. Her thoughts were of Adam, as they had been all last evening: after he called; when Paul arrived; during every orgasm Paul wrenched from her; and after Paul left, until she went to sleep.

She was both puzzled and thrilled over the new feelings Adam inspired in her. Only once before in her life had she known anything like it. There had been a sliver, a mere hint of it with Paul when they first met, and she had thought then that nothing in the world could be better.

Mirella waited for the light to change and then rushed with the crowd across the avenue and down the street. She was relieved to see, a hundred yards ahead, the restaurant's sign, MISHIMO, and she slowed down. Her last thought before she entered was, if there was to be nothing else between Adam and herself but his flowers, his call, this lunch, meeting him would have done one thing: reminded her how good it was to feel, *really* feel something beautiful between herself and another human being. It was then and there, on the pavement in front of Mishimo's, that Mirella dropped Paul, finally, and forever.

She pushed the door open, leaving the chaos of the city and the sunshine outside behind her, and was swallowed up for a second by the quiet, sensuous beauty of the darkness within.

Her eyes adjusted to the interior light as she stood on the deep, soft beige carpet. The period brownstone house had been left just as it was and the dark mahogany walls and ebony staircase and balustrade, rising steeply up to the first floor, gleamed from years of care and polish. A large bronze

Shinto temple lantern hung in the center of the hall and a huge, ancient, fearsome-looking bronze shaggy dog, famous for once guarding an emperor of Japan's palace, leered out from under the elegant curve of the same beige velvet-carpeted stairs.

There was not a sound to be heard, nor a person to be seen. Mirella walked over to the pier mirror near the entrance door and rearranged the few strands of hair out of place, when a pretty young Japanese hostess appeared from nowhere.

"Miss Wingfield?" she asked in a hushed voice.

Mirella turned around and said, "Yes," in what was nearly a whisper—which came naturally in the templelike atmosphere of Mishimo's.

The young woman, dressed in a simple light-gray kimono and an obi of gold- and silver-embroidered cranes, smiled, bowed low from her waist, and said, "Mr. Corey is here. Would you like to freshen yourself, or would you like to join him directly?"

"I'm very late, and had better join him directly," she answered and quickly stole another look in the mirror, adding, "I will have to do."

Mirella knew, as she said it, that that was underestimating the way she looked. She had on a deep violet silk dress with very full accordion-pleated sleeves that finished in a narrow cord of the same material tight at her wrists. By contrast the bodice clung to her and revealed that underneath were naked voluptuous breasts and a very small waist. The dress had a narrow belt that matched her jacket, and the accordion-pleated skirt, reaching to just below the knee, flared out provocatively as she walked.

Her jacket was magenta-and-cream-checked linen, whose sleeves finished loosely at the elbow, allowing the luscious dress sleeves to show. Her large gold Mayan frog lay grandly on her chest from the ring of gold around her neck, and her feet were shod in bone-colored high-heeled shoes. Her matching calfskin handbag hung from her shoulder on a handsome thin gold chain.

Mirella's rich raven-colored hair and white skin glowed because she was excited and happy. She was aware of looking especially pretty, not only because women know very well when they do, but because of the whispers of approval she had heard from Ossario and Hymie while she had eaten her bagel at breakfast, and because of the way the male delegates

at the U.N. had given her lascivious looks. Women had checked out her clothes and men on the streets had turned to take a second look.

The hostess smiled sweetly and led her up the stairs. Mirella took a deep breath, let it out slowly, and tried to compose herself. She was not so much nervous as she was eager to see Adam again.

He was standing in front of a mahogany and ebony bar, one foot on the brass rail, listening to a man standing beside him. Mirella saw him before he saw her. He was more handsome and virile-looking than she remembered, and bigger too. The delicate-looking Japanese man in a crisp white jacket who was tending bar leaned forward and whispered something to Adam, who turned around as she approached with the hostess.

They looked at each other across the room and Mirella felt that same rush of warmth flow through her as she had during their first encounter. The hostess stepped to one side and they moved toward each other; more, they seemed to be pulled together by some invisible force.

Mirella and Adam met in the middle of the small, nearly empty room. They smiled. Slowly, hesitantly, both raised their hands and reached out to each other simultaneously. They held hands. Adam broke the spell when he lowered his head and kissed first one of her hands, then the other. Mirella's heart was pounding so hard that she imagined he could hear it. He released her, stepped to her side, and put his arm around her shoulder. He crooked his index finger and ran it ever so gently, tenderly up and down the side of her cheek. The first words he said to her were "I love you," whispered in her ear as they followed the diminutive hostess to their table.

The first words she said to him were when they were alone, seated next to each other on a low beige velvet banquette.

"I'm a linguist, and not supposed to be at a loss for words, yet whenever you speak to me, you leave me speechless."

"Speechless good or speechless bad?" he asked with the hint of a tease in his voice, a serious look in his eyes, and a smile on his lips.

"There, you've done it again," she said, and they both laughed at themselves, softly and good-naturedly, never breaking the spell of intimacy between them.

Their laughter was something of a relief for Mirella: it helped her to regain her balance enough to say, "I'm sorry I'm late, I don't like being late, but the traffic was dreadful and I ended up walking—well, actually, it was more like Olympic walking—the last four blocks."

"I don't care about the time as long as you're here. Time doesn't matter. That we're together matters, wanting each other matters, feeling the real thing with *you* is what matters to me. And for you?"

"Yes, for me too," she said, unable to hold back her feeling for him. Once Mirella had declared herself, she was so overcome with emotion, there was nothing for her but to go on. She turned around to face him better and put her hand delicately on his arm. He covered it with his own hand.

"I wanted you so much the night we met," she said in a hushed voice with a slight tremor in it. "I was shattered when you left me. The flowers, the *wonderful* flowers you sent me. When the roses arrived at my office, I could feel only pain, the pain of your words, the pain of my loss. And your card offered me no reprieve. Finally, I came to terms with it.

"When I arrived home and saw the daisies and the azaleas, trees of them, all over my living room, I knew it was all right, you still wanted me. You turned my room into a garden, and filled it with love; only after I understood *that* did I realize how much we almost lost. I think the basket of violets you sent is the most tender lovemaking I have ever known. When you called and I heard your voice, it all became *real*, certain. I put the receiver down and cried, releasing so much stored-up love and passion, feelings I had long ago forgotten to use in these jaded, nonromantic times of ours. Adam, you make me feel mellow and ridiculous, and I'm not so sure I want that. I love you, but—"

Adam touched her lips with his finger, as if to silence her, then he caressed them by tracing first the outline, then the provocative soft flesh, and sliding his finger along the crack between, where he felt the warm moist velvet of the inside. He said, very slowly and clearly, as if he were saying it once and for always, "I want you as much as you want me, but no *but*'s. Remember that for the rest of my life all the flowers in the world are for you."

He took the silk handkerchief from the breast pocket of his gray pinstripe jacket and picked up a tear that lay precariously in the corner of each of her passionate violet-colored eyes.

"I think you'd be relieved," he said, "if this luncheon culminated in a fabulous afternoon of sex, and was the beginning of a terrific, romantic, erotic affair, and nothing else. Anybody can do that, but not everybody can feel the real thing. Be brave." He gave her a warm, open laugh, adding, "How about a little sake, for courage?"

Mirella smiled at Adam. "How about a *lot* of sake for courage?" She made a little turn on the banquette in order to snuggle up closer to him, slipped her arm through his, and squeezed it close to her breast.

Adam gave a discreet signal. A waiter and waitress approached their table and gave the traditional Japanese bow. The kimono-clad woman carried a little square crimson lacquered tray with two small, scented, steaming hand towels tightly rolled up on it. From the front of her obi she withdrew a pair of ivory sticks, which she nimbly used to pick open the hot towel, shake it loose, and offer it to Mirella. She repeated the act for Adam.

Mirella and Adam cleansed their hands and returned the now-crumpled towels to the tray. The waiter draped a large crisp white napkin across first Mirella's lap, then Adam's. The warm rice wine arrived in a small porcelain carafe, and was served in tiny cups. Saucer-size cream-colored plates of sashimi arranged like minute bouquets of flowers were placed on the low table before them.

They were served swiftly, efficiently, silently in the small quiet dining room, conspicuous for its serene beauty and lack of decoration. They dimly realized there were two other tables with people dining at them. They picked up the tiny cups, touched the rims together, and took their first sips in silence.

"Have I told you that I think you're beautiful?" he asked.

"No," she answered.

"Well, I do, I think you're gorgeous."

"Oh, that's nice," she said, feeling flattered and happy.

"You know, Mirella, you're not the only one surprised about how we feel. I've known you approximately forty-eight hours and I find it hard to believe that you haven't been with me all my life."

They sat there sipping their sake and looking into each other's eyes. Mirella said, "It's all been so fast, furious and fast, that I have only just realized I know nothing, absolutely nothing, about you, except your name, that you're an archaeologist, and that you obviously like flowers."

Adam refilled their cups and handed hers to her.

"I am forty-eight years old, I am a considerably wealthy man, I am an adventurer, an explorer, a big-game hunter, a corporate businessman, as well as an archaeologist. I use my money to excavate lost wonders of the world. I live what is considered nowadays to be an exotic life, in a white marble palace on the Bosporus in Istanbul. When I'm not there I am usually on an expedition of one kind or another in some remote part of the world, trekking through the Amazonian jungle, through the highlands of New Guinea, up the Himalayas, or I am here in my apartment at the Sherry Netherland. And I have five wonderful children ranging in age from twenty-five years down to seven years, whom I enjoy and hope enjoy me."

Mirella drank her cup of sake in one hard swallow, and said in a low desperate voice, "I can't bear it! You're married."

Adam put his cup down, took her hand, which had gone quite cold, and rubbed it.

"No, I'm not," he said. "I merely told you I have five children. I didn't say anything about a wife. I *was* married, but that was twenty-five years ago. It didn't work out, we divorced after three years and two children. My other children were mothered by women I've lived with. I've always liked having sex and relationships with beautiful, erotic women and have always liked fatherhood. I have been a great disappointment to my mistresses in the past, who assumed I would marry them because they were pregnant. I did that only once, and *that* was a mistake. I am not a man to make the same mistake twice.

"Please don't look so worried. You'll love them, they aren't babies anymore, and they really are terrific kids. They'll be playmates for you as they are for me, when I can find them. They do have lives of their own, except of course for the two youngest."

"This is all mad, quite mad. What's happening to me? I thought my life was set—worked out and set."

"And what about me?" Adam asked. "I lived a happy bachelor-father life, ignorant of what I had been missing until I found you. I've enjoyed my work, my shooting, fishing, hunting, erotic lovemaking. But everything that I like to do pales when I think of loving you. I want to take you . . . in your lovely room, in my apartment, in my house on the Bosporus, everywhere. Oh, how I look forward to exquisite, delectable, erotic sex with you. I wish we were alone, really alone, right now, so we could lie down together in each other's arms and talk, feed each other erotic food, do erotic things, and make love, tender and delicate, wild and passionate, heart-rending love, over and over again all afternoon."

A pair of ivory sticks lay on the table in front of him; with them he picked up a morsel of the excellently prepared sashimi, dipped it in a sauce, and offered it to Mirella.

"I hope you like sashimi," he said, holding a sliver of the shiny white raw sturgeon against her lips.

She sucked the delicacy from between the ivory sticks and it disappeared between her soft, rosy lips. She ate it while he watched. After she swallowed, she said, "I like sashimi, I like sake, and I like your idea for this afternoon. I like the spare beauty of this room, but I wish we were home, under the flowering trees, having a picnic."

He refilled their cups again, sipped from his, and said with a smile, "We're on our way."

Adam beckoned to the waiter and asked him to pack up their lunch as quickly as possible, plates, sticks, cups, napkins, sake, and all. Then he asked Mirella, "Do we have the afternoon?"

"No," she said, "but we will."

They scarcely spoke until they were in the backseat of Adam's Rolls. He picked up the car telephone and said, "What's your office number?"

Adam put the call through for her and listened with some admiration to the way she managed to delegate her afternoon appointments to others. He further appreciated the authoritative manner she took and the quick decisions she made when presented with a problem from the other end of the line, as the car negotiated the midday traffic to her house.

Adam liked this side of her: he found it exciting. It led him to ponder why, being as obviously secure as she was within herself, and so good at spontaneous changes, as she was clearly demonstrating, she was so adamant against her legacy, or anything else, for that matter, that threatened her life with change. He took her hand while she was still on the telephone and held it. At one point he kissed her on the cheek.

When she handed the receiver back to him, he said, "You're wonderful."

"Am I? Oh, that's good. I want you to think I'm nothing less than wonderful. You have no idea how hard I've worked at it. Do you know why?"

She bent her head forward to give him a playful kiss on the lips. He reached out, put his arms around her, pulled her roughly tight up against him, and took over the kiss. Mirella felt herself dissolving, and when he released her, she said in a low, husky voice, "Because nothing, but nothing, in this world feels as good as being wonderful, unless it's both being and having you, like now."

They stood beside each other in front of her door. Mirella fumbled in her handbag for the keys. As she reached out to put the key in the lock, she looked up at the handsome man watching her. His strength, power, and masculine warmth took her breath away. This very sexy man emanated *the* ultimate adventure and it made her feel inarticulate and clumsy.

She couldn't manage to put the key in the lock. He stepped behind her and slipped his arm past her waist. She felt it press against the side of her breast as he reached up under her arm and guided the key in her hand into the keyhole. She felt not only clumsy but weak and embarrassed because of their mutual need for each other. She could feel the outline of his body pressing up against her back when he put his other arm around her in order to reach the doorknob, turn the key, and push the front door open. She trembled.

Having opened the door, they were confronted by Moses, aiming a twelve-bore shotgun point-blank at them. Adam's first instinct was to protect Mirella. He pushed her to one side, and grabbed the gun before anyone knew what happened. It was all over in seconds, and all three began shouting and rebuking each other at the same time. Mirella screamed at them to stop and when they did they burst into peals of laughter, at themselves and at the sight of John, the chauffeur, who had followed them up, standing passively on the threshold holding the basket of food.

Mirella, who had somehow landed in the horn chair in the hall, managed to say, between fits of laughter, "Moses, what a performance."

He, having curbed his laughter, replied, "Well, you should have called. I thought it was a burglar. You never come home at lunchtime: I've never known you to come home in the middle of the day. You usually call to tell me if you are going to be early or late, even if it's a matter of twenty minutes. Who could have guessed it was you? What's happened? Why have you come home?"

Adam, who had cracked the gun open, found it empty. He

began to laugh again, shaking his head from side to side in disbelief at the whole farce.

"We've come home to have an amorous lunch and an assignation," said a still-laughing Mirella. "We were going to have a magical picnic in our flower-laden room," she said and pointed to the basket containing the supposed romantic alfresco meal still being held by the poker-faced John.

Moses took the basket from him, thanked him politely, and closed the front door.

"If your great-uncle Hyram had seen this," he said, "it would have given him a good laugh. He liked a little drama, and he had his assignations, too, but I can't remember one starting off like this. Maybe I did overdo it. I should have used his handgun. I think I must apologize."

"Never mind, Moses," Mirella said, trying to keep the suppressed laughter out of her voice. "I guess liking a little drama runs in the family, and Mr. Corey might just as well know what an eccentric bunch we are."

Adam was amused by the easy banter between the two. "Moses," he said, "sorry if I overreacted, but it was a hunter's instinct. A keen shot never likes a gun aimed at him, especially one that could take out an elephant."

"Well," said Moses, who had regained his composure and taken up his housekeeper role, "if this is the picnic lunch, I think I had better leave it to you, Mr. Corey. I'll just put it upstairs in the living room. Will you be wanting dinner in, this evening, Miss Mirella?"

Adam saw a look of embarrassment cross Mirella's face, and the hint of a blush on her cheeks. There was a moment of awkward silence, as if she were unable to answer the simple question. Adam came to her rescue; he went to her, put his arm around her waist, looked into her eyes, and said in a low voice, "First let me give you lunch. Who knows? It may stretch on through dinner and breakfast, and forever. We might want to dine here, there, or anywhere. It's not a problem."

They started up the stairs behind Moses and Mirella said, "Moses, we don't know," and was somewhat surprised to hear herself saying "we." So many years with Paul and it had never been "we." It felt so strange but so right; yet, when she told Moses she would call him on the intercom if she wanted him, she reverted to "I."

Adam's first reaction to the living room was sheer delight.

He was thrilled to have made a contribution to what he thought was one of the most bizarre and enchanting rooms he had ever seen. Here dwelt the eccentric side of Mirella and he loved it, as much as any of the other things he saw in her.

The room was dappled in sunshine pouring in from the window facing the street and the light from the window overlooking the garden at the far end of the room. Mirella saw that Adam was completely overawed by the room, and she watched him as he walked around the chairs and tables, the packing cases, the desk, the tall potted azalea trees. She saw him look up at the flowers cascading above his head from trees that had been placed on tables, on the piano, a packing case, a pedestal, and she thought: he has given me the hanging gardens of Babylon.

Mirella pulled the settee cushions onto the floor in front of the fireplace, then opened the basket and spread a tatami mat over the rug for their picnic. She arranged a few of the dishes and then went to join Adam.

He was standing near the piano when she went up behind him and slipped her arms around his waist and leaned her head against his back.

"Thank you again for the flowers," she said.

He turned around and arm in arm they circled the room together. Near the window overlooking the street, he tilted her chin up, as if to have a better light, in order to drink in every drop of her beautiful being, because for him that was exactly what she was, and would always be, he felt, for the rest of his life.

Very slowly and carefully he slipped her jacket from her shoulders and put it on a packing case nearby. He touched the large flat golden frog of her necklace that rested on the violet silk of her dress. He reached around the back of her neck and unfastened it. Once removed, he held it in the palm of his hand and admired it, then laid it carefully down on the piano.

Adam began stroking her gently, ever so tenderly, first under her chin, as one does a cat, until she wanted to purr. Then he stroked her chest and her breasts; he fondled them, cupped them in his hands and caressed them, he embraced them where they swelled into perfection under the soft silk. He kissed her. Lips grazing lips, lightly, sweetly; parted lips against parted lips, allowing tongues to lick, to give the kiss within a kiss. They were two people so moved by passion that only silence was possible.

The incredible attraction they had for each other increased even further when, as they were about to sit down to have their meal, Mirella removed his jacket and vest, undid his tie, and slipped her arms around him, leaned her face against his chest, and reveled in his warm scent—a mingling of tangerine, orange, and lime, sandalwood, patchouli, and cedar. Armani cologne mixed with Adam's unique perfumes to create for her the most heavenly of scents.

She caressed him, ran her hands lovingly over his torso, unbuttoned his shirt and kissed and licked him through the hair on his chest. When she felt him rise, she gave him light, quick kisses as she moved her face down and laid it over the large hidden erection, nestled it by pressing her face against it and moving her head lovingly from side to side.

Adam sank slowly to his knees, taking her down with him, and rolled her around into his arms. He removed her shoes, placed them neatly to one side, then bent down and kissed the top of her ankle, slid his hand up her leg and under her dress and found the garters holding up the sheer bone-colored stocking. He unbuckled the garters, raised her leg in the air and slowly, caressingly, rolled the stocking down and off, and did the same again to the other leg, adding kisses to both her naked legs and thighs with the tip of his tongue.

When Adam ran his hand farther up under her dress and caressed her, fleetingly grazed the small silk triangle covering her mound with his palm, and gently stroked her soft flat stomach, Mirella, trembling with excitement, had to turn on her side and hide her face against him. So strong was her passion and feeling of love for this man, she felt quite ridiculously innocent again.

He deftly unhooked first her garter belt, then the bikini silk panties, and slowly slid them from her body. Adam fondled her lovely, round, firm bottom, naked and unencumbered now under her silk dress. He could feel her body give in to his hands as fingers explored the furrow dividing the cheeks.

Mirella, lying on her side against him, pulled her knees up and hugged him even tighter. With one arm, he held her close, bent his head down and kissed the top of her head, her ear, the side of her neck, as his hand continued to caress the luscious orbs and his fingers explored. He found the tiny tight puckered opening, caressed it, and reached down even farther until, at last, he was where he so wanted to be, with the fleshy lips that covered her slit. He had scarcely separated them with a gentle prodding, when he remembered he wanted more, much more from Mirella, than the great afternoon bang. So he decided to defuse their lovemaking with sake, food, and conversation.

It was only after a considerable time and much sake that Mirella and Adam, still in each other's arms, feeding one another morsels from their sumptuous Japanese picnic, were able to talk.

He kissed her, and while stroking her breasts and playing with her erect nipples through her dress, asked, "Will you tell me about your lover?"

"Why do you assume I have a lover and why do you want to know about any men in my life?"

"Because, for one, a woman as beautiful, desirable, and sexy as you always has a man in her life, no matter how busy and successful she is. Unless of course she has a woman in her life, which I doubt is the case. And for another, because he's part of your life, and I want to know all about you."

"And will you tell me about the woman in your life?" she asked.

"Yes, of course I will. In fact I want to. I want you to hear from me everything about me."

"I don't know where to begin," she said.

"At the end, I hope," Adam said, as he smiled at her, and cuddled her in his arms.

Mirella slipped her hand under his open shirt and caressed him. She loved the feel of his skin and running her fingers through the blond and gray curly hairs on his chest. She was sensually lost to him, and she knew it and liked it. She half raised herself from his arms and cupping her hands around his aureole she opened her mouth and kissed his erect nipple, then licked it with her warm wet tongue. As she slid back down into his arms again, she saw him close his eyes and a tremor of passion cross his face.

"All right," she said.

Adam kissed her on her lips, took her hand and opened it, raised it to his mouth and kissed the palm.

"He's married. He has been my lover for ten years, he is the only man I have ever loved except for my father. I came to terms with our relationship years ago, and it suits me just fine. We are marvelous together in bed, probably because we were lovers in college and lived in a permissive society, where we tried it all, and still do. We have no hang-ups in bed, but we have innumerable ones about each other out of bed, which we tend to ignore in order to stay together. I was head over heels in love with him until the Oujie inheritance and you erupted into my life. From that moment two days ago, something went very wrong. Everything in my life seems threatened by change.

"When Paul called the morning after we met, his voice was a reminder of how happy I still was with the life I had created for myself. The interference of a legacy and you entering my life got put into proper perspecfive. Nothing needed change: my life was intact, and working."

Adam never stopped petting her while he listened. She put her arms around his neck and pulled herself up to him, kissed him, nibbling at his lips, then slid back down to where she was in his arms, and continued.

"I wiped you out of my mind. At least I thought I had, until I came home to all this." She waved her arm, as if to illustrate her point.

"Did he take you to bed?"

"Yes, directly to bed. We had an undeniably splendid two hours of debauched, depraved sex, in which I lost myself completely and fantasized that you were with me. Do you think the less of me for that?" she asked rather nervously, worried that she had confessed too much.

"Quite the contrary. If anything, I think the more of you for it, and how lucky I am."

"Why lucky?" she asked. Aroused by the answer she anticipated, she reached out and slowly pulled his shirt up and out of his trousers, then stripped him of it.

He watched her every move, and felt the sexual electricity between them rapidly gain power over them. Mirella was amazed at how—naked to the waist now—he appeared even bigger, more muscular, more rugged. Her hands and eyes devoured him.

"Ah," he said, as he bent down and untied his shoes and removed his socks, "because when I take you into my erotic world, I'll have a partner who is as sexually free as I am, and sex, debauchery, depravity will be infinitely more thrilling because we *really* care for and love each other. Because the corner of our lives that has been waiting for something we didn't even know we were waiting for will be filled."

Adam stood up, bringing Mirella with him, took her in his arms, and kissed her passionately.

"I love you, Mirella," he whispered in her ear, and felt her body and soul open to him, as she whispered back, "Yes, yes."

He stepped away, reached out and ran his fingers through her hair, pushing it away from her face, looked into her eyes, and willingly lost himself in them. He unbuckled his belt and slowly slid it from the belt loops on his trousers. Mirella watched him, and was mesmerized by the black alligator belt. He put the two ends together, making a loop, and slipped it over her head and pulled her to him, giving her another long electrifying kiss.

He released her by opening the loop and sliding the belt slowly off from the back of her neck. Mirella closed her eyes for a moment, and tried to hold back the tremor she felt before the rush of her first orgasm with Adam. When she opened them again they were riveted on his hands, which were unzipping his fly. She reached up in back of her neck and slowly unzipped her dress, undid the cuffs, wriggled her arms free, and slid her dress down to her hips and let it drop to the floor.

They stood silent and naked, examining each other lasciviously. Like young lovers they touched and played with care and tenderness that in itself was overwhelmingly erotic. They took turns, watching one another revel in their discoveries.

Being able to see Adam's obviously infinite enjoyment of her, and at the same time being the recipient of his ardent attention only increased Mirella's lust and love twofold, as when he caressed her naked breast for the first time and told her, "You have just the type of breasts I like the most, large, heavy but firm, and they swell so beautifully at the sides."

He took one in his huge handsome hands, petted and stroked it. With his fingers he circled round and round the just faintly darker area. And, just before he put it in his mouth and sucked, he added, "I love breasts, all kinds, but none more than ones that are large and heavy and culminate in smooth conical cups, their aureole just a shade deeper than the skin, the nipple long enough for my lips to suck easily on. Breasts exactly like yours."

Watching Adam's handsome mouth, licking and sucking, feeling his tenderness, his need and his desire for her, as he sucked harder and filled his mouth with her pale mocha nimbus, was sublime. He moved from there to her other breast, then stood back with her nipples between his fingers and rolled them, stretched and pinched them, moved his hands sensually over her, and caressed the triangular patch of dark hair covering her voluptuous mound.

Mirella could feel her intimate inner lips moist with her orgasms. She took Adam's hand from her mound just before he separated the lips hiding her clitoris, kissed it, and placed it on her hip, then his other hand on the other hip. She went down on her knees before him and stroked his flat, rock-hard stomach, took the massive, erect penis in her hands and tenderly, sweetly, licked and stroked it. It rose even farther up against him and she gasped with pleasure at the sight of his beautiful distended testicles. She reached under them, cupped them in her hands, and licked them, then fed the warm raunchy-scented sacs, slowly and carefully, one at a time into her mouth and sucked, rolling the ball within over her tongue and around in her mouth.

She kissed him like that there and everywhere, and when he finally took his eyes from her for a second, and caught a glimpse of themselves naked, Mirella making love to him, among the masses of flowering trees in the exotic room, reflected in the mirrors resting against the wall, he thought he might almost be in paradise.

He drew her attention to the vision, and together they moved from place to place around the room making love and new discoveries about their bodies and how to caress them, and always in front of one of the great mirrors so they could see themselves in the Garden of Eden they had created for each other.

Continually they delayed the final act of coupling, holding off the consummation they both wanted for the sheer joy and pain of making love without it. He had come between her breasts, the cheeks of her bottom, across the nape of her neck and down her back, had bathed her with his orgasms, and now, having come in her mouth, he carried her to the settee where they lay down.

Mirella tasted the light, salty ambrosia of Adam's semen and shivered with the thrill of the sensuous flavor, and felt a rush of warmth and ecstasy as she swallowed. Adam saw it in her face and knew at once what was happening. He laughed, threw his head back, and still laughing, said, "Oh, my darling, how lovely, how wonderful you are, and I've only just begun to make love to you." And he kissed her on the cheek. "Wait, wait until we stop playing and I take you." And he kissed her again. "We're going to make love and fuck beyond any ecstasy either of us has ever known, everywhere, and in some of the most romantic and erotic places in the world."

"Is that a promise?" she asked, laughing.

"No," he answered rather more seriously. "That's a vow."

The afternoon had passed and dusk had brought long shadows to their Eden, so Mirella had Adam light the fire, while she went to the far end of the room where she found an old worn beaver car rug, lined and edged in brown satin, draped over the side of a packing case.

Mirella and Adam stood, still naked, holding hands in front of the dancing flames, and were bathed in firelight. Then Adam kissed her forehead, bent down, and pulled the tatami mat with all the remainder of their picnic on it slowly and carefully across the floor and behind a Japanese tiger screen. Mirella clapped her hands.

"Well done, my love," she said, hardly believing her own words.

He bowed low, insinuating he was her servant, then rearranged the cushions on the floor, putting them in front of the fire. Adam took the beaver rug from Mirella, shook it out, and laid it over the cushions, made a gesture with his arm, and said, "And now, madam, your bed of furs."

"Oh," she said, "I brought that to cover us if we should get cold."

"We don't need that," he said, "you have me to keep you warm." And he lay down on the furs facing the open fire, with knees drawn up, legs wide apart, and arms outstretched, waiting to receive her.

Mirella was about to lie down on top of him. "Wait one minute," she said. "I have an idea. I just wonder if . . ." She went to the door leading to the hall and opened it a crack. *"Voilà! Il est merveilleux!"*

"Who's wonderful?" Adam asked as he rolled over and watched her bend down and walk backward into the room, slowly dragging a silver tray.

The sight of her naked in that provocative position delighted Adam. He leaped to his feet, and went to Mirella, bent over her and rubbed himself up and down against her bottom, his chest resting on her back. The scent of their body perfume mixed with the raunchy perfume of orgasm, and Adam felt something akin to pure animal lust.

Lordly beasts mating in the bush that he had watched while on safari came to mind. He made a mental note to take Mirella someday to the jungles of Malaya on safari, where he would mount her and take her like one of the great bulls of the wild. His erect cock throbbed between her legs, where it nestled against her moist closed lips, and Adam reached around for her breasts, and held them in a fierce grip.

Mirella kept walking backward in that position, pushing him along with her. She had to bite her lip in order to hold back from begging him to take her right then and there, and tried to concentrate on getting the tray intact to the hearth.

Adam reluctantly moved his hands away, stroked her back, and kissed it. Then he bit her hard on one buttock, slapped her on the other, and gingerly stepped in front of her, before she could strike back.

Her eyes were shiny, watering from the sharp bite and the stinging slap Adam had lustily dealt her. When their eyes met, the look of indignant surprise in hers quickly gave way to smoldering passion. It was then he understood that her sexual appetites, just like his own, were accustomed to tasting everything. She never said a word, but her silence was telling him she wanted him to know that. Never taking his eyes from hers, he said, in his deep, resonant voice, "Oh, I see," and then they both said, at the same moment, "It's Moses who's wonderful." They laughed, as he bent down to pick up the heavy tray laden with an ice bucket, a decanter of malt whisky, a graceful silver thermos of chilled martinis, a syphon of soda water, a glass-domed dish of small, neatly trimmed sandwiches, two large 1930's Lalique martini glasses, and the same tumbler Adam had used the night they met.

After placing it on the floor in front of the marble hearth, Adam sat down on the beaver rug again, facing the leaping flames, his feet resting flat on it, knees drawn up, his arms wrapped around them, and his back against the settee. Mirella sat on her haunches facing him and poured a large whisky with just a splash of soda for him, and a martini for herself. Then she pushed his knees apart and sat in between them with her back against his chest facing the fire. He kissed her on the side of her neck, and they watched the flames leap into the air in silence while they drank.

Adam held his glass up to the firelight and slowly turned it. The etching of the couple lying together in the soft warm rain held a fascination for him. His heart leaped, like a young lover's, for the joy that had been and the joy that was yet to come. He took a great swallow of his drink, and with his free hand delicately stroked Mirella's shoulder, then leaned back and closed his eyes.

Mirella caught a glimpse of them in one of the mirrors at the far end of the room. Naked, sitting by the fire, one fitting into the other, in the furniture-filled flowering orchard, they were a masterpiece, a live Renoir. It was too perfect even to put into words. She listened to the crackling fire, and took another sip of her drink. After a few minutes, she broke the silence.

"What are you thinking about, Adam?"

"You."

"Oh, that's nice, very nice. Am I allowed to know what you were thinking about me?"

"Of course. To be more accurate, I was thinking about you and me. Us, and how Turkey and chance have brought us together, and marveling at the poetic justice of it all."

"How so, poetic justice?"

"To understand that you would have to know about the love affair I have with Turkey, and have had for the last thirty years. I first went there with my father and my sister when I was seventeen. My mother had died in a fire the year before. Her death was a terrible loss. None of us was over it. Father took the year off so we could travel and hunt big game around the world, before I entered college and my twin sister, Jane, went off to a finishing school in Switzerland. He thought it was just what was needed to jolt all three of us into enjoying our lives again. As always he was absolutely right. We all found ourselves, and life became very sweet once more.

"After eight months of traveling we arrived in Istanbul. My father knew the city well, and had kept up his Turkish contacts. The city and his friends were very welcoming. My sister and I took to Istanbul at once, and we were intrigued by the country and the Turkish people. Father was delighted to stop traveling from country to country for a while, so he bought an old marble palace on the Bosporus, and we settled in. The three of us scoured the bazaars and the countryside, buying things for the place, and took a hand in what my sister called 'playing house,' with the idea that it would be our holiday villa for years to come, a base from which to explore—the country, the Aegean islands, Iran, Iraq, Syria. But what happened was we made a home, and became a happy family once again.

"Some of the most significant things in my life happened to me in Turkey. I was taught how to appreciate the erotic pleasures of the body and the soul there, by men and women whose knowledge was handed down to them from keepers of the sultan's seraglios. I became an archaeologist because of my love for the country. My professional reputation is based on the finds and excavations I've made there. And, after years of studying the Turkish mystics, and the Sufis, I think I have acquired a degree of awareness. Three of my children were conceived and born in Turkey. My favorite home is there. I keep my favorite women there. And now it has yielded true love to me, the one love beyond all other loves that can happen between a man and a woman, a treasure I honestly never believed existed."

Mirella turned and gave him a tender kiss. They finished their drinks and she refilled their glasses. Then she turned around and faced the fire again, leaning against him as she had before.

"For the last thirty years I have championed Turkey and have become one of its benefactors on quite a large scale, for no reason but fascination and affection for the country and its people. Don't you think it is poetic justice that the woman I have fallen in love with should have an inheritance that makes her, to the very heart and soul, a Turk, and probably one of the wealthiest, most influential persons today?"

Mirella turned to face him more fully and rested her hand on his arm. "Adam," she said. "The more I'm with you, the more amazing I find you. I have never known a romantic such as you are. Poetic justice and us? I don't know about that, it's too fanciful for me even to contemplate. What I do know is that you are sweeping me off my feet with romantic love, and that surprises me enough."

"Why should that surprise you? Don't you think a born-and-bred Missouri boy can have romantic fantasies, and go out and live them? We may be a Saint Louis family that loves our Midwestern roots, but we have managed to escape them."

"Yes, I guess you have. It's just that I had this image of you as a man whose ancestors crossed the great Western plains in covered wagons and tamed the land, and I liked that."

"Well, we did, my dear, but that's not to say we didn't become cultured and cultivated, or were impervious to romance and love," he said, cupping a breast in his hands and bending his head down to suck tenderly on her nipple.

Mirella slowly removed his hand from her breast and brought it to her mouth where she opened it and kissed his palm.

"Adam, do you think I am a romantic?"

"Yes, I do. But you keep it hidden. You've buried it under the façade of 'self-made single woman makes good,' probably because you had to, to get where you are. I chose to cultivate the romantic side of my nature: you are just about to."

"How are you so sure you're right?"

"Because when two souls meet as ours did the other evening, they can read each other. They can, that is, if they're not afraid. You are afraid, I am not."

Mirella reached out and poured what was left of the martinis into her glass and refilled Adam's. She lifted the glass dome covering the thin smoked salmon and brown bread sandwiches, and put two on a white linen napkin edged with ecru lace and offered them to Adam. They ate their sandwiches in silence. Mirella finished her martini in one big swallow. Adam put his glass down and drew his arms around her tightly and held her to him, rocking her gently in his arms.

"I think you should be warned," she said. "I find submission to you exciting, because it's strange and new, and I reap untold pleasure from the rewards. It's a sexual role I enjoy playing. But I'm all for rebellion. I've been a rebel of one sort or another throughout my life, in bed and out of bed. A romantic? I'm not sure you're right about that. Romanticism is not a luxury I have ever been able to afford."

"Well, you certainly can now. Not that I agree with you, by the way. Everyone can afford to be a romantic, if they want to be, and they're not afraid where it will take them."

Adam continued to rock her gently back and forth in his arms, and she said, "Oh, and by the way, I also want you to know that I certainly *do not* feel, to my very heart and soul, like a Turk, as you have suggested. I am a true-blue American through and through and of only one-quarter Turkish extraction. So if you want me, you will have to take me as I am."

Adam laughed, and stroked her hair. "Oh, I *will* take you all right, and just as you are. It's you who doesn't accept you exactly as you are, but you will. One day, you will."

"Now what precisely does tha—"

Adam cut her words off with a long and passionate kiss.

"That was for the submissive you I adore," he said. "This is for the rebellious you I find so enchanting, and look forward to seeing more of." He quickly gave her another long, luscious kiss.

"This one is for the all-American girl you," he added and kissed her for the third time.

Mirella felt herself melting through his kisses and under his caressing hands, and kissed him back with a wild passion which drove his hand to her mound, his thumb to her clitoris, and his fingers inside her where he felt the rush of a lovely warm orgasm.

He loved the silky smoothness of her come and left his hand where it was, massaging her with it, while he teased her. "A quarter of a Turk only gets this much kiss." And gave her a peck on the cheek.

Mirella was too happy and content in his arms to care about the tease. She lay there, looking into his face, and marveled at what a remarkable man he was. She wanted to know more, a great deal more about him.

"Will you tell me about the woman in your life now?"

"The women, not woman in my life," he corrected, and told her about them, and the life he led with them in Turkey. She was not so much surprised as confused as to how she could fit into the life of a man who kept a modern-day harem, involving not only three favored women and the children they mothered for him, but also a number of beautiful girls who lived in his house, who were there to serve him erotically, and to act as servants and companions for his women and children.

He explained how he had bought them a marvelous *yali*, a large, early eighteenth-century pine-boarded manor house, on the Bosporus, backed by a spacious garden and thickly wooded hills from which cypresses towered up. They all lived there. He maintained a private bedroom and sitting room for himself when he went to stay with them. His own home, the Peramabahçe Palace, was only five miles away, ten minutes by speedboat down the Bosporus, and there he kept rooms for them all.

"I told you I live an exotic life. You'll like the life in Turkey. It's a wonderful place to live and work and to travel from, and I'm sure you will get along well with the family. They may not be family in the conventional American way you know, but we all like each other and take care of each other. I want so much to show it all to you." And he kissed her once more.

"You've left me speechless again," she said.

"I must admit, I thought I might. Mirella, everything will fall into place. You'll see. Time will do it. There is so much in my life I want to share with you, and there is your life that I want to become a part of. I know that none of this can really begin until you arrive home in Turkey."

"Adam," she said. "I *am* home. New York is my home. America is my home, remember?"

"Of course I remember, it's my home as well. Mirella, I am just as much an American as you are, even more so because I have no Turkish blood in me. Surely you can conceive of being an American and a Turkophile at the same time?"

Her sudden slight stiffening in his arms told him she would have none of that.

"Hey, what are we going on about?" he asked. "I'm being so unfair. You haven't seen your estates; I haven't shown you some of the most marvelous sights on earth . . . riding over the blue waters of the Bosporus in an old *kayik* and watching the green shores lined with marvelous old houses, and small fishing ports, with glimpses of medieval castles poking up above their rooftops, turning black against a red–gold sunset. The Golden Horn at sunrise. Istanbul, a city of breathtaking beauty that tumbles down to the water's edge, still as romantic and erotic as in the days of the great Ottoman Empire. . . . Once you've seen all that, we'll make love under the full moon beyond the Valley of the Pigeons in Cappadocia, where we'll look across windswept, cone-shaped hills that were once a thousand small Byzantine churches. We'll go to Mount Ararat and look for Noah's Ark. I'll make love to you in the wild dark night among the colossal heads of the Olympian gods, lit by massive bonfires. Gods that have been waiting for us since the first century before Christ, on the remote stony summit of Nemrut Dagi. Oh, and more, so much more. When will you come to me? What are your plans? Have you begun reading the papers about the legacy? When do you leave for England, and when may I expect you? And when will you be mine, so I can be yours?"

8

Mirella had no idea how long she had been lying naked across her bed, where Adam had unceremoniously dumped her. Nor had she any idea how long after he left the house the shock of his departure gave way to fear of loss, and the fright drove her to panic and tears.

Between sobs, and fits of coughing, she tried to piece together how their feelings for each other had turned against them. But she couldn't. She was too fragmented. For the moment all she could remember clearly was that one minute she was in his arms listening to his declarations of love, and the next minute he had gathered up his clothes, picked her up, and carried her to the bedroom. His actions and his words upset her so much she was unable to move or speak, either when he left her to take a shower, or when he returned and dressed in front of her.

His last gesture after leaving the bedroom was to walk back into the room, gather up the violets from the basket on her dressing table, and, standing over her, thrust them into her hands. Then he walked away from her without a word. Or was it without a word? Her distress was so acute: everything he said to her and everything he did was a jumble of words and actions she couldn't sort out. All she was really sure of was that this time there would be no flowers the next day.

Mirella's distress caused her to feel sick. She rushed to the bathroom and hung her head over the sink. After a few minutes the feeling subsided and she poured herself a glass of water and drank it slowly, while looking in the mirror. She was quite shocked at the sight she saw: eyes all red and swollen from crying, a chalk-white face streaked with mascara. But the thing that distressed her the most was the misery she saw: undeniable emptiness, despair, and misery.

The shock stopped her crying at once. Still leaning against the sink, she put her hand to her head, closed her eyes, and took half a dozen deep breaths. She had a terrible headache. With shaking hands she rummaged through the medicine cabinet to find the aspirin and took three. She picked up the towels Adam had left on the floor and draped around the room. She thought she had regained her composure until she picked up his distinctive scent from one of them. Her heart skipped a beat. She didn't want to let it go.

She turned the taps on full for the bath and the overhead shower, climbed into the tub, and stood under the hot, steamy water. It poured down over her, and with her face buried in the towel, she inhaled every bit of his scent she could, wanting to remember it for the rest of her life. When she could no longer smell the perfume of his body, she slowly slid down into the bath and sat there, the towel heavy in her hand, wondering what to do.

What was happening to her? She was falling apart. Suddenly her life was a mess. How could this happen to her? How could she meet a man and allow her emotions to rattle her like this? Deena—she would understand. She must talk to Deena. Only that seemed to make sense.

Mirella dropped the towel in the bath, and looked up into the stream of water pouring over her from the shower head above. The powerful spray beat against her skin and brought color back into her face. She reached into the recess of black marble and took a jar of Perlier Almond Cream Bath from one of the shelves and sloshed it all over her body. She stood up under the shower and massaged the rich Italian cream made from almond seeds into her skin, then rinsed it off. It made her skin shine like satin and the scent was heavenly, not unlike walking through an orchard of almond blossoms. She wrapped herself in a terry-cloth robe, wound a towel around her wet hair, and hurried into the bedroom to call her friend.

When Deena rang the front doorbell it was only eight o'clock. Moses let her in.

"Hi, Moses," she said. "How's it going? Are you cooking or Mirella? I sure hope it's you, I'm famished," she said breathlessly, as she removed the sweatband from her forehead and wiped her face with it, remarking, "Boy, will I be glad when this keep-fit fad is over. It will be over, won't it, Moses? I'd hate to do this for the rest of my life." She put her hand on her hip and bent over double, trying to ease the pain of her marathon run from her apartment on Central Park West to Mirella's house.

Moses put one hand on her shoulder and slipped the other massive black hand under her curly, long honey-colored hair, and massaged her neck.

"Slow down the breathing, girl, just slow it all down. How's it going? Dramatically, that's how. Who's cooking? Me. I expect the keep-fit fad will be over for you when you run down a husband, but for some who don't see it as a fad I expect it will go on forever."

"Oh dear, touchy, touchy, bitchy, bitchy. My own fault. I should have known better than to ask a body builder that one. How goes your body-building classes with those kids in Harlem?"

"Fine, just fine. Thanks for asking. Sorry, I guess I was out of line, but you know me: I take physical fitness and education very seriously. Come on, Miss Deena, Miss Mirella's in the kitchen."

She followed behind him. "Really dramatic, Moses? Something really dramatic has happened in this house? Boy, that's hard to believe. How did Mirella let something like that slip in? Not like her, not like her at all. Come on, give me a hint: you know Mirella will tell me anyway."

"Well, let her tell you then; it's not my place to gossip. All I will say is that maybe the shotgun should have been loaded."

Deena Weaver's eyes were out on stalks as she entered the kitchen and repeated, "Shotgun?" Mirella was tilted back in Moses's rocking chair, her feet resting on the edge of an antique pine hutch, one thinly sliced piece of cucumber placed neatly over each eye. She was finishing the drying of her hair.

"Good god, what's going on around here?"

Mirella turned off the dryer and heard Moses say, "She hasn't told me, but my guess is it's either 'money-corrupts time,' or 'assignation-gone-wrong time.'"

Mirella removed the slices of cucumber from her eyes. "I bet you think that's funny, Moses. Well, it isn't. I haven't even got the money, and as for the assignation, that is not funny either."

"Okay, okay. I'll drop it, but you must admit the shotgun was funny."

The fury in Mirella's swollen eyes softened and then changed to a smile. She finally burst out laughing and so did Moses.

He slapped his thigh and said, "Man, you should have seen your faces. And did I ever feel a fool when you saw mine."

"And what about you?" she said, between gasps of laughter, "the hero of East Sixty-fifth Street, who forgot, or was too chicken or too clever—I'm not sure which—to load the thing."

Moses, the handsome middle-aged gentle black giant went to Mirella and put his arm around her shoulders. He smiled at her.

"Now, that's better, isn't it?" He gave her a fatherly hug.

"Yes, much better, Moses, thanks," she said and wondered how she could have been so very lucky to have Uncle Hiram drop Moses into her lap, so to speak, and remembered how Uncle Hiram had said he would be a devoted friend as well as a houseman. How right he was.

"Hey, remember me? Is someone going to tell me what's going on around here? Money, gun? You've been mugged. My god, look at your eyes. It'll take more than a couple of slices of cucumber to get *that* swelling down. Tea bags, that'll do it, lots of soggy tea bags. Mirella, seriously, what in god's name has happened? Why, you didn't have eyes as bad as this even when Paul jilted you."

"Oh, Deena, always the soul of discretion, the subtle diplomat. If we had you at the U.N., I wouldn't have a job." Mirella went to her friend and kissed her on the cheek.

"No, I haven't been mugged," Mirella continued. "There's so much to tell you! I'm so glad you're here. Do you want to have dinner first, or hear what's happened in the last four days since I've seen you?"

"Can't we do both?"

"Oh no," said Moses, "you're not going to get into all sorts of serious discussions and ruin my meal. I made a special dinner, simple but special. So it has to be either food now and talk later, or talk now and food later. Make up your minds, ladies. And is it to be here in the kitchen or up in the dining room?"

The two women looked at each other and automatically went together to the hutch to take down plates, and said in unison, "Food now, talk later."

Deena put her arm around Mirella and said in a really concerned voice, "Are you all right?"

Mirella nodded her head, implying that she was; but she had to bite the inside of her lip to keep from crying, No, no.

"Honestly, Deena, it's okay. It will all wait until after we've had our dinner."

The kitchen was a large room, a chef's delight, with an open working fireplace, and an electrically controlled iron spit in it for roasting. Down the center of the room was an old wide nine-foot-long scrubbed-pine worktable with all sorts of appealing things on it: bowls of nuts, duck and chicken eggs, and fruit. Pedestal dishes of dried apricots, mounds of tangerines, and pyramids of chocolate rum balls covered with white chocolate sprinkles—all looked delicious.

They were arranged down the center of the table, along with earthenware jars of all shapes and sizes containing green olives and black olives, pickled radishes, capers, greengage plums in their own syrup, white peaches in brandy, whole grain flour, white flour, Demerara sugar, molasses, and golden syrup. Clear golden honey from France, dark rich honey that smelled of rosemary from Greece shone like amber in their glass jars. Crocks of mustard from France and England were there next to a bottle of Log Cabin syrup, a giant jar of peanut butter, a tall earthenware crock with two long, thin baguettes of French bread, made with whole grain flour, and a family-size jar of Marshmallow Fluff.

Above the table, hanging from hooks, were bunches of dried herbs and giant sunflowers, copper and cast-iron pots and pans, ladles and spoons of wood and metal in all sizes, and several different hard cheeses from Italy, the most prized of which was a nine-year-old Parmesan.

"Are you eating with us, Moses?" Mirealla asked as she took quilted table mats from a drawer and began to set the table.

"No, thank you, I'll eat later," he said.

Mirella's invitation was one she always extended when she dined in the kitchen, since she considered the kitchen to be Moses's domain. It was one of many polite little rituals she had with Moses. But she could not remember his ever accepting the invitation when there was a guest in the house, not even Deena.

During the first course, a delicious smoked salmon mousse, homemade melba toast, and a cooled bottle of white wine, an excellent Pouilly-Fumé, courtesy of Paul, a wine snob who kept the cellar well stocked, Mirella listened to Deena rattle on about herself and her work.

Mirella held up well through the first course, but was only able to peck at her food. The second course was one of Moses's truly magnificent Louisiana dishes—chicken, sausage, and shrimp gumbo prepared without the traditional *roux* base to make it lighter and less filling. It was served with

Cajun-style rice, and a fresh green salad of romaine and Boston lettuce and watercress tossed lightly in an excellent vinaigrette dressing. Mirella's mind kept wandering back to Adam and the events of the afternoon. Several times during the meal, she nearly lost control of herself and burst into tears. One time was when Deena said, "Moses, this is divine, a dish for the gods, or to impress a lover. If I ever find a man who deserves a meal like this, will you come and cook it for me?"

She realized from what Deena said that Moses had probably spent the afternoon creating the meal for Mirella and Adam, on the off chance they might want to dine in. Of course! It had been prepared and waiting. If she had not called down for something simple for supper, for herself and Deena, Moses would have kept it for the following day, or put it in the freezer. So *that* was why he had discreetly suggested they have a proper meal.

"The trouble with me," Deena was saying, "is that I live in a shallow, superficial New York life, not because I'm a top advertising executive and have to, but because New York values still amuse me. *Style* is a hell of a lot easier to cope with than substance; *glamour* is always just around the corner. But you have to really look for beauty, and if what people wear is more important than what they are, all I have to deal with is the visual label, not a person.

"I was at the Russian Tea Room the other day for lunch. It was filled with the usual crowd: a few Hollywood executive types, Dustin Hoffman and his agent, all the publishing and media people who weren't lunching at the Four Seasons. Do you think I was bored? Not one bit. After hundreds of lunches there I still get a buzz from the place."

Mirella's attention began to wander away from this monologue on a subject Deena agonized over repeatedly: Deena's inability to dislike the New York style-and-status syndrome.

"Listen," Deena went on, "you would think that, if anyone had seen as many stockbrokers, transvestites, hookers, and gigolos trying to get with it at the Area as I have, they would never set foot in that place again. Not me. Just the hint of a suggestion and I'm the first one in the taxi.

"I was at the Surf Club the other day, it was filled with Yuppies and Euro-Trash. You know about them, don't you? The Yuppies are young urban professionals and Euro-Trash are rich Europeans who come to New York to be seen at parties. I watched those Yuppies at play: they're lethal—even more lethal at play than in business. They're so hungry—and I mean hungry—they want to devour everything. They're nothing but really dangerous puppies who want to grow up to be big human-eating dogs. But they won't make it. Do you know what's going to happen to those Yuppies? I'll tell you what: they're going to disappear, devour each other, in their quest to 'make it big.'"

Deena's words were to Mirella like pleasant background music that one puts on to drown out the silence and keep one from thinking or feeling. But her words this time offered little more than a scant lulling effect. Mirella almost came to tears again when she remembered entering the kitchen earlier in the evening, with sunglasses on, her hair dryer in her hand, and saying, "Moses, I hope we have a cucumber in the fridge," trying to keep her voice steady. After she found one and tried with a shaking hand to slice it, he had gone to her and removed her glasses, and looked at her swollen eyes.

"He didn't hurt you, did he?" Moses had asked, with a mean look in his eye.

"Only my pride."

"That's all? You're telling me the truth?"

Mirella had nodded her head, and Moses had said, "Well, that's not so bad then," and patted her on the shoulder. "We all know what it's like, we've all been there one time or another." He had shaken his head and sighed, then took the knife and sliced the cucumber for her.

"Too bad," he said. "I liked him. Would you feel better if you told me about it?"

"No," she had answered. "I liked him, too, but he's gone and that's that, and I honestly would like to forget I ever met the man, so let's never mention him again."

Mirella made a supreme effort to enjoy her food, and concentrated on Deena and what she was saying. She had to, she simply could not bear the thought of making a scene by breaking down at the dinner table. She had had quite enough scenes and upsets in the past four days to last her a lifetime.

Mirella even managed to ask Deena, "Are the Euro-Trash fun?"

"More pretty than fun. More decadent than fun. The Euro-Trash men are very attractive, a little too arrogant. They're not great givers of themselves, but very good takers and charmers. Euro-Trash women look as if American women could eat them for breakfast, but, believe you me, I wouldn't try it. They're undigestible. Like Jewish cooking."

Mirella started to laugh.

"My God, you actually laughed, Mirr. That's the first sign I've had since we sat down to dinner that you *have* been listening. I was beginning to think I was dining with that jar of Marshmallow Fluff, and the jug of daffodils in front of me."

Deena bent forward and picked up the jar of peanut butter from the middle of the table and said rather sentimentally, "Mirr, one thing Euro-Trash would never understand is how we could have gone through Vassar on peanut butter and Marshmallow Fluff on Jewish rye bread, and still made a success of life. *God*, were we poor! Thanks to you—classy and eccentric too. Strange, isn't it, that we still sneak a taste of the stuff every so often. We sure have come a long way since then. Except for one thing: we are still attracted to inferior men. I just wonder, if a good one came into our lives, whether we would even recognize him."

Mirella felt the blood drain from her face, but remained calm.

"Mirr, for goodness sake, you've gone all white."

Moses moved really quickly from his rocking chair near the fireplace to the table and stepped in between the two women. He removed the yellow-glazed pottery tureen containing the gumbo, a signal that the meal was nearly over.

"Dessert is fresh strawberry sorbet and my homemade praline nuggets," he said, much to Mirella's relief. "Why don't I bring them and coffee up to the living room for you?"

Deena was dazzled by the transformation of Mirella's living room. The two women sat opposite each other on the settees. Mirella kicked off her sandals, plumped up a few of the small decorative cushions, and put them at one end of the settee. She rested against them, swung her legs up and stretched out.

She knew the crisis was over, finally over, because, although she had dreaded entering the living room, afraid that she might be upset again because of Adam, it was quite the contrary. As soon as she saw the room a feeling of calm and well-being swept over her. He had given her a gift, so special that nothing of the unhappiness and confusion she felt was able to sustain itself.

Deena said, while bending over and untying her New Balance running shoes, "How stupid I am. How thick-skinned I've become. Now that I've seen these flowers, I realize you're upset over a man. Quite a man I would guess, by the quantity of flowers, and the imagination he had in choosing them for this room. So that lets Paul out. Sorry, Mirr, it's so long since either of us has had a man in our lives who has meant enough to us to cry over, I forgot that it was possible. That's what happens when you're into Gucci track suits and not what's in them."

Deena stretched out on the settee facing Mirella and the fireplace, and looked at her friend with a humbled expression.

"Hey, there's no need for a look like that," Mirella said. "How could you have known? And besides, the man is only just part of it. You know better than anyone, except maybe for Dad, how ambitious I am to succeed in whatever I take on, how I like to have my life running in perfect order, how hard I've worked to accomplish those ends, and the price I've paid for it. You've been chastizing me for it for years, and warned me enough times about repressing the adventurous side of my nature, and about the romantic restlessness and sheer dissatisfaction I am capable of that used to make me cut and run."

Deena began to interrupt Mirella, but Mirella stopped her, saying, "Let me finish, Deena. What you have not understood is that I had put a life together that gave me a great deal of satisfaction, happiness, and security, and I thought I had made very few concessions for such rewards. In the last four days I've seen my whole little world broken in two, destroyed against my will. Things have happened that have changed my life and there is very little I can do but try to salvage what is left of the peaceful existence I led until a few days ago. But let me tell it all to you right from the very beginning, so you will understand why I was in such a state when you arrived." And then she launched into her tale.

Moses carried the tray into the room at a moment when both women were silent. He took one look at them and was amused to see that Mirella was obviously waiting for Deena to take in the significance of what had happened to Mirella since the two women last met. He put the tray on a Louis Philippe table and carried it over to where they were, and placed it in front of Mirella. He made a small wager with himself that Deena was recovering from the news of the money. Although he himself had no idea how much was involved, by the look on Deena's face he figured it must be considerable.

He offered to Deena a handsome antique crystal stemmed

coupe of sorbet, with a small royal blue Russian enamel spoon stuck in it, and a few of his succulent nuggets—something between a candy and a cookie—on a small Sèvres dessert plate, and smiled. Deena was too stunned to smile back. He went to Mirella and handed hers to her. Mirella smiled at him, and he said, "I guess you've told her about your inheritance."

Mirella nodded her head, confirming that she had. Moses stood over the tray and filled the small cups from the Queen Anne silver coffeepot. Then he stood back and waited to serve the coffee.

Deena looked at Mirella and rolled her eyes as if to ask "Can I speak in front of Moses?" Mirella indicated that she could and said, "It's okay, he knows about the legacy, although he doesn't know how much money is involved, but I did tell you we would be fairly wealthy, didn't I, Moses?"

"Fairly wealthy, Mirella! I know you are naïve about money, have no idea about the value of money or how to handle it, and although you respect the need for it, put it very low on your list of priorities. I have happily bankrolled you enough times to know that. But surely you must understand that having forty million dollars a year is not 'wealthy,' it's being fucking fabulously rich."

With that Deena jumped off the settee and handed the half-emptied *coupe* to Moses, kissed him on the cheek, ran to Mirella and kissed her, then did a few cartwheels from where she stood into the hall and back again. She let out a joyous, rumbustious cheer and then retrieved her sorbet from Moses, sat down, and began firing off questions. Mirella and Moses were laughing, and their laughter was infectious. She caught it, and when their laughter finally petered out, she looked hard at Mirella and Moses.

"My God, you two really haven't grasped the reality of the situation, have you? It's just a lot more money than you have ever had. That's all it means to you, isn't it?"

"All I know is that Miss Mirella won't ever have money worries again and that can't be bad," said Moses, who collected the empty sorbet dishes and handed them each a demitasse of black coffee laced with cinnamon. "And we'll probably have the builders in soon because now we have the money to fix the roof." After asking if Mirella wanted anything else, he said good night and left the room.

"And all I know," Mirella said, "is that I am thrilled about the money, but it has already disrupted my life, and I am far from happy about that. Not to mention the fact that in order to go get the will probated, I have to ask you yet again to lend me money."

"Sure. Of course. As much as you need. You know that. Mirr, I have a million questions but I don't want to miss a thing, so carry on with what happened. So far, we are at the part where this dishy man, Adam Corey, saved you from fainting over the news. Go on from there." And Deena made a mental note to remember to look in her Dun and Bradstreet first thing in the morning to learn more about Adam Corey.

It was well after midnight when Mirella finally finished telling Deena what had happened to her in the last four days. In the telling, Mirella was able to see some things that had happened and her reaction to them more clearly *and* she was able to piece together the events that sent Adam away so abruptly and finally.

Deena looked at her friend and felt a pang of compassion for her suffering, her having been forced by Adam Corey's criticism to face herself. Mirella's world and the life she had led for the last eighteen years were well and truly shattered, and Deena could understand the ambivalence she felt about the legacy, as well as Adam. She went to her, put her arm around her shoulder.

"The whole thing is fantastic," Deena said. "I couldn't be more thrilled than if it had happened to me. One reads in the newspapers about people who are left unexpected legacies but one hardly ever has a best friend who's the recipient. We all dream, search all our lives for the real thing in the love stakes, between ourselves and a man, and it sounds as if you really had a taste of it for a few hours—enough to show you it's what you never had before, and it's what you haven't got with Paul. And now your maternal family roots, which have evaded your mother and your grandmother, have surfaced for you. You'll never be able to ignore them, no matter how much you may try. I think your friend Adam is right about that."

Deena gave Mirella a hug, then walked to a table and poured two snifters of Armagnac from a crystal decanter, said, "As I said, it's all fantastic, but what is even more fantastic is the steps you have taken so quickly, and, as you yourself admit, against your own will. Frankly, I'm surprised but thrilled that you've moved so swiftly—taking the vacation, allowing yourself to be receptive to a man other than

Paul, and, most of all, dropping Paul. Have you really dropped him once and for all?"

"Oh, he's been dropped all right. He hasn't been told yet, but it *is* over for us." Mirella accepted the brandy from Deena, who was standing in front of her, and continued, "That's not to say I'm happy about it. He has been the only serious love affair I've ever had, the other lovers as you well know were erotic one-night stands. It really hurts to think I've been deluding myself for so many years with the idea that what we had was true love.

"I can see now that when Paul and I first met we were romantics, passionate romantics about everything, like so many people in the late fifties and all through the sixties. When he killed that in himself, I allowed him to influence me to do the same. I've been so busy all these years dealing with the harsh realities of our togetherness that I've been living in a nonmarital, nonblissful state that has colored my whole life. For a supposedly very clever woman I have been very, very stupid."

Deena sat down again on the settee opposite Mirella. "Jesus, Mirr, I can hardly believe what I'm hearing. It may have taken a mysterious, magical miracle—like a long-lost legacy of gigantic proportions, and a great fuck from what sounds like one of the last of the extraordinary men in the world—but it's done. They have cracked your carefully organized life right open and enlightened you."

"Deena, he didn't do it with a fuck. He never fucked me. I told you we made love to each other for hours, and then it all started to go wrong: we had words and he walked out on me, assuring me he would never come after me again. But I never said he fucked me."

Tears welled up in Mirella's eyes and she forced them back. Her voice began to crack and she pulled all her energies together and controlled it and herself. Deena started to get up to go and comfort her, but Mirella stopped her by holding up an outstretched arm and indicating to Deena to stay where she was.

"Oh dear, oh, dear," Deena commiserated, "maybe you had better tell me the part you've left out. Would you feel better if you did that, got it all out in the open?"

"Yes," she said, "I think I would. Now that I am more calm than when he left me I think I can remember most of it. We were lying together naked in front of the fire and he had finished telling me all about his life in Turkey. You remember—I told it to you just the way he told me. Then he got carried away with where he would take me in Turkey, and how and where he would make love with me, all the while kissing and petting me, keeping me in a constant state of readiness for him with exquisite orgasms brought on by his hands and his fingers and his mouth.

"Deena, from the first moment we saw each other, we liked each other, wanted each other, loved each other, and it was that way all the time we were making love. I felt emotionally fullfilled as I have never felt before. He did too. He was generous about telling me that all the time. He exuded so much love and caring for me, it was impossible to hold back how I felt for him. I made the most beautifully erotic love to him and it only doubled my pleasure. We had everything going for us. He wanted to give me love, intimacy, companionship. There was sharing, communication, and equality, and I wanted it all, and I accepted it all from him.

"It's rather embarrassing for me, telling you this next part. But you might as well know it all. For hours, I wanted him to take me. He has a very large, magnificent cock, and fantastic testicles, and I wanted him inside me. I knew instinctively that all the playing and sex we had had through the afternoon was nothing compared to what was to come, once we had consummated our feelings by his fucking me. I suppose we both knew what an extraordinary commitment that would be for us, because we came close to it so many times, and delayed it.

"He was on top of me, I could feel the throbbing knob of his penis. He was there and ready to begin his entry. He kissed me. We were both trembling with emotion, love, passion. He said, 'When will you come to me? What are your plans? Have you begun to read the papers about the legacy? When do you leave for England, and when may I expect you? When will you be mine, so I may be yours?'"

Mirella took a large gulp of the Armagnac and saw an anguished expression appear on Deena's face.

"I kissed him," Mirella continued, "told him I loved him and begged him to take me right then and there. He kissed me back, passionately, and I felt myself opening to him. I waited for him to push farther, thrust us into oblivion. He whispered in my ear, in a voice brimming over with emotion, that he loved me, and said, 'Answer me. Until I know the answer to those questions how can I make plans for us?'

"I remember so clearly the weight of him on top of me, his skin, his scent, how much I wanted him—so much it was painful. He raised himself up just a little to study my face, and I ran my fingers through his hair and told him, 'I'll come to you, but—' He interrupted me and said, 'There are no buts between us, I told you that,' kissed me again, and waited for my answers.

"I told him I had read some of the documents, and they made me realize how much work it will take to liquidate the estate. That I leave for England in four days' time, and how wonderful it would be if he could come over during my ten-day stay. He asked, 'And what about Turkey? Do you mean to tell me you won't come and look at your legacy before you liquidate?' I told him no, that, if I ever went to Turkey, it would be when he took me there to make love in all the places he had told me about."

Mirella stopped talking. She sat looking at Deena. The room was very silent. It was as if the two friends were absorbing the effect of Mirella's words on Adam. Mirella sighed heavily and Deena finally broke the silence, asking in a very concerned, soft voice, "Then what happened, Mirella?"

"He caressed my hair, and kissed me lightly, sweetly on the lips and said, '*That's not good enough*. You may throw the legacy away without becoming involved with it, or considering the ramifications of what you are doing, because all you want is the money, and not the responsibilities of such a legacy. That sort of stupid, narrow-minded, and destructive behavior is bad enough. Must you compound it by throwing me away along with it? You can't behave like that. You decided on liquidation and noninvolvement before we met. Are you so foolish as to not understand that one taste of loving and being loved, and nothing is the same? Do you honestly think I will allow what we feel for each other to be turned into an affair? No, what you offer is not enough. I want it all, not just part of what you are. Mirella, you're a role player. You have probably confused role playing with real feelings all your adult life. Too bad. You should have learned to balance them. I thought you were a woman who could take on enormous responsibilities, like real love. It could have been wonderful for us for eternity. I won't return to you a second time.'

"Then he removed my arms from around him, picked himself up off me, and went to find his clothes, and returned and lifted me up into his arms. I wanted to say something, but I didn't know what to say. He asked me where the bedroom was and I told him. I kept thinking while he carried me up the stairs that it was all going to be all right, that he wanted to make love to me in bed. I kept thinking, 'When he's inside me, he will never leave me, any more than I will be able to leave him.' It never happened. He merely dumped me on the bed, found the bathroom, showered, and left. He won't come back, you know. He meant those last words, 'I won't return to you a second time.'"

"What a story. What are you going to do about it?"

"Nothing. I don't believe there is anything to do."

"You could call him."

"That's impossible. Look, Deena, he has made it patently clear that he is a loner—albeit a loner with an unconventional family—and has been all his life. We met and he was prepared to love me, but he left me because, as he pointed out, what I offer is not enough. How can I chase after a man who says that?"

"You can't. All you can do is go to him, and give him what he wants. He sounds like a very smart fella to me. Unless your feelings are as strong as his, though, and there really are no 'buts,' nothing good will come of your running after him. Your Adam Corey is a man who holds his ground, and you either meet him on his turf or you don't get him, period. This guy is no flawed American hero like Paul, who puts his soul on the auction block and waits for the highest bidder."

"What should I have done? He didn't even give me a chance to discuss our relationship and how I could work it into my life, as he would have had to work me into his."

"*I* can understand his point of view."

"Which was what exactly?"

"That there was nothing to discuss. I can't speak for him, but I think most men are not preoccupied with relationships and emotions like women are—unless they're gay. He was thinking like a man, and you were thinking like a woman. Your Adam believed that together you were the real thing, and everything else was details to be dealt with.

"You're talking about 'his life, my life'; he was talking about *our life*. Most women live under the delusion that they are open to intimacy, but when it finally does come to them they are terrified of being taken over and losing what hold on separateness they have. I am afraid you're an excellent case in point. Adam Corey offers you himself, romance, a ready-made family, a sense of belonging, and you insinuate you would rather forego the belonging, liquidate the legacy, and have a good fuck than the responsibility of real love with him."

"You're saying that I've made a terrible mistake."

"I've said no such thing. I've only said in a roundabout way this Adam is no Paul—who was a terrific excuse not to take on the responsibility of sharing a life with someone."

"Well, if he loved me so much, Deena, then why was he so quick to let me go? You weren't here, but I promise you, he was angry but very cool about it."

"What did you expect him to do—rage at you? The man said what he had to say, and all he wanted was to go away and get on with his life. He behaved with a degree of decorum and good manners, and left you to get on with your life."

"But, Deena, I loved him so much," said a sad Mirella.

"Not enough, old girl, not enough."

9

Mirella was feeling disoriented. She sipped from her glass of champagne, and looked across its rim at the man sitting opposite her.

He was watching her, and she was aware of a glint of anger in his eyes—or was it annoyance? With Paul it was always hard to tell.

Very few words had passed between them since they left her bedroom. An atmosphere began to build then, and grew stronger when she said good-bye to Moses as he loaded her luggage into the trunk of Paul's red Ferrari. It had increased when he held the door open for her and she slipped into the soft cream-colored glove-leather seat, and heard him say to Moses, "Thanks, Moses. Oh, by the way, I'm sending over two cases of Château Margaux for you to lay down in the wine cellar. Will you take care of it?" He closed the car door much more firmly than necessary.

When he turned on the engine, shifted gears, and shot down the street, she had said, "Please don't. Don't send the wine or drive like you're out to win the Monte Carlo Grand Prix."

The atmosphere was explosive when he snatched her ticket from her at the check-in counter at Kennedy Airport. With an American Express Gold Card he paid the difference between her economy-class ticket and a first-class flight to London. Just as she was about to protest, he challenged her with a look that silenced her. He had taken her firmly by the elbow, briskly walked her to the first-class waiting room, saying through clenched teeth, "Not a word, not one word about my changing that ticket."

In stony silence he raised his glass and toasted Mirella, then drank the glass dry and reached out to the ice bucket and took the bottle of Dom Pérignon, topped up her glass, and refilled his own.

"Why are you so angry with me?" she asked.

"Not angry. Damned annoyed with you for playing tedious female games with me."

"But I'm not playing games with you."

"You could have fooled me. I made my usual morning call—the same call I have been making for the last ten years— to your office on Wednesday, Thursday, and Friday and you were never there to receive it. When I wanted to see you on Thursday night all I was granted was an hour's conversation on the telephone, at which time I was notified about your vacation and the news of your departure. Then I am inundated with bullshit about us stopping seeing each other for a while and see how it goes, at least until you are installed in Southampton. God, how I hate the deviousness of women."

"Now, just what do you mean by that?"

"You know very well what I mean. For example, you could give me some time on Sunday afternoon before you leave for the airport, you said. You know how difficult it is for me to get away from Sunday lunch with the family. You deliberately made it very inconvenient for me, and we both know you could have flown just as easily tomorrow instead of today. I suppose it must have come as quite a shock to you when I said, 'Wonderful, I'll take you to Sunday brunch, eggs benedict, the Edwardian Room at the Plaza, half past twelve. Also, I insist on driving you to the airport.'"

"Yes, as a matter of fact it was a surprise. I told you it wasn't necessary. I was having lunch with Deena, and Moses was going to drive me. You didn't have to miss your Sunday lunch *en famille*."

"You weren't saying that during the time after brunch and before this vintage wine." He took another great swallow of the perfectly chilled champagne and continued, much to Mirella's embarrassment. "Your twelve minutes of 'Paul, it's over' drowned in a powerful sea of orgasms that lasted a hell of a time longer than twelve wasted, ridiculous minutes." He checked his watch as if to prove his point. "Four hours, give or take a few minutes. Four hours of lust so violent and exciting I never heard another 'Paul, it's over.' What I did hear was: 'More, more.' And words like 'marvelous,' 'exquisite.' Expressions like: 'take me any way you want,' 'I'm coming again,' 'fuck me until I die,' primal cries of excruciatingly painful pleasure. And what did I see? You reveling in your own come and my sperm, orgasms we climaxed in at exactly the same instant, so powerful and mind-bending we died together for a split moment and were reborn."

Mirella stood up and he hissed across the table to her, "Sit down! Mirella, sit down until they call your flight. If you don't, I'll make a scene. And you know me. That's no empty threat."

Mirella sat down. They drank their wine in silence, then Paul filled their glasses again. They looked at each other, and slowly the stormy atmosphere began to subside.

"Mirella, I don't know what that business of 'Paul, it's over' was all about, and I don't want to know. It's unimportant, because I proved to you in the bedroom that it is not over for us."

Mirella said nothing. She knew he would never believe that when he had torn the dress from her back, forced her onto the bed on her stomach, and tied her by her wrists and ankles to the four posters of the bed with the remnants of her dress, mounted her from behind, and fucked her into submission, he had raped her. That all they had done was add yet another few loveless, lustful hours to an already-dead relationship.

What could she say to him? That she had left him days ago, on the pavement in front of Mishimo's? That what had happened in the bedroom was nothing but sublime sex for the sake of sex, something she could get from any number of terrific studs who enjoyed the delights of eroticism?

Hardly. She could say none of those things—any more than she could tell him the only reason she even allowed him in the bedroom while she finished packing was that she wanted to let him down easy, without offending him, and in the hope that they could at least remain civil to each other. How stupid, how *naïve* she was, she thought.

"What happened to us, Paul? Have we really changed so much? What happened to the wealthy Glen Cove, Long Island, boy who was the loving, caring radical at the Harvard Business School, and the poor, young Vassar girl, working her way through college? What happened to those two kids who fell in love? The day we met I was tutoring your roommate in Arabic, and you sat there hardly taking your eyes off me. When the session was over and he paid me three dollars an hour, you took the money from my hand and handed it back to Arthur, called him a cheap prick, and told me to get my coat. You told Arthur off for exploiting me, because I needed the money and he didn't, and said how disgraceful that was. I was so upset at losing the money, I cried and told you to mind your own business, because that was food money. Before we left the room Arthur agreed to pay seven dollars an hour. You apologized for interfering and told me you couldn't bear injustice of any kind, and where you were taking me to dinner.

"Those were wonderful years, Paul, when we were the privileged, educated flower children who were going to save the world through peace and love. We expanded our consciousness with and without drugs. We were secure lovers, who believed in freedom and the human being, and entered wholeheartedly into a drug culture that was supposed to add to our lives. And we were lucky: it did. We were vulnerable and open to everything: we experimented with sex, and embraced all sorts of alternative religions and philosophies and learned from all of them, because we cared and we loved.

"We were active participants in a time when idealists had a chance, existentialists were on the march, and everyone we knew believed there could be one world and peace without violence. What happened to us? Did the caring burn out in our years in the Peace Corps, the march on the Pentagon, the bus trips to Georgia, the endless demonstrations and protests? I guess it did, and that doesn't say much for us."

Paul reached into his breast pocket and pulled out a crumpled pack of Camels, removed the last cigarette, and put it in his mouth. He made a fist around the empty packet, crumpling it into a little ball that dropped into the ashtray.

Mirella thought he looked extraordinarily cool and detached as he stared at her while he picked up a book of matches, struck one, held the flame up to his face, paused for a moment, and lit his cigarette. He blew the flame out when he exhaled, dropped the dead match into the ashtray. It was all so exaggerated that Mirella found it strangely compelling.

"What happened to us, Mirella? Before I give you my answer, let's clear up a few things about those two young lovers who met on that snowy day in Cambridge.

"In the first place the poor beauty who was so dumb about money, the victim of Arthur's greed, turned out to be—hidden under her shabby but frightfully chic hand-me-downs—a brilliant Vassar student, an impoverished Boston socialite, as eccentric as the rest of her family, who wasn't poor at all except in cash. The wimp I felt sorry for that day was a sexually liberated girl with passion, potential, and courage who swept me off my feet. In the second place the Lochinvar of those days turned out to be—underneath his radicalism—very interested in power, money, and success—especially his own—and able to afford to be swept along by the times and the liberated girl who held him with sex, her joy in life, and her love of adventure. What happened to us? What do you think happened to us? The very same thing that happened to Jerry Rubin and Abbie Hoffman and a million others. We woke up from one hell of a self-indulgent dream into reality. We traded all that flower power and peace for success and money. We joined the establishment. We grew up.

"What we were died and was buried long, long ago, when the flowers wilted and the peace we dreamed about for the world was boring and unprofitable. I thought you knew that, and accepted it, when I returned to you, ten years after I jilted you. The love and caring only comes, for us, through eroticism. You know that as well as I do. Why, after ten years of building a life together around sex, do you suddenly question 'what happened to us?'"

A soft silky-smooth voice came over the intercom, announcing that flight 0794 for London was boarding first-class passengers immediately. Mirella and Paul stood up and for a minute faced each other in burning silence. The last vestige of illusion had been swept away. She had no idea where she got her strength to stand there, because her knees were so weak.

"Because it's just not good enough," she said, turned on her heel, walked away from him, and never looked back.

Mirella was horrified, devastated. Those had been Adam's very words to her. Using them on Paul only doubled the pain she felt when she thought of Adam and of her own inadequacies.

Waves of emotional exhaustion swept over her. Every step down the corridor to the waiting aircraft was agony. Her eyelids felt heavy, she could hardly keep them open. Her legs felt as if they were made of putty, and her feet felt swollen, and as if made of lead. Yet she stood up straight and forced herself to walk slowly and steadily. The effort caused her to break out in a heavy perspiration, and she was so hot and out of control she began to hyperventilate.

At last she was inside the plane, and greeted by a flock of flight attendants with wide, open airline smiles that made her think of Pepsodent toothpaste; young, fresh complexions, courtesy of duty-free French cosmetics, that looked straight out of a Coca-Cola ad; crisp, well-fitted, and pressed uniforms that reminded her of American haute couture designers and nannies and nurses. Their clean, pretty hair shone, and conjured up the image of a bottle of Breck shampoo.

Each one, individually, greeted her with "Good evening." She was obliged to repeat more than half a dozen times the same greeting in response, and she stopped hyperventilating. They reeked of so much purity, and such good intentions; projected so the image of the airway's Little Sisters of Mercy that Mirella sniffed, imagining she smelled iodine and camphor. All she received was the heavy scent of airplane freshener, and she coughed and sneezed a few times, knocking herself off balance, and leaned against one of the aisle chairs, and began to breathe erratically again. Wryly she savored the detachment of the flight attendants: they certainly knew how to turn a blind eye to overemotional, overstressed women. Mirella buckled herself in, and all at once the attention and marvelous service of first class enveloped her. One thousand nine hundred and twenty-nine dollars worth of it. And that was only one way. She still had to return.

Mirella opened her canvas shoulderbag and took out a handkerchief and gently wiped her face, then applied some face powder to dull the shine. She caught the image of herself in the little mirror trying to regain her breath and made a concerted effort to calm herself down by closing her eyes, while taking long, deep breaths and exhaling slowly.

When she asked herself why she was experiencing such

anxiety, Adam Corey and his words were the answer—not the loss of Paul, or the fact that the great love story of her life was all an illusion perpetrated by her. Her last conversation with Paul made Mirella think all the more about what she used to be and what she must seem like now to strangers. She felt haunted by Adam's words, and her anxiety was not just disorientation: she felt wounded and vulnerable as well. Mirella was both angry and hurt at the same time.

"Excuse me, Miss Wingfield."

Mirella slowly opened her eyes and saw one of the airline angels smiling over her.

"Yes," she answered.

"This envelope has been sent through to you from a gentleman in the first-class waiting room. If you read it quickly and there is an answer, I might be able to get it back to him, because we are still taking on passengers in economy class."

Mirella opened the envelope. Inside was a check for one thousand dollars and a note telling Mirella to buy herself a pretty new dress to replace the one ruined during the afternoon, and that he would call her, in London, every day at one o'clock, London time. It was signed "Paul."

"Is there an answer to the note, Miss Wingfield?" asked the flight attendant, offering Mirella an open leather-bound correspondence portfolio.

Mirella was so angry that her anxiety diminished and she stopped breathing abnormally. She looked at the various envelopes, the different sizes of stationery, the postcards, and the plastic ball-point pen laid out before her. She slipped the check back in its envelope and tore it in half, then in half again, and again, and again; picked up a large envelope, opened it, and scattered the tiny pieces of paper into it. Once it was sealed she picked up the plastic ball-point pen and wrote on the envelope "Mr. P. Prescott" and handed it to the stunned attendant—whose smile at last had slipped—saying, "Was that quick enough . . . er . . . what's your name?"

"I'm Wendy," she answered and the airline smile swept again across her face, as if it were in some way connected to her name or her voice box.

"Well, was that quick enough, Wendy?"

The woman looked at her wristwatch. "Yes, Miss Wingfield. With time to spare." Wendy disappeared down the aisle and Mirella unbuckled her seat belt and went to the bathroom to wash her hands and face. Mirella returned to her seat far more composed than she had left it because of the effects of a cool wash. She even had removed her dress and given herself a sponge bath.

It was a marvelously smooth, steep takeoff. Mirella actually felt a surge of excitement as the powerful jet engines thrust the airplane forward, up into the sky and the unknown. She heard herself say softly under her breath, but aloud, "The adventure begins." And her heart felt glad, and slowly her soul began to soar, and Mirella Wingfield was set free as she had not been since she was a young girl at Vassar.

There were only nine people in first class and only one woman other than herself. A very pretty young thing with a handsome middle-aged man, trend-setter types that Deena would have loved and been able to identify by every chic item of clothing they wore. Except for the couple, every person in first class had their row to themselves to stretch out in. She took note that all the men on board were very attractive and thought the fact that she noticed was a good sign. The other good sign was that half of them had definitely taken notice of her.

There was very little to-ing and fro-ing, except of course by the flight attendants. The passengers seemed quite content to stay in their seats and be waited on, with endless streams of champagne, cocktails of their choice, or any other alcoholic or nonalcoholic beverage they desired. The magazines, earphones, newspapers, hors d'oeuvres, dinner, dessert, after-dinner drinks, and mints came in volley after volley, until at last the booties for their feet and the sleeping masks for their eyes arrived and were followed by the extra pillow and the blankets, and the start of the movie.

The passengers settled down in darkness and muffled silence. Mirella put the little foot warmers on her feet and fixed the eye mask on top of her head, ready to be slipped down over her eyes as soon as she felt a wave of sleep approaching.

The movie came on and ran silently, and the light from the screen and the changing colors were eerie in the nearly empty cabin. There was something sensual about the atmosphere inside the plane then. Enveloped by the cushioned drone of powerful jets, they were suspended in space and borne forward through the night. She felt that her fellow passengers, cocooned in their own dreaming, were sharing the same mystery of aloneness and drifting. Who knew what was in store for these strangers whom chance had brought together for a few hours, and who were, in a sense, trapped together until released again on landing in London? They hadn't made contact with one another yet they were all bound together as if each had done so.

Mirella turned in her seat and looked up the dark aisle to the rear of the first-class section of the plane, where the couple was sitting. All she could make out were two shadowy, entwined figures covered with a blanket, and she guessed they would have sex some time during the night: quiet, discreet fornication was, for sure, on their flight plan. Mirella smiled to herself, remembering how very sexy it had been when she did it, over the Fiji Islands, with a news-magazine photographer.

She went to the bathroom. On returning to her seat she stepped aside and leaned against the aisle seat diagonally opposite her own in order to allow a steward to push his liquor-laden cart past her. She lost her balance and slowly, casually she slipped over the arm of the chair and into the seat. Her back touched the side of the man sitting in the seat next to the window. She turned to apologize as he reached out to steady her. He was a handsome man, young, undoubtedly Arab. Their eyes met in the eerie light. His were pools of darkness, large, seductive black dots. They were mesmerizing.

She quickly made her excuses and returned to her seat and decided to bed down for the night. She lay on her side across the seats, her legs tucked in under the blanket, and cuddled up against the window of the plane, a pillow behind her head. She watched the movie screen from an acutely lopsided angle but saw nothing of the film, only the changing of the light it cast out into the interior of the cabin of the plane. The eyes of the handsome Arab across the aisle burned into her imagination. The seductive black spheres turned into a black dot. She watched the black dot trot, trot and prance itself out of the horizon across the desert, in a straight line, under a burning sun, and turn into a young Omar Sharif. Swathed in black so that nothing but his chocolate-pudding eyes showed, he rode his black-tassel-draped camel right up to her.

It seemed very beautiful and exciting; a faintly wicked and extremely sensual ride that promised a great deal. The scene from *Lawrence of Arabia* played on in her mind. The absence of surging music, or any sound at all, made her visual experience, played through memory, strangely realistic and highly erotic for her. She liked drifting in and out of the scene, becoming part of the romance of the desert, the madness of Lawrence, and fantasizing over a dark Saharan prince with whom she could exercise her sensual desires.

Mirella was nearly overcome by her urge to be swept away into an erotic sexual encounter where she was spoiled, pampered, and adored by a handsome man who would explore with her every avenue of sensual delight. A man who would play with her and take her on the ultimate adventure of life, an adventure of shared love, for eternity. She wanted what she could have had with Adam Corey, if the timing had been right, if she had not still been living in the illusory world she had created for herself, and if her courage had not failed her.

She slipped the sleeping mask down over her eyes. In time the thought of Adam Corey would not hurt. She would be able to think of him with gratitude as the guide who pointed her to the path of real love. Mirella closed her eyes under the mask and ceased battling against waves of uneasy half sleep.

He had the same chocolate-pudding eyes as Omar Sharif, but was very much taller and came riding out of the sunset, kicking up a cloud of dust, on a magnificent black polo pony, instead of on a camel under the hot sun. He was not swathed in black, but wore a white polo shirt and jodhpurs, very expensive, magnificently polished leather riding boots, and carried a handsome handmade Hermès riding crop of the finest tanned leather. He swung his leg over the horse and dismounted, dropped the reins over the horse's head, and left them to trail in soft, white, powdery sand.

He struck his thigh with the whip, and some dust rose from his jodhpurs as he walked toward Mirella, who was standing next to her father's favorite car, his Bugatti Royale, one of the biggest and most expensive cars made in the early thirties: the car that, according to her father and Christie's car expert Robert Brook, was the greatest car ever built. She was waiting there with Donald Davies for her handsome polo-playing lover.

A shiver of excitement went through Mirella as he walked toward her. He was smiling. And he was so young and handsome. His thick, silky black hair was worn long, his features were rugged. His costume showed his amazing physique: fantastic biceps bulged from the short-sleeved polo shirt that fitted like a second skin, and his huge muscular chest rippled under it. The Hermès leather belt around his slim waist and the top stitching that outlined the very long flap covering the fly opening of his jodhpurs, the strong, firm, slightly bowed legs striding up to her made her open her mouth a little and slide her moist tongue around her lips. She found him utterly delicious.

He raised the riding crop and caressed her with it under her chin, and looked at her with lascivious eyes, but eyes that at the same time told her he loved her and adored her. She returned the same look. He ran the riding crop slowly, in a straight line, down under her chin and neck to her chest and lifted the white silk lapel of her wraparound dress and looked at her bare breast. He removed the riding crop and put a question to her with his eyes. She knew his meaning and nodded: yes, she was stark naked under the silk dress that was cinched at her waist by an antique Macedonian silver belt encrusted with coral and pearls.

He sat in the driver's seat, Donald next to him, and Mirella on Donald's lap, and they drove down soft sandy roads through vast orange groves in a cloud of dust. A tilt of his head and a raised eyebrow gave Donald the hint to kiss Mirella sweetly on her face and cheeks. Mirella looked at her lover, their eyes met and she slowly pulled the top of her dress apart, exposing her breasts for Donald to caress and kiss. Once or twice during the ride her lover reached over and pinched her erect nipples, then rubbed his hand up and down the length of his semierect phallus.

Mirella ran her hand over the taut skin of his bulging bicep and down his arm, and she quivered at the feel of his smooth skin and hard flesh, and in response to Donald's expertise in sucking her breasts. They arrived at a small clearing in the grove, and through the trees they could see an emerald sea lapping against the white powdery sand beach.

Dusk was upon them, and with it a strange, warm mist rolling in from the shore. There were eight handsome young men standing and sitting in a group, some lighting a large bonfire, others expertly aiming and drinking red wine from a bulging goatskin. They were naked except for the huge, ornately decorated codpieces that all of them wore. And under those were magnificent phalluses, all selected with care for Mirella's pleasure by her lover.

The three were received with enthusiasm. One of the men began to undress Donald. Mirella, her lover, and three of the men sat down on a huge white marble slab that was supported by a set of carved angels with wings. It was something between a bed, a table, and an altar. The men passed in front of Mirella and kissed her first on one cheek, then on the other, and each offered her his codpiece by arching his back and thrusting himself out in front of her, and she accepted by pulling a string to remove it. Mirella all but wailed with pleasure at the sight of one handsome cock after another, knowing full well they were all there for her. The men sitting next to her jumped off the table and begged to be released as well.

Mirella and her lover watched all the men licking and sucking the array of phalluses until the magnificent cocks were erect and waiting for her. Mirella's lover stood up and they converged upon him and stripped him. He was more glorious than any man there. She watched the men, all heterosexual libertines, admire her lover's body, caress him, with hands and tongues, and mouths that tried to take in all of his eleven-inch phallus, so superb to look at because of its six-inch circumference and its huge knob, the angle of its throbbing erection and the magnificence of the testicles, so perfect in proportion to the rest of him. A living sensual god.

Mirella was wet with her own orgasms long before any of them touched her. She slipped off the marble table and out of her sandals, unbuckled her silver belt with trembling hands and let it drop on the sand, then opened the white silk shirtdress and removed it, crumpled it in her hands, and rubbed her body with the sensuous material, then dropped it to the sand as well.

She opened her arms wide and offered herself to her lover. He went to her surrounded by the other men; they touched her, kissed and licked her all over—on her arms, and in their pits, between her fingers, under her breasts, between her thighs, her pubis, between her buttocks, her nipples, and even her toes. Two men lifted her up level to her lover's mouth, and spread her legs wide apart. Two others gently stretched the outer lips of her cunt open as far as they could and her lover tongued and nibbled her clitoris, sucking up the juices that flowed copiously from her. She cried out and shivered with orgasm after orgasm, but none of the men stopped. With no warning at all her lover grasped her by the waist, lowered her, and, with one powerful thrust, he penetrated her nearly to the hilt of his cock.

Two of the men held her in that position as her lover penetrated her again and again, while others continued their kissing and licking. Neither Mirella nor her lover took their eyes from the glorious sight of his cock pounding into her again and again. Each time he withdrew fully, their need grew greater: she, to be powerfully pierced and filled; he, to be squeezed and sucked dry by her vagina. At some moment he had opened her sufficiently for one of the men to reach in and fill her with an exquisite scented cream that made her crave him even more, if that were possible. Then he continued to fuck her until, at last, she had taken all of him inside her, swallowed him whole with her vagina. When they climaxed together, their cries of pain and pleasure rang through the orange grove, and were echoed by those of several of the men as they came in and on other parts of her body.

Her lover bore her to the table and lay down on it, cradling her in his arms. He kissed her passionately on the lips, then sucked on her sensitive nipples. They declared their love for each other, as they watched each of the nine men take her in turn, and fill every orifice of her body with warm sperm. She called out to him that it was wonderful, wonderful . . . and enough.

"Whatever I give you," he said, "will never be enough. I want to give you more, and *will* give you more and more. I wanted you, wholly and totally, and you gave yourself to me just that way, without any *buts*, from the moment I met you. I will love you until the day I die for giving yourself to me, Roxelana, and accepting the responsibility of our love and our marriage."

Mirella wondered why he called her Roxelana, and turned in his arms and looked into her lover's face. It had changed. He was Adam Corey. The shock woke her with a start, and she hit her head against the airplane window.

Rubbing her head and frowning, she swung her legs down onto the floor, sat back, and stretched. She raised the small window blind and looked out. The sun was rising and lighting up the sky. There were great flat wedges of white cloud floating in space like slabs of whipped cream against a cold blue sky streaked with yellow and pink. Mirella's disorientation was complete.

She stared out across the vastness that lay before her and

recalled her dream with a great deal of amusement and pleasure until bitterly, she reminded herself of the gulf between fantasy and reality. Her sex life with Paul had been, in a different way, as liberated and wonderful as that of her dream, but it was over. She had had a taste of real love twice—once with Paul, and it had turned out to be five percent real love and ninety-five percent illusion and selfishness . . . and then with Adam. She couldn't say that had died, because it never really began. Every second with him had been a promise that the love of a lifetime was *about* to be realized. Mirella wondered if she would ever experience real love. It seemed to her unlikely.

10

The wheels hit the tarmac with a bounce and Mirella was in England. The moment she walked out of the plane into the morning sunshine she shivered with excitement. She followed the other passengers without thinking where she was going and felt like a dumb sheep. It wasn't a bad feeling.

When she lined up for immigration, her disorientation disappeared and reality hit her—she was in a different country and with a mission. Mirella decided then and there that she should have a good time while working through the details of her legacy.

While waiting for her suitcase to appear on the circling steel luggage carousel, she remembered the name she had been addressed by in her dream. Roxelana. The same name as her benefactor. With New York behind her, no work to think about, no man in her life, Mirella was free to speculate about her legacy. And, so, for the first time since Brindley Ribblesdale arrived with his fantastic story, she thought it might, after all, be interesting to know something about Roxelana Oujie, her great-grandmother, who from the grave had wrought so much havoc. Since she had made this journey, she might just as well examine in detail the contents of the legacy and read the family archives.

She saw her old battered Gucci suitcase—even more battered for having been victimized by baggage handlers yet again. Its sturdy leather handle was broken and hanging off at an angle, and much to her amazement, a thick piece of rope was tied around it. As the bag glided toward her on the merry-go-round she saw that the zipper had broken as well as the handle and she knew she would have to have the twenty-year-old valise repaired.

At last she had her bag on a cart and was pushing her way through the crowds of people, past the customs agents, who waved her on with hardly a glance. She went through the automatic doors and into the reception area of Heathrow terminal.

She had yet another attack of disorientation when she saw the crowds pushing against the barriers, waving and calling to the red-eyed, air-weary travelers arriving from all over the world. She was astonished by the mob of Asians, Africans, Chinese, Arabs, and a smattering of Caucasians. That crowd was a sorry lot in saris and Rastafarian hairdos and Pakistani bloomers. There were women heavily draped in black cloth, only their eyes showing, men in banana and turquoise colored suits wearing lots of cheap cologne, their hair slicked back. A great many children of all shapes and sizes with runny noses and distressed faces, dressed up like adults, were doing a great deal of tugging and clinging, crying and sniffling. Worst off to Mirella were the ones with dead rubber nipples, pacifiers, in their mouths.

She could have been in an airport terminal in Bombay, Dubai, or Jidda, by the look of them. Only the sight of a well-turned-out chauffeur in a Rolls-Royce cap, holding up a white card inscribed "Lord Albermaryl," and another driver twenty feet along the barrier whose card read "Mr. Walters" and another next to him, whose sign read "Donald Munson," reminded her she was in London.

Mirella pushed her luggage cart along, following the signs directing her to the exit, and was surprised to see how much more dirty and shabby Heathrow was since the last time she had been there. She was astonished to hear her name blared out over the terminal's intercom system, and she proceeded immediately as instructed to the information desk. There she was even more astonished to find a chauffeur from the Turkish Embassy waiting to take her to her hotel in Mayfair. He presented her with a letter from the ambassador apologizing for not meeting her himself due to a previous engagement. On behalf of the Turkish government, he welcomed her to London and offered her the services of the embassy and in staff.

Mirella sat back in the car and tried to work out why the embassy would go to all the trouble it had for her, and who had alerted them to her arrival. At first, she thought it might have been Roland Culver who had asked someone from the Turkish delegation at the U.N. to call London and have their embassy assist her in any way it could. Then she crossed that idea off, because she realized that Roland didn't know of her involvement with Turkey. Brindley, of course! It had to have been Brindley, who must be in contact with the embassy because of the estate's holdings there. Satisfied that she had solved that little mystery, she sat back and relaxed.

The ride in to London was dreary until the Museum of Natural History came into view. The huge Victorian pile made her warm to London again. They rushed through Hyde Park past the Hotel Intercontinental, the Hilton, and exited in front of the Dorchester Hotel. The driver took South Audley Street to Grosvenor Square. As they were passing the American Embassy Mirella realized the car was flying two small Turkish flags, from little poles of steel mounted on each of the front fenders. She considered that very strange. She had been at the U.N. long enough to know that this was usually done only for the highest officials of the country or for very important visiting dignitaries. She found it disconcerting.

The traffic jammed up on Brook Street as they inched their way to the entrance of Claridge's. Mirella was really looking forward to staying there. Many times she had dined in the hotel, and had had drinks there, listening to a quartet play music that created a kind of genteel elegance that transcended time, but she had never been a resident of the hotel. The Wingfields had always stayed at the Berkeley.

At last the car pulled up to the curb in front of the revolving door. Two doormen, wearing their smart uniforms and shiny black top hats trimmed in gold braid, approached the car with a grand flourish as the chauffeur opened the door. Mirella stepped out onto the pavement. She was wearing an ensemble designed by Adolfo. On her head was his handsome wide-brimmed mocha-colored hat made of the finest felt. The narrow band around the crown was made of braided ribbons of white velvet, satin, and chiffon. Her dress was a long mocha-colored linen tunic. It hung to six inches above a narrow white linen underdress that finished a few inches below the knee. On her feet were a pair of Manolo Blahnik white alligator shoes with a sensible heel.

Mirella knew that she looked beautiful and elegant, in spite of jet lag and travel grime, and had Deena to thank for that.

It was Deena who insisted that she buy the expensive outfit, emphasizing that it was perfect for traveling: she could hang the tunic up or lay it out on the luggage rack, and look fresh and elegant when she slipped it on over the white underdress, wrinkled from eight hours of sitting, twisting and turning, sleeping and eating, while flying across the Atlantic Ocean. Deena had bought her the hat as a gift.

"Not one woman in 'Dynasty,'" she had said, "would have gone to pick up forty mill without a hat on."

"This is no soap opera, Deena, this is my life," Mirella had answered.

"I am beginning to think," Deena had shot back, "the only difference between your life and a soap opera, Mirella, is you haven't made the radio or the TV yet. God knows, you have the family, the background, the life-style, and now this inheritance, all the ingredients that soap thrives on."

Mirella smiled to herself while watching a doorman heave the messy-looking piece of luggage from the trunk of the car. Deena would have been so embarrassed for her, yet Mirella couldn't have cared less. She thanked the Turkish driver, gave the doorman two pounds, and then stepped into and pushed the revolving door, while Deena's last words to her went through her mind:

"Remember, old bean, you'll be all right if you just think 'Joan Collins's Alexis Colby' when you're negotiating anything to do with men or money, not 'Mirella Wingfield.' And, if you can't think 'Alexis,' then think 'Winebaum.' Marcus Winebaum has always been so clever in advising you and your family when it comes to dealing with the outside world. Call him."

Mirella's attention was caught by what she thought was an instantaneous bright flash. She looked over her shoulder, back toward the embassy's car, where she thought the flash came from, just as the revolving door began to turn. The car was pulling away from the curb and all she saw was the two doormen talking to each other, and the back of a man, before she was gently spun into the lobby of Claridge's.

She walked up several marble stairs into what must be one of the most discreet lobbies of any of the grandest hotels in the world—large, with an extremely high ceiling and very elegant; a great hall, with two period wing chairs and a small, comfortable, nineteen-thirties-style settee tucked under the curve of the grand staircase. A fire burning in the fireplace left a faint scent of wood smoke that blended with that of beeswax from well-polished period pieces placed sparsely but decoratively, and whose surfaces bore huge handsome vases filled with opulent arrangements of fresh, long-stemmed flowers.

There were no guests, no bellboys in sight, no bank of elevators, and the quiet was sublime. Directly ahead, Mirella saw the grand salon, where drinks were served, and the string quartet played. The deep, comfortable sofas and chairs, arranged in small groups and around tables, were all deserted behind glass and doors. The hall porter was placed so discreetly against a wall that Mirella hadn't seen him on entering, and only found him when she turned around and made a decided effort.

When she gave her name and asked to be shown to her room, she was ushered around the corner from the hall porter's desk to where several tailcoated men were rushing about. There was something farcical about the way they darted back and forth through a pair of closed doors, where the telephones kept ringing softly and the precious "reservations" were kept. It was Chaplinesque: grand and elegant and necessary, but still Chaplinesque.

Mirella was well received, but then pleasantly ignored for nearly five minutes before one of them finally read the note with her name on it placed in his hand by the hall porter. He reacted as if he knew the name, and was most apologetic for keeping her waiting, fawned over her, and himself guided her to her room.

The porter who accompanied them slipped the key card into the slot in the door and swung it open. He went ahead of them to check the room out. Mirella knew at once a dreadful mistake had been made. She had reserved the least expensive single room available in the hotel, and clearly the room she had been brought to was the drawing room of one of the exceptional suites Claridge's was famous for.

She had a good look around the room before she turned to the man in the tailcoat to tell him a mistake had been made, but before she could say anything the room began to fill with people. The first arrival was the maid, whom he presented to her, assuring Mirella the woman would attend her at any time during her stay. It was at that moment that the luggage porter arrived with her shockingly shabby suitcase and carried it, somewhat awkwardly by the rope around it, past her to the bedroom. Following on his heels was the waiter who served her room, carrying a silver tray covered in a crisp white cloth, with a silver coffee and tea service on it and a plate of biscuits. He was followed by another waiter wheeling in a service table laden with everything to form a drinks bar that included a champagne bucket with a bottle of Krug chilling in it. He was followed by a young boy in livery carrying a large bowl of fresh fruit. The valet arrived and stood discreetly at the entrance of the suite waiting for instructions. It was somewhat of an assault, as if someone had called "action—stations" . . . and Mirella felt embarrassed to tell them they had the wrong lady.

She sighed, as she took a last look around the handsome room filled with bowls of beautiful white poppies and orchids. For a fleeting moment she thought of Adam Corey and her own flower-filled room at home. Then, somewhat sadly, she spoke to the tailcoated man who had introduced himself as Mr. Trafford.

"This is all very embarrassing," she said as softly as she could without whispering, "but you see there has been some mistake, I reserved—"

Mr. Trafford looked appalled as he interrupted her.

"But madam is not pleased? I assure you this is one of the very finest suites in Claridge's. Please, allow me to show you the dressing room, the bathroom, and the bedroom. If there are any minor details about the rooms that do not meet with madam's approval, we will, of course, change them."

He led the way across the magnificent drawing room with its antique Chinese wallpaper, and its Chippendale furniture. Mirella followed Mr. Trafford, feeling even more foolish because he had misunderstood what was wrong. She stopped him just in front of the bedroom door.

"No, no, you misunderstand. I think this suite is magnificent. It's just that I have reserved a small single room, not a suite. There has been an error in the reservations."

A look of relief passed across Mr. Trafford's face, and then a smile. He pushed open the bedroom door and Mirella stepped into a huge bedroom, filled with sunshine. A magnificently grand double bed was draped in one of the loveliest floral fabrics she had ever seen: tiny miniature yellow daffodils, bright green stems, leaves, and all, printed on a cream-colored watered silk taffeta that blurred the flowers ever so slightly, softening the line of the usually stiff-looking blossom. The windows were festooned and draped with the same material.

"Miss Wingfield, there has been no mistake. These rooms have been reserved for you. Your reservations were changed two days ago and your arrival confirmed yesterday. I can assure you this suite is yours for the duration of your stay in London. Now if you will excuse me, I will leave you to settle in. If there is anything, I repeat *anything,* you need, I am at your service."

Mirella followed Mr. Trafford back into the drawing room of the suite. She wanted to stop him and ask who had changed the reservations, but it would have made her look like a fool, so she hesitated. She knew that whoever it was would make himself known soon enough. She guessed that it had been either Paul, trying to sweeten her up, or extravagant Deena trying to tell her she had a new role to play, the role of heiress.

She watched Mr. Trafford leave her rooms. The waiter, still fussing over the drinks table, asked her if she would like a cup of coffee or tea. Mirella removed her hat and dropped it on one of the pair of sofas in the room and sat down on the other, accepting a cup of coffee from him. She was told where the service buttons were in the suite, and one by one the staff left.

Alone at last, Mirella kicked off her shoes and poured herself another cup of coffee, then returned to the sofa and drank it slowly. The coffee table in front of her had an exotic floral arrangement—dozens of white poppies and fine long stems of white moth orchids. She had never seen the combination before and thought it extremely sensual and provocative. No matter how many times she distracted herself by the other beautiful things in the room, she was constantly drawn to the flowers, like a moth that's drawn to a flame.

Then she noticed, tucked among the flowers, an envelope. She opened it. It was an invitation to dine with the man who had arranged it all: the car from the Turkish Embassy, the suite, the flowers. *She* was amazed to read that she was there as his guest, and that if she would like to know more about why, she should join him for dinner that evening. He would be waiting for her in the dining room at eight o'clock.

The note was written by hand on a stiff white card with a handsome border of two heavily engraved black pencil lines, a thicker line of gold leaf in between, and was signed *Rashid Lala Mustafa*.

Mirella was amazed. She stood up and walked around the room looking at the various bowls of flowers, the card still in her hand. *She* was the guest of Rashid Lala Mustafa, the world-famous society playboy, a handsome Turk with a Cambridge degree, known for his business acumen and notorious for his womanizing. His name was never out of the society pages of the *New York Times*. It was he who wanted to have dinner with her this evening. This was all too much, yet an offer she could hardly refuse, and, she said to herself, he knew that when he wrote the note. She sank into one of the deep wing chairs in front of the black and gold marble fireplace and placed her hand to her head in despair: the legacy was proving even more complicated than she had ever imagined.

It was almost noon when she called Brindley to tell him of her arrival. He seemed surprised when she said she would shower and change and be right over to begin working with him. He suggested that she take the day off and relax, try to get over her jet lag, and that they should begin their work the following morning. Much to her own surprise, she heard herself agree that it would be better that way.

She went into her dressing room, and noticed that her things had been unpacked and put away. She found the clothes that she was going to wear that evening and rang for the valet to have them pressed. Then she ran a bath and lay in the pink marble tub for the next half hour, admiring the enormous Art Deco bathroom.

The need for sleep caught up with her. She was just about able to ring for the maid and turn a corner of the bed cover down and slip in between the sheets. Her eyes were closing when the maid arrived. The last thing she remembered was the woman removing the bed cover and tucking her in, while Mirella asked her to see that she was not disturbed until six that evening, and if Maria would please see that her things were back from the valet by then.

Mirella was woken up gently from a deep dreamless sleep by the pleasant Portuguese maid dressed in her neat black uniform and crisp white apron, and offered a cup of tea. She had no feelings of disorientation, all she felt was good. She pulled herself up on the pillows and admired the room. She was famished and asked Maria if she could get her a sandwich—anything would do—and bring a banana over from the fruit bowl to tide her over until it came.

After her light repast, she dressed carefully, and slipped one of the small white moth orchids into the buttonhole of her suit as a gesture of appreciation for her host's generosity. She felt a flicker of her old adventurous spirit that she had been keeping under strict control for the last ten years, and she walked from the suite of rooms with a rekindled zest for life, and a new jauntiness to her step that tapped out "Watch out, world, here I come."

11

At a few minutes after eight o'clock Mirella walked through the nearly deserted lounge, paused at the entrance to the dining room, and announced herself to the maître d'hôtel. She was immediately escorted to Rashid Lala Mustafa's table in a quiet corner by the window on the far side of the large dining room.

The room was filled with handsome, well-dressed diners, mostly American and English, sitting in large, comfortable upholstered armchairs around tables set far apart from each other. Flocks of waiters served them. As she crossed the room, she recognized his face immediately—how many times had she seen images of that magnificent head in newspapers and magazines and on television? So many times that not only were Rashid's magnetic dark looks instantly familiar to her, but she had that odd feeling one sometimes gets of knowing someone who is a total stranger.

When he rose to greet her, Mirella found him much taller than she had imagined him to be. She was further surprised that he was so slim for a man with such broad shoulders. He was impeccably dressed in a gray, Savile Row bespoke suit, and a red Turnbull and Asser shirt that was dashingly set off by a black-and-blue-checked tie of raw silk. His shiny, straight black hair was perfectly cut, though worn full and long. It shone as brightly as the strong white teeth that he revealed to her as he smiled.

He held out his hand to greet her, and she could not help but note the perfection of his face, with its olive skin, high, wide forehead, and prominent cheekbones. The dark, soft eyes, set at a subtle slant, gave him an exotic, clever look, and were separated by the bridge of a classical Roman nose. She saw him at once as the East and the West, and his seductive gaze reflected a male sexuality so animalistic that even before their hands touched Mirella had the extraordinary feeling that he had already marked her with his scent.

Rashid took her hand and kissed it. Sex emanated from him. "Lady Killer," one of the names conferred on him by the press, came to mind. He exuded mischief—and fun as well; and another of the press labels, "The Ladies' Delight," came to mind. At last she *really* sensed what "playboy" meant, favorite label of the gossip columnists for him.

Mirella blushed at the thought of what she was wearing. Her B. Altman gray flannel suit with its pleated skirt, and her Yves Saint Laurent silver silk blouse with the soft neck ruffle had never let her down before; they had always felt chic and right with any man in any restaurant anywhere in the world. Until now. She suddenly felt as if she looked dowdy. She thought to herself, as he guided her by the elbow to the chair being held away from the table by a waiter, "My only hope is that he will notice my shoes."

They were high-heeled black snakeskin shoes, sensuous from the heel down the seductively curved arch to the provocatively pointed toe. They were elegant and undoubtedly tarty. Mirella wondered how a woman could seduce a man who had already seduced her, and gave him a broad smile. Then she answered her own question: It couldn't be done. At best the game to play would be: Hold that line and have a good time.

He looked at her from across the table. All they had done was exchange names, and she felt ridiculous that she was so enthralled by this handsome man. Handsome was really incorrect: beautiful was the better word, but seemed wrong for such a sexy, macho man. Yes, beautiful. Rashid Lala Mustafa was the most physically beautiful man she had ever met.

"Will you have a drink? A glass of champagne? What would you like?" he asked.

"A martini, very dry, with a twist of lemon," she answered, and, to herself, added, "He never saw my shoes."

After he ordered the martini and another old-fashioned for himself, he sat back in silence and gave her a long, searching look that undressed her, evaluated her, and sexually seduced her all at the same time. Then he said, "Thank you for accepting my invitation to dinner."

"I don't imagine you get many rejections, Mr. Mustafa," Mirella said.

He gave her a dazzling smile and laughed. Mirella smiled back at him and said, "That wasn't very gracious, was it? Well, I can do better than that. I can thank you for asking me to dinner, and for sending the flowers." She touched the small white orchid in her lapel and he tilted his head to one side, as if to say, "A pleasure." "And, of course, there is the magnificent suite you magically conjured up out of a reservation for one small single room. Mr. Mustafa, you certainly know how to get a woman to come to dinner. Of course, the burning question is, why this woman?"

The drinks arrived at the table at that moment and they were served. He lifted his glass.

"How very, very nice for me, Mirella Wingfield," he said. "You are a very beautiful and clever woman, and I adore beautiful and clever women. I drink a toast to you."

She raised her glass to her lips and told herself she was having dinner with one of the smoothest, most charming men in the world and she had better be *very, very* careful. But she was also aware that, careful as she might try to be, he was pulling her toward him by the sheer power of his looks and his sensual magnetism. She thought she had better find out what his generosity toward her was all about, at once, before she became involved any more than she was.

"Mr. Mustafa, much as I would like to think I am here having dinner with you because you saw me somewhere across a room and found me so wonderful, so remarkable that you had to get to know me, we both know that's not true."

He began to say something, but Mirella held up her hand to stop him and continued, "No, please, no chivalrous compliments; let me go on. Since that is not the case, I can only assume this has something to do with my visit to London, and, if that is so, I would appreciate an explanation."

"And you shall have one."

He was interrupted by several waiters who arrived at the table with a glass-lined silver-plated server containing a half pound of the best Russian beluga caviar. They presented it to Rashid for inspection and he nodded his approval and asked Mirella, "Will caviar do, or would you prefer something else?"

"Caviar will do just fine."

The waiters served Mirella and Rashid, and offered nothing more than toast points with the caviar.

"Since this beluga is as fine as a jewel," Rashid said, "I suggest we spoon it onto our tongues and forget the usual accompaniments, the chopped onion, egg, or sour cream. It would be a pity to disguise the delicate flavor of this delectable roe, do you agree?"

Mirella agreed with a nod, and Rashid removed from his jacket pocket a slim five-inch-long brown velvet packet tied with a satin cord. He opened it and removed two thin lapis lazuli palettes and handed one of them across the table to Mirella.

"It's not so much an affectation," he said by way of an apology, "as it is a desire not to spoil the taste of the caviar. Gold, wood, or semiprecious stones will do: anything but silver: it leaves a bad taste in the mouth. Shall we have vodka with it, or champagne?"

The vodka arrrived at the table at that moment and was offered to them in a small carafe, set in a miniature ice cooler. They both chose the vodka, which was served in small stemmed glasses. They drank it neat, between palettes full of the Caspian sturgeon roe. Without a doubt there was something terribly romantic and exciting about the combination of the man, the Russian caviar, and the vodka. They were redolent of legend and magic, and the question of why she was there only made their rendezvous more mysterious.

She tapped the caviar onto her tongue from the lapis lazuli palette. Having the dark gray eggs in her mouth and rolling them on her tongue, crushing them between it and the roof of her mouth, having the exquisite, unique flavor caress her taste buds, was extremely sensual, and Mirella could well understand why caviar is claimed to be an aphrodisiac.

"Well, Mr. Mustafa, I am waiting for that explanation of what this is all about and I do wish you would tell me, so that I may stop worrying about the cost of the rooms, and how I will pay for them if I decide I cannot accept your hospitality."

"And why might you do that, Miss Wingfield?" he asked.

"I would have thought that self-explanatory: I might not like your motives."

He began to laugh and said, "First of all, I would like your permission to call you Mirella." She nodded her consent and then he went on. "Secondly, if you don't mind my saying so, your thinking is so provincial, so American-provincial. How does it follow that you cannot accept a man's hospitality if you do not like his motives for wanting to meet you? You did not have to accept this invitation to dinner, you know. I would still have extended the hospitality of the suite and the flowers. But let's not have a purposeless dispute over the codes of Eastern hospitality as against those of Western hospitality. Instead let me answer your question.

"I am rather well connected at the Turkish Embassy here, and they received notification that you have been discovered to be the sole heir to several large, prosperous estates, comprising many varied companies and properties, which have been for years all part and parcel of one enormous, until-now-undiscovered holding known as the Oujie legacy. I am familiar with certain aspects of that legacy and for as long as I can remember have heard legendary stories about some of your distant relations.

"Word has it that you have no interest in Turkey, that you have a successful career in the United States, and that it is your intention to dispose of your legacy and all your holdings in Turkey without going there.

"My curiosity got the better of me. Here was a real live human being, the heir to the romantic legends and places of my youth, some of which have colored my whole life. I felt, since you are so removed from it all, I would like to extend a hand of hospitality, on behalf of myself and my country. I happen to be in the unique position of being a wealthy, successful, international man, with the peasant's deep love of his country. In a strange way I feel somewhat like an unofficial ambassador, duty-bound to welcome you to your legacy and your country, for the short time that you will be involved with it.

"That you're liquidating you legacy is understandable: you and your family have been removed from Turkey for generations. Istanbul is not New York, Antalya is not Nice or Cannes. Turkey is wonderful—but so are a good many other places in the world—to play in. I only return for short visits myself, because underneath the gloss of a Cambridge education, and the life-style of a world-famous playboy, I am drawn to my country. It's still very much a part of me. I have family and friends who live there, and I maintain considerable business interests there. *I* am after all a full-blooded Ottoman who is passionately interested in Turkey and her people. Well, there you have it, your explanation. I hope it's sufficient for you to accept the hospitality of the East, or at least the hospitality of this Eastern man in Western clothing."

He refilled their glasses with vodka and their eyes met. Mirella thought of the man with chocolate-pudding eyes in her dream, and she smiled at Rashid and wondered just how much of a "Lady-Killer" he was.

The next course, a bird's nest filled with small cream-and-brown-spotted Japanese quail's eggs on a silver platter, was put down before them. They cracked the shells, peeled them, and ate the delicious eggs with celery salt and paper-thin slices of buttered brown bread, and washed it down with an outstanding bottle of chilled white wine, a Premier Cru Meursault. They talked not about Mirella and her legacy but about how much pleasure it gave him to arrange the flowers and the rooms, the meal they would have together, and how much it amused him to do it for a perfect stranger. He laughed good-naturedly when she told him she thought he was probably a pathological seducer of women.

When Mirella unbuttoned her jacket and began to slip out of it, he rose from his chair and went around to help her. He snapped his fingers and two waiters arrived at once, and brought an empty chair to lay it on, then placed the chair close by, but out of their way. He returned to his seat after he had smoothed the silk blouse over her shoulders, and arranged the back of her hair where it had been messed by the collar of the jacket.

Mirella had never met such a charming man before. He made the suave foreign diplomats she had met through her work at the U.N. who had tried to seduce her look like adolescent schoolboys at the game. She was enchanted by his manners and fascinated by the stories he told her of his homeland.

She had asked him quite bluntly what he would have done if she had turned out to be disagreeable, stupid, fat, and ugly. She was surprised to see the look of dismay on his face, and felt quite embarrassed by his answer.

"Mirella, I think that's a dreadful question," he said. "How do I know that you're not all of those things under the façade of a very beautiful sensual face and body, your wit and your charming intelligence? But I will answer it. If you had turned out to be visibly those things, or do in fact turn out to be invisibly all of those things, then I will have enjoyed your company to the extent you will have allowed, by your looks and your actions.

"You see, for me it's easy, because I find all women interesting, at least for one dinner. An evening with a woman is not just *the woman*. Do you think the caviar would have tasted differently because you weighed two hundred pounds? Do you think I would have enjoyed peeling a quail's egg for you any the less because you were stupid? That you have turned out to be the woman I think you are is a bonus for me, but was not expected. Had you had all the defects you mention, we most probably would have parted sooner rather than later. You would still be my guest, and I would be happy to have you, and I would still have been pleased to meet you."

"Rashid, I am so sorry and terribly embarrassed. Please accept my apology. I don't even know what made me ask such a horrid question."

He gave Mirella a winning smile, and said graciously, "I know what made you ask that question. It was a hidden lack of respect for me, someone you don't even know. I do of course accept your apology and we will talk about it no more."

It was then that they were served the main course, rack of lamb, purée of celeriac, and creamed spinach, followed by a crisp green salad, with a light, delicate olive oil and lemon dressing. The claret they drank was the color of the darkest, most mysterious ruby, and it was like a nectar for the gods: a Château Margaux. It was a bottle from one of the superior harvesting years: one could tell by the delicacy, and the sweet haunting perfume that makes it the most exquisite claret of all.

During their meal Rashid said, "Mirella, I would like to tell you something about Turkish men, the Turkish sultans. It may help you to understand the kind of blood that, even though thinned out, still flows through my veins. It always amazes me how little women understand men and their desires—their love of beauty, their sexual appetites, and their love of the sensual and of power; the love-hate emotion they can have for a woman, the evil they are capable of, and their need for luxury in a hard and unbending world. The Turkish men of our class have inherited it all and still enjoy these same passions, but in a different style from our ancestors.

"How else could you explain the garments our forefathers wore; they were stiff with pure gold and silver thread, tooled leather and jewels. Men who crowned their turbans with egret feathers and precious jewels the size of pigeons' eggs, whose armor and helmets were jewel-studded, whose every possible utensil and weapon was encrusted with diamonds and pearls.

"Gone may be the gold paving that once covered the floor of the royal reception room in Topkapi, but you can still see the luxury that once was in the museum, the two uncut emeralds weighing six and three pounds, which dangled from the ceiling of that palace, like green lights. The fantastic firework displays of dragons and castles that used to light up the dark sky over the sultan's fabled tulip garden may be gone forever, but what remains is that a Turk, Sultan Ahmed III, gave the tulip to Louis XIV first, and thus to the world.

"The palace of Topkapi, as I am sure you know, was built on a triangular piece of land, high up on a slope that leads down through gardens and terraces to the shore, between the Bosporus and the Sea of Marmara. In 1639 the Sultan Murad IV, to commemorate his recapture of Baghdad, built a magnificent kiosk at the far end of the marble terrace. It is the loveliest of all the pavilions in Topkapi, superbly decorated inside. From there he had magnificent views over the Golden Horn, Galata, fishing-snaks, kayiks, islands, mosques, domes, crescents, and shining water that turned bloodred as the sun set over my Istanbul—what was then called Constantinople.

"The man who could commission that was also the same terrible Murad IV who spent the last years of his life making love to his favorites in this pavilion, and who on his death bed at the age of twenty-eight, as one of his last acts, ordered the execution of his brother Ibrahim, making the Ottoman race extinct and giving the throne to the favorite he chose.

"We are talking of men whose passion for the tulip, a mere flower, was infinite, as was their passion for bloodthirsty murder. Ahmed III was known as the Tulip King and had his grand vizier beheaded during a campaign in the Aegean and the putrid head brought back to him for burial. These were men so sensitive to beauty that they designed the tulip vase in honor of the flower, yet would throw women who displeased them over the cliffs and into the Sea of Marmara, tied in a sack filled with stones. These were men who indulged themselves—like Sultan Murad III, who was a weak and ineffectual ruler but was potent enough to have fathered one hundred and three children.

"Passions and intrigues were their life. When Ibrahim—who had managed to hide from his brother Murad IV long enough for Murad to die and Ibrahim to succeed him on the throne—had no children of his own, word went around that the dynasty was in danger of extinction. The rumor in the harem was that he was impotent. It was his own mother who, with the help of her eunuchs, took control of things. He was dosed with aphrodisiacs, and brought the most sexually exciting women from the slave market of Istanbul. In time sons were produced and the dynasty was safe. He spent the remainder of his life addicted to lust.

"When nature flagged, new and fresh remedies were found: he made love on a bed of sables; the walls of rooms used for his sensual delights were covered with mirrors, so that the sight of himself performing sexual acts stimulated him yet more. His pillows were both filled and covered with the finest Russian wolf, lynx, chinchilla, and ermine skins. He ravished all at one time several virgins who were made to kick and struggle as if they were being raped. He had voluminous books of pictures—pornography. He tried everything, and even invented a few things not heard of before, in his debaucheries—some much too bizarre for me to tell you over dinner.

"He was not the only one. They all had their lustful histories. But these were also the men who waited for the full moon to rise over Topkapi at the time the tulip garden was in full bloom. They would have all the lights extinguished in the palace, while they dallied in the love pavilion, the Baghdad Kiosk. They gazed at the tulips. A thousand small white candles attached to the backs of tortoises that wandered through the tulip beds lighted the flowers from below while the full moon lit them from above. These are your Turkish men. We have something in common, Mirella Wingfield: these are the sort of men who sired the ancestors of both of us."

Mirella was utterly enthralled by Rashid and his evocative tales. He made it all sound so real, not at all like "history," and his dark eyes and the smoldering looks he was giving her made it quite plain to Mirella that he wanted her, and she knew she would not resist him.

12

Rashid Lala Mustafa was an inveterate seducer of women. He knew it, his men friends knew it, the gossip columnists and glossy magazines writers knew it. Only the women in the throes of being seduced didn't know it, or, if they did, never accepted it. Rashid put that down to the vanity of women, who, for the most part, always believed they were different in some way from the women who preceded them. From the moment his seduction had been successful and each had fallen in love, each always assumed *her* love would conquer all: "all" being possession of, and marriage to, Rashid. That was *the* fatal mistake.

Rashid thrilled to the chase. What he told Mirella was true: He loved women, everything about women. The female mind, its cunning and vanity; a woman's body; and most of all the female genitalia. He enjoyed spending time and money on women, and had infinite patience when drawing out their secret smoldering desires and needs. He liked stripping them of their protective covering, until they were raw and vulnerable. And he would go to great lengths to satisfy their newly uncovered desires and needs.

Once that was accomplished Rashid would begin to make demands on his women. They had to allow themselves to be stretched in many directions, pushed to the limits of what they could and would give, intellectually, socially, emotionally, and most of all sexually. Never was he less than charming, attentive, generous in his inventiveness to seduce, not even at this stage of the game. Only when he had broken them on all those levels did a hint of the evil in him enter the relationship: the first sounding of the death knell for the affair. It tolled when he was no longer amused.

From the moment he saw Mirella walking across Claridge's dining room with the maître d'hôtel, he made up his mind to seduce her. Her immensely beautiful voluptuous looks, so obviously played down by her New York style—the smart suit that would take one anywhere—and her efficient, cool, somewhat arrogant air of success, were perfect game for him. When, as he was evaluating her body, he checked out her legs, he was delighted and somewhat amused by her shoes. He quickly assessed them as her concession to the erotic in her costume, and categorized them as the shoes of a chic, respectable tart, who was probably kept by one man.

Her having pinned to her jacket one of the orchids he had sent to her told him she was a woman of charm and an adventurous spirit. As she came closer to him and he saw the movement of her luscious silky black hair, and her elusive violet eyes, he was already thinking, she must wear her hair longer, instead of only to the shoulder, and she must give up the subdued makeup. He liked the idea of her eyes and lips being accentuated. He wouldn't mind people seeing them clearly as the sensuous lips and mouth that served him.

True, a seduction of sorts of Mirella Wingfield began three days before, when his embassy spy had leaked the news to him that a portfolio had arrived at the embassy with a list of major holdings in Turkey that would be coming up for sale: their owner an American named Mirella Wingfield. Rashid and his family had been trying to obtain control of those holdings for years. They had never been able to crack the mystery of who the real owner was behind the dummy companies controlling them. But the seduction began in earnest, and on a different level, when he had kissed her hand upon meeting her.

Now for dessert, there was first, a skinned fresh white peach, poached in Pomerol, a rich young Bordeaux wine with a deep color, and served on a bed of crushed Pomerol ice. That cleared the palate and was followed by a sliver of Stilton and a biscuit. Mirella sliced through the firm but supple flesh of her peach with her spoon, holding it in place with the prongs of her dessert fork, and listened to Rashid talk about London, the place he considered his second home.

"Rashid, would you mind terribly if I asked you a very blunt question?"

"No, please ask anything you like. But understand I shall feel entitled to be just as blunt if I ever want to ask you anything."

"That's fair enough. It's just that there is no use pretending I don't know that you are one of the world's most sought-after men. You have replaced Ali Khan, Rubirosa, Gunther Sachs, the present Aga Khan. They say that both Niarchos and Onassis were your mentors, and then they say there has been no one, ever, like you. Do you hate playing the role of the international society playboy? What's your life really like? What do you do with your life?"

Rashid hesitated for a moment, finishing his mouthful of peach, then he placed the spoon on the underplate of his dessert dish. He looked at Mirella and smiled, then said, "You know, Mirella, there is something very refreshing about you. I think it must be a naïveté, a sort of American innocence. It's almost as if you have a vein of New England puritanism running through you, which on occasion breaks out like a spot on the surface of your skin. Are you from one of the New England states?"

Taking note of his deductive ability, she answered, "My father's family arrived in America on board the *Mayflower*. My mother and father still live on the land that his forefathers stepped onto, and claimed, in 1620."

"I thought so," he said. "Well, to answer your questions: first of all, *they*, whoever *they* may be, are correct; there never has been anyone like me in the society jet set. I do have the same playboy mentality that those men you mentioned had, I am a hard-working, shrewd businessman in the manner of the Greeks you mentioned. Similar, but also very different. I don't *hate* playing the role of the playboy, and for two reasons. One, I am not playing a role, I am living the life I choose to live; and two, I enjoy every minute of it. When I don't, I simply stop for a few weeks, and retreat into one of my houses in Turkey.

"You ask, what is my life really like? What do I do with it? Because I am extremely clever and ruthless in business, and know how to delegate, I only have to work hard about twenty percent of my time. I play twice as hard the other eighty percent. But that isn't really what you want to know. What you long to ask me is, am I the rapscallion *they* say I am? Am I the 'Lady-Killer,' the cad who leaves a trail of broken hearts wherever I go? Well, be warned, Mirella Wingfield: sometimes I am."

Not for the first time that evening, Mirella was amazed at how direct and forthcoming he was about himself and his life-style. She thought it was odd that he had asked absolutely nothing about her or her inheritance, but she welcomed the omission because not to think about herself or that legacy was such a relief.

The cheese plates were whisked away and demitasse cups of strong black coffee were placed on the table in front of them.

She watched Rashid sweeten his coffee with three heaped small spoons of Demerara sugar and she smiled.

"I consider myself warned," she said with a naughty twinkle in her eye that he did not miss. She then added, "Ah, I have found out one of your vices, Rashid. You have a sweet tooth."

He smiled back at her.

"That is quite true, I love sweet things. Would you be shocked to know that it's my only vice? I don't consider the other things I do, or the things the columnists accused me of doing, vices."

They talked for a while about how he did not consider his occasional drug-taking, drinking, cigars, or smoking the nargileh, the Turkish water pipe, vices.

"Rashid, what about your sexual vices?" she boldly asked him.

He laughed in the most open and engaging way. "Mirella, I don't consider anything sexual I do a vice. Absolutely nothing, because it's good for me—unlike sugar—in any form."

Mirella couldn't help but laugh at him. Rashid Lala Mustafa was the most perfect cad she had ever met in her life, she was very sure of that. They were both enjoying themselves, and were aware of the sexy sparkle in each other's eyes. He snapped his fingers and the waiter appeared at once to refill their cups. He sighed and shrugged his shoulders as he filled his spoon three more times with sugar and sprinkled the grains into the fresh hot coffee. The waiter approached the table again.

"Ah," Rashid said, "here comes the best part of the meal."

They were served tiny pots of dark chocolate mousse, so extravagantly rich and delicious that Mirella called this final touch to their meal *wicked*.

They took their after-dinner drink sitting on a sofa in a quiet corner of the lounge, where the musicians were still playing. They both chose Calvados. Mirella had had too much to drink and was very aware of it.

"Rashid, I want to thank you very much. This has been the most unexpected and charming evening I've had for a very long time. May I make the toast?"

He nodded his consent and she raised her snifter of clear white liquid, and swirled it around, brought it closer to her nose, and inhaled the faint scent of apple. He followed suit, and then she touched her glass to his and said, "To my host, you, Rashid Lala Mustafa."

"So," he said, with a teasing smile on his face, "you find my motives allowable, therefore you accept my hospitality. How very nice for both of us."

They lifted their glasses at the same time and drank, gazing at each other, but said no more. The musicians packed up to leave the reception room shortly after that, and a few of the other guests left for their rooms.

"Would you like to go to Annabel's?" he asked.

"Who's Annabel?"

"Not *who's* Annabel, *what's* Annabel's. It's the best night-club and disco in London."

"Is it really the best, or is it the poshest, the most chic? The society night spot of which you just have to be a member? The place where all the beautiful people go?" she asked teasingly.

"It's all of those things, *and* the best," he answered and then added, "Does that bother you? You're not one of those inverted snobs are you, Mirella?"

"No, Rashid, hardly. But frankly, if it's all those things, I really don't feel I can go. Here comes my vanity. All evening I have felt drab sitting opposite you. Do you always bring out the peacock in a woman? Do they always feel as I do right now, wanting to be gorgeous and glamorous? Do women always want to sparkle for you?"

He smiled and said in his most charming manner, "Yes, most of the time, and why shouldn't they? I always find that if you give a woman what she wants, she's happy, and happy women sparkle. As you do right now."

"Can you really see the beauty and glamour, the frivolous and amusing Mirella Wingfield I would like to project through all this chic gray flannel and composure? Or are you saying that I am sparkling because you, Rashid Lala Mustafa, are giving me all the luxury and charm most women crave and would enjoy?"

"I'm not blind, Mirella. It's true you are dressed with a chic that is New York, that is to some extent smart. You have the look of an ultrafeminine women's libber, that look that resembles Gloria Steinem, which some men find mightily attractive. You project the image of the successful, intellectual, liberated single woman—successful and liberated being the operative words. I am guessing that you are, probably, an executive of some kind, with an academic background. One of those women who reads *New York* magazine at home and *Vogue* at the hairdresser's; one who subscribes to *Art News, Architectural Digest, Gourmet,* and *The New Yorker,* but never gets the chance to read them.

"I see you as a lady who keeps up with the world via the *New York Times* and the *Washington Post* every day, and sneaks a look at the glossy fashion magazines at her friends' houses and the dentist's office.

"Mirella, I may be wrong, but I think you are a glamorous lady who is just about to come out of the closet. And if that's true, I am all for it. Glamour and gloss are fun. Maybe it's about time you made a success of them as well."

"Oh, Rashid, you're good, very good," she said with admiration. She finished her Calvados and placed the empty brandy snifter on the table in front of her, and sat back, relaxed and agreeably tipsy. She put her hand on his coat sleeve, gave him a smile.

"Maybe you're right, Rashid, maybe it should be good-bye, gray flannel; hello, silver sequins. So long, academia; hi there, Hollywood. Bye-bye, adios, adieu, and toodle-oo to the American work ethic; hello, playtime. How does one go about gathering glamour and gloss to one's bosom? It has to be done right, you know. I'm not a woman who likes half measures."

Rashid was enchanted by her playful outburst. The more time he spent with this woman the more he delighted in the prospect of seducing her.

"Ah," he said, "that's a good beginning. In fact, you have two good beginnings—that attitude and me. Please let me be the man to unlock the door for you and bring you out of the closet."

"Can we do it in four days?" she asked.

Then they looked at each other and began to laugh together. He reached around her and helped her into her jacket.

"We can give it a damned good try. All I can say is: Watch out, world, here comes the new Mirella Wingfield."

"Funny you should say that; I said something very much like that to myself earlier this evening."

Mirella was not surprised, when, after leaving the reception hall, Rashid asked her for the key to her suite. They gazed at one another, and for a split second the tension sparked between them. Faint smiles crossed their faces, as Mirella, without a moment's hesitation and without a word, reached into her black snakeskin bag and handed over the key to her suite.

Rashid slipped his arm through hers, and gave her a look calculated to make any woman want him. Her eyes were riveted to his sensuous mouth and when she saw him nibble at the side of his upper lip and hold it for a second between strong white teeth, then let it go, she wondered what indeed Rashid Lala Mustafa had in mind for her.

The couple remained silent during the ascent in the elevator, and they did not speak while walking down the corridor to her suite. The silence between them was not an awkward one. Nor was it one of anticipation or excitement. It was a glamorous, powerful, sexual silence vibrating between two erotically secure people. Mirella had rarely known anything like it before. No words were necessary. He used nothing more than his physical beauty and the power of his personality to make her feel passive, open, and vulnerable, joyously ready to receive and satisfy his every sexual demand.

The lamps were lit when they entered the living room. It looked so welcoming, and even more beautiful than Mirella had thought it to be. She noticed at once, on a coffee table, in front of the fireplace, two champagne glasses. And, by the shape of the bottle, chilling in the bucket, a magnum of a very rare vintage of Krug champagne. There was a pretty pedestal dish there, too, with a pyramid of Godiva chocolates on it.

Mirella was quite overwhelmed by the certainty with which Rashid Lala Mustafa carried out his seduction. At no point had the man left an inch of space for her to maneuver in, and she found that thrilling. He had her exactly where she wanted to be.

She watched Rashid open the bottle and pour some of the bubbling wine into the sparkling Baccarat champagne flute, taste it, declare it to be superb, and then fill the two glasses. He handed one to her across the coffee table, and they raised their glasses and drank as one. It was as if their actions were synchronized.

He picked up one of the dark chocolates and bit into it as he walked around the table to her, then offered her the other half. He took another swallow of his wine; she did the same. Then he removed the glass from her hand, and placed it together with his on the table to walk in back of her and help her off with her jacket, which he draped over a chair. He refilled their glasses and handed hers back to her. He slipped his arm around her waist and together they walked into the bedroom.

The bedside lamps gave off a lovely soft light. The bed had been turned down and on one side her nightdress had been laid out. It was a pale violet silk gown, the top of which had a black lace inset just large enough to cover the breasts that continued on down to the waist; its straps were made of two strings of black satin. On the far side of the bed, Rashid's black silk moiré robe was none-too-discreetly draped at an angle across the bottom of the bed. On each nighttable was a small pedestal dish stacked with Leonidas white chocolates. Mirella was neither surprised nor annoyed that he had taken her for granted.

Rashid thought it was much to Mirella's credit that she hadn't said a word to him when they entered the living room and she saw the liberty he had taken in having the wine and chocolates sent up. He watched her closely in the bedroom. There was not the least hint of surprise in her face when she saw his robe or his favorite chocolates waiting to satisfy his craving for sweets.

Again they moved together as if in sychronization. This time when they placed their glasses on one of the tables, held hands and then raised them, each of them kissed the other's hands. They stepped back a few paces, eyes examining each other as they undressed.

Mirella was quite overwhelmed by Rashid's naked body. His nakedness seemed to dominate her even more. His slim but muscular body was more like the sculpture of a young Greek god than of a man in his late forties. He was narrow and slim-hipped, but with small, voluptuously rounded, tight buttocks, and his long legs and his thighs were strong.

He stood, one foot resting on the bed, the other on the floor, bent slightly forward, hand resting on his thigh, watching Mirella. His long, thick penis and ample testicles hung between his legs, large, and magnificently formed. Mirella could not take her eyes off him. Although his handsome head and his perfect genitals dominated his devastating good looks, she realized that even his feet, long and narrow, and his hands, large with long slim fingers, were perfectly beautiful.

Mirella reached for her nightgown, and he said in a firm, sharp voice, "No."

She dropped it as if it were red-hot. He stood up straight and they walked toward each other. They stood together at the side of the bed and he caressed her. He ran his hands over every inch of her skin, lightly, tenderly. He began with her face and then down over her neck and shoulders. He missed nothing, not even the crease between her thigh and her mound—not even the furrow of her bottom, when he had turned her around and had begun again from her neck to her toes. He used his fingertips like feathery brands to inflame her, consciously and calculatedly.

She stood there as if she were made of stone. That was on the outside. Inside she was melting to the very marrow of her bones. She was mesmerized now, by his body, his magnetism, and his touch. He walked away from her to the table next to the bed and returned.

"Open your mouth," he said.

She did, and he fed her one of the large delicious white chocolates with a soft vanilla-and-chocolate filling made of fresh cream, and ate one himself. Then he took her in his arms and kissed her. Their lips touched and opened and their first kiss was filled with sweet and wild passion.

As they kissed, their arms enveloped each other. He picked her up and put her on the bed. Before Mirella realized what was happening, he had dragged her, somewhat roughly, onto the middle of the bed and placed her the way he wanted her: on all fours. He made her comfortable with cushions under her elbows and had her raise her buttocks high, her legs wide apart. He exclaimed at her beauty, how magnificent and beautiful her genitalia were from that angle. In one powerful thrust he entered her and felt himself caressed by a moist warmth and soft sweetness that lured him on.

Mirella was taken by surprise and with such a fierceness and force that she called out in pain and ecstasy. He filled her so swiftly and fitted into her so tightly, and stretched her open so powerfully she came in a gigantic wave that made it easier for him to pull out and reenter her again and again. He was a master at fucking: he was able to create and prolong tingling intensities of pleasure for both of them.

He was a commanding lover, to whom she happily submitted, and the more she did, the more she wanted to. When they came together the first time she was already near to swooning, she had had so many orgasms. When still filled with the juices of their lust, he slid several of the white chocolates up into her and then sucked them out slowly one by one and ate them, feeding the odd one to her, right from his own mouth into hers. Mirella came again and begged him to stop, at least for a moment so she could rest. She dozed off lying in his arms.

He came with her twice more after that, and with the same intensity and in different ways, before he declared that they could finally go to sleep. She woke up twice. Once when the room was in total darkness and she could only see the outline of his features in the dark; she listened to his quiet even breathing and admired him. The second time was when she turned onto her side, and leaned on her elbow facing him. She studied his handsome face in a shaft of early morning light that fell through the not-quite-closed draperies.

Tears came to her eyes and slowly seeped out and ran down her cheeks, for no reason other than he was so beautiful. He was the most beautiful man she had ever woken up with in her life. He was indeed a "Lady-Killer."

She was well aware that there was, in the man sleeping next to her, beauty, eroticism, and glamorous charm, a certain degree of danger and possibly evil. She had already had proof of the passion and a hint of the wild erotic lengths to which he extended his indulgence and could drive her also. And she knew she wanted to go there with him, and she would. There were no flashing lights warning her to stay away: only good feelings about having a great vacation romance with one of the world's most glamorous, amusing, sexy playboys.

Her last thought before she dozed off to sleep again was, Thank you, Roxelana. You may have wrought havoc with my life, ah, but with what style! She smiled to herself in the half-light, and murmured aloud in a dreamy whisper and half sleep, "I really mean it. Thank you, Great-grandmother. I hope I won't let you down."

13

"There are very few glossy annual reports and company prospectuses for us to show you on the businesses in which you own shares," Brindley said. "Most of them are privately and closely held. But what we do have is an excellent listing of your assets along with simple reports of their value. I don't know how knowledgeable you are about business and money, Mirella, but I thought I had better explain why we don't have a great raft of glossy portfolios ready for you."

"Oh, Brindley, what a relief that you don't! I know virtually nothing about business and money. My family and I aren't very clever about it, but we do have an advisor, and if I am really confused about something I can always call on him. But frankly, Brindley, I don't see why you and I cannot handle everything between us. The Oujie legacy has been your baby, so to speak, for so long that I think you should remain in legal command, with me at your side. And, if you think I'm making a dreadful mistake about something, I want you to say so. I'm a very practical woman; in some cases too practical. So you speak up. Fight with me if you have to, because I'm a fair person and don't have a problem about being wrong and changing my mind. Now, where do we begin?"

What was so different about her, Brindley wondered. And almost instantly got his answer: softer. Mirella Wingfield, away from her work and that frenetic city, was a softer person. He had liked her right from the first. He liked her even more sitting in his antique-pine-paneled and somewhat worn and seedy office, with cardboard boxes and stacks of briefs piled everywhere. If she meant what she said, and he had no doubts that she did, then he would indeed stand up and fight her, whenever he thought she was making a mistake in the handling of this magnificent gift.

"Well," he said, "let's begin with procedure. First, we must legally hand over the estate to you. You must read and understand the contents of the will, and sign documents that release the estate to you. Then we must arrange for each of the companies, corporations, all the stocks, property, and so forth to transfer ownership into your name—or into the name of the Oujie corporation as the parent company with you the managing director and sole stockholder, if you prefer. In other words, there are a hell of a lot of papers for you to sign."

She laughed and flexed her fingers. "I think I'm up to it, Brindley. Is that all?"

"No. Once everything is legally yours, we go over each of your assets one by one and decide what to do with it. For that we have outside advisors to sit in with us. All these I have lumped together, calling them business assets. The other assets, the personal items, works of art, jewelry, the family archives, private houses, et cetera, I have grouped together, as personal property. It seemed the easiest way to handle things. Does that seem agreeable to you?"

"It sounds fine, Brindley."

"What I suggest is that we divide the day between both. The mornings for the business, the afternoons for the personal. Agreed?"

"Agreed."

"This morning I would like to brief you about some things that might make it easier to understand the reports we have on your business assets, because then you can take some of the papers back to your hotel and work on them there if you like."

Mirella couldn't help but smile to herself, because she somehow felt that there would be little time to read anything in her hotel now that Rashid had come into her life.

Rashid—his name reminded her how surprised she was when she woke up and he was not there lying next to her. He was gone: his robe was gone, his clothes were gone. All that was left of him was the faint scent of his cologne, a musky sandalwood on the pillow next to her, and a very strong aroma of chocolates.

Sitting opposite sweet Brindley, in the overcrowded office, reeking of honorable English law, it was hard not to laugh when thinking of those chocolates, which had to be the sexiest chocolates in the world. The very thought of them being sucked out of her made her squirm in her chair and grow very warm. She distracted her thoughts from Rashid and concentrated on what Brindley was saying.

". . . you start from the back."

You start from the back! "You start what from the back, Brindley?"

She felt her face grow red with embarrassment. She had lost all concentration, and hoped she wasn't going to make a fool of herself over Rashid Lala Mustafa. She gave herself a split-second lecture and was assured that she most certainly was not going to make a fool of herself over a vacation romance with a sex-mad scallywag.

"I was saying, Mirella, that an investment analyst gave me a few hints on how to read an annual report. It might be good for you to keep these in mind when going over the documentation of the business assets. You always start from the back.

Forget the front: what you really want to know, what is relevant, is in the back. So read the report backward, starting with the auditor's report. If it says anything like 'in our opinion, the statements present fairly the company's financial position,' you need not worry."

She grinned. "And when am I to worry?"

"When you run into 'except for' or 'subject to.' Let those words be a red flag and send you to the footnotes. It's usually there you find large contingent liabilities—a bid, debt due, a suit for damages, that sort of thing.

"The next thing to read is the analysis of operations. Here is where management tells you if the company is doing well or not, and how it intends to do better. If we follow these few rules we should do all right. If we can't work out what we want to know from these few hints on how to evaluate a report, then we should get expert advice. My goodness, you look hot, Mirella, shall I open the window?"

"Yes, if you would, Brindley."

He opened the window a few inches, and the papers on his desk began to rustle, a few blew off the desk and onto the floor. Mirella reached out and caught one in midair, just as it passed in front of her, twirling down toward her shoes. Brindley went to his desk and tried to move things around so that they wouldn't be caught by the breeze. Mirella said, with a tone of amusement in her voice, "I think you had better close the window, Brindley, before we lose part of my legacy among all these papers."

He did, and gave her an embarrassed look. She laughed and said, "Brindley, don't look that way. You saw my desk at home, didn't you? I'm sure you're just like me; you can find what you want in the mess far better than if it were filed. Besides, I like your office this way: it's very Charles Dickens. I feel comfortable here; it makes me think of every English solicitor's office I've ever seen in a movie or read about."

"We don't call them offices here, Mirella, we call them chambers. Solicitor's chambers." Then he began to smile and said, "And, if you think these rooms are typical, wait until you see the rest of the chambers. And you will. I am to take you around to the conference room for tea and biscuits, and to meet the other members of the firm in half an hour. Some of the men, such as my father, are older, retired members of the firm who have all been involved with your legacy in some way. One or two of the more elderly gentlemen knew and can still remember, as my father did, several of the custodians of the estate. I am sure you will find it fascinating to meet them, and they are looking forward to meeting you. But, before that, why don't we go over, just summarily, the list I've prepared of the business assets?"

Brindley walked around his desk and presented Mirella with a copy of the list, then carefully moved aside the papers on his desk and sat on the end of it while she read.

If there was one specific moment when the enormity and the responsibility of the legacy finally struck home to Mirella, it was when she read the five-page list. It was not the quantity of business assets that daunted her. They only took her by surprise. It was the quality and the variety, their importance, and the fact that, with the exception of just a few, the estate had the controlling interest in them all.

Twenty-six banks, five in Turkey, nine of which were in the Islamic world, and then names like Hambro's in London, the Morgan Guaranty Trust Company of New York, the equivalent in Paris and Amsterdam.

Three pharmaceutical companies, all of whose brand names Mirella recognized. The twenty-fourth largest construction company in the world, whose head office was in Istanbul, builders of highways, bridges, tunnels, pipelines, power plants, refineries. Turkish exporting companies of agricultural and industrial supplies. A large Turkish shipping fleet, several shipyards, ferry companies, airlines, transport companies from small bus lines to vast trucking companies shipping all over Europe and Africa. Some of the major share holdings in Turkey included bridges, the most famous one being the suspension bridge that spans the European and Asian sides of the Bosporus. A company that had the lion's share of all but twenty percent of the country's domestic oil production.

Mirella stopped at the agricultural listings, the tobacco companies to be exact, too stunned by the fact that one of her companies had three-quarters of the tobacco harvest of three hundred and fifty million dollars in 1983.

"I had no idea, Brindley, absolutely no idea."

Brindley took the list from her hands and saw her shiver slightly. He rose, went to the clothes stand tucked away in a corner of the room, took her jacket from the wooden hanger, brought it to her, and draped it over her shoulders. Then he returned to the edge of the desk and sat on it.

"I know you didn't. I did try to tell you in New York,

Mirella. That's why I left all those documents for you to read. Obviously you haven't had a chance to read them because if you had, you would have been a bit more prepared for all this."

"Brindley, I simply cannot understand how it could have happened, how it could have grown into this enormous fortune, and be mine."

"That's why you must read the archives. It's such a remarkable family history and story of intrigue, power, politics, money, and sociological and religious changes."

"I don't think I have much choice, Brindley. I feel a moral obligation to know and understand what this is all about, now that it's mine."

"I think that's what Adam Corey and I were trying to suggest to you."

Brindley saw Mirella flush with embarrassment and it suddenly came to him that more had gone on between Mirella Wingfield and Adam Corey than those few words in her drawing room. He thought they must have had words when he went up to get his fountain pen and upon his return found Adam in the car, and not where he had left him, with Mirella at the front door. He said, in order to cover her embarrassment, "Now, Mirella, you are in an excellent position to read the archives because you speak all the languages they're written in—English, French, Arabic, and Greek. But interesting as they are, to read them is a considerable task. I could give you a synopsis if you like and then you could read them at your leisure."

Mirella thought it was a good idea. Brindley suggested they do it that afternoon, before they began working on the personal assets, some of which he said he would be able to bring to her hotel, because before she left the chambers of Rumbold, Grumthorp, and Ribblesdale that morning, the will would have been probated. She wanted to, but realized she couldn't because she had another appointment. A date with Rashid for lunch and a promise of a marvelous afternoon and evening, about which she had not been allowed to ask anything.

The date had been made when, after she had found him gone without a trace, she had slipped on the peignoir that matched her nightgown, and had gone into the bathroom. There she had been greeted by a mass of used towels dropped and draped all over the bathroom. She had noticed at once his robe lying over a chaise, his shaving things used and still there, and various toiletries: cologne, aftershave, shampoo.

After her morning ablutions, she had gone through the bedroom to the drawing room to order her breakfast, and there she rather expected to find a note of some sort from Rashid. Instead, she had been surprised to find him, dressed and looking very handsome, speaking on the telephone.

He had been talking in Turkish, and she had understood that it was a business call. He had smiled at her and it was as if he sent out some sort of invisible tentacle because she had felt immediately drawn to him. She had been going past the breakfast table that had been set for two, and had a large shallow bowl of white roses in the center, and the remnants of his breakfast on it, when he had held up his empty cup and motioned to her to fill it. As she had filled it she had become aware of his looking her over, slowly, every inch of her, more like assessing her, with a slight smile on his lips.

Mirella had lifted the silver-covered lid of one of the serving dishes and picked up a cold strip of bacon, on which she nibbled as she brought the cup of coffee to Rashid.

He had tucked the telephone between his shoulder and his neck and with one hand he took the cup of coffee; with the other he motioned for her to sit on his lap, which she did, and he took her into his outstretched arm. Mirella had leaned her head against him, comfortable in his arms, while he had drunk his coffee and finished his conversation.

After he had put the receiver down, he picked it up again immediately to ring room service, and Mirella had ordered her breakfast. Rashid had then greeted her with all the charm and suave manner he had shown her during dinner, with no reference to their erotic night together. It had been then that he asked her to have lunch with him and to spend the rest of the day and evening with him.

She, of course, had accepted, helpless to do anything else . . . and, besides, she wanted to be with him.

It was quite obvious to Mirella that Rashid Lala Mustafa had power over women—the sort of power women look for, dream about, fantasize they will experience once in their lifetime. She had reminded herself that she must at all times remember to keep her head in this little affair.

"Brindley, much as I would like to make it this afternoon, I can't. I made a date from luncheon onward for today. How about tomorrow afternoon?"

They agreed to have a working lunch on the following day in Mirella's suite at Claridge's, and work straight through the afternoon. Brindley allowed himself a smile, which widened into an open grin, and he stated, after looking at his watch, "Well, Mirella, in approximately forty-five minutes, you will be a multimillionaire. An independently wealthy lady. We will now go into the conference room where tea awaits you and the necessary documents are ready for your signature, where you will meet all the members of the firm concerned with your affairs. I hope you don't mind but it is a proud moment for all of us, and we still feel very protective toward the estate, and now the legacy.

"You do know that, after tomorrow, your news will probably no longer be private and personal. The press will most assuredly become aware of it through the law courts, and the Turkish and other governments will most probably make contact. Tomorrow we can discuss how you want to handle that side of it, but today everything is relatively simple and you are still a very private client under our protection."

The firm of Rumbold, Grumthorp, and Ribblesdale was located in an imposing Georgian building on Grosvenor Street, about a hundred yards from Grovesnor Square. It and its most discreet brass plate were extremely well kept on the outside, and, though very elegant with all the antique furnishings of the correct period for such a house, it was dark, seedy, and somewhat shabby on the inside.

Mirella had seen only the lobby, with its excellent cantile-vered curved stone staircase, and handsome balustrade of wrought iron, topped by a walnut handrail, its black and white marble floor, and a large round Georgian table with a celadon bowl of daffodils on it. Two pairs of tall, dark, well-polished walnut doors with Georgian brass hardware, and especially finely carved architraves, were very impressive. Then she was whisked up in a tiny lift to the top floor, where Brindley's offices were.

Nothing could have prepared Mirella for what she saw or for what took place in Rumbold, Grumthorp, and Ribbles-dale's conference room. She and Brindley walked down the stairs to the first floor. There he politely asked if she would like to see the library. She accepted, and was astonished by the room. It was twenty feet high, with a gallery around it, and all the walls were solid with books, in between mahogany Doric columns, and windows draped in tattered red silk, whose folds had faded into stripes of burnt orange, and were tied back with large black and gold silk tassels that had faded into a bronze brown and dull silver. A period pair of library stairs was fixed to a brass rod, and was capable of sliding along wherever needed. The spiral staircase to the gallery was of wood and carved as finely as a Chippendale chair.

The sun poured in rays through the window, turning the particles of dust in the air to silver. Brindley whispered, so as not to disturb the elderly librarian and one of the younger solicitors with the firm, who were engrossed in several open volumes and busy taking copious notes on cheap yellow foolscap paper.

"We're very proud of our library. It's one of the finest libraries on international law in the world. And we have another, a twin to this room, on the other side of the hall, on political and military law."

They entered the conference room. It was a fine pine-paneled room with three tall French windows leading out to a narrow balcony overlooking the street. The walls were covered with portraits of the senior members of the firm, going back to the original founder, Vivian Rumbold. There was a life-size portrait of the reigning monarch, Queen Elizabeth II, over the fireplace at one end of the room, and over the fireplace at the other end of the room a portrait of Napoleon Bonaparte.

They were an impressive, formidable lot, painted in the robes and wigs of Her Majesty's Courts of Law, and for the most part painted by the famous artists of their day—several Sir Joshua Reynoldses, two Whistlers, a few Millaises, an Augustus John, a Rossetti, two Graham Sutherlands were only a few that stood out before Mirella's eyes lighted on the Stubbs. Of all the paintings it was the most enchanting: a romantic picture of an English landscape with a man dressed in flowing black robes, and a long white-powdered wig, holding the reins of a black stallion in the foreground. All of the pictures were set in deeply carved gilt frames.

A pair of Georgian sideboards stood against the walls, with an impressive collection of silver on them, and the conference table, which seated twenty-six and was five feet wide, ran down the center of the room. There were ten Georgian wing chairs, five on either side of the table, covered in worn and tattered but still bright yellow silk damask that matched the curtains. These were equally tattered, and tied back with very faded olive-green-colored silk tassels.

All the chairs were occupied by men, some of whom looked quite feeble. An empty chair had been placed at the far end of the table, a wing chair just like the others, and laid out on the table in front of it was a stack of documents ready for Mirella's signature and a fountain pen. A matching wing chair had been placed at the near end of the table and Mirella was escorted to it by Brindley.

There she stood and received each of the men in turn whom Brindley introduced to her. After the introductions, they all returned to their seats. A Georgian wooden chair, covered in the same worn fabric, was placed next to Mirella for Brindley by the elderly, wispy-haired butler in a well-worn tailcoat.

When they had entered the room, the butler, Cookham, had been standing next to an equally elderly waitress in a black uniform and a white organza pleated band, with a one-inch black satin ribbon through its center, that was tied neatly across her forehead.

Mirella felt like an Alice who had just walked through the looking glass. It was as if she had stepped back in time. She kept thinking it must be the nineteen-thirties, just before the Second World War. Then, as Cookham the butler and Beryl the waitress served tea and biscuits, with trembling hands so that the teacups rattled, Mirella fancied she was at the Mad Hatter's tea party.

It began as a somewhat stiff and formal affair, where Mirella kept having the fantasy that they were a club and that she was up for membership. That at any moment they would pass around the dreaded wooden box where each of them was to cast his vote with a tiny black or white ball. She was really concerned that one of them would blackball her, and she would never belong.

It may have begun like that, but after tea, and when she had signed seven documents, a sigh of relief rippled through the occupants of the chairs, and slowly, one by one, the men began to tell Mirella about the custodians of her affairs, and the part each had played at some time in the extraordinary events connected with them. Mirella was riveted by what they told her, and one door to the past after another gradually opened for her, and she found herself readily wafted back in time.

A whisper in Brindley's ear by Mirella, and soon champagne appeared and was served in hundred-year-old goblets that Beryl produced from the Georgian sideboard. Before she left the conference room Mirella Wingfield, probably the world's newest multimillionaire, knew she had not been blackballed from this group of remarkable men. Far from it: by the time she had to say her good-byes Percy Rumbold was telling her how Whisley Ribblesdale had had a good war, saved Monty's skin more than once. Beverly Grumthorp had had a bad war—that was World War I—the Red Baron had shot him down twice. Thackery Grumthorp had shot himself over Gallipoli, the only suicide in the firm's history. One of the firm, Devlin Rumbold, interpreted English military law to Napoleon on St. Helena; and she was told a few stories about that by Bertram Rumbold. And just as she was walking out the door, the ninety-eight-year-old Hannibal Grumthorp whispered in her ear to come and visit him in his house in the wilds of Derbyshire, because it was his father who was said to have had a long-time liaison with her great-grandmother Roxelana, and to have become persona non grata in Turkey in consequence.

Brindley walked Mirella down the stairs. They looked at each other: in that moment they both knew they were friends, and that Rumbold, Grumthorp, and Ribblesdale would continue to act as her solicitors for as long as she lived and for generations to come, as they had for generations past. He smiled at her and said, "Mirella, I hope you don't mind my getting personal, but it was wonderful to see you with the senior members of the firm. I don't think I shall ever forget it. It was a lifelong ambition of every man in that room to tidy up and hand over their various responsibilities one day to something more than paper companies. And I could tell you were no disappointment to them. Well, how do you feel? Any different?" he teased, referring to her being now an heiress.

"Yes, I do as a matter of fact. First of all, having had tea with those men, I feel I have just had a most extraordinary experience, maybe even profound in some ways. There were moments there when I felt as if I had entered other worlds: as if I had come alive for them as various different people, and in various different times. It was like stepping back into generation after generation, taking a quick breath of lives lived then, and moving both backward and forward at the same time. It was strange, surrealistic in some ways. I suddenly felt another part of myself—an Oujie—and it didn't feel wrong; it felt familiar and right.

"I know that what you meant is, do I feel different having

become an heiress? Even that feels right, but it will take a great deal of getting used to. Mostly having all that money. You said something to me before, something about being independently wealthy. It made me think of two American feminists I once met. I spent a wonderful few hours talking to them. They were making the point that women would never be liberated, be truly their own, until they were financially independent and knew how not only to earn but also to handle their money. I understood and agreed with what they were saying then, but now I *know* what they meant."

14

Walking the short distance from Grosvenor Street to Brook Street and Claridge's, where she was going to freshen up before meeting Rashid for lunch, Mirella had but one thought: to call home—not her house, but Wingfield Park. And then she would call her brother Lawrence. This was, after all, a family affair.

Mirella smiled to herself when she thought about talking to the family, and trying to explain to them the immensity of her legacy and what it meant in monetary terms. Only Marcus Weinbaum would really understand. The others, like herself, held money in such low esteem they would most probably react as they always had to money—something quite necessary but awkward and just a little too embarrassing to talk about.

Her father, Maxim, who understood money the way he understood everything else in life—from a philosophical standpoint—would take her news in, comprehending and dropping it simultaneously, almost before she had finished telling him. Mirella could understand that, because Maxim had been born into money. In the Wingfield family, for generations, one son went into the church or the state's judicial system, one son went into the army, and one went into business. By Maxim's generation, the church had been replaced by scholarship for three generations, and the business had turned into money, the same way the Pulitzers', the Du Ponts', the Cabots', and the Lodges' had, and was dealt with behind closed doors as nothing more than a vulgar necessity.

And so, because he had been born into it, and had taken it for granted all of his life, just like his father and his grandfather before him, it had meant very little to him when he inherited the family possessions, but no cash. Having or not having money had made no difference to Maxim. He simply carried on living his life, and working the way he always had. And his children were just like him in that respect. Until now, Mirella thought.

What would Lili, her mother, say to the news? "Oh dear," murmured Mirella, whose relationship with her mother had always been a problem. Lili was going to be upset. She was going to be upset because, for one thing, there really was a legacy, which Lily had insisted was impossible, and Lili could never bear being wrong. Second thing, it came from her side of the family, and the legacy had skipped over her. Another reason, it was worth a vast sum of money, and although Lili behaved as if money was low on her list of priorities, that was only because she didn't have any. The real truth was, Lili loved money, and was madly envious of anyone who had money to spend.

The list of reasons why Lili was going to be upset kept growing longer in Mirella's mind. Most of the reasons on the list worried her, but none more so than power. Lili had a pathological need to feel herself the most powerful member of the family, which she wasn't. Her need to have control over everyone and everything she was involved with was obsessive. She lived in a fantasy that she had control of herself and everything that touched her and that she was the only real power in the family; but of course, she wasn't.

When Lili's will, which was formidable, was at its strongest was when she was at her most evil. She could show the most appalling indifference to others. The things she could do when in the grip of her semiconscious fantasy were horrifying. But there were the other times, too, when she exercised her will with moderation and was able to keep her altruism intact. At such times the family and everyone involved with her always strove to keep her like that, because then Lili was a joy to be with.

All the family—including Marcus Weinbaum, who was considered family, and who lived with them—suffered in some way from Lili's fantasy. She drove her children away from her, then pretended they abandoned her. She showered them with love and affection when it suited her and ignored them when they needed her. She would have driven them from Wingfield Park, but, try as she might, they clung on to their ancestral home and family regardless of what she did. They loved their mother in spite of herself—as did their father and Marcus.

Lili was the only frustrated failure in the family, and everyone worked very hard to keep it from her. Not a very difficult task, since Lili, who was a beautiful, self-centered, mediocre amateur concert pianist, had sufficient vanity to ignore the *Boston Globe* and declared it or any other newspaper that ever gave her a bad review merely jealous of her success and unable to accept that a great beauty could also be a great pianist.

When Lili married Maxim Wesson Wingfield, it was a love match. The fact that it was a social and financial coup as well was a bonus, but one that Lili took very seriously. That he was well on his way to becoming one of the three most important philosophers of his time had been interesting to her, of course, but hardly an important factor in their relationship. Lili had thought she made the perfect marriage. But then things began to change swiftly and drastically, just before Mirella was born.

The change in their financial circumstances caused by her father-in-law's death and Maxim's inheritance was a shock. She had become quite spoiled by having all the money she wanted. It made up for her having been the "poor relation" before she married Maxim. Then there was Maxim, who kept stepping back from his social position in Boston society as he kept stepping forward in his work and became increasingly important on an international level, with some of the greatest and most interesting men and women of the times.

Though she enjoyed his success immensely, and was happily part of the famous circle of intimate friends who were always gathered around him, Lili somehow felt cheated. She loved and adored Maxim and his success, and waited impatiently for him to win a great prize. She knew he deserved one and was bound to get it. But she also considered him to be an unfortunate failure, because he was never able to earn the great sums of money they needed to keep up their inheritance and their life-style. And there was a part of her that could not forgive him for making the decision never to sell any of the valuables left to him, for the benefit of his wife and children, and standing stubbornly by it.

Lili believed as no one else in the family did that money was real power. She also believed that lack of it was the only thing that kept her from being as powerful and as important as she wanted to be. In her sometimes warped mind, she, periodically, blamed her family, whom she loved, for standing in the way of her success, and sometimes she hated them for it.

Telling Lili was a frightening prospect, and Mirella wondered if it might be kinder to all concerned, including herself, to have the news broken to her by Marcus, who was able to reason with her far better than anyone else. When Lili understood that the inheritance she had claimed didn't exist did in fact exist, and that Mirella was to have, at the very least, an income of forty million dollars a year, Lili would see her daughter as successful at last. She would then see Mirella as trying to usurp her mother's position. In other words, Lili was bound to go crazy, and be driven at once to her psychosomatic bed. That was always the stage that preceded her unhealthy, willful pursuit of control and omnipotence. Lili would react to the news in the most evil manner she could muster.

The thought engraved a deep frown on Mirella's forehead. She was reminded of her own first reaction to the legacy. Crossing Davies Street, she was almost run down by a black Daimler, so distracted was she in wondering how many times she had rejected important things in her life in order to spare her mother and herself the wrath Lili could hurl so mercilessly.

The shock of the Daimler's screaming horn brought her mind back to the problems of the phone call she was about to make, a phone call that should not be problematic, but a sheer joy to make. Yes, the way to make the call was: Dad first, then Marcus, then her mother, and (depending on what Marcus said) maybe not her mother, then Lawrence. The greatest fun would be talking to Marcus about the money.

Marcus Weinbaum was an art historian, with a master's degree in philosophy, who had arrived at Wingfield Park as her father's assistant, and eventually had taken over and run their lives and their estate for them. He had for years cared for the vast collection of works of art and artifacts, vintage automobiles and biplanes, had kept the family out of debt, and loved and cared for them all; and he still managed to assist Maxim, one of the most brilliant minds of the century. What a joy it would be to say, "Marcus, how many millions do you need to fix the hangars, make a motor museum, have the roof fixed, and so on?" Or just say, "Here's twenty million: let me know when you need more."

She thought about Marcus, whom they all loved, and reminisced about the endless speculations she shared with Lawrence about whether Marcus was her mother's lover and her father's, or whether he was their mother's lover and just in love with their father. Neither of them thought it at all unusual that Marcus should be in love with both of them: they were all so deeply involved in each other's lives. Nor did they . think it strange that Marcus might be their father's lover, because they knew their father's views about sex and love, which he felt should have no discriminating boundaries. They had seen any number of the other men and women who periodically fell in love with Maxim, and could understand it, because both of them were themselves in love with the handsome, discreetly promiscuous, brilliant man themselves. They finally decided that Marcus was in love with their father's mind, their mother's body, and both of their personalities.

There was also an enormous bond between Marcus, Mirella, and Lawrence, sealed forever when in Mirella's late teens she had a torrid sexual affair with Marcus that lasted for nearly a year, and Lawrence was taken into their confidence. The affair came to an end by mutual agreement, when they began to feel guilty about their secret meetings—made so by fear of not Maxim but Lili finding out. They were afraid of Lili and what she might do. They gave up their sexual affair in order to keep their family affair, which they knew to be so important to all their lives.

She went through the door at Claridge's, and thought she got an extra smile from the doormen but wasn't sure. Yes, she told herself again, the minute I get into my room it's Wingfield Park first, then Lawrence. Dear, clever Lawrence— as promiscuous as his father, as handsome as his mother was beautiful, almost as brilliant as Maxim, and still as naughty and adventurous as Mirella was twenty years ago. His best friends were his father and sister, and his great love was his mother, whose every fault he knew too well, and chose to ignore. Dear Lawrence, who was always so brutally frank with himself, and a jury, he was a natural success in everything he did.

Mirella put the key card in the door to her suite and she

pushed the door open thinking, No, I will call Lawrence first, then Deena, then Wingfield Park. She stepped into her room. The sight she saw swept all thoughts of telephoning anyone right from her mind.

There were big beautiful dress boxes tied with wide, brightly colored satin ribbons, several large and small hat-boxes, a dozen or so shoeboxes, deep square boxes, huge rectangular boxes, some open, erupting glaciers of tissue paper and beautiful mountains of fabrics, others closed, calling out to be torn open and have their surprises revealed.

Dresses and gowns were draped over the sofas, and chairs and shoes and handbags were sitting on the tables and the floor . . . and Rashid Lala Mustafa was standing by the fireplace, a glass of champagne in one hand, a high-heeled silver kidskin sandal in the other. The twinkle in his eye and the smile on his lips said it all. He was certainly enjoying himself.

Mirella walked into the center of the room, hardly knowing what to say. She put her handbag down on the first empty space she found, and walked toward Rashid, who was pouring her a glass of champagne.

"Rashid, you have gone mad!"

"Yes, I have, haven't I, but nice mad. Fun mad, extravagant and indulgent mad," he said as he handed her the glass and put his hands on her hips and kissed her, adding enthusiastically, "Where have you been? I can hardly wait for you to see all the marvelous things I have had brought here for you to choose from. We'll choose together, yes?"

"Yes," she said, smiling and nodding her head in disbelief, then added, "But it will take me all day to try on these things. How am I ever going to choose one dress from all this? You don't make it easy do you, Rashid?"

"Oh, don't I?" he said, hardly able to suppress his laughter. He pushed some of the boxes and dresses off the sofa and took her by the hand and sat her down next to him.

"You have no idea how easy I have made it for you. First of all, the only things you have to send back are the things you really don't like. I have conditionally bought them all for you, the condition being that you like them and want them."

He leaned against her, and began unbuttoning her jacket, and whispered in her ear, "A little present to say thank you for all the pleasure you gave me last night." Then as he bent down and removed her shoes from her feet, he continued,

"Secondly, you have twenty minutes to decide, and lots of people to help you do so. . . ."

He clapped his hands loudly and the bedroom door opened and half a dozen dazzlingly beautiful, wonderfully dressed models strutted into the drawing room, followed by four salesladies.

"My own fashion show," she gasped. "Oh, Rashid, what a fabulous gift. I don't know where to look first. And the clothes! I have never seen such clothes. Can it be true? Have you really bought them all for me? It's too much! How can I possibly accept all this? How did you do it? Did you choose them yourself?"

Rashid laughed, overjoyed at her reaction to his gift; it was almost exactly how he had imagined she would react. He helped her off with her jacket and began to unbutton her blouse, first one cuff, then the other, and then he began at the neck, almost as if she were a doll he was playing with.

"You can and will accept all this because you're a woman, and want to give me pleasure. And yes—I did choose every item in this room myself. I went from shop to shop and chose every glamorous thing for all sorts of occasions that I thought you would look marvelous in, and I must admit I've had great fun doing it. Then I got the shops to send the models so you wouldn't have the boring job of jumping in and out of clothes to see how they look on a body—unless you want to—and I have arranged it so you can have any fittings needed at your convenience."

Mirella threw her arms around Rashid, and gave him a big hug. She was a little surprised when she realized that she had taken him off guard, and for a split second he had become flustered. She turned back to the women in the room, who were all watching her carefully, and she saw the look of delight for her on their faces.

They dazzled her with what Karl Lagerfeld called "the ethnic Milanese sloppy look," and then Lagerfeld's own magical and inventive luxurious sporty pieces designed for Fendi. Furs, spectacular in both the treatment of the pelts and the workings, were combined with denim, gossamer silk, linen, and leather, soft and supple, yet tough and serviceable. Every piece was a work of art.

Giorgio Armani's stunning Prince of Wales sequined and sparkling bead studded tartan evening jacket over a checked taffeta ball skirt, and his camel-hair coat that wrapped around the body like a bathrobe, and the cut and shape of the Versace and Ferre evening dresses left Mirella with nothing to say but yes, yes, yes!

After the marvelous Missonis, and the amazing Comme des Garçons, and the Saint Laurents, and the Chloés, and the Ralph Lauren trousers, and the Cartier handbags, Gucci handbags and Loewe handbags, and the shoes and the boots from Blahnik and Charles Jourdan, Mirella thought it would never end and she would never be able to put together outfits that looked right.

By the time Zandra Rhodes's clothes appeared, the models, salesladies, Mirella, and even the maid Maria were all working on her wardrobe with her. Within ten minutes the models gave up the idea of going back and forth to the bedroom to change, and were climbing in and out of clothes in the drawing room with Mirella, under the watchful eye and direction of Rashid.

Wherever one looked there was someone's naked breasts being exhibited, or a naked back, all skin and muscle with vertebrae so prominent they were easy to count. A bikini-pantied beauty in nothing else but a pair of five-hundred-dollar Maud Frizon black patent-leather boots strutted around assembling bits and pieces of the luxurious clothes to model. Luscious, near-naked ladies pulling on boots, stepping into shoes, or climbing in or out of something, appeared to fill the room and would have made a magnificent study for De-gas . . . or a fabulous De Kooning, in the Women series he painted in the fifties. There was a great deal of talking and laughing and at some point Mirella realized Rashid had created an extravagant female-clothes orgy. At the end of twenty minutes the whirlwind shopping spree was over. The doorbell of the suite rang and four men flowed through the room, waving to Rashid as they were shown by Maria to the bedroom.

He went to Mirella and said, "Time's up, I will take care of everything with the salesladies. They have been keeping a record of what didn't fit or what you didn't like. Now you go into the other room because Leonard is waiting to do your hair. We only have an hour and ten minutes left to get to the luncheon I'm giving at the Connaught, and we're going to be on time, and I am going to walk into that dining room with the most beautiful and glamorous woman in London. Maria, get Miss Wingfield one of her new dressing gowns. I think the dark blue Ralph Lauren silk velvet one with the white ermine lapels should do."

He helped her out of her new Miyake and into her dressing gown, and tied the silk cord belt, giving her one of his seductive looks that seemed momentarily to enslave her. Then he put her into the hands of a new hairdresser, whose only directive, delivered by Rashid, was to give her the hairstyle most flattering to her—anything but what the successful businesswoman would wear—and a makeup artist who had been told to "teach her what to do with that magnificent face: I want the world to gasp."

The next time Mirella saw Rashid was when she stepped out of her bedroom all dressed and ready to leave for the Connaught. He was seated in the drawing room of the suite, which had been cleared of the fashion happening. There was not a trace of the shopping spree left. All the women were gone with the exception of the two most attractive models, who Rashid had kept there to amuse himself with. They were drinking champagne as she entered the room.

As Rashid's and Mirella's eyes first met she thought she caught a sly glint in his. The two women looked embarrassed, as if they had been surprised doing something they shouldn't have been doing. When her eyes met Rashid's again the glint she thought she glimpsed was gone, and the look of complete admiration, the hint of adoration he bestowed on her drew Mirella to him with only one thought in her mind: to do anything to please this man who had indeed kept his word and transformed her into the most beguiling and irresistible of women.

Mirella had hardly known herself when she had stood in front of the mirror and looked at the finished product of so many people's imaginations, and care, and of so much money. True, she had the same face, the same body, was the same person, but an air of great and rare beauty about her had now surfaced. It was the same sort of romantic, mysterious, refined beauty possessed by Greta Garbo, Carole Lombard, Romy Schneider, Charlotte Rampling. She had something of the beauty and glamour of Elizabeth Taylor, Raquel Welch, Sophia Loren—but more so because she didn't carry the stigma of flash and glitz that movie stars are burdened with, and most of all because she was still untouched and unaffected by this new image of herself.

What she had seen in the mirror was still the international

civil servant at the U.N. in New York, who was having the time of her life. London's most famous hairdresser of the sixties, Leonard, had not lost his touch with the years. She couldn't understand how he could have cut her hair and yet still make it look longer. But he had. He had layered the top and the sides and swept it all up and away from her face, so that it was soft and full. It was long and straight in the back and at the sides of her neck, turning under in a soft pageboy to just below her shoulders. There was just a hint, a mere wisp of a fringe that fell casually on her forehead, as if the wind had misplaced a few strands of her hair. It gave the effect of her never having been to the hairdresser at all. It was the chic, casual hairstyle for the natural beauty with the right bone structure that it takes a world-famous hairdresser to create.

She had a difficult time choosing what to wear to lunch. She was going to wear an alluring Miyake outfit of linen, but chose instead an equally eye-catching Zandra Rhodes two-piece dress, whose skirt was a pearly-mauve suede as thin as a piece of paper, and whose top was a skin-tight, dull black taffeta jacket with huge puffed sleeves of cabbage roses made of the same material, with the edges topstitched in rust. It nipped in tightly at the waist and had a short peblum that was reminiscent of the fashions of the forties; its deep V neck was softened by a short stand-up ruffle around it. It was romantic and charming, chic and a little wild, elegant and utterly young and feminine. She chose rust-colored Maud Frizon high-heeled shoes and a small crazy-looking handbag that matched the sleeves of her dress.

Mirella thought she looked terrific—a little mad for her, impractical for her, too many labels and famous names for her—but a hell of a lot of fun. She really loved the way she looked. That had been in front of the mirror. Now in the drawing room, walking toward Rashid, she *knew* she looked terrific. She began to smile, tossed her head back ever so slightly and to one side, then laughed softly. It was a somewhat shy, happy laugh that had a lilt to it, and was filled with a coquettish, feminine charm that was irresistible.

The two models gushed over the way Mirella looked. She did a pirouette for them, then walked away and back to them, one hand on her hip, head thrown back, chin and nose stuck up in the air, as if she, too, were a model. What Rashid saw was a mature, ripe beauty. He admired her grace, her new flair, the violet-colored eyes, the voluptuous lips—made even more seductive and beautiful by her new makeup—and her amazingly fair, pearly complexion, her sensual femininity. There was something gay and wild and adventurous about her that he had not seen clearly before.

Her inner personality had surfaced and was decidedly attractive—forthcoming, frank, and completely natural. It surprised him that although she was one of the loveliest, most intelligent and successful women he had ever known, there was hardly a trace of vanity in her. He reveled in what he saw, and could hardly wait to show her off to the world, and take the seduction of Mirella Wingfield one step further.

The following days and nights with Rashid were heady with romance. Their candlelit dinners alone, the luncheon parties with jet-set friends, the elegant formal dinner parties, the ball at Buckingham Palace were always punctuated with some intimate, amorous gesture known to them alone. His romantic seduction of her never let up for one minute.

Every day he presented her with a gift. The morning after the fashion show she found on her breakfast tray a velvet box with a pair of baroque pearls the size of peach stones, mounted in slim gold frames and made into earrings. One afternoon while walking through St. James's Park, he asked her the time, and when she looked at her twenty-five-year-old Bulova watch with its worn-out leather wristband, he took her wrist and held it while he removed the watch and replaced it with one from his pocket: a stunning custom-made Cartier, with an octagonal white porcelain face with black Roman numerals, and a gold band.

While on top of her, during one of their sexual encounters, he penetrated her with a particular fierceness, and when she called out in pain, that special kind of pain that is mixed with passion and pleasure, he pulled her up to a near-sitting position, and, still embedded and throbbing within her, he took from under his pillow a long rope of perfectly matched ten-millimeter pearls and slipped them over her head. He withdrew and penetrated her again and again, even more passionately and violently, as if he wanted to whip the very life right out of her. When she woke up the next morning she had three exceptional ropes of pearls around her neck and nothing else.

That very same evening before they went out to dinner, he

presented her with a short single strand of pearls, each the size of a small hazelnut, whose luster was luminous. They were extraordinary, and lovely. He closed the large diamond bumblebee clasp at the back of her neck and declared that the pearls, fitting like a dog collar, were safely locked in place, and could only be removed by him, unless the string of priceless beads was cut from her. He made her promise that as long as she wore them she would obey him as if she were his sexual slave. And he instructed her to imagine there was an invisible chain linked to her collar of pearls, which he held always in his hand and by which he could always exercise sexual control of her.

Their erotic life was just as extravagant as his gifts and his romancing. His intimate wooing of her alternated drastically between charm and affection and a wild, demanding passion, and was always entertaining and satisfying—sometimes experimental and unusual. He was clever in drawing out every sexual fantasy and desire in Mirella, extending those she indulged even beyond her own imaginings, making her feel sexier than she had ever felt before in her life, because the self, the ego, and the id were swallowed up by the fun, and the dazzling erotic pleasure Rashid elicited from her. She reveled in it. He turned many of her sexual fantasies into realities and removed layer upon layer of defenses, leaving her the most raw and vulnerable of women.

The gossip columnists wrote about them, photographed them everywhere. They remarked on Rashid Lala Mustafa's latest lady, and then named the unhappy ladies that he had ditched for the American who worked at the U.N. and who had become the world's newest millionairess. And always the question asked by them was how long she would last before she, too, was thrown aside for another beauty, to be spoiled and pampered by a man they styled one of the world's most eligible bachelors and most wicked playboys.

That was a question that never entered Mirella's mind. It didn't have to, because Mirella was levelheaded and reminded herself that her affair with Rashid Lala Mustafa was merely an exciting vacation romance that would end when she returned to New York. However seduced she was by him, or allowed herself to be enslaved by him and his attentions, she never lost sight of what she and Rashid were *not* to each other . . . just as she could not lose sight or understanding of how deeply in love she still remained with Adam Corey. The memory of pure bliss their love generated wedged itself between Rashid and herself. No matter how firmly she put Adam out of her mind, all too often he was there. Without a choice she was condemned to wear him and the love they felt for each other like an invisible second skin. He had become a part of her. She was ruthless with herself about not fantasizing that their relationship was something other than it had been. She was dealing with it in real terms, exactly as she was her affair with Rashid, which only worked to draw the Turkish playboy and Mirella closer together, and allowed her enough of a clear mind to use every spare moment alone to deal with the affairs of her legacy.

And even if Mirella wanted to get lost in this interlude with Rashid—which she didn't—there were some harsh reminders that kept interrupting and alerting her to the new responsibilities of having become an important, rich, and powerful woman.

15

Most of the harsh reminders that kept Mirella on balance and in touch with the reality of who and what she was, and from slipping totally into a world of glamour and frivolity during the five heady days she had spent under the romantic and erotic spell of Rashid, had to do with human relationships past and present.

First came a phone call, just after Rashid had given her the new look and wardrobe. She and Rashid had been leaving for their luncheon at the Connaught when the telephone had begun to ring.

"Let it ring," he had ordered, then had softened his tone and added, "We don't want to be late."

"I can't do that. I never have been able to walk away from a ringing telephone, it goes against my grain, it makes me feel irresponsible, weak for not being able to cope. I have to answer it even if it's to say I can't talk."

She had walked to the telephone at the far side of the room and picked it up. The conversation had been short.

"Hello."

There had been a moment of total silence. Then Paul had

said, "You're behaving in a very stupid and bitchy female way with me, Mirella, and it's not worthy of you, or our relationship. I took the house at the beach for you, so we could have more time together this summer, and I intend to see that we do. I warn you now, it could be our last summer, unless you shape up. I won't call again; I'll wait for *your* phone call."

She had said only three words to him: "Hello" and "Don't wait," and had hung up. Then with a last look at the new image of herself in the mirror, she had slipped her arm through Rashid's and they had left for the Connaught.

That phone call had done Mirella great service. It had made her realize what love wasn't: it wasn't Paul Prescott and it wasn't Rashid Lala Mustafa. And it had made her realize that whatever a relationship was, good or bad, it always affected you and stayed with you, even when it was over. Like a sharp needle-prick in her flesh came another painful reminder. If a relationship worked in satisfying her needs and desires at a given moment in her life, and served her and her partner well—as it had with Paul, as it was doing now with Rashid—she was quite capable of twisting and turning it around, fantasizing that it was more than it was. Seeing that selfish flaw in her character enabled her to admit to herself how she had used endless female rationalizations in order to label her relationship with Paul as "love," because that was what she was looking for. Having had a glimmer with Adam Corey of what real love might be like, she was prepared now to wait for the real thing, while dealing with the realities of her relationships, instead of fantasizing them into something they were not. She vowed that she would never do that again. And now, five days later, she was still with Rashid and still having her romantic interlude and being levelheaded about it.

When Mirella and Brindley had met, as they had planned, to have their working lunch in her hotel suite, on the day after she had legally become the heir to the Oujie legacy, he had brought with him her family's archives, as he had promised he would. Rashid had been annoyed with Mirella when she would not break the date with Brindley to go riding in the country with him, and so had remained with her until Brindley's arrival. That was how the two men had come to meet each other.

To say that Brindley had been overwhelmed by Mirella's transformation would have been an understatement, and to say that he had been surprised to find her with a handsome Turk in her suite would have been another.

The meeting, though short, had been illuminating for Mirella. While Brindley could not take his eyes off her, Rashid could not take his eyes off the volumes of archives Brindley and two of Claridge's porters trundled into the drawing room. Rashid had kept stealing glances at them with a look that was something less than romantic. It disappeared when he turned his gaze on Mirella.

For the first time she had realized it was very odd that since their first meeting when he had acknowledged he knew she was the heir to the Oujie estate, he had never mentioned it again. Mirella didn't have sufficient vanity to imagine he had forgotten it, once he had bedded and enjoyed her.

A little red warning light had flashed within her. She had introduced Brindley to Rashid as her solicitor and the man responsible for finding her and having made her an heiress. For no particular reason that she could understand herself she had added, "In all the excitement yesterday and last evening I momentarily forgot that I had become an important, rich, and powerful lady. You didn't know that, did you, Rashid?"

"Of course I knew that: one look at you and any man would know that" had been his answer.

He had bent down and kissed her hand. He'd given her an unquestionable look of adoration that told her he wanted her, the same magnetic look that drew her to him. The man was irresistible. When he had said he would be back for her at seven that evening, she was sorry to see him leave, and his manner had simply extinguished the little red light.

That meeting had told the three of them something. It had underlined for Mirella how essential it was to stay centered with this man, in sex, in love, as Mirella Wingfield, woman, U.N. executive, heir to the Oujie legacy. Rashid could not be allowed to think her a fool, blind to the undercurrent of something not quite reputable, something secret and mysterious in his remarkable courtship of her.

What Brindley Ribblesdale had seen when she introduced him to Rashid was not the stubborn, unbending Mirella Wingfield whom he had met in New York, and who had been so determined not to have the legacy interrupt her way of life. She was a more youthful, vivacious Mirella, dressed in a black sleeveless cashmere sweater and a pair of provocative honey-colored leather Ralph Lauren trousers. A sleeveless vest of the same leather, an antique silver Navajo belt, studded with chunks of turquoise, and high-heeled boots only added to the sensuality of her costume.

This was the same Mirella Wingfield who had been in his office the day before, but something had happened to her. Now she had the look of someone totally secure in her own sexuality. He had never seen that in any other woman before, and found it exciting and very powerful.

He, too, had sensed the interest Rashid Lala Mustafa had in her family archives and admired the way she had subtly and diplomatically challenged him. The meeting with Mirella and Rashid had confirmed not only that she was a clever, formidable, powerful woman, but that, dazzled as she might be by a man or a fortune, she had excellent basic primal instincts and emotions.

The encounter with Brindley had told Rashid a great deal too. First he had learned from her challenging him about whether or not he knew of her inheritance that she might doubt his motives, despite their night of lovemaking. That did not suit him. The way she had phrased her question had also told him that she was very clever, and he liked that. It made the chase more thrilling. He had watched closely her reaction to his answer, and what he had seen had delighted him. His charisma and charm had seemed to extinguish her doubts, and he had been satisfied that, clever as Mirella Wingfield might be, she was no match for him. Only one thing disturbed him about that meeting: why she was receiving the family archives. He didn't like that one bit.

Brindley had been much too discreet to ask anything about Rashid, and Mirella had offered no information about him. Brindley had no idea who the man was, and, because he was never mentioned again, Brindley had registered Rashid's name in his memory bank and dismissed all other thought of the man.

The most caustic reminder Mirella had to keep a tight control on herself was Lili's reaction to news of the legacy. It was much worse than she could possibly have imagined. It also highlighted the recent change in herself.

On the day that all three had met, she and Brindley had decided that, after they had their lunch, it would be best to call and break the astonishing news of her good fortune to her family. They felt that it had to be the first order of business because the documents had been registered in the courts and the newshounds would be on to it at once.

At their lunch, served in her suite, Mirella extravagantly had ordered two bottles of Château Latour 1945 to mark their first business lunch together, and to thank Brindley for all he had done for her. They had talked at length about how much happier she was feeling about the legacy, and Mirella, with a modicum of embarrassment, retracted the ridiculous position she had announced to him in New York, that the legacy was not to change her life-style. She had then made the first of her phone calls, with Brindley by her side for moral support.

The phone calls had gone pretty much as she had thought they would . . . only more so. And in the four days that passed after she broke the news to them and the newspapers broke the news to the world, there had not been a day on which she was spared the misery and wrath of Lili and her calls. They had come at all hours of the day and night and, if some were less hysterical than others, almost all mingled love with hate, abuse with adoration. They were at moments pitiable, but more often the ravings of a tyrant.

Mirella sighed deeply as she eased herself slowly into the steaming hot bath. She reached out and took the bottle of Armani bath oil from the marble shelf and poured some in her cupped palm, inhaled and savored the sensuous perfume. She closed her eyes, gave another deep sigh, and languorously spread the oil over her arms and breasts, careful not to come too near the collar of pearls still locked in place around her long, slender neck. When she had finished massaging the rest of her body with the oil, she lay back against the bath cushion in the soothing hot water, and let the heavenly scented mist settle over her, closed her eyes and allowed her mind to drift.

What bliss, she thought: a few minutes alone. She had just returned from yet another meeting at Brindley's chambers, this time with some business advisors. If anyone had told Mirella that she could be fascinated by money and business, she would never have believed it, nor would anyone who knew her have believed it. But she was absolutely infatuated with the boardroom, the excitement of deals, both buying and selling, that had been recommended to her during the past two days. And the money—what unthinkable amounts of it! Only now did Mirella truly understand how very attractive power was.

She thought about her mother and suddenly understood

Lili's frustration and unhappiness at not finding the fame, fortune, and power she wanted and needed.

Mirella knew now that one day she would be able to go to her mother and confess that she had not truly understood her own ambition for success until the collapse of her affair with her longtime lover, and her inheritance of a vast fortune. She wanted to settle her differences with Lili, to let her know that her daughter realized they were very much alike in wanting success. More, Mirella realized she had achieved where Lili had not because she had never given up anything for the love of a strong and powerful man the way Lili had. But at the moment no such confession was possible because of her mother's anger. Lili was deaf to anything but her own words.

Mirella picked up the large, soft sponge and squeezed the water in it over her breasts, then dipped it into the bathwater again and repeated the process several times. The telephone conversations she had had with her mother over the last few days came to mind.

Her father had been wonderfully supportive, and so had Marcus. Both had given her short and simple advice on how to handle herself. Marcus had been more interested in the monetary aspect of the legacy, and the arts and artifacts that were left to her. This was normal and right. Typically, Maxim had been more interested in the ancestral background, and the thinking behind the accumulation of such a long-hidden fortune, and was disappointed she knew so little about it and that she had not yet read the archives. Both men agreed she must be the one to tell Lili, and there would be no easy way in or out of it. Maxim, a New England sailor, gave her the best advice: "Get on with it, keep it simple, bolt down the hatches, and ride out the storm." Then he had gone to get her mother.

The conversation began well enough.

"Hi, Mother, how are you?"

"Oh, hello, Mirr, I'm fine, very busy, trying to talk your father and Marcus into turning Wingfield Park into another Tanglewood, but they won't. They never want to do anything with this old, worn-out place. They're so protective of Wingfield Park, it makes me ill. They never do anything to lift us out of the penurious grandeur we live in, and they never will."

"Well, maybe I can. In fact not maybe, Mother, I can, and I will."

Lili began to laugh. "You, Mirr? That's a joke. You're a

civil servant, with a civil servant's salary. You're just as bad as your father. You never think about money, you know even less than your father about the value of a dollar or where to put it. If not for good, old faithful Marcus, I don't know how we would have survived, where we would be. But any idea I come up with to try to make money is always shot down by those two, as well as you and your brother. I'm just your mother; to others I'm just the beautiful and amusing wife of one of the world's most interesting philosophers, a dreamer who thought she would grace the concert stages of the world and didn't. Well, I could if I had my own Tanglewood."

"Mother, I can buy you a Tanglewood if you really would like to have one, but not at Wingfield Park."

"What are you talking about, Mirella? Stop trying to joke me out of this, I am furious with all of you. I know I usually forget my dreams after a while and grow calmly into happiness because I love you all, but just once I would like to see one of you give up as much as I have for love and marriage. I wish I could divorce you all. Now, what is it? What do you want?"

"Lili, remember when I spoke to you a few days ago, I told you I was going to England to investigate this legacy left to me by your grandmother?"

"Oh yes, that fantasy forty-million-dollar story. Well, dear, not to worry, we're all taken for a fool one time or another in our lives. It's a good thing you listened to me and didn't waste the air fare."

Mirella had immediately picked up the change of tone in her mother's voice, the anger had gone, and was replaced by a saccharine sweetness. The volume had been turned down and the softer, condescending tone irritated Mirella. She reacted by doing the worst thing she could have done: she gave her news to her mother hard and straight, and in a tone of voice that was sure and emphatic. It was the tone Lili usually reserved for her family and one she resented anyone else using, especially on herself.

"Lili, do be quiet and listen. I'm in England talking to you from a suite in Claridge's. My solicitor is here next to me. The legacy is real. I have inherited a very large fortune, worth far more than an income of forty million dollars a year. We are very, very wealthy, Lili. Your days of living in penurious grandeur are over. You need never use that odious expression you love throwing at us again."

Lili's answer to the news had been to slam the telephone receiver down with such force that Mirella had felt a ringing in her ears. The phone calls Lili then harangued Mirella with ranged from the ridiculous to the sublime. The first came twenty minutes after Mirella's call to her. She had said in a hard, sour voice, "Mirella, we were disconnected. I order you not to take that money. It isn't rightfully yours. If you take it, you will be no better than a thief, a fraud."

"Mother," Mirella said, "that's ridiculous. I promise you it is all legal. Just think: You always wanted to be rich, and now you are."

"*No I'm not!* You are, and it's unjust, it should have gone to my mother and then me. I will not have you touch that money, or have anything to do with that legacy. How can you stand by and see me cheated like this? Will you give it up?"

"No, but I will happily share it."

"Not good enough," Lili had answered and banged the receiver in her ear again.

Mirella let some of the water out of the tub and ran more steamy water back in again and gave herself a harsh rubdown with the sponge, while a few other bits and pieces of Lili's conversations came to mind.

"Since you've chosen to take my family's money and become so rich, you have no need to come back to Wingfield Park. I'll just have all your things burned. With all that money what need do you have for the worn-out rubbish we have sacrificed to buy you?"

Mirella thought that she was weathering the storm because of the last phone call that had come from Lili, at five that morning.

Her mother had said, weeping and crying into the receiver, "I think I forgive you," and hung up. That was also when Rashid announced they were moving into the six-room suite he kept all year round at Claridge's on the floor above, if her mother woke them up one more time. He was exasperated with Mirella for refusing to have her calls held.

Mirella picked up the hand mirror from the small table standing next to the bath. She took a dry facecloth from the shelf under the tabletop, and wiping the mirror clear of steam, looked at herself in it. Gently, she dabbed the moisture from her face and neck, then her collar of pearls—smiling slightly—dried her hand and touched the pearls.

They were only just loose enough for her to slip the

diamond bumblebee around to the front. She did, and the lifelike giant bee, which was about the size of a walnut, sparkled in the mirror. Mirella mused about Rashid, his overwhelming generosity, and the happy time they were having together. She loved the *collier,* as he called it, and enjoyed—more than enjoyed, she reveled—in being Rashid's sexual slave, as the collier implied, though they both knew it was to some extent a game. She would miss the necklace when he either unlocked it or she cut it from her neck when the game was over. But she had to admit that her feelings for Rashid had become stronger than she'd expected, and knew she wouldn't be able to just discard him. She was intrigued by the dark, mysterious side of Rashid's nature and she was intensely curious about his background.

Then and there she decided to go and see Turkey, the home of this mesmerizing seducer of women, her extravagant lover. She turned the clasp to the back of her neck again and admired the luster of her pearls once more, then dipped the facecloth into the bathwater, wrung it out, and wiped her face with the steamy hot towel.

Mirella had never been happier. She felt more free and secure in herself. She had fame, fortune, and power, as well as glamour, sensual love, and a great deal of opulent fun . . . and she didn't feel the least bit guilty.

Things her father had said to her some twenty years before suddenly came to mind.

"You have the heart and the spirit of a great samurai warrior, trapped in the body of a clever, sensuous female beauty, Mirella. For a father, that is the ultimate one can ask for in a daughter, but for a mother, and especially a mother like Lili, I'm not so sure. Most mothers like to control their daughters, just the way most fathers like to control their sons. Only really remarkable men will be able to see the samurai qualities in you, my sweet Mirr, and may not even know what it is they see, but they will love you for it. Those who don't will drop you by the wayside, or you will drop them. As for your dear mother, have compassion for her. I think she sees the noble qualities in you but has to blind herself to them, because she's too busy looking for them in herself. I love Lili, as you well know, but I love her tenfold more for giving me a daughter like you."

And from that day he called her Sam, short for samurai, and no one else in the family ever knew the reason.

Thinking about Maxim and being a female samurai released a chain of thoughts in Mirella as she stepped out of the bath and into a large, luscious terry-cloth robe, wrapped it around her, and thought again of the business meeting she had had that afternoon. Her first decision was not to dabble or to play the role of the dilettante in the business affairs of the Oujie estate, because that was no way to win in business. The idea of liquidation was not abandoned, just held in abeyance. The Rothschilds in London and Lazard Frères in New York would continue to manage her investments.

The second big decision was that she would not accept the offer made for all her Turkish holdings by a well-recommended Turkish conglomerate that was prepared to act instantly, conditional on an immediate sale. Mirella felt she had nothing to lose and could therefore take all sorts of risks. She would sell in her time, not someone else's.

She went to her dressing room and chose a sensational-looking, one-shouldered long dress made entirely of clear crystal bugle beads sewn on a white crêpe de chine, and selected a pair of white high-heeled silk shoes. She would wear that with her collier, the other three strands of pearls, and the magnificent baroque pearl earrings that Rashid had given her. Mirella wanted to look her very best because Rashid had taken a box at the Covent Garden opera house for them, and she knew he really had no great love of the opera. She did, and especially when she could hear from a box artists of the caliber of Caballé and Luciano Pavarotti in an opera like *Mefistofele*.

Mirella relished the comfort of being in a box at the theater, a concert, or the opera, the feeling of seclusion, yet also of being seen. The intimacy of a box afforded her the luxurious feeling that she was being accorded a private performance. The whole occasion was uplifting, and she, too, out of some sort of gratitude, always wanted to rise to it, and be grand like the opera.

Maria appeared at just the right moment to help her finish dressing and to tell her that Mr. Mustafa was waiting for her in the drawing room. Mirella's heart skipped a beat, in anticipation of seeing him yet again and of being drawn into and absorbed by him.

The long slit of her body-hugging Galanos gown opened as she took graceful strides across the room. But she was stopped before she could reach her bedroom door by the ringing of the telephone. Damn, she thought: Lili. Reluctantly she went back to answer the phone.

"Mirella, it's your mother."

Mirella could tell by the tone in Lili's voice and her authoritative announcement that the storm was not over.

"Mother, I can't talk now, I'm just leaving for the opera, I'll call you back tomorrow."

"That won't be necessary, what I have to say won't take long. You tell me that you cannot give up this legacy for me. Well, you don't have to, no more than I have to face the resentment you have for me anymore. Keep the money, discard your family for a lot of dead ancestors. We here at Wingfield Park can get on without you and *my* family's money. Don't come home, with or without your legacy; wait until you are invited, and that won't be for a long, long time, at least until I can accept your deceit. I have nothing more to say to you."

Then silence from the other end of the telephone. Lili was obviously waiting for some reaction. Mirella gave one.

"Thank god for that!" And she hung up.

Mirella sighed. She was sorry about the phone call, but not upset. She had heard it all a thousand times before, in various forms, different words. What a relief that it didn't hurt anymore.

She walked into her drawing room. Rashid, deep in thought, was standing near the fireplace. When he saw her, he said nothing, just smiled and waited for her to reach him. Mirella detected an emotion in Rashid's expression that she had never seen before.

"I'm overwhelmed," he said. "You're a vision of opulent loveliness that thrills me."

His tone was cool, devoid of passion, yet Mirella found it devastatingly erotic coming from the lips of this handsome, sexual man. She wanted to raise her skirt, leap into his arms, and wrap her legs around him, have him take her then and there, once, quickly, the way the man in her dream had taken her. That was always the way she felt when they met, always wanting to be taken by this mysterious dark man, who, as she knew from her sexual encounters with him, could be ruthless, brutal even, and all the more irresistible to women. It was then that Mirella finally realized that Rashid's elusiveness was the key to his sexual charisma. In his love affairs it was Rashid, not the woman, who was the sex object, no matter how much he might pretend otherwise.

16

The curtain came down on the second act of Boito's *Mefistofele,* to ecstatic applause from the glittering audience. The applause continued for a considerable time before the houselights went up and the music lovers moved to the crush bar for refreshments.

It was a knock on the door to the box where they sat that released Mirella from the spell of the music and the ringing voices of Ghiaurov, Pavarotti, Freni, and the glorious Caballé. Until the knock at the door Mirella felt a sense of perpetual ascent from the celestial music of the prelude, rising yet further through the chorus's *"Ave, Signor degli angeli."* And even when the music subsided, she still felt as if she were in heaven.

She turned and smiled at Rashid, who appeared to her at that moment yet more handsome and mysterious—possibly even a little more dangerous—than usual. He had been looking out over the opera house, and turned back to her and caught her smile as he stood up to answer the knock at the door.

"Ah, you're back with us, my beauty," he said as he raised up her hand and lowered his head to kiss it, then turned to the door that was just opening.

Two waiters entered carrying a table between them covered with a white cloth. The center of the table was resplendent with two dozen white orchids in a tall, slim trumpet-shaped crystal vase. There were two tulip-shaped champagne glasses and two bottles of Piper-Heidsieck *cuvée* Florens Louis chilling in ice coolers, and a large dome of sandwiches of smoked salmon on paper-thin brown bread, small white plates, and white linen napkins. Rashid ordered the waiters to pour two glasses for them, and to wait outside the door in case he should want something more.

Mirella stood up to stretch her legs, and the two looked

down across the opera house at the audience. She noticed that Rashid attracted some attention from the occasional woman who obviously knew him or wanted to know him. They turned almost simultaneously to face one another.

"I need not ask you if you are enjoying yourself because it's so obvious that you are."

"I know you're not an opera buff, and I do thank you so much for bringing me."

He gave her one of his more lustful looks. "I had no idea you could become so excited by a performance," he said. "Will you allow me to arrange one for you? One that I would find extraordinarily exciting?"

Looking deeply into her eyes, he reached out and ran a finger across several of the pearls in her collier and gave her a look so lascivious that it was as if he had indeed pulled on the invisible sexual chain he held her by. There could be but one answer.

"Oh yes, if it gives you pleasure, I would like that very much."

Rashid handed her a glass of the rare vintage champagne. They smiled, then touched the rims of their glasses, and sipped their wine. Mirella was tingling with sexual excitement from erotic signals he was transmitting to her. She suddenly realized they were presenting a glittering display in the opera box, and that any number of eyes were upon them. She was relieved to think no one could read their thoughts, but still she stepped back a few paces from the edge of the box as if to be less conspicuous, and Rashid chuckled, knowing very well what made her do it.

"Rashid," she said with a twinkle in her eye, "you make me feel like Margherita in the opera when she has become entranced by Faust, with his air of distinction, his ardor, and his gentleness. And then, after Faust has turned her head, she is enslaved by his wishes, good or evil."

It was just this sort of talk that Rashid relished. It made the chase more amusing for him.

"Ah," he said, "but am I Faust? Are you so sure I am Faust and not Mephistopheles? Am I the man who made a pact with the devil, or am I the devil, the king of darkness?"

Mirella knew he was teasing her and enjoying each detail of it, but she also knew very well that it was one of those teases that point to a great deal of truth. She couldn't help but laugh at him.

"Are you implying I have supped with the devil, a chocolate-addicted devil, no less? My goodness, that makes me a remarkable woman, because if so, I have come out of it unscathed and liking my devil enough to buy *him* something for a change. Something to get him through the remainder of the opera."

Mirella went to the chair where she had put her silver kidskin envelope evening purse, opened it, and withdrew a long, flat rectangular box wrapped in silver paper and tied with a black velvet bow. And handed it to him.

"Oh, for me?" he said, and pulled the end of the ribbon. The bow dissolved and fell to the floor. He lifted the cover and smiled. A tray of Neuhaus Belgian white chocolates wrapped in attractive Italian foils were arranged in an enticing pattern in the box.

"You are a clever girl. You can have the sandwiches. I'll have the chocolates. Thank you, Mirella, that was thoughtful."

They sat down, she with several of the tiny sandwiches on a plate and her glass of wine, and Rashid with several chocolates that he proceeded to unwrap and eat.

"You do know what you have done, don't you?" he asked, still in his teasing mood. "Casanova and Madame Du Barry, those celebrated lovers, believed as I do that chocolate is an aphrodisiac. Be prepared for what is to come after I've eaten these."

He bit into the first piece, and Mirella began to laugh, because, if truth be told, she did see a look of real pleasure come into his eyes as he ate it. He could not resist and quickly ate another saying, "Delicious, I will save a few to eat in bed with you tonight. Just the thought of it gives me an idea. Why don't we both cancel all previous engagements for tomorrow and stay in bed and have sex all day?" And he put a chocolate in her mouth.

She chewed it slowly, giving him a most sensuous look.

"I can't do that, because I won't be here in England tomorrow. But if you are in a position to cancel your appointments, then why don't you? Come away with me for a few days. I'm going to Turkey."

Rashid was visibly taken aback. Mirella was not surprised. She had, after all, sprung it on him with no previous suggestion that she might be moving on, to Turkey or anywhere else, and they were, anyway, in the throes of a still very exciting affair.

It was the very last thing Rashid expected. He knew she had registered his shock at her announcement, and because she had, he felt he could reveal his feelings.

"I think I'm quite disturbed at the idea that you can just pick up and leave without giving any warning of your plans to me."

"Well, I couldn't very well, could I, Rashid? I only decided this evening in the bath."

"Oh. Well, why this decision to go to Turkey? I thought the only interest you had in Turkey was to sell off your assets. And surely there is no need for you to go there for that. I was under the impression, with all the meetings you have been having, that a sale was imminent. Do I have my facts wrong?"

"No, you have your facts right."

"Then what's the problem? Aren't you going to sell?"

"Yes, I am."

"Then why don't you just sign the documents and be done with the whole tedious business and stay here and play with me? Why have you decided to go to Turkey?"

Mirella finished the wine in her glass and held it out for Rashid to refill. He drank his down and poured two more glasses for them while Mirella answered, "First of all, for some reason I no longer feel any immediate need to rush into disposing of anything. I intend to do it in my own time. A few more days is not going to change anything. And, secondly, business is not the reason I want to go to Turkey—you are. I would like to see your country, the legendary city you love so much. To see some of your roots, and maybe see some of the things that helped make you what you are. I've met few men who compare with you and I'll not meet many more. In a week's time I'll be going home, and we both know this affair will change then, if not end. So I guess I want to visit the romantic East before that happens, and experience you even more than I do now, here. It would be more wonderful for me if I could be there once, in Asia Minor with you. If not, I'll go anyway. I suppose that if I am going to be there at all, I might just as well take a look at some of my estate. But in truth that is not why I'm going."

In the five days they had been together these had been the most direct revelations of their feelings, other than sexual ones, that had been expressed between the lovers. Rashid wanted to accept her sentiments in the same way any man would who was out to seduce a woman, and had won. But he couldn't. He knew it was only a token win: Mirella had only partially surrendered to him, and that was not enough. The chase was still very much on, and he had to admire her: she was giving him good sport.

The last thing that Rashid wanted was for Mirella to go to Turkey, and certainly not before she signed the documents selling all her holdings there. It would not be advantageous for him if she were to find out that he had dubious connections with her legacy. He knew he would be unable to dissuade her from going without her realizing he had some motive for keeping her out of Turkey. There was only one thing to do: take her to Turkey as his own guest so as to control her visit as much as possible. And besides, he reflected, he was very much enjoying his relationship with Mirella. And he was confident that nothing could impede his plans anyway.

Rashid rose from his chair and put his box of chocolates and his glass of wine on the table, then walked around in back of Mirella's chair, where he was partially hidden from view by the heavy velvet curtain draped to the side of the box. He put his hands on her shoulders: she reached up and placed a hand over one of his, as he bent down and kissed her on the side of her neck.

"I am very touched by your feelings, Mirella," he said. "Of course I will come with you; I want to be the one to show you Istanbul, my Istanbul. Please leave everything to me." And he kissed her on the side of the neck again, then slipped a finger under the bumblebee diamond clasp of her collier and gave it a tug.

Rashid felt a tremor pass through Mirella's body. It delighted him to control her sexually, to know that she would always obey him as long as she wore the pearl collar. There was no question in his mind that Mirella Wingfield was a sexual adventuress. She might even be in his league. Finding out was, at the moment, his greatest pleasure.

He remained standing behind her, and slipped his hands from her shoulders over her arms, and increased the pressure. Mirella felt it like a passionate kiss transmitted through his hands. His caresses—no matter how innocent they appeared—were on display in the opera house and made Mirella blush, the more so because only she knew what they really meant: Exquisite, erotic joy, tinged with the forbidden they both reveled in.

Soon the curtain rose. Pavarotti sang Faust's impassioned plea for deliverance from Mephistopheles, and from all temptation, then Faust expired. Mephistopheles, who was left writhing in frustration, had lost his wager with the Lord, because he was finally unable to catch and hold Faust's essential being, thus landing him in his net. A hail of roses descended upon the body of Faust, while Mephistopheles, whistling in defiance, sank beneath the ground defeated—though not, of course, for long.

The huge velvet curtain closed, and the members of the audience rose to their feet in an ovation that reverberated throughout the opera house. After a few seconds the artists came out from behind the curtain—musical magicians holding hands and smiling as they bowed, whom the grateful audience showered with flowers until they lay thick at the performers' feet. Altogether, there were seventeen curtain calls, and at last Pavarotti took his solo bow.

More than a few tears were shed there that evening. Mirella was no exception. She finally turned to Rashid and said, "Oh, Rashid, we should have thought to bring flowers for them. They were stupendous. What a night!"

"We did," he replied, and took the orchids from the center of the table, bent down, and picked off the floor the black velvet ribbon from his box of chocolates, and tied the stems of the flowers together with a neat bow. He handed them to Mirella, who was delighted.

"Come here to the corner of the box," he said. "I think to Pavarotti, yes?"

She nodded her approval. He adored her enthusiasm, the excitement in her eyes. That was, in fact, when he liked her best, when she held nothing back, and gave herself up completely to her emotions, as she did with him in sex.

"When I get his attention, be quick and throw well. Aim for his chest, and he will catch them; we are so close to the stage you can easily make it. Ready?"

She nodded, and he thought to himself that Pavarotti could not miss spotting her because she shone like a diamond in her glittering dress and had to be the most beautiful woman in the opera house. Then he shouted in Italian, "Luciano, Luciano. Maestro, it's Rashid. Thank you, Luciano." The moment the tenor turned and saw him, Rashid waved the magnificent orchids at him and then quickly placed them in a surprised Mirella's hands.

"Throw quickly," he said, "and Pavarotti will catch them."

Luciano Pavarotti flashed a smile up at Rashid and Mirella as he reached out and caught the flowers. The audience went wild. Mirella saw his lips move, and she read "Thank you, Rashid," and then the tenor made a gesture of admiration for the beauty of the orchids, by waving his right hand in a small circle, and bowed his head to Mirella.

The audience was now pounding its feet. Pavarotti opened the crack in the curtain and disappeared, then immediately reappeared leading Caballé, who was leading Freni, who led Ghiaurov by the hand. They all took a bow and then Pavarotti, still carrying the orchids, pulled the ribbon and let it fall to the stage and gave a spray of the large white orchids to each of his fellow artists. The opera house all but rocked with the audience's enthusiasm. They bowed and left the stage.

For ten minutes no one was able to leave, so electric was their recollection of the performance. They just remained in the auditorium until finally their applause died away. Very slowly a degree of composure settled over those in the opera house, and they began to leave Covent Garden.

"You never cease to amaze me, Rashid. I had no idea you knew Luciano Pavarotti. I thought you didn't like opera?"

"I don't. I know Luciano. We've met at several parties, and I like him, and his voice, as I like all kinds of wonderful music. I just don't particularly like to attend an opera."

He slipped his arm around her waist and slowly turned her to face the door, and they started to leave the box. On the way, she bent over the chair to take her purse. All evening he had been besotted by her in that dress. The provocative bare shoulder, the tight fit over the flat hips, and the high, voluptuous bottom he was so enamored of. It was more than he could bear to see it presented to him so alluringly, so he quickly stepped up behind her, pressed a hand on her tummy, and pulled her tight up against him, then swiftly stepped with her behind the curtain of the box. He put his lips on her bare shoulder, opened them and kissed it, while pressing her bottom so tightly to him he could feel his erect penis throbbing the length of the luscious furrow between its cheeks.

"Tomorrow night in Istanbul I will arrange a performance for us such as you have never dreamed of. You will see and do things, and want things done to you, that you never imagined before, things that would have delivered even Faust into Mephistopheles's net forever."

He lifted her hair from the back of her neck, and kissed her there; then he bit her with such a passion, she felt her nipples stiffen, and she whispered, "Pull me tighter, pull me tighter to you."

He did, and he felt her whole body contract, and actually go rigid for a second. She picked up his free hand and sank her teeth into the back of it, to stop herself from letting out a cry of passion as she came in a breathtaking orgasm. Mirella had been helpless to do otherwise: the danger he promised in Istanbul, and that of being discovered in such a compromising position in public was half the excitement. He of course was the other half. When she released his hand from her mouth, she whispered a soft whimper of contentment. Her knees were so weak she had to sit down, and try to compose herself, and so, playing for time, she asked, "Have you decided? Are you Faust, or are you Mephistopheles? Or do you still not know?"

He sat down next to her, rubbing the top of his hand. An oval-shaped mauve bruise was coming up rapidly on his satiny olive-colored skin. She could see in his eyes, and by the huge bulge straining against his trouser leg that he had lost none of his desire for her. With hypnotically dark, soft, sexy eyes holding her to him, he said, "I am Faust, who," and then he quoted almost verbatim from the libretto, " 'has desired and enjoyed, and then desired anew, but has never yet said to the fleeting moment, Remain, for thou art fair!'

"I say as he said, as Luciano sang, 'Every mortal mystery I have tasted, the Real and the Ideal, the virgin's love and that of the goddess . . . Yes, but in Reality was pain, and the Ideal was but a dream.' And, who knows, Mirella, maybe like Faust I think of being 'A King of a boundless country, a land that knows no strife. To a prolific people I would consecrate my life,' Perhaps. I've skipped some bits and haven't got it quite right, but yes, I am Faust. But a Faust who prefers to play the role of Mephistopheles."

Rashid had surprised her yet again, with such an insight into the contradictions inherent in life. There was no response she could give to what he was implying. He rose from his chair and helped her up from hers. He kissed her sweetly on the lips, and gave her a broad smile, and slipped his arm through hers. As he opened the door to the corridor, he stopped and said to her, in his husky voice, "I *will* have you, you know, I won't fail like the Mephistopheles of the opera, I *will* take you, I *will* break you, tomorrow night in Istanbul."

Then, with a mischievous, teasing smile on his lips, he slipped all the fingers of one hand over the slave collar of pearls locked around her neck and tugged at it a few times, as if to pull her along by it. She stumbled. He released her and took her by the hand and they stepped together into the corridor, and joined the crowds flowing out of the opera house.

Rashid's car was awaiting them among the numerous Rolls-Royces, Daimlers, and Bentleys parked in readiness for their owners. They made their way through the throngs of people standing looking at other people looking at other people, and hurriedly slipped through the car door held open by Rashid's gray-liveried chauffeur and into the backseat of the car.

The first thing Mirella did, once seated, was to open her purse and tap Rashid on the arm. He gave her all his attention as from her purse she produced a small, pointed, very sharp pair of darning scissors in the shape of a stork, on the end of a narrow bright-red satin ribbon.

"I thought you might like to see these," she said. "I always carry them with me, at the ready, even when we are in the midst of our more flagrant intimacies. I love my collar of pearls, and what they represent. But remember, we can, either one of us, remove it, we both have the means: you, the little golden key you wear on that gold chain around your neck, not unlike a trophy; and me, my little scissors." And she put her thumb and forefinger through the oval holes and teased him by opening and closing the blades close to his face.

They began to laugh, then filled the back of the Rolls with uproarious laughter, and they both wondered to themselves which of them would master the other in the end. Rashid pulled her close to him and he kissed her. Then he bent forward and from a compartment built into the back of the front seat he removed a long, slim box.

"I was going to give this to you in a much more sexy way in bed tonight, in not quite the same fashion as I have given you chocolates. But you are so clever and I adore you so much, and I think those tiny scissors you carry for protection are so amusing that I want you to have your little present now."

Mirella looked at the emerald-green velvet box and wanted to protest, but she had learned better. He had told her that her objections to his generosity only robbed him of some of the pleasure he received from spoiling her. She could only show her thanks for his extravagant gestures where he wanted them most—in bed. By the shape of the box, it was quite obvious what was inside.

"Well, it's obviously a handcuff," she said. "You'll not be satisfied till you have me bound and gagged in pearls and jewels, will you?"

God, he thought, there was no woman to hold a candle to this beauty. Surely she had the legendary Oujie courtesan blood in her. It was no wonder those women had amassed and held on to such fortunes. He opened the box still in her hands and took out the diamond and pearl bracelet, which was indeed like a three-inch-wide Art Deco Cartier handcuff.

He eyed her as he helped her out of the car in front of Annabel's and thought to himself, she deserves to be draped with the finest pearls in all the world. He wondered what passions would stir in her if she found out that she was not the only member of her family to have worn those particular pearls around her neck. But he hoped never to know because it was imperative that she never find out that for centuries the Lala Mustafas had been robbing the Oujies, the wealthiest and most powerful of the Ottoman Jews.

It was four-thirty in the morning, and Mirella couldn't sleep. It had been yet another awesome evening and night with Rashid. After the opera, it had been dinner and dancing at Annabel's, then Tramps, with some of his international jet-set friends, all of whom had been only glamorous names to Mirella less than a week before. Names she had no interest in, and would never have considered wasting an evening with, and there she had been—laughing and dancing, and, if truth be told, having fun with them, and all because of Rashid.

She had been dancing with Prince Ahmed Sahid Whabi, whom she had recognized at once as the man who had been on the make for her at the U.N. party, and whom she had been introduced to by Donald Davies. Then she had been wondering how long she would continue drifting in such glittering but shallow social waters. Her heart skipped a beat when by contrast she thought of the real, the pure, things solid and deep, beauty and continuity: Adam Corey.

It was irrational to feel hurt, as she had felt earlier in the day when he had called Brindley's office and she had overheard their conversation, and learned that, like her, he was getting

on with his life. He was in London only for a day to get his
son at Eton, to take two of his former mistresses on a
shopping spree, to read a paper and receive an honorary
position at the British Museum, and to invite Brindley to an
early dinner before flying back to Istanbul. He hadn't even
asked about her or how things were going with the Oujie
legacy.

What would she have done had she known that Adam
Corey was very busy putting his emotional attachments in
order, making space for a new woman and a great love in his
life?

Alone in bed now—Rashid having just left her for his own
apartment upstairs, because he had so many arrangements to
make for their arrival in Istanbul—Mirella thought about that
again. She turned on her side and closed her eyes; she was
exhausted, but sleep eluded her.

She thought about Ahmed who had been utterly charming.
What a snob she had been about men for such a long time,
because of her so-called love for Paul and their alliance.
Mirella could see now it was one of the many ways she used
to keep her freedom. A perfect device to stop her from finding
a man she could love enough to build a whole and complete
life with.

She remembered a few things Ahmed had said to her . . .
something about him and Rashid being both friends and
partners. They had both teased her. Ahmed asked Rashid to
sell Mirella to him, and he had answered that she was not for
sale, *yet*. She would have worried about the "yet" except that
he had said with a decadent look in his eye that she was, for
the moment, still a free woman. If she wanted to go to
Ahmed of her own accord, Rashid would not deprive her of
one of Ahmed's orgies, he would in fact join them. Mirella
found the idea repellent. She declined the invitation with just
as much charm and lightheartedness as the two men had used
in trying to entice her. Charm was one thing, trust another.
She trusted Rashid to some extent, Ahmed not at all.

She tried to calm her mind and drift off to sleep. It was
impossible. She was too excited about seeing Istanbul with
Rashid. Ah, Rashid! He was as sexually besotted with her as
she was with him.

True as that was, she knew he would never master her as he
had mastered other women, because she was not in love with
him. She was merely seduced by him, and she had the advan-

tage of knowing and facing it. The music from the opera resounded in her head and she visualized some of the scenes she had seen performed earlier. She could never do what Margherita had done in the opera: slip a heavy sleeping potion into her mother's drink at the request of a lover. Poor Margherita, she had lost her mother in death and her lover in life, and suffered a glimpse of hell as her reward.

All hope of sleep was gone now. Mirella slipped on her dressing gown and went into the drawing room. She picked out two of the journals from the archives she had been reading and put them to one side to take with her to Istanbul. Then she went to the commode where she had locked away the personal effects left to her by Ottoline Sinan and Oberon Winslow-Ward and took some of the jewelry she thought she might like to wear. She sat down in one of the deep, comfortable chairs next to the telephone and stared at the Gérôme portrait of Ottoline Sinan that Brindley had fallen in love with. There was no question about it, there was a close resemblance between Ottoline and her grandmother, and something of both lived again in Mirella's face. For the first time since this phenomenon of the legacy burst upon her, Mirella felt the thrill of being descended from these romantic women of another era, her kin. Suddenly she was proud to belong to them, have their ancestors and their legends as part of her life. Her sense of history took over. She must find her own place in it.

It suddenly came to her why she, Maxim, Lawrence, and even Marcus loved Wingfield Park and all its possessions; why none of them ever thought of selling off the things there for a stake in the future. The house, their things were part of the past. Knowing them, and being part of them was a response to the past that made sense of the present. Some things had to be permanent to create a solid foundation from which to raise oneself.

Her poor mother, why did she try so hard, waste so many years trying to deprive them all of their heritage? She had never made any headway with her father or her brother, not even with Marcus—he had managed to hang on to everything for them in spite of her pleas. Only Mirella had weakened under her assaults—weakened but never had been beaten. But she had to admit she had been lucky, saved by the men in the family, and by Uncle Hiram saddling her with the house. And now, a great-grandmother and her legacy. Without them she might have become completely absorbed in her own little world and swallowed up by it, as Lili was.

She shuddered when she thought of what she had been like just two weeks ago, how clever she had been in fooling herself that she had the perfect life. How absolutely extraordinary, she thought—it took the legacy, glamour and gloss, and a fortune, to allow her to feel humility and a love for herself that might be fruitful. The same kind of love she allowed herself to feel for Lawrence and her father and Marcus and Deena, and had always wanted to feel for her mother.

She went to the bedroom and found her wristwatch: it was two minutes past five in the morning, two minutes past midnight in Massachusetts. Everyone at Wingfield Park would still be up, no one went to bed before one in the morning. She wanted to call and tell Lili she loved her. That whatever problems there were could all be worked out. She wanted to tell Lili how grateful she was for the legacy and that it had taught her how important it was to invest something of oneself in one's past, and how good she felt about it.

She picked up the telephone and dialed Lili's private number. It rang a half dozen times and finally Mirella heard a click. Lili had picked up the receiver. There was a pause and then at last Lili said, "Hello."

Mirella said, "Hello, Mother, I just called to say I love you."

"Who is this?" asked Lili in an ice-cold voice.

"Mirella Wingfield, your daughter, Lili," said Mirella, shaking her head in disbelief and thinking that Lili was incorrigible.

"I don't know any Mirella Wingfield, and I don't have a daughter." And her mother slammed down the receiver.

17

Mirella was on her way to Turkey with Rashid on board his private twelve-passenger jet, the interior of which had been converted to his specifications. It was divided into three sections: the cockpit and galley, the sitting and dining areas, and a bedroom and bathroom.

It was luxurious and in good taste, planned and executed by

one of the best of the contemporary Italian designers from Milan. The walls and comfortable sofas and armchairs were covered in soft beige and fawn colored leather, and the decorative cushions scattered around the cabin were covered in tiger skin, white Persian lamb, leopard, and black panther skins. The tables were carved and honed smooth from blocks of beige travertine marble.

The staff of four—an American pilot, the copilot, and two Sudanese stewards—were the only other people on board. As soon as the plane was airborne, Rashid unbuckled Mirella's seat belt, took her by the hand, and led her to the bedroom, instructing the stewards to wake them a half hour before landing.

They were both exhausted from the rush to leave London. That had been at Rashid's insistence because he had made arrangements to have lunch in Istanbul. And so, with hardly a word said between them, Rashid and Mirella undressed and slipped between the peach silk sheets on the bed and pulled the blanket made of chinchilla skins over them. Both having missed their sleep the night before, they had scarcely put their arms around each other and got settled before they fell into a deep sleep.

Three and a half hours later they were awakened by a knock at the door from the stewards, who brought them glasses of champagne that they drank in bed. Mirella watched Rashid break open and suck out the flesh of two succulent fresh figs, and once again was mesmerized by the beauty and sensuality of the man. Sensing her admiration, he smiled at her, broke open a fig, and held it to her mouth so she could suck the fruit from its skin. It was as sweet as sugar and as sensual a taste as sex itself. She wanted to take him in her mouth and eat him as she had the fig, but that was not their way. They only had sex the way *he* wanted it and directed, and Mirella had no complaint about that because it was always satisfying for them both.

He kissed her lips, rather dispassionately, she thought, then licked the lingering sweetness from them, and ordered her to hold in abeyance the sexual ardor he detected in her gaze because it was time to dress.

She obeyed his order and slid from between the sheets and began dressing. Rashid remained in bed eating some of his favorite Leonidas white chocolate creams and watched her put on the same outfit she had worn on the plane from New

York. It was obvious that he derived infinite pleasure from watching her and was generous in his approval of how she looked. Rashid asked her to wear all her pearls, saying he wanted her to enter Istanbul adorned as its newest and most regal empress. And he thought wryly that this still naïve and unspoiled American didn't realize she actually could be a modern-day empress with the power her legacy had given her.

When she had put the last touches to her makeup, brushed her hair, and pinned her lovely Adolfo hat on, she stood up from the dressing table and turned to face him, obviously seeking his approval. He hopped out of bed, and stood naked in front of her, put his hand on his chin, rubbed it, and looked at her thoughtfully. She was perfect, a vision of beauty, elegance, and wealth.

Mirella felt silly standing there all dressed up, while he stood before her splendidly naked and regal. It made her feel like a tourist admiring a live statue of Adonis. He went to her and adjusted the longest strand of pearls.

"You are perfect, a goddess." He smiled and added, "But, what I want is an empress."

He reached around her, and from a drawer of the dressing table behind her he withdrew a velvet case, opened it, and said, "This is my gift to welcome you to my Istanbul."

He pinned an antique Russian diamond sunburst, its center a huge round cushion-cut diamond, onto her tunic high up near her shoulder.

"I dub you the new empress of all Turkey," he said.

Mirella turned to look in the mirror. It was almost impossible for her to reconcile the woman she saw draped and garlanded in jewels before her with the Bonwit Teller, B. Altman-suited woman she had been all of her life. Almost but not quite. She knew that she had changed and that she could now accept being both those women. When she turned from the mirror back to Rashid, she saw a subtly altered expression in his eyes. She wasn't quite sure what it meant and lost her sudden sense of identity as she put her arms around his neck, thanked him profusely, declared herself taken aback yet again, and kissed him passionately.

She felt his lips open and his tongue find hers, and felt his body rise and throb against her. Her heart began to pound as he gently grasped her by the chin and began moving her kisses down his splendid naked body. He ordered her to her knees and guided her lips to his magnificent cock, and for the first time since they had been together, he allowed her to take him in her mouth. She felt him push deeper and deeper down her throat as he flicked away her hat, and it dropped on a chair close by. He was now able to watch her sucking him, to see the unbridled lust in her eyes. They were both surprised by the swiftness of his command not to move her lips but to grip him tight with her mouth and hold him firm, remain absolutely still and just keep swallowing as he poured forth down her throat.

Once spent of his seed, he ordered her to keep sucking, telling her he wanted her to milk him dry. When he was ready to withdraw, he did so very slowly. It was all he could do during that act to hold himself back from his urge to strip and whip her for being now not like a goddess or an empress but like the most accomplished of whores. When he finally stepped back a pace from Mirella, he was still fully erect and throbbing. There was not a drop of his semen on her lips.

Mirella was trembling with passion, her knees felt weak. She raised her hand and silently asked to be helped to her feet. She wanted to undress and be taken by him, wanted desperately to feel his exquisite, rampant rod deep inside her, but he would not allow it, feigning there was not time. There was now a degree of pleasure for him in not satisfying her.

The final stage of the seduction of Mirella Wingfield had begun: all was working according to plan, with the exception of their being in Istanbul. But Rashid had no doubts that he could work even that to his advantage. He was well aware of how much she wanted him to fuck her, bring her to the climaxes she dissolved in. It was apparent in her eyes. He sensed it in her whole body, he heard it in words from her own lips, and he had been delighted, and in his perverse way liked her almost as much as he disliked her for it.

There was, however, one factor that Rashid had not bargained for. He regretted not fucking her, not being inside her. He longed for her orgasms, the exquisite juices he was capable of extracting from her. And he wanted, too, to be inside her erotic soul.

They landed at a small airfield on the outskirts of Istanbul and were met on the tarmac where two cars were waiting for them—a dark gray Rolls-Royce and a black American Cadillac, two chauffeurs, and two men Rashid called "assistants."

Mirella was impressed by their very dark, olive-colored skin, very Oriental eyes, massive bald heads, and bullish necks. Both were of average height but were extraordinarily broad-shouldered and -chested. One had a long, mean-looking scar that just missed his eye but took a slice of his eyebrow away, and the other had one, as if to match it, that went from behind his ear, down and around his neck to disappear somewhere under his shirt collar. They were dressed in dark, well-tailored suits and crisp, white shirts and wore black wool ties, which made them appear even more sinister. If they had found employment before Rashid's, it could only have been as Turkish wrestlers. They staked out as the toughest, meanest bodyguards anyone could ask for.

Mirella thought little about the men as they traveled from the airport, with Fuad hunched in the front seat of the Rolls with the chauffeur, and Daoud a sinister presence in the Cadillac used to carry the luggage that followed them into the city and to Rashid's house.

The magnificent mansion with its imposing, sturdy stone façade was set in a shadowy cypress wood and garden, and was surrounded by a high, finely wrought iron fence and massive decorative gates. It stood on the highest point of the exclusive Mesrutiyet Caddesi, where were to be found the once-sumptuous mansions that were formerly the British, French, and Russian embassies to the Ottoman Empire.

But she was surprised, as the day wore on, by the constant hovering of the two bodyguards. They discreetly shadowed Mirella and Rashid as the couple walked through the enclosed gardens of his house. Inside the mansion they disappeared and were replaced by two other men, who looked much less threatening. There was a splendid lunch of the finest Turkish cuisine, with several gorgeous, well-dressed Turkish women, a very elderly Russian prince with exquisite manners and watery eyes, and two handsome Egyptians who appeared to be playboys in the same class as Rashid. The less-menacing pair of "assistants" stood on guard in front of the set of doors at one end of the grand dining room.

After lunch, when Rashid's guests left, he said, "Go and change into something simple and comfortable because I am going to take you on a tour of the Misir Carsisi. It's the Egyptian Market. Most people know it as the Spice Bazaar. A good way to begin to see my Istanbul. You will like it because it's one of the liveliest markets in the city. It still retains the flavors and scents, color and atmosphere of the Oriental bazaar of times long past. From there I will take you to see some of the finest of the old mosques. Few tourists ever get to see them. But they're the jewels of Ottoman architecture.

"Later, much later, we'll meet friends at an excellent restaurant called Pandeli's in the domed rooms above the entrance to the bazaar. And after dinner we will all go deep into the huge Kapali Carsi, the Covered Bazaar, one of the largest and most intriguing marketplaces in the world, where we will see that exciting performance I promised I would arrange for you. Something very unlike the opera last night. Your first night in Istanbul will be one to remember all the days of your life."

Rashid's bedroom was impressive. Done in raw white silk, gossamer white silk, and yet another nuance of white in a taffeta handwoven in Lyons, it featured several pieces of heavy Biedermeier furniture and some exceptionally fine and huge eighteenth-century Kashar portraits of Persian princes. Rashid's manservant brought him a pair of gray flannel trousers and a navy blue cashmere blazer with handsome gold buttons inlaid with silver that once adorned one of Sultan Suleiman the Magnificent's court robes. Rashid wore the blazer over a gray cashmere polo-neck sweater.

A diminutive maid brought Mirella a Miyake dress and jacket of very thinly quilted stiff cotton, cut in a masterly fashion, yet looking like the most elegant rags ever made, which, she decided, they probably were. She emerged from the bedroom adjoining Rashid's that for reasons of "propriety" was assigned to her for her stay in his house. She found it too hypocritical for words, and said nothing to Rashid about it, not wanting to offend him.

She was somewhat surprised when Rashid told her to wear no jewelry of very great value, and to make sure her pearl collar was covered by a scarf, since their evening's excitements might transport them to some pretty rough places. And Rashid was surprised in his turn when Mirella made a request.

"I'm all yours, but there is one thing I ask. I want to stand in the middle of the Galata Bridge some time around sunset when the *muezzin* calls the faithful to prayer."

Byzantium. Constantinople. Istanbul. What other city in the world has had its name changed three times, and in the changing has lost nothing of what it symbolizes—the exotic, the erotic, opulent wealth?

Byzantium. Constantinople. Istanbul. By any name the city

always has evoked myriad images: source of every kind of pleasure, glistening water, Asia Minor and the Asiatic life, dark cypress groves, the jewels and pearls of potentates, mosques and minarets, adventures and dangers. Upon hearing it, the listener may conjure visions of the palaces, the yalis, austere wooden summer mansions weather-beaten gray from the sun and salt air, rising above stone steps washed by the Bosporus. Or the listener's imagination may be stimulated to summon the reclining odalisques, the intrigues of the harem, or to recall the sound and sight of bubbling fountains, a legendary river named the Golden Horn, or the fragrances of magnolias and jasmine, the spices of the East and their seduction of the eye, the nose, the taste buds.

What other city stands astride two continents and two worlds, the East and West? The Istanbul of today is still an Eastern city with an Eastern people influenced by a Western world—an influence always limited because the city has an Oriental past, an Islamic religion, yet retains the heart and soul of Asia Minor. It is one of the truly great cities of the world, populated by a people who live in the shadow of the Byzantine and Ottoman empires, and made even greater because its qualities are all framed by a setting of infinite beauty.

The city is bounded and divided by water. And what waterways! The Bosporus, the strait that flows from the Black Sea to the Sea of Marmara, cuts through Istanbul, leaving the city in Europe and its surburbs in Asia. It joins the Golden Horn flowing seaward from Thrace, and once met, they merge and dissolve into the Sea of Marmara.

The Galata Bridge spans the Golden Horn. On its left bank is Galata, the Levantine port quarter, while on the right is Stambul, the imperial city built on seven hills. To stand in the center of it is to stand at the heart of the city and feel its pulsing daily life, and at the same time to have a view of Ottoman Stambul. Seven hills of mosques, palaces, and pious foundations. Voluptuous domes and vastly high and needle-like spires beckon to the heart and mind with the sheer beauty and power they generate. And to see them as imperial, dark, brooding silhouettes against a flaming red sky at sunset, just before the light dies, and the sky bruises mauve and then purple, and finally, after turning dark blue becomes inky black night, is to have straddled four worlds: the East and the West, and today, and all Istanbul's yesterdays back to Byzantium.

The thought of spanning time and cultures went through Mirella's mind as she stood next to Rashid, flanked by his two "assistants," in the middle of the Galata Bridge. They were Adam Corey's ideas—spoken to her in New York two weeks before, when they lay naked in each other's arms making love.

Mirella was no longer perturbed by Fuad and Daoud. She was even grateful to have the two bodyguards, who practically had to use hand-to-hand combat in order to shield Rashid and Mirella from the throngs of street peddlers hawking their wares, small shopkeepers and café owners, and restauranteurs making their pitch for business. It was as if the whole population of Istanbul was crossing and recrossing the bridge.

There were a thousand unforgettable sights: the sellers of *simit*, the doughnut-shaped bread sprinkled with sesame seeds, pushed through the crowds and were followed by the sweetmeat peddlers. There were the makeshift stalls that popped up anywhere and everywhere for selling peanuts and pistachios, and roasted marrow seeds, and chick-peas, and almonds and hazelnuts. The sherbet vendors, with their handsome leather bottles wrought with brass, chrome, and ironwork, elbowed their way through the sea of people.

Small boys appeared as a community all of their own. There were masses of them, carrying tiny cups of coffee or glasses of tea on ingenious brass trays that remained level as they swung back and forth on chains from a hand-held ring where they converged. There was, too, the vast population of shoeshine boys who took their customers whenever and wherever they found them.

Small, dark, unshaven men trundled along under massive loads of timber, cartons, bales of wool, sacks of coal, as high as ten feet, which they carried cross-strapped and tied on to their backs, bent double under their loads. Burdened like donkeys, they hooted and hollered to clear the way. These human cargo vessels shirked nothing Mirella realized as she saw a battered upright piano move across the bridge on a pair of skinny, hairy bowed legs stuck in a pair of worn-out black rubber shoes and no socks. He was saved by Daoud from a crash with a massive and ugly walking modern cupboard with mirrored doors. She saw a pitiful accident, a head-on collision between a five-foot pile of flattened oil drums and a six-foot-thick load of metal rods fifteen feet long that had been springing through the crowd. The sound of the crash was like a newly discovered percussion instrument in the symphony of human chatter and giggles, shouting and hawking, jostling, elbowing, touching, and peering.

Mirella found it incredibly dusty, gray, grim, the people poor, shabby, and not smiling very much, a maelstrom of confusion. She saw nothing of the glamour, nostalgia, and beauty that Adam's words had promised, or that the archives of her ancestors suggested. She looked at Rashid, and could not equate him with the Turks engulfing them on the bridge.

She leaned against the rail and saw below her fleets of ships in all shapes and sizes plying the waters of the Bosporus and the Golden Horn. The line of ferries sailing from berth to berth and depositing streams of people. Caïques loaded with cargoes of fish, fruit, and fresh vegetables for the local markets, playing aquatic dodgems with huge, rusted, and battered ships or tankers flying Liberian, Greek, Turkish, Russian, Iranian flags. A streamlined ocean liner let out blasts of its horn and scattered sailing boats and yachts of all sizes, sleek speedboats, and Turkish naval vessels. Mirella listened to the river and its chorus, as it merged in with the Galata Bridge symphony, and she discovered yet more mayhem. All along the water's edge the quays were studded with cranes, both mechanical and manual, loading and unloading ships, and hundreds of overloaded porters running back and forth like parts of a human conveyor belt.

Quite suddenly the light changed. It rolled slowly over the bridge, and bathed everything a Byzantine gold color for a few seconds. Then the dying light faded further and it all switched again. Everything in sight was dusted in a glowing golden-rose color, and the sky was streaked with garish pink, coral, and flaming red.

It was after all, as Adam Corey had promised, an inescapably romantic setting. Diffused was the sad seediness of human cargo milling across the bridge, and that undercurrent of chicanery one sensed. The mysterious reflected light of Istanbul stirred Mirella's romantic imaginings, and her heart cried out not for Rashid, who stood watching her closely, but for Adam Corey. She thought of him and her heart lifted, she felt a sense of heightened life, as the memory of being with him surged back to her. She felt closer to him than to the man standing next to her, in fact closer to him than to any other living human being. Here was the moment of truth, and it was not to be ignored.

The haunting chant of the *muezzin* calling the faithful to prayer echoed over the city, and pierced Mirella to the heart. As she looked at Rashid, her eyes filled with tears, so touched was she by the beauty of the moment and place, so devastated by her sense of aloneness and the absence of the loving relationship that had eluded her throughout her life.

The magic of the moment, as in a fairy tale, rescued her, caressed her, and she was warmed, in the same way she had been warmed when she met Adam Corey for the first time. She looked across the Bosporus, now a wide avenue of shimmering silver-black water, and imagined she saw a misty shadow part from her own being and float up and away. It took a vaguely human form. Mirella reached out as if to touch it, but it suddenly became birdlike as it disappeared over the river toward the Black Sea.

And, astonishingly, her sensation of utter aloneness vanished. Mirella instinctively felt that she was loved by Adam Corey with a love till then unknown to her. It made her heart flutter, and enabled her to release her own love, greater than any she had ever imagined herself capable of. She was thrilled as she thought of sharing so much, so much of herself with a man who truly wanted all of her.

Rashid grabbed Mirella's hand and squeezed it as hard as he could. It was warm, almost hot. He had the most dreadful feeling that something had happened to her, that she was suddenly somehow transformed, and that she might be abandoning him even now. He sensed that something profound had stirred in her, there, just a moment before. Whatever it was he didn't like it. She stopped gazing at the Bosporus to turn and look at him.

"Don't leave me!" he ordered.

There was an ear-shattering blast of a ship's horn as it passed under the bridge that obliterated his words. He pulled her close against him by her hand and looked into her face.

"I couldn't hear you," she shouted. "What did you say?"

He was too late. He caught a subtle change in her eyes, a softening, and he knew that in spirit she had already left him. The question now was whether she was emotionally still with him at all. He would know after what he had in store for her tonight. For the first time, Rashid began to believe he might never master Mirella. He saw her now as the first woman who might be a threat to his way of life, dangerous to him. The idea that he was capable of falling in love with her disturbed him. The sound of the ship's horn died away.

"What did you say?" she repeated. "I lost you."

He squeezed her hand even harder and said, "We have to leave now, that's what I told you."

"You're hurting my hand, Rashid," she said, wincing in pain, then frowning at him.

He raised her hand to his lips before he eased his grip. He smiled at her, patted her hand, slowly released it, slipped his arm through hers, and together they continued their crossing of the Galata Bridge, Daoud elbowing a path through the crowd and Fuad protecting them from the rear.

"Istanbul has given you one of its best sunsets to bathe in, and as you wanted, while you stood in the middle of the bridge. Even the muezzin's call came at the perfect moment for you. Is it everything you expected?"

"Oh yes," she answered. "And more, much more." Then she squeezed his arm against her breast, looked up, and smiled at him.

Portable gas lamps were being lit, and small pools or eerie white light dotted the stalls and the shops and cafés, lighting up the bridge. Their constant hiss was another new sound added to the symphony around the bridge, just as hot candle wax and kerosene from alternative lighting became part of its aroma. Then the street lights of Istanbul, scattered over the hills, were turned on and seemed, from where Mirella stood, like small fires scattered over a vast primitive but exotic landscape, and lighting the city and its monuments, transforming it into a strange and exciting metropolis.

Mirella adored it all. She stopped Rashid.

"It's such a special city, and I am thrilled to be here. I might never have come if not for you, if you hadn't seduced me in the dining room of Claridge's. Rashid, I think I am having the best time of my life, and I will always be grateful to you for it. 'Thank you' sounds awfully trite for such a gift."

"It is," he said, "but it will do," and they both laughed and continued walking.

When she discovered how compelling was her love for Adam Corey, Mirella had quite simply forgotten Rashid, even though he was standing next to her. She was therefore surprised to feel, after their exchange, that her affection was if anything even stronger for Rashid than it had been before her discovery. It confused her, but only for a fleeting moment, because Rashid again charmed away from her all thoughts of Adam, and the sheer power of his presence repossessed her.

Rashid sensed that all was not lost: he still held Mirella emotionally, even though he was not sure to what extent. He was ebullient, he doubled their pace, and called out to the vendors who peddled their wares alongside the couple, pushing through the crowds.

By the time they reached the end of the Galata Bridge and were in Eminonu, he had filled her arms with long-stemmed black and red Turkish tulips and fed her sherbet, and simit, *bulbulyuvasi*: "nightingale's nest," a sweet similar to baklava, in the shape of a nest, made with pistachios and honey, and filled her hands with paper cones of hazelnuts, toasted almonds, raisins, and roasted marrow-seeds.

They walked on through cobbled alleys of the market quarter that had been there since the earliest days of the city, and saw monuments and mosques hidden down labyrinths of narrow winding streets flanked by old wooden houses, romantic for their carved balconies and gables that tilted dangerously toward each other. They were dark and mysterious byways with names like Street of Nafi of the Golden Hair, or Elephants' Path, or Street of the Bushy Beard, or the Avenue of the White Moustache. The pair was followed now not only by Daoud and Fuad, but one of Rashid's cars, on old American Chevrolet.

In one such dark and mysterious cobbled street, which hinted of forbidden Byzantine delights and fabled decadence, Rashid pushed on a pair of ancient worn wooden doors with huge iron studs imbedded in them. They opened and he pulled Mirella into a courtyard lit by nothing more than one small candle in an old lantern. Mirella could hear the sound of water, a fountain. Rashid pushed her up against a wall and pinned her there with his body. There was barely enough light to see each other; he took her face in his hands and he found her mouth with his and kissed her passionately. Then with one hand he ran his fingers through her hair and pulled on it as he kissed her again, tongues kissing tongues. He licked the roof of her mouth and ate at her lips as he whispered the many ways he wanted to take her and how much he sexually adored her. She answered him back with kisses as desperate with need as his own. He slipped the scarf from her neck and put it in his blazer pocket and kissed each of the pearls in her collier, then he tilted her chin up and looked into her eyes.

With a tremor of passion in her voice she answered the

question he didn't even have to ask. "Yes, yes. I am like a captive in your harem. I am still your sexual slave. I wear your collar proudly, as a woman absolutely in your power, and I am ready to share your illicit delights with you."

"I had to know, I had to be sure. Now we can go forward into your first night in Istanbul," he whispered.

Then they kissed a few more times until their acute passion and need for each other slackened and they quietly left the courtyard and the wooden doors closed behind them.

Adam Corey was having lunch with five Turkish men from Kahta, a village located in the wild and difficult country of eastern Turkey. Every year between May and October he made two ascents with them—one to Mt. Ararat and one to the 9,193-foot Nemrut Dagi. A week before their first excursion Adam always brought the men down to Istanbul as his guests, to make final plans and to give them a treat.

His passion for eastern Turkey and the years spent there excavating made him many friends among the country people, who always looked forward to his return. For these men who had originally excavated with him on the mountain, it was not only a treat but a proud moment for them and their village to entertain Adam, and share their mountain and a view of its ancient treasures with him.

The luncheon was held as usual in the garden on a marble terrace close to the edge of the Bosporus, because the men were intimidated by the grandness of the house. A happy event, with enormous quantities of food and delicacies—along with water pipes of hashish to make up for the absence of alcohol, since they were all devout Muslims—it greatly pleased Adam to host it. He delighted in talking with them of past adventures they had shared and anticipating the ones to come in the future. Therefore, when he saw his houseman Turhan approaching through the beds of white-, pink-, and peach-colored tulips, obviously bringing news, he instinctively felt that whatever news it was could only be good.

It was a phone call from London. Adam took it in the seventeenth-century, triple-domed pavilion in the garden. When he replaced the receiver in its cradle, he sat quietly for a moment, thinking. Brindley Ribblesdale wanted to see him. He was concerned about several aspects of the Oujie fortune and was coming to Istanbul. He asked if he could impose on

Adam for some advice, and they made a tentative appointment to meet.

The telephone rang again just as Adam was returning to his guests. He sat down on the low cushions and picked up the telephone, assuming it was one of the servants ringing from the house. It wasn't; it was Brindley again.

"I don't know why, Adam," Brindley said in an embarrassed tone of voice. "But I think you should know that Mirella Wingfield is in Istanbul. She is there as the guest of a man called Rashid Lala Mustafa."

Brindley had put down the receiver quickly after that last clipped message. Adam smiled at the phone. What an out-of-character thing for Brindley to do, Adam thought. Yet he had heard the relief in the man's voice and knew Brindley had felt better for giving him that message.

18

Rashid, Mirella, and half a dozen of Rashid's friends were replete with food and drink. They were quiet, lulled by *kef*. The men smoked it in nargilehs, and the women smoked it in cigarettes, only because it was unseemly according to custom for them to smoke a water pipe in public. The kef induced a state of voluptuous nothingness and was the perfect Oriental retreat from reality. Timelessness was theirs, they drifted in dreams that carried them far away from the people and noise of the busy restaurant.

Rashid bent forward and whispered in Mirella's ear, "Oda-Lala." Then he turned to the woman on the other side of him and repeated the words. Mirella saw the young Circassian beauty perk up, bend forward, and pass on the word.

"Oda-Lala."

The whispered name went through the party and revived them. Mirella knew that Oda-Lala meant "master of the chamber" but had no idea what else it might mean. Before she realized what was happening they were all whisked away in cars that took them as close to their destinaton in the Kapali Carsi, the Covered Bazaar, as possible. There the party left the cars and was met by several men who discreetly surrounded and led them on foot deep into the bazaar that was a city in itself. Faud and Daoud stayed conspicuously close to Mirella and Rashid.

There were hundreds of shops along the apparently endless twists and turns of the narrow streets they passed by. Some still were filled wth people; others were quiet, dark, and deserted. They passed teahouses and stalls, scores of cafés, ateliers, a bank, a police station, a tomb, even an information center for lost tourists, closed of course for the night. The streets still carried names of the guilds that had been located there over the centuries: the Street of the Turban Makers, the Street of the Sandal Makers.

Mirella felt as if she were floating through the bazaar, sorry that so much of the Oriental atmosphere had vanished. She was heartened when they came to the Old Bedesten, the five-century-old domed hall at its very center. The great antiquity of the market suddenly became a reality. This part of the market was securely locked and guarded every evening, as it had always been for five hundred years, because it was here that the most interesting and valuable objects in the bazaar were sold. Rashid's party stopped only for a minute while one of the men who had met them unlocked the gate and hurried them through an entrance into the hall.

A woman in their party approached Mirella as she had when they left the restaurant and again in the car, and offered her yet another delectable slim wafer that melted on Mirella's tongue. It heightened her awareness almost instantaneously—she felt as if she were floating on her way with the others.

By the time they reached the small dark alley, and were let into and through the deserted antique shop called Oda-Lala, Mirella knew herself to be floating in a dreamy world far from reality. One of the swarthy men leading them swung open a secret door, which was faced with a marble wall and a fountain spurting water from a lion's mouth into a large marble basin in the shape of a half shell. As one by one they slipped through the door, Mirella knew that the forbidden was upon her. The night Rashid had promised her was here.

Completely under the influence of drugs and aphrodisiacs, she could fathom only the moment, only the experience, only the here and the now. Rashid put his hand out to help her down two stairs and then through a long, dimly lit corridor. She saw a pair of doors open at the far end and watched the others disappear through a pool of light. When it was her turn Rashid stood next to her and together they looked into a huge, high, covered courtyard, surrounded by two stories of twenty-foot-wide archways, hung with silver or gold gauze curtains as fine as spiders' webs. They drifted with the movement of the air, undulating like the naked and nearly naked women roaming through the courtyard, or rising from the pool and gliding up the marble steps in its center.

Rashid slowly raised the curtain; the scene was like a great Ingres painting come to life. Mirella had never seen anything, never dreamed of anything, so beautiful. Delectable odalisques lay naked, some with just a ravishing turban of gold brocade wrapped around their heads, one nude except for her waist-length auburn hair entwined with tiny diamonds; another, a six-foot-tall black-black Ethiopian, with hair smoothly twisted up onto her head, wore nothing but a thick white four-inch-wide ivory bracelet on her upper left arm and another on her right ankle, and moved like a panther. A shimmeringly beautiful blonde girl who looked like Botticelli's Venus, all her pubic hair removed, danced slowly on her toes with a sheer white silk shawl for a partner. Occasionally she tossed it into the air, and it floated above her, teasing her like a lover.

Mirella saw a woman, no longer young, but more beautiful than any she had ever seen. Her golden red hair, cream-colored skin, and clever and seductive green eyes were captivating. Hers was a sensuously alluring face with a proud, patrician nose and a bone structure such as sculptors idolize. Her long, slender neck tapered into a wide-shouldered, tall, lean body dominated by extremely large, firm breasts. She had a narrow waist, and was slim-hipped from the front, and carried full and voluptuously round, tight buttocks. She was naked, with henna-dyed arabesque designs tattooed on her nipples and the halo around them, and on her voluptuous mound where her pubic hair should have been.

Wound around her neck was a long silk chiffon scarf embroidered in gold and studded with emeralds, tied to one side and draped to below her knees. She was opposite Mirella and Rashid in the enclosed courtyard.

Mirella looked at Rashid, who smiled at her.

"She is Humayun," he said. "And this is only the courtyard. There are things to see behind each of those curtains, one more erotic performance after another. The most deliciously depraved acts of passion merging into the most gentle and refined lovemaking possible. And all for us."

While he was talking she could only glimpse the proud,

copper-haired odalisque walking toward them. She tried not to see her, distracted herself with other sights: two handsome, naked, blond-haired men, or two Arab men lying on white marble chaises at the edge of the pool bidding for a girl who appeared no more than twelve years old. She was a lovely child who displayed herself for them, danced and laughed, and finally was bought by one of the men, who handed over a wad of bank notes to her former owner. The reality of what Mirella saw kept slipping in and out of her mind. She was too drugged to really grasp it. Slaves. It wasn't possible . . . or was it?

She was about to ask Rashid when the copper-haired woman reached them. Mirella could actually feel a sexual excitement coming off Rashid. She watched both him and the woman closely as the woman went down on one knee, picked up his hand, and kissed it, saying only one word, "Master."

Rashid watched Mirella's expression as the woman, Humayun, rose and stepped back, waiting for Rashid's bidding. He ignored her and took Mirella by the arm, ushering her to one of the empty chaises under a huge papyrus in full bloom. He took off his jacket and helped Mirella out of hers. Two naked young men brought champagne, opened it, and poured some for them. Mirella and Rashid had not spoken since the odalisque had approached them. They kept looking into each other's eyes and a tension both sexual and extremely emotional continued building up between them.

Mirella was sexually excited, desperately wanting his lust. The thrill he felt at this prospect and at the slow degradation of her that must follow before he abandoned her convulsed him with a sadistic shudder.

Their eyes met, and something broke. Not in Mirella, but in Rashid. It was suddenly impossible. He couldn't do it. He could not subject her to the despotic depths of the dark side of his nature. He dropped the curtain and the scene continued as if under a soft lens. He took Mirella by the arm, called for her jacket as he walked her through the *hamam* again, past the lovely ladies languishing among cushions on marble chaises. At the curtain where they had entered the courtyard he sent an attendant through the dark passage to bring Fuad and Daoud to him. He helped Mirella on with her jacket, and took her in his arms and kissed her.

"I'm sending you home with Daoud and Fuad," he said.

"I'll see you there later, Mirella. Don't wait up for me. Get some sleep."

She was confused. She was still in his arms, and, from the way he kissed her and caressed her breasts, slipped his hands under her dress and stroked her bottom, she knew he still wanted her. She couldn't seem to concentrate on anything. She shook her head, trying to clear her mind. Rashid was sending her home. That was all right. Yet it wasn't all right. She wanted to stay, to be part of the erotic scene, but she wasn't unhappy about going. That was the kef speaking, the orientalist's fatalism speaking, and that was acceptable. She wanted to be ravaged by Rashid, to swoon in a pool of their orgasms. That was the effect of the aphrodisiacs pressed into paper-thin wafers that had melted on her tongue. But she was being sent home. The kef spoke again and told her that was all right too.

Rashid slipped a thin gold chain over her head with a golden key hanging from it.

"Mirella, listen to me," he said. "I want you to have the key to your collier. I want you to have the collier without the invisible leash attached to it. Mirella, the pearls are a gift. A person cannot be a slave unless he agrees to be. You don't want to be a sexual slave. Your body may, but your heart says no, at least for me it does. I saw that in your eyes, and I don't want to do to you what I would have to do to make you one. I'll see you at home later."

Mirella was suddenly exhausted; she slumped against his chest, and floated in and out of what was happening. She saw his face when he picked her up in his arms and handed her into Daoud's, ordering him to guard her with his life and to carry her to the car because she was exhausted, to put her in his room and have the maid undress and put her to bed.

"I think something important has happened—is that right?" she asked, slurring her words as she drifted into half sleep.

"It certainly has."

For the next twenty-four hours Mirella never quite understood what had happened between Rashid and herself at Oda-Lala's. She drifted in a world somewhere between fantasy and reality. In her waking moments while being carried by Daoud through the back streets of the Covered Bazaar, she felt fragile and childlike.

Was it a dream or was it real when two women bathed her with sponges of soothing, warm, scented water, and helped her into a nightgown, brushed her hair and dressed it with small white jasmine blossoms? Or when she slipped between the pearl-colored silk sheets, and was cradled in the arms of a young woman who held a goblet to her lips while she drank? The kef and the wafers were doing their work. She was sensitive and vulnerable in the extreme, filled with passion and lust at one moment, then lulled and made dead to the world and to her own senses by the warm potion she drank that provided her the luxury of deep sleep.

She opened her arms and no one was there. Through a veil of faint light she imagined she saw, in the distance, a huge, fierce-looking man with a scar down the side of his face, standing, legs far apart, arms folded across his chest, with his back against the door, and she drifted away again. The next time she opened her arms, Rashid was there. Whether in wakefulness or in sleeplessness, in fantasy or in dreams, when she saw his face, touched his skin, and was enveloped by his scent all her senses cried out for him, and her need was to be ravaged, satisfied. She saw herself, as in some hazy dream, pull him down on top of her, and from that point on reality, fantasy, dreams, desires, and needs, all were quenched.

Mirella opened her eyes. She stretched her legs against the smooth silk, and it felt good. She closed them, wanting to dive back down into sleep, but quickly opened them again and sat up instead, because she couldn't remember where she was. For a moment the room looked unfamiliar to her, then suddenly it all came back. She was in Rashid's room in Istanbul. She slumped back on the pillows and tried to put together the fragmented vision of the night before. It wasn't easy.

Some of the memories of her first night in Istanbul filled her with an excitement about the city. She would never forget her first sunset there, her realization of a mutual unconsummated love she and Adam Corey had for each other. Other fragments of the night deeply shocked her. But she had to admit to herself that she would not have missed going to Oda-Lala's for anything. It was an experience she would carry with her all her life. She could understand why men wanted, even needed, Oda-Lala's. They exercised their fantasies there. Mirella was not sure she didn't envy those men; men free enough—or was it sexually deviate and self-indulgent enough?—to climb out of themselves and into their erotic needs. And the women . . . Mirella had almost forgotten about the women. Not the ones who were sexual slaves but the female counterparts of Rashid and the other men who were sated at Oda-Lala's.

Another fragment of the evening came to Mirella. She had wanted to stay with Rashid at Oda-Lala's, and go sexually as far as she could allow herself. Why hadn't she? She put her hand to her neck: her collier was gone. She stroked her neck, and then it all came rushing back—how he had sent her home, because she would never be his slave, and had made her a gift of the necklace. How she had taken the key from her neck and unlocked the necklace. Mirella looked at the side table next to the bed. Her pearl collar was there, just where she had put it the night before. She picked it up and looked at it, played with the bumblebee clasp, and realized that the sexual game she and Rashid had been trifling with until now was over between them.

Something new had begun for them when he gave her the key to the necklace. Was it a new game or was it something else? She had no idea. She thought they had confirmed the sexual ardor they felt for each other in Rashid's bed after he had returned from Oda-Lala's. This was only a gut feeling because, deliberately drugged and overstimulated for sex by Rashid as she had been, she couldn't be sure of anything that had happened to her after he had sent her home.

She lowered the sheet covering her breasts and saw faint bruises; she touched her nipples and realized she was not sore but tender all over, wherever he had made love to her. The soreness brought back memories of being sodomized by him while being caressed by a beautiful woman, of being kissed and fondled by him while he and another man made love to her, and all three came at the same time, in orgasms that seemed to go on forever. If Mirella's mind was unclear about the hours of ecstasy Rashid had arranged for them, her body knew them to be real. Her feeling of joy, and well-being, her enthusiasm for the new day, told her so.

Mirella was in the bath soaking the remnants of ravishment from her body when she looked up and saw Rashid leaning against the doorjamb. Her heart skipped a beat and she asked, "How long have you been there?"

"Oh, about five minutes." He went to her, tilted her chin up, kissed her on the lips, and gave her a little tap on the end of her nose, saying, "Good morning," and returned to the door that led to the bedroom and leaned against the jamb again.

"Hello," said Mirella, thinking how amazing life can be, that you could unexpectedly meet a stranger who swept you off your feet and into another world, brought gifts of pleasure after pleasure and adorned you with priceless ornaments; that you could find him devilishly attractive and irresistible, and yet not be in love with him. She smiled at her handsome lover who looked relaxed and happy.

"How do you feel this morning?"

"I think very much like you, relaxed and happy, looking forward to a new day."

"Good," said Rashid. "I'll go and ask the maid to bring your breakfast. You must be famished, having had nothing but a few chocolates to eat since dinner the night before last."

As he started to turn away, Mirella casually said, while raising a leg up out of the soapy water and lazily washing it with a large sponge, "You mean last night, Rashid. And yes, I'm ravenous."

He turned back to her and, with a wicked twinkle in his eye, he said, "No, I don't, Mirella dear. I said what I meant. You haven't left my bed since Faud and Daoud brought you home the night before last." Then he left her and called for her breakfast.

Mirella was still puzzled about that when he returned and took a bath sheet and shook it out, held it for her, and watched her as she stood up and rinsed the soap from her body. She stepped out of the tub and let him wrap her in it and tug her over to the chaise where he sat down, unwrapped her, and dried her off. She kissed the top of his head and realized there was affection between them that had not been there before. He made her place one foot up on the chaise and dried her feet, with infinitely gentle care, drying even between her toes. Then quite suddenly he stopped and said, "Come, we have to hurry." He held her robe open for her.

Over breakfast served on the balcony off his bedroom, he told Mirella he wanted to take her with him to a dealer from whom he had purchased many antiquities found in Turkey. The man had Greek and Roman pieces of museum quality that he was offering to Rashid, before anyone else. He explained to Mirella that all export of Turkish antiquities was illegal without a permit, and permits were rarely given. Since whatever Rashid rejected ended, eventually, in some famous

Western museum or private collection somewhere, it was not only illegal but a dangerous business. He would therefore take her with him and show her an Aladdin's cave of treasures, but she would have to reveal to no one what she had seen.

Mirella assured Rashid she could be silent, as silent as the dead, when she wanted to be, and he had nothing to worry about. It was a bright and sunny day. She stretched, feeling the warmth in her bones, and gave a contented sigh.

He was staring at her as he smiled and with a serious note in his voice said, "You do have a way sometimes of talking in graphic images, Mirella. Often too graphic. Silent will do, but I never want to think of you as 'silent as the dead.'"

"How *do* you want to think of me, Rashid?" She had no idea what made her ask so leading a question.

"That's a question far too complex to go into over breakfast, for many reasons, not the least of which is, I don't want you to know."

He laughed, and had a twinkle in his eye and a tease in his voice when he continued. "Will it suffice to tell you that one of the ways I will always think of you is sexually, and especially as you were here in bed with me for the last twenty-four hours? Oh yes, to recall you lost in sexual licentiousness will be my favorite way of thinking of you."

Mirella had the grace to blush and he laughed at her again, reached across the table, and opened the top of her robe. Mirella poured herself another cup of coffee and said, "I will always think of you in that way too. Maybe that's why I can't understand why you sent me away from you at Oda-Lala's."

"But you *can* understand why I released you from our game of 'let's pretend you are my sexual slave and I am your master'?"

"Yes, I can. It was because it *was* a game. That was the reason, wasn't it?"

"Precisely. Now surely you can figure out the rest from that?"

Mirella took another sip of her coffee and then stood up, adjusted her robe, and walked to the balcony rail. She looked out on the lovely garden blooming with spring flowers—tulips, hyacinths, daffodils by the thousands, wild primroses, and crocuses. The bouquet filled the air with spring. She turned back to look at Rashid and then went to him.

He scraped his chair back on the marble floor of the balcony and patted his thigh. Mirella sat down on his lap, put an arm around his shoulder, and leaned her head on it.

"Sexual slavery is no game for you, is it? It's the real thing, a part of your life you enjoy to the full. When you realized it was only a short-lived game for me, and nothing more, you released me. I can understand that. But you knew I was not only ready but desperately wanting to go through the night with you at Oda-Lala's. Instead, you sent me away. Would the sex I might have had at Oda's have been somehow more degrading in your eyes than what we've shared together here? Is that why you sent me home? It was because you were afraid to let me see to what lengths you will go in order to satisfy your lust, wasn't it? You were afraid to take me into your hell, because of what you might do to me, what might happen afterward. That's it, isn't it?"

Rashid opened Mirella's robe again. He stroked her body lovingly, he kissed her tenderly on the cheek and slipped his hand between her legs, separated her outer vaginal lips, played with the tender soft flesh between his fingers.

"For a woman with all the answers you certainly do have a great many questions. Leave things the way they are for the moment, Mirella. You are treading on dangerous ground when you talk to me about my deepest feelings and desires. If you go on, you could be made to pay dearly for what you learn. Is it not enough for you that we are having a thrilling erotic affair?"

They looked deeply into each other's eyes, and she felt herself give way—whether from what she saw or from his caressing fingers, all of which were now pushed high inside her vagina, fondling her in search of a fresh orgasm. Which it might be scarcely troubled her.

"Yes, Rashid," she answered as he saw the all-consuming passion appear in her eyes and her body yield even further into his hands.

"More than enough."

He bent his head down to her lips and kissed her tenderly first, and then their mouths opened and they kissed with a greater passion and understanding than they ever had before.

19

"**Y**ou do me proud, you know, you look lovely," Rashid said. "You'll be the most beautiful and talked-about woman at Princess Eirene's picnic."

Rashid had been pacing back and forth impatiently at the side of his waiting car, the old Chevrolet. She knew that, because she had seen him from her bedroom window while she had been dressing.

He raised her hand and kissed it, smiling his approval as he stroked her cheek. His obvious admiration for the way she looked delighted her. Mirella was not stupid: she knew very well that part of the excitement of being with Rashid was that he could be as generous and tender as he was passionate and violent.

Ever since she met Rashid he had always managed to give her infinite pleasure by the sheer power of his will to do so in the way *he* chose. Mirella was constantly surprised that he could hold her so completely by his charisma. But he could. He blocked out the real world she was used to. Yet no matter how far he took her into his world, there remained something unreal about it. It was his reality not hers, and they never really shared it. She was always his guest. It didn't seem to matter, because she was enjoying every minute of her excursion.

That was why it made her so happy that he approved of the way she looked. She wanted to please him. It was one of the small ways in which she could say thank you for so many things: releasing the ultimate woman within her, seducing her to break free of her bonds, teaching her that luxury and being carefree were not crimes. Most of all he had taught her that she could have a vibrant sexual affair with a man, yet not *have* to be in love with him. Her Ottoman lover was a decadent but wonderful teacher, and her puritanical New England background had a great deal to answer for.

When he had told her that after their visit to the dealer of antiquities they were going to a huge, sumptuous picnic on the hills above Bosporus, she had seen yet another enchanting day awaiting her.

211

The picnic, he had explained, was an annual affair given by a Romanian princess on the anniversary of her husband's death. It was the first and one of the grandest parties of the season in Istanbul. He would therefore help her to choose a costume for it. She had surprised them both by not allowing him to. Yet she had not disappointed him.

They traveled in convoy as usual to the dealer's cave of unearthed treasures. There Mirella had seen wonders of art so powerful and rich in perfection they left both Rashid and Mirella speechless, long after he had made his purchases and they were in the car and on the way to the picnic.

The car, after leaving the ugly, dusty, poor, and depressing section of the city where the dealer hid himself and his treasures, wound its way down through green hills and drove through a small picturesque village nestling in one of the bays that frequently indent the shores of the Bosporus. They walked to the quay and boarded a handsome, long and sleek black yacht, whose shining brass and teakwood displayed the infinite care that had been bestowed on her for the last seventy-five years.

Once aboard they pushed off before Mirella and Rashid could even get to the stern, where a table and lounge chairs were arranged for them. Half the village was out to wave them off and Mirella and Rashid stood together and waved back. He turned to her and put his arm around her shoulder. They watched the crew, dressed in white turtleneck sweaters, white trousers and shoes, and black felt vests elaborately embroidered in rust silk, rush around the deck, raising sails and tossing over the sides boughs of spring flowers attached to brass rings so that they hung in great swags all along the hull of the boat.

There was hardly any wind but what there was picked up and filled the rust-colored sails. The sound of them flapping and wheezing while being stretched taut was a music Mirella had been brought up with, off the shores of Massachussetts. It was always, for her, one of the most evocative sounds in the world.

Eight men appeared carrying brass poles wound with ropes of wisteria, and a thick canopy made with mimosa that they carefully erected at the stern above the lounge chairs. The scent was a hymn to the senses.

"I wish you could see the surprise on your face. I think that must be one of the many reasons I like doing things for you," he said. "But, to be fair, I must tell you that we do this every year for the princess's party. The flowers are never the same and are always arranged differently, but we always try and make the *Aziz* splendiferous for the event. It's our version in the eighties of how our families dressed their barks and boats for a special occasion. In the days of our grandmothers and great-grandmothers and all our ancestors before them, they had long and lovely boats with many rowers dressed in elaborate costumes of the time, and the boat itself was completely draped in silk and embroidered in gold and silver. The draperies hung over the sides and into the water."

"How fabulous," Mirella said.

"I can remember stories even more fabulous. My grand-father told of your great-grandmother, the Kadin Roxelana, who, when she traveled on the Bosporus, used a cloth of royal blue embroidered in pure silver and sewn with diamonds on her boat. The edge of the cloth that was under water had silver chains, at the end of which dangled exquisitely made silver articulated fish with diamond eyes. She was rowed by twenty men in silver livery, and when the sun shone upon her boat it was as if she were carried by a shoal of fish to her master, because the sun pinpointed the hundreds of glittering fish just below the water gliding with her up the Bosporus.

"My grandfather saw her only once, when he was a young boy. His father, my great-grandfather, was a favorite caliph of the sultan. The sultan was besotted with Roxelana, so much so, that he actually bestowed the name Roxelana on her, after the wife of Suleiman the Magnificent, who reigned in the mid fifteen hundreds when the Ottoman Empire reached the peak of its greatness.

"Her arrival in the boat was the most splendid sight he had ever seen, until she disembarked and walked the length of the carpets on the quay and prostrated herself before the sultan. When she was ordered to rise, she did and sat on a low seat at his feet. It was then he was able to savor this vision dressed all in white, silver, and diamonds. He was so impressed by her beauty and her figure, her dress, and above all her face—and those eyes, looking out above the transparent white silk veil edged by diamonds covering the lower part of her face. For his entire life all beauty was measured by what he saw in her."

That was the first time Rashid had mentioned her family to Mirella since their first meeting at Claridge's, and it served to remind her how little she still knew and understood about her remarkable and exotic relations. She realized that she had somehow lost track of time and the work connected with her estate, and she made a mental note to call Brindley as soon as possible, and to continue reading the journal she had brought with her.

Rashid swept all such thoughts from her mind, though, when he took her by the arm and led her to a chair under the flowering canopy.

"Everyone who can arrives by boat at the *déjeuner sur l'herbe*," he said. "Afterward we make a pilgrimage to Eyup. We sail from the princess's yali on the Bosporus under the Galata Bridge, where we stood the night before last, and then up the Golden Horn to Eyup. Do you know about Eyup?"

"Only that it's one of the most sacred places of pilgrimage in the Moslem world."

"Quite right," Rashid said. "It is thought to be the burial place of the Prophet Muhammad's standard-bearer Eyup Ensari. Pierre Loti, the French novelist, a devoted Turkophile, used to sit in the teahouse at the top of the hill above the cemetery to gaze on his beloved Constantinople, as it was called in his day." Rashid paused, then added, "The picnic goes on all afternoon until midnight, with people coming and going in their boats on the pilgrimage to Eyup all during the day. I, like Loti, adore the view from Eyup at sunset, so I and my guests always make our yearly pilgrimage at that time, when it is particularly romantic. The waters of the Golden Horn from that vantage point are tinted the constantly changing pastel colors of twilight. The distant view is wondrous—a thousand pious needles piercing the sky among a tangle of hills and houses, mosques and domes."

"You obviously like this day very much, don't you, Rashid?"

"Yes, very much. It's a day of resurrection, new beginnings, meeting old friends, the best day of spring, the day I pray over the bones of a saint, and confirm to my lord Muhammad my love for Islam. I am always profoundly touched, as I am sure you will be, by a visit to Eyup.

"Wait until you see the two courtyards of the mosque with its gnarled old plane trees, its innumerable resident lame storks mingling with devout pilgrims, and peddlers hawking religious trinkets. It is never less than awe-inspiring to see the *turbe* of a saint in the inner courtyard. I will challenge you to tell me that you are not deeply moved, as in no other way before, by the walk up the hills above the shrine and through the turbaned tombstones and cypresses of the great cemetery of Eyup.

"We'll have tea, and smoke the best Lebanese Gold and float with our dreams over Eyup. And then we can do one of two things: sail or drive back to Eirene's, where the hills above her house will be lit with torches and lanterns, and we can dance, or dine in kiosks of velvet or under the stars; or we can go home. The Rolls and my driver will be in Eyup waiting for us. Shall we wait to see how we feel?"

"Yes, do let's wait and act on the feeling of the moment," said Mirella, puzzled why money should offer so many more choices in life. But she knew now, after these days with Rashid, that it did. Why had she taken so long to accept that fact? Maxim had often told her money was nothing more than a fact of life, but an important one only in as much as it had to be dealt with in the proper manner.

One of the crew arrived with a tray: a double martini on it for Mirella and an old-fashioned for Rashid. They sat under the mimosa drinking and eating small pieces of octopus grilled over an open charcoal fire in a brazier, watched over by one of the crew.

"Well, the Greeks did have some good ideas," Rashid said. He speared a morsel of the delicacy with a long slim wooden skewer and fed it to her. Their near-empty glasses were exchanged for fresh drinks, and Mirella's attention was taken up completely by the villages and harbors lined with waving people. The weather-beaten wooden mansions all looked deserted behind closed shutters, until you were upon them and saw through the odd open window that they were teeming with life.

Her attention was drawn by the haunting sound of the horn of a cabin cruiser, whose hull was draped in red felt profusely dotted with the emblem of Turkey—the crescent and the star, embroidered in gold thread. It pulled up level with the *Aziz*. Rashid stood up and waved to the dozen or so people who called to him. A megaphone was held up by someone on a Turkish kayik skimming across the water toward them. The flat and wide craft tapered inward at both ends, and the gunwale almost formed a half-moon. It was painted an ocher color and manned by a crew dressed in black and ocher, and was filled with masses of silver-foil balloons, one of which would occasionally break loose and fly up into the air. From the bow they shouted their greetings to the *Aziz*.

"The man with the megaphone is an old childhood friend, and that kayik is the best boat of its kind in Turkey. The three women with him are his wife and his two mistresses. You will like them. They are very sweet but a little too intent on being trendy."

Rashid barked orders to his captain to go all out and beat the other boats to the party. When the captain reminded him that the vessel was dressed for the party and not for racing, the captain was told not to be ridiculous. And then before Mirella knew it they had made their sprint, and had brilliantly maneuvered past all the river traffic before them and won.

The princess's yali was a tall, two-story-high, wooden mansion painted an oxblood red that was faded and bleached pink in parts from the sun and the salt air. It looked like a decadent fantasy hideaway made on a grand scale but with a low budget, which in fact was hardly the case. It was long and rambled along the water's edge, with a number of interesting architectural features—windows of pierced wood in the harem quarters, bays of glass windowpanes, miniature square towers. Built on a limestone base over stone arches where water ran through and boats bobbed up and down in the wash, the yali made Mirella think they were in the Venice of the East.

The mansion had a vast garden that meandered lazily on either side of the house and behind it to the banks of the canals of fresh sweet water flowing past into the Bosporus. Far to the back of the mansion the garden gave way to well-wooded, rich green hills punctuated by the high needle-shaped dark cypresses, terebinths, and umbrella pines rising in tiers high above the house.

The woods were alive with color. The red-pink of the flowering Judas trees mingled with the red and white flowering candles of the huge chestnut trees, and the delicate mauve flowers of the old twisted and gnarled wisterias. From the water it looked like a doll house set in a fairy-tale garden. The sun sparkling on the water flowed like rivers of silver sequins around three sides of the palace and only added to its fantasy appearance. It seemed a poor man's castle, languishing on its own in a cultivated Garden of Eden.

Rashid's two-hundred-and-fifty-foot-long, three-masted schooner sailed right up to Princess Eirene's quay, dodging the many vessels of all shapes and sizes that were moored in front of the yalis, beating across the length of the entire yalis frontage one way and back the other. She came in all standing and didn't drop her sails until, to the onlookers, it was dangerously late. Mirella, an excellent sailor herself, let out a sigh of relief. They had come in so fast, and had cut so fine the moment to drop sail, that she had already seen in her mind's eye their crash into the stone wall.

Rashid found the whole thing exhilarating, and very amusing. He picked from her hair some of the mimosa blossoms that had broken from the canopy, and laughed.

"You should know by now I always like sailing on the edge of danger," he said. "You should also know by now that you will always be safe with me. Now, you had better fix your hair, and make ready for your debut among Istanbul's elite."

He heard someone call his name and he turned his attention to the hills above the house. He waved and smiled at friends walking along the terraces, climbing up the hills, standing in groups, sitting under purple and gold silk umbrellas shading their tables and chairs, and dancing and dining in a series of pretty domed and pinnacled gazebos dotting the flowering wood. The sound of music drifted down from the musicians roaming the hills and mingled with the orchestra playing in the garden near the house.

Rashid put his fingers through Mirella's hair, like a comb, and then removed the large white silk shawl wrapped around her and draped across her neck and over one shoulder.

His delight at what he saw shone in his eyes. She had put on her pearl collier.

"Thank you for that," he said, touching the pearls. "I was rather hoping you would wear these for me, because you chose to do so."

Mirella was also wearing the ropes of priceless pearls he had given her. Her white silk Christian Dior dress had long tight sleeves that puffed up on the edge of her shoulders and then plunged down in a sharp straight line, and it was cut straight across the breasts to form a low square neckline. It bared her entire chest to a hairline below the swelling of her breasts. To one side, at her waist, she had pinned the diamond sunburst he had given her. It set off the brilliant bias cut of the dress and the perfection of the skirt that moved seductively with every step she took.

It had been a wise selection because the effect was elegant

and quite simple with the shawl on. It had been just fine at the antique dealer's, and would be perfect for a pilgrimage, because she would be well covered, offending no one by her dress. Now, here at the party, without the shawl, she was all that Rashid wanted her to be—dazzlingly sexy, beautiful, elegant.

News of her appearance with him, and who she was, would sweep through the party like a wildfire in the wind, but Rashid had no anxieties about that because he had her well protected against anyone approaching her with more than an introduction in mind. She knew only about Fuad and Daoud, and was under the impression that they were there for him. She still had no idea that every person she had met so far in Istanbul had been chosen to help keep her isolated from anyone interested in exploiting her new and powerful position in international money circles. Rashid had brought her to this party not only because he would never have missed it, but also because at this point it was important that certain of his associates see he had her well in hand, well under his control. It would pacify them and their anxieties over the fact that she had not yet signed the documents of sale to their conglomerate—something they were becoming increasingly nervous about.

"You look lovely. I remember when I bought that dress how much I thought it would suit you. It's the devil that's always right," he said teasingly. "Too bad you haven't a diamond chain to wear among your pearls. I should have thought of that."

"But I do," she said.

She reached into her handbag and withdrew the two diamond link necklaces with the Oujie seal cut into the huge emerald of the one and the ruby of the other. She held them in her hand for Rashid to see, and caught the look not only of utter surprise, but of something more—she thought it might be anger—before he covered it up with his sleek charm.

"Good God, you certainly do. How magnificent they are," said Rashid, as he offered to slip them over her head and arrange them among her pearls.

Mirella was not quite sure but she thought his hand trembled ever so slightly. When he had finished to his satisfaction and took her by the arm with just a little too tight a grip, she was sure he had seen before the necklaces left to Ottoline Sinan and Oberon Winslow-Ward by her great-grandmother, but thought it best not to probe.

She was quite right. Rashid had seen them in the portraits of his great-grandfather and his great-grandfather's two brothers, who were stripped of the necklaces by the sultan when they fell from grace, for plotting against the sultan's favorite, the fabulously wealthy and clever Jewess he later made the Kadin Roxelana, Mirella's great-grandmother. That act was the beginning of the decline of the power of the Lala Mustafas. It was now another reminder to Rashid that Mirella *must* accept their offer. Until the holdings he wanted from the Oujie estate were his, he would never rest.

He took Mirella by the arm and together they joined the party. They were accompanied as always by Fuad and Daoud, who kept their discreet distance but were readily available, and several of Rashid's friends who had been waiting for them when they disembarked. Mirella was surprised once she was at the party that there were only about two hundred guests in all. From the *Aziz* it had looked like much more. Since the party was spread over a hundred acres of house, woods, and gardens, one hardly felt the presence of so many people. It was more like going to a series of small intimate parties one after the other, and was utterly enchanting.

The guests were followed about by liveried servants offering a selection of Turkish delicacies to eat and every sort of drink, both alcoholic and nonalcoholic. There was a sit-down luncheon for all two hundred guests. They dined at a series of circular tables, linked together like large interlocking rings across the top of the hill overlooking the house and gardens below. The service was of sterling silver plates, the cutlery of vermeil, the goblets of Baccarat crystal, placed on specially made gold lace runners on the tabletops, with napkins of fine white linen edged in a two-inch lace border of gold and silver. In the hollow center of each ring of the tables were small trees of mimosa and azalea in full bloom, arranged on pedestals of different heights to look like huge flower arrangements. Fifty gypsy violinists and twenty balalaika players wandered around the tables playing soft Russian love songs, sometimes accompanying an old stout woman with a voice like a nightingale. The sheer beauty of the affair and the people was as dazzling as the setting itself.

Princess Eirene, when not strolling with her guests, received them in a luxurious kiosk on a small promontory midway up the hill. Rashid and Mirella found her there after lunch, surrounded by handsome courtiers of all ages. They ranged from ninety years down to twenty-five and danced attendance on her. She was guarded by two huge Sudanese eunuchs of considerable age, dressed in the white jackets and striped trousers of an authentic English butler, and with white and black fabric entwined and wound around their heads in magnificent turbans. The women who came to pay their respects were usually dismissed without their escorts as soon as the princess was bored with them, usually within ten minutes at the most.

Rashid whispered in Mirella's ear just as they were about to enter the kiosk, "She is reputed to be in her nineties, but no one really knows, and they say she still wears out three men a day in one way or another. You will adore her, she will adore you, and I adore you both."

Mirella had no idea what to expect of Princess Eirene. It therefore came as quite a surprise to her when the princess turned out to be a diminutive delicate-looking woman who might have been no more than forty-five years old. Only her hands gave her age away, though even those were remarkable for the lack of liver spots the old usually develop. She was dressed in a long, narrow white crêpe de chine skirt and a top of black and white candy-striped taffeta with long, tight-fitting sleeves and a simple oval neckline. The belt around her waist was of gold and inlaid solidly with square-cut pigeon-blood rubies. Her earrings matched the cabochon ruby she wore on a simple black ribbon high on her neck, only they were smaller than the sixty-five-carat gem. After her mother, Lili, the princess was the most accomplished flirt Mirella had ever met.

The twist of a wrist, the way she used her hands, the tilt of her head, and the language of her eyes were all lethal weapons of seduction in this woman's armory. Her lips and the many ways she used them to smile—not smile, almost smile—to pout, and even to laugh were instruments to torture her victims with. She teased with her eyelashes, the movements of her body, and a soft, sweet voice that was like a whisper on the wind. She commanded like a queen with a look, and dismissed her public with a word as soft as feather, and everyone loved her, wanted to be near her, and was afraid of her.

She sent everyone away soon after Rashid and Mirella arrived, except for her turbaned Sudanese. It was quite obvious to Mirella that the princess adored Rashid, and she was puzzled when she dismissed him after ten minutes by saying that she had a lovely surprise waiting for him in the music room of the house, and that she would take it upon herself to keep Mirella amused while he went to collect it. She made it quite clear that he was expected to return in an hour's time, and not before, explaining that by that time she would have learned all about Mirella's grandmother, her long-lost childhood friend, and how she had passed her last years. Rashid left reluctantly, and was further annoyed when he was told to take Daoud and Fuad along with him. He had little choice but to obey, but did leave the two bodyguards on duty just out of sight of the kiosk.

Once the two women were alone, an awkward silence fell between them in the kiosk. Princess Eirene rose from her chair and said, "I have the most charming wild English garden down the path from here. Come, let's walk there. It is especially lovely in bright sunshine and when it is very warm as it is today."

The two women walked down a neat and narrow path paved with bricks through a dense wood of pine trees, small wild tulips and daffodils in clumps beneath them, the two Sudanese walking fifty paces behind them. Mirella complimented her hostess on the enchanted world the princess had created for her guests, and the princess surprised Mirella by asking, "Why have you come to Turkey with Rashid?"

She stopped walking and looked into Mirella's face and waited for an answer.

"Are you in love with him, or merely sexually infatuated with him?"

The princess waited for her to answer. Mirella looked at her, and although she wanted to think the princess rude for posing the question, somehow she couldn't. Mirella had no idea how the princess had done it, but she had won Mirella into her confidence by her very presence. And still the princess waited for her answer. There was the slight tilt of the head, a knowing look in her eyes, and the soft, sweet curl of the lips, silently commanding an answer from Mirella, who at last said, "I came to Turkey because of Rashid, but I am not in love with Rashid nor am I sexually infatuated with him to the point of no return. But I only found that out the night before last."

"Ah, that must have been when you left Oda-Lala's."

The princess laughed when she saw the surprise in Mirella's face. It was a light, sweet laugh like that of a young girl.

"Would you have stayed had you been in love with Rashid, do you think?" asked the princess, as she resumed her walk, Mirella at her side.

"An interesting question, Princess," answered Mirella. "To be honest, yes, I would have. I am obviously a sexual adventuress or I would not be with Rashid in the first place. That I am quite sure you have guessed. It's to Rashid's credit, Princess, that he recognized I had to be sent home."

"He sent you home! I find that very intriguing. That does surprise me. But then, Rashid is clever, and always gets what he wants. That, my dear Mirella, means he knows you are not in love with him, and that could be dangerous. On the other hand, it could mean that he is falling in love with you, and that is potentially more dangerous. Are you in love with someone else?"

Mirella was about to curtail any further questions, but hesitated. She stopped and stood still. The princess stopped, too, and looked into Mirella's eyes.

"I am a very old lady, Mirella, I have spent a lifetime being loved and adored by men. I was a child of the harem and have learned the wily ways of love, seduction, passion, cruelty, the erotic, and what they entail. Love is the jewel of anyone's crown, and I could see in your eyes when we met, there is a bright jewel in the crown you wear. You need say nothing more. I understand more than you think. The intrigues of the heart are my specialty. Come, let's walk in my secret garden."

With that the princess took Mirella by the hand and together they moved down the path. At the end there were two huge yew hedges of topiary. A pair of birds with beaks touching sculpted from the yew formed the arched entrance to the English garden. They walked through it and down an arbor of climbing roses in full bud. Everywhere they looked there were wild spring flowers and tall grasses of every variety. It was a mass of delicate pinks and magentas, yellows and whites mingling with blues, purples, and lavenders, and dramatically accentuated with blood-red, papery wild poppies, among the tall, fragile yellowy and beige, pale soft green- and lime-colored grasses, growing on the slope of the hill.

They left the path and walked among the wild flowers. The princess separated some tall grass and carefully caught a large bright yellow butterfly in her cupped hands and showed it to Mirella. She watched the princess play with it and then release it to flutter away. The two women were an incredible sight—dressed in Christian Dior and Jean Patou dresses, and a million or so dollars worth of jewels, playing with a butterfly in a fragile field of wild flowers above the banks of the Bosporus. The childlike interlude was broken by the laughter of a man walking with a woman down the path.

Mirella's heart leaped, touched at once by a laugh she knew.

"Come," said the Princess Eirene. "Come and meet some of my guests."

Mirella heard scarcely a word that was said during the introductions. She found it difficult to take her eyes from the man. Her heart was glad. Yet again she felt that special warmth that only he had ever been able to kindle in her. All the days and nights, all the new and thrilling events that had happened to her were swept clean away.

When Adam Corey raised her hand and kissed it, Mirella closed her eyes for a split second to compose herself. When she opened them a smile of such bliss crossed her face that he gave the hand he still held an extra squeeze as if to say, "Thank you, my love."

She felt the princess take her arm and she forced herself to listen to what her hostess said.

"I should so like Mirella to see the remainder of my garden, Adam. Would you mind terribly escorting her through it? I am rather warm and just a little tired, and there is still a long day ahead of me. And why don't you, Carla, come and let me show you my favorite kiosk?"

The group had just parted when Princess Eirene turned back to Mirella and Adam, who had not moved. She looked up at the sky and said, "It is just possible we are going to have one of our sudden spring showers. If you should get caught, remember the tree house at the bottom of the garden, and shelter there. Adam, I expect you to bring Mirella back to me not a minute after five o'clock."

It was then that Mirella realized that Princess Eirene was indeed a woman who delighted in the intrigues of the heart. There was no question in her mind that her meeting with Adam had been arranged by the princess: hence the questions not from a disinterested gossip, as she had thought, but an interested friend of Adam Corey.

"How entirely lovely you are," he said, touching her hair, raising a lock of it to his lips.

He took her by the hand and they wandered through the

field of flowers and down the gentle slope. He stopped, pulled her to him, and she slipped her arms under his jacket and around his waist. His body scent affected her at once and she felt herself overwhelmed with love for him.

His voice was husky with emotion when he said, "I can hardly believe it's true that you're here. I am so happy to see you. You look exactly as I imagined you would when I dreamed of bringing you to Turkey and laying this land at your feet. All that inner beauty and passion I recognized in you the moment we met glows now. You have clearly set yourself free from whatever was restricting you from living your life to the full. I love you, and you are glorious. The most glorious of all women."

Then he gently put his lips to hers and kissed them. Her lips became his. It was as if everything she was, had ever been, or would ever be flowed from her into his being. He drew back and smiled at her, a smile full of love and adoration. Pure joy suffused his face. Adam took her by the hand and pulled her along, and they laughed like carefree young lovers.

The relief Mirella felt at Adam Corey's friendly feelings toward her after their disastrous encounters in New York was far more intense than she could have imagined. It only proved, yet again, how much this man meant to her.

They stood holding hands gazing across the Bosporus to the other shore.

"Look," he said, "that's Asia Minor. There are wondrous things there for us." Then they turned and looked at each other.

No words came. Slowly and ever so gently he gathered her in his arms, and placing a crooked finger under her chin, raised it up. Longingly, savoring every moment of her, he lowered his lips to hers and they kissed.

A warm rain fell softly from the cloudless sky, and, for a moment, their separateness dissolved and they became one. They parted and, still holding hands, looked up at the sky, and felt the spring shower on their faces. His desire to lay her down naked in the grass and make love to her under that soft warm rain was as strong as ever. But now was not the time, nor the place. He was consoled that at least they had come closer to it. He removed his jacket and held it over her head.

"Come on," he said. "The tree house."

It was only a matter of a minute, two at most, until they reached the wooden stairs winding up and around the huge old apple tree in full blossom. Just then the rain ceased. The sun was as bright as ever and the air exactly as it had been all day, very warm.

"I think it's a miracle," she said.

"I *know* you're a miracle. Come on, we have only a few minutes before we must get back to Eirene."

He pulled her by the hand behind him as he climbed the tree. It was a small, proper old-fashioned tree house with walls and a roof, a door and windows that opened. Adam could just about stand up straight in it without hitting his head. He pushed the windows all around the odd-shaped room open and showers of apple blossoms fell into the room. There was a fine old Turkish brazier, a low table in the center of the room with a bowl of fresh fruit, a glass decanter filled with peach juice and two glasses, and deep comfortable soft cushions on the floor, all along the walls.

Adam took Mirella in his arms and kissed her. This time love and tenderness turned into passion, their erotic feelings for each other surfacing again, as they had in New York. He pulled her down with him onto the kilim-covered cushions and held her in his arms. They could see nothing but apple blossoms thick on the branches of the tree. A gentle gust of wind blew some through the windows into the room.

"It's like hiding in the eye of a snowstorm," she said.

"Mirella, look at me. I think I know, but I have to ask: Are you in love with Rashid?"

"I have feelings for Rashid, but no, I'm not in love with him. I was completely captivated by his gaiety, his generosity, his charisma. I didn't think of love. Love never has or will come into my feelings for him."

Adam helped Mirella up. He plucked some blossoms from her hair and kissed her deeply with tender care as he caressed her. But he had to murmur, "We cannot be late. We must go. I'm sure you have guessed that Eirene arranged for us to have a few minutes alone together. I couldn't bear to meet you again casually with a group of strangers around us. I had to know that there is peace between us; and I had to know about you and Rashid. We'll work it out. I have never had doubts about that."

When they were back on the paved brick path leading to the kiosk where the princess awaited them, Adam looked at her and said, "I will wait for you to come to me, Mirella. Remember, the name of the house is the Peramabahçe Palace."

20

Mirella stood on the deck of the *Aziz* still filled with boundless joy at having met Adam Corey again. She felt humble, grateful that there was another chance for them. New beginnings. Just as Rashid had foretold, Princess Eirene's party and the excursion to Eyup were always occasions for new beginnings. Mirella could not help but marvel at the things happening to her. It was as if some mythical god had called across the heavens, "Look on this woman and give her everything she has missed in life, and give it in abundance."

She waved good-bye to those ashore, her gaze sweeping the slopes in search of Adam, but she couldn't find him. On board was a large party of people to whom Rashid had offered passage for the pilgrimage to Eyup, and he was busy playing host to them. Mirella was thankful for the few minutes she had to herself that gave her an opportunity to go over the events of the last hour.

She didn't think either Adam or herself had had the intention of deceiving Rashid, but they had, simply by doing nothing to dispel Rashid's assumption that they had been introduced to each other for the first time by Princess Eirene. It had come as somewhat of a surprise to Mirella that Rashid knew Adam. The two men had seemed quite pleased to see each other, and it was Rashid who had said to Mirella, "How nice you have met Adam, a countryman of yours, a patron to *my* country, and an old and very good friend of mine. We have been friendly enemies for years. On occasion, we womanize together and travel together."

"And," said Adam with a big smile on his face, "we are fierce opponents on the tennis and squash courts."

Together the two men were devastatingly attractive. The contrast in their looks, the unequivocal sexuality they emanated, and the open and seductive charm they displayed could have overpowered the strongest of women.

"And you, my dear, are wearing them like a pair of earrings," whispered the princess, who had been sitting next to Mirella.

The two women had smiled. The princess had continued aloud.

"Mirella, there you see two friends who respect one another as men, but dislike each other for their moral, political, and business differences. I find the friendship between the two an interesting one. In many ways they admire each other, but Adam detests the ruthless streak of evil Rashid displays on occasion; and Rashid hates the way Adam curbs Rashid's impulses and always appears so faultless. They have been trying to change each other for years. And I, Mirella, adore them both and am deeply attached to them for their very dissimilarity."

The two men had laughed, and each had picked up one of the princess's hands and kissed it. Mirella had been confused at first, then momentarily upset over their friendship. If Adam knew Rashid that well, then it was a reasonable assumption he was aware of the intense sexual relationship Rashid and she were having. Adam must have come to terms with that, because—he had made it quite clear—all that mattered to him was whether Mirella was in love with Rashid or not. Now that he had his answer, he expected her to come to him. She marveled at his calm trust in their love, which allowed him to wait securely for her to take the final step and go to him.

The *Aziz* left the princess's yali behind and a bevy of sailors began pulling the boughs of flowers into the boat and tying them in wreaths that they tossed over the side into the Bosporus. Mirella watched the wreaths float in a line one after the other behind the schooner. Rashid came up in back of her and put his arms around her waist. It gave her a start. He placed a kiss at the nape of her neck and pressed his body tight to hers, pinning her to the rail. They silently watched the rings of flowers drifting from the boat. Then Mirella said, putting her hands over his, "What a marvelous day. There are so many things to thank you for, I don't know where to begin."

"But you do thank me, as you did today, simply by rising to the occasion. To watch you enjoy everything we do together is all I need in the way of thanks."

He slipped his hands from under hers, cupped her breasts in them, and kissed her on the side of the neck where the warm breeze had blown her hair back. Her most pressing desire was to thank him for inadvertently giving her and Adam a chance to come together again. It was Adam who was very much on her mind, and yet, in spite of her mind and her heart, she felt her body reacting to Rashid's.

He moved his hands up onto her shoulders and then under her necklaces, and caressed her bare chest. He felt her relax against his body, and slipping the puffed sleeves from her shoulders, he kissed first one, then the other, and under the loosened silk of her bodice, he fondled her naked breasts.

Mirella closed her eyes and sighed. She leaned back even further against Rashid, aware of how difficult it was going to be to leave him. She had come to Turkey because she had stronger feelings for him than she expected or wanted, but she did not mistake strong feeling and gratitude for love.

She was concerned that something more was developing in their relationship when he sent her home from Oda-Lala's. It was almost as if a love was growing in each of them that neither wanted. Mirella knew she would have to leave him as soon as possible, but made up her mind that they would part as lovers who have run their course and remain the best of friends.

"Rashid, no, not here, one of the crew, one of your guests might see," she said.

He misunderstood the emotion in her voice for passion, and pressed his advantage. He laughed, and searched out her nipples, toyed with them, tweaked and teased them until they stood hard and erect, and placed his pointed tongue behind her ear and licked. He tickled the spot by blowing gently on it, then licked it again, his hands still busily caressing her breasts. He felt her body yield to him yet more. Surely it was she, not he, who rocked her pelvis almost imperceptibly against his trousers. Mirella seemed ensnared, yet again, as she always was when Rashid was anywhere near her. She felt again the impossibility of resisting him in spite of her love for Adam and her fears of the eyes that might detect them.

"That's the first time you have ever said no to me, and we both know you don't mean it. The last of the ship's sails have just been unfurled and hoisted, the crew is busy. All they can see is that we are standing one behind the other watching the wreaths trail behind us, my greeting to the god Poseidon."

She tried to distract him. "You're such a romantic. Even your gestures to the gods are poetic and beautiful ones. What other man would think nowadays to appease Poseidon, the Earth-Shaker, with spring flowers cast upon the waters? And what of the canopy of mimosa?"

"They're just taking that down and folding it. We'll bring that to the turbe of the saint and lay it there."

He pushed against her and she could feel through the thin silk of her dress the bulge in his trousers press against the furrow dividing the cheeks of her bottom. He stretched her nipples between his fingers and whispered in her ear, "Feel that. I want to take you, here at the boat rail, in the middle of the Bosporus, while the boat is in full sail, and with all the crew at work around us. They will not see us. But if they do, I find it thrilling. Admit to me, it would delight you to be fucked by me, now, while the wind takes us across the water."

Rashid bent his knees slightly and tucked them under her bottom, wanting her to take in the swell of his penis nestling between her cheeks. He removed an earring from her ear and kissed her earlobe, licked and sucked on it, while pinching the elongated nipple of the breast held still in his other hand. How could she not yield? Passion was in her moan, her whimpered surrender. Her responses to his sensual demands were his sexual feedback. She excited him further by the small circular pelvic movement she added to her rocking back and forth against him, and they were lost in their sexual enthrallment with each other.

"I've got you like a bitch in heat now, haven't I, Mirella? If I didn't have guests below, I would take you now myself and then have my crew fuck you one after the other, in this position, while we sail to Eyup. You would be the envy of every man and woman watching from the shores of two continents, Europe and Asia. Fifty anonymous cocks beating into you, their come streaming down your legs onto that polished deck."

He felt her movements quicken and he kissed her gently on the ear. He had her now, as he always had her, by the power of his looks, his charm, his erotic being, and her sexual freedom and fantasies, and he knew it.

"If you do just as you are told," he said, "no one will see. Trust me? Tell me you want me to fuck you. You trust me?" he asked again as she felt his hand easing down the zipper of his trousers.

"I trust you," she said with some fear and a great deal of urgency.

Rashid placed sensuous kisses on her neck as he released her breasts. He adjusted her sleeves back on to her shoulders, and placed one hand on her waist, while pushing her legs further apart with his knees. He slipped the other hand under her dress and between her legs. She had come and was warm and wet. She aroused him to such a passion that he took her earlobe into his mouth, bit into it, and whispered sexual obscenities into her ear, as much to drive himself wild as her.

"Please, please, Rashid," was all she could manage to say.

He knew from other experiences with her what she wanted. She wanted him inside her. Her urgent need to take cock inside her and make love to it with her vagina was what the tremor in her voice signaled. He raised her dress up to her waist. She felt the breeze caress her flesh like a strange and exotic kiss and she came again. Rashid ordered, "Bend, just a little, over the rail. Ah, perfect," he said, and stroked her luscious naked orbs.

At last his erection released, and he swiftly, roughly pulled the opulent cheeks of her bottom as far apart as he could. In one lustful swoop, he thrust himself into her up to the hilt, at the same time quickly arranging her skirt so that her nakedness was covered. She held back a scream by biting into her hand, and he felt her contract the muscles of her vagina. She squeezed and released, squeezed and released, in a series of what he called her cunt kisses, which drove him into an erotic frenzy, and then came in an orgasm that trickled over his cock. The sensation was so compelling he almost lost control to climax with her.

"Don't move again, not a muscle, darling. If you do, I'll be unable to hold back and give you what you want. Oh, I love your cunt," he said in her ear.

He cautiously straightened up, and ordered her to do the same. Then with his hands on her hips he fucked her standing up and from the rear. He manipulated her with his hands and his penis into various positions with only a nuance of change to them, but enough for her to feel him in a new and different way with every thrust.

The men calling orders to each other on deck, the flap of the sail in the wind, the spray and sound of the water slapping the hull incited them. Rashid had no idea how long he had been humping Mirella. He only knew that he was unable to stop, each entry was more sublime than the last. He could only guess he had made at least forty or fifty deep thrusts by the way her cunt and his cock worked together as one.

When he was ready to climax he whispered in her ear,

"Together, when you're ready," and kissed her on the side of her neck and at the nape. And when they did come together, it was with such powerful orgasms, and they were both so out of control, that he seized a fistful of her hair and pulled as hard as he could, calling out, "Save me," as if he were dying.

And Mirella, heart pounding, eyes brimming over with tears of passionate emotion, whispered to the wind, "How glorious."

Rashid had achieved it again: he had whisked her away from all thoughts of anything but eroticism, and his personal power. And he never let up, not for a minute. Eyup had been all he had promised and more, much more. It deepened her enchantment with Turkey, and had done something else: It had touched her spiritually.

The days seemed to melt one into the other and she seemed lost from time. After the usual sights of the city, there were private formal dinners and dances in Topkapi, and evenings in opulent private palaces. He showered her with gifts of Turkish antiquities. There were introductions to the last of the aged beauties from the harems of the Ottoman Empire, who related stories of their erotic lives and loves, the sexual abuses they tolerated, and the tortures on their lovers with which they retaliated. Night after night Rashid created sensual soirées in his own house where he kept Mirella distracted with sex and mysticism.

And each new day Mirella would make an attempt to cool down their liaison, but Rashid was too quick, too clever for her. Finally, several days after their arrival in Istanbul, the indolent life of luxury and pleasure began to wear thin, and she tried yet again to call Brindley on the telephone, feeling the need to talk with him about the progress he was making with the settlement of her estate. For the first time Mirella suspected something odd was going on because she was told, as she had been told on a number of occasions, that all lines to London were busy. She became somewhat annoyed with herself for having been so negligent, and that annoyance acted like a beam of light that focused things she had not been aware of.

Mirella had been all but a prisoner since her arrival in Turkey. Not one call of the many she had wanted to make had ever gotten through. She had never been out of Rashid's sight or Daoud's and Fuad's since her arrival, except for the few minutes alone with Princess Eirene and Adam, and that had been accomplished only by subterfuge. Not one phone call had come through to her since her arrival. Mirella had been cleverly cut off from her own life, and the outside world, and had been too dazzled by Rashid and what he created for her to realize it.

And there was something else very odd. She had made it quite clear to Rashid that she had fallen in love with Turkey and now had a keen interest in seeing some of the properties and companies she owned there. Yet, he had turned aside her every suggestion of making a visit to one of those places. And what steps had she taken about going to Adam? None. She could hardly believe that, feeling as she did about the man, he had scarcely come into her thoughts. She had been so absorbed by her great romantic interlude with Rashid, there had been little time for anything as mundane as thinking, she reflected facetiously. All this would have to change! At once! She had made up her mind to it.

Mirella had finished dressing, and was buckling on a pair of ankle-strapped high-heeled black satin sandals, when all these revelations came to her. Now she held her leg up and looked at the shoes and could not help but smile. In style they were the shoes of a real, low-class tart but their price and designer label made them most respectable. She stood up and straightened the black satin Halston evening dress. Without a second glance in the mirror she went to the dressing table and removed the pearl choker and her pearls from around her neck, put on the Sinan and Winslow-Ward necklaces and then looked in the mirror.

The image that looked back at her was that of a sensuous and ravishing beauty in a black satin halter dress cut on the bias and down the front, between the breasts, to the waist. What she saw surprised her, as it had been doing these days ever since she met Rashid.

She picked up the emerald and the ruby in her hands and looked at the seals. The hundreds of diamonds in the links of the two necklaces twinkled against the black satin. She turned to have a side view: provocative as hell, she thought, then turned more to see the back. She was barebacked to below the waist, and had to admire herself not only for looking sensational but for having the courage to. It softened her anger against Rashid for what certainly must be secret motives for keeping her all to himself.

"Are you ready?" he called from his room where he was

tying his white tie in a bow. "We must be on time, it's an official reception, hence the white tie. Come in here and let me see how you look."

"Yes, I'm ready," she said, walking into his room and up in back of him.

Mirella's anger softened even further as she watched this incredibly beautiful, exciting man in white tie and tails preening himself in front of the mirror. Was he perhaps the most dangerous man she had ever met, because he was so easy to fall in love with? When he worked at it, as he did with her, he was absolutely lethal. She felt a pang of sorrow for the many women before her who had succumbed and gotten little but broken hearts for the pain of loving him. Mirella knew she could have been just another one of those women had she not met Adam Corey. Rashid smiled at her in the mirror, and her anger dissolved—but not her determination to get on with her own life, work, and friends, and to find out why he had found it so necessary to isolate her from those things.

"When the papers write you up as one of the most handsome, eligible playboys in the world, they certainly are right," she said.

He smiled at her again in the mirror, then went back to his tie.

"Don't you ever call your offices?" she asked.

"London, Paris, New York, Hong Kong, every day at least once."

"Then how is it I can never manage to make a call out of this country?"

She saw his fingers hesitate for a split second before the final tweak of the tie, and he looked into her eyes through the mirror.

"I hope you're not going to embarrass us both by putting it down to something like bad timing, are you?" she asked.

She caught the look in his eyes reflected in the mirror. It was one of relief . . . as if he were happy she had discovered what he was doing. But that was before he turned around and faced her. That look changed in a flash when he saw the jewels she was wearing around her neck. It turned to anger—mean, hard anger.

Mirella felt a chill run through her. She rubbed her naked arms with her hands as if to get her blood to run warm again, and stood her ground.

"Because I don't want to share you with anyone or

anything." He raised up her hand and held it, adding, "You look devastatingly attractive. I will be the envy of every man tonight. Now turn around and let me see you, all of you."

He lifted her arm high above her head and held her that way while Mirella made her pirouette. When they came face-to-face again she asked, "And because of your possessiveness, anything I might want must be excluded from my life?"

"I thought I was giving you everything you wanted. Is all this fuss because I have saved you from some boring conversations with your solicitors, and opened up a world for you that few people have had the good fortune to be a part of? Must I apologize for that? I thought we ran away together, here, for a few days, because you wanted to see something of my life in Turkey, the place I came from. And so that we could continue an exquisite erotic interlude that is molding and stretching you from past fantasies into sensual realities you yearned for. Listen, Mirella, I have had, am still having, a terrific time with you, and I know you are with me. But, my darling, if the good times, the fun times, are over for you, and you want to go back to London, and are ready to sign those papers liquidating your complex business interests, then we go tomorrow morning, first thing, without fail. "No one will be more delighted than I to see you get all that out of the way. I am only sorry you put off signing those papers before, because it delayed you from taking your newfound financial resources and getting used to being the millionairess, rather than the civil servant. The good times we have had together and will always have, in one way or another, can become part of your new life and not just an interlude."

Then he took her in his arms and kissed her. She draped her arms around his neck and said, "You make me feel foolish, and yet I know I'm not foolish. There are moments when I think you have deep feelings for me and other times when I think a part of you hates me. You manipulate me beautifully, Rashid, you are a master at it, but I am loath to call it manipulation because I indulge myself in your games, and you treat me splendidly. But the day you try to manipulate me against my will, Rashid, God help you. I have too much inbred freedom in me to stand for that. It's what allows me to play the game of the submissive female and enjoy every minute of it. Now, may I make a phone call to Brindley, and will you please see to it that there are clear lines open for me from now on?"

She had found the very sort of words that kept Rashid interested in Mirella for reasons other than the age-old family vendetta of sorts involved with her legacy, and that made the game of seduction he played with all women so much different and better with her.

He kissed Mirella again but found her lips unreceptive, and kept kissing them lightly, sweetly, until they responded in kind, and she gave in to the passion their kisses generated. He stopped and removed his caressing hands from her bare back.

"Make your call to Brindley, Mirella. Tell him you will be in his office to sign the papers by noon tomorrow."

They were walking together, arms around each other's waists, toward the telephone when she surprised him.

"I'm not ready to go back to London yet," she said. "I'm going to ask Brindley to come here tomorrow, if he can, and to bring along the documents for me to sign, as well as any other work that can be done while I'm here. You've done your job too well, Rashid. Not content to seduce me for yourself, you've managed also to have Istanbul seduce me. Now I want to see more of Turkey and the magnificent estates I've inherited that so many people have told me about. I want to become properly involved in my inheritance and examine the details more carefully than I have until now."

Rashid covered very well his surprise over her change of heart about the Oujie estate. He knew better than to oppose her plans. There was too much to lose if he overplayed his hand, and, besides, it mattered not to him where she was when she signed those papers, as long as she did sign them and quickly. So he said, "What a good idea. Tell Brindley to call back with his flight number and the time of his arrival, and we will pick him up at the airport. Of course, he will stay here with us."

Mirella was insistent that Brindley should stay in a suite of rooms at the Hilton, where he might carry on with the business affairs in hand. When she casually suggested that it might possibly be better if she, too, moved from Rashid's, the idea was thrashed out between them, and Mirella agreed to stay with Rashid for the time being. The fact of the matter was that, much as she wanted to leave Rashid's house and go to Adam, she couldn't, so strong still was his hold on her.

Hours later, while dancing with Rashid, at the French Embassy, Mirella whispered in his ear, "It's a lovely ball, Rashid, and I'm having such a marvelous evening. I'm really

pleased Brindley is coming tomorrow. It makes me feel I still
have some control over my life. When I'm with you, I'm
constantly being swept away from my old familiar self and
into new worlds within your life, until I'm almost lost in
you."

"As far as I am concerned there is only one thing wrong
with that—the 'almost,'" he replied. And then gave her an
extra squeeze as he waltzed her away, whispering in her ear,
"There is no 'almost' for me, when it comes to you."

21

When Mirella woke the next morning she had several
things on her mind she wanted to do that day. First and
foremost was to buy a really memorable and beautiful gift for
Rashid. She had an overwhelming desire to surprise him with
a token of her affection for him. It would not be an easy thing
to accomplish because as usual Rashid would have the day
filled with things for them to do together and places for them
to go. Brindley was arriving by chartered jet at eight o'clock
that evening. She thought she had summoned him by her
telephone call and had no idea that he had planned this trip
several days before when he had been unable to reach
her . . . and when he'd felt he needed Adam's advice.

Mirella became more enthusiastic over her idea of a gift
when she decided on the perfect thing for Rashid: the nearly
life-size white marble Hellenistic statue of Apollo she had seen
among the antique dealer's treasures. She needed a plan to get
away from Rashid for a few hours. But what? How?

She formulated a plan, setting it in motion over breakfast
by telling Rashid that she would like to go with him to the
Hilton and find a suite of rooms she and Brindley might use as
their Istanbul office. Then, making it sound like an after-
thought, she had added that while she was there she might
just as well spend the afternoon in the beauty salon and have
her hair done, get a facial, a pedicure, a manicure. She had
added prettily, "If it doesn't spoil your plans for the day, of
course."

As she anticipated, he had tried to persuade her to have the
salon assistants come to her at home. He only gave in to

Mirella when she finally consented to allow Fuad and Daoud to wait outside the salon for her and bring her home afterward. Her evident irritation sparked his temper.

"As long as you are with me," he had snapped, "and in my care, you will go nowhere at all in Turkey without those two bodyguards. Stop thinking like a clerk. For heaven's sake, Mirella, you are a perfect target for any number of people. Wake up, woman. You are a beautiful foreign girl, alone. That in itself is enough to provoke men to snatch you away. Add to that you are one of the richest women in the world, and you become the perfect target for a ransom. An American and a woman, with a great deal of power as a result of inherited wealth in a politically nervous country such as mine, you also are a perfect target for a political kidnapping. And, if that is not enough reason for you, how about being one of the richest women in the Moslem world, a Jewess, with the controlling power of Moslem millions owned and controlled secretly by Jews for hundreds of years? There must be any number of fanatical Moslem factions that would be prepared to assassinate you for that alone."

Mirella began to laugh. She really thought he was being ridiculous, but could hardly say so. What she did say was, "Don't you think you're laying it on too thick, Rashid?"

He frowned derisively and did not immediately answer her question. He thought that, indeed, he was *not* "laying it on too thick," not given what he knew and Mirella did not. He felt a twinge of mild regret that he'd kept even the newspapers from her, along with so much as a shred of the gossip about the furor she was causing that he had gleaned at the end of each of his business calls abroad. Ah, in fact, he had well and truly encapsulated Mirella within a passionate, exotic orb. She hadn't the least notion what was going on concerning her in the outside world. She hadn't the slightest clue that the press was camped on the doorstep of her home on East Sixty-fifth Street in New York, and that her houseman, Moses, and her best friend, Deena, were doing a masterful job of handling those men and women of the fourth estate. And, of course, she could not know that he and she were the hottest item in all the rags, nor that the Wingfield family flatly had refused to comment on her love affair or her inheritance.

"Rashid?" she prompted. When he still did not answer, she said to lighten his mood of angry concern for her, "Oh, and just for the record, I am not a Jewess. Not that I would mind being one, I just don't happen to be. For what it's worth, I'm a nonparticipating Protestant who, if religion became an important factor in my life, would choose to become a Buddhist."

"You decline to be serious about this, Mirella. You are still appealingly innocent, but I can assure you that's only because you have not been a millionairess long enough to become paranoid. Now come here."

Mirella went to him and sat on his lap and leaned against him. He pierced a piece of the ripe mango on his plate with a silver fork and fed it to her.

"Maybe I did exaggerate a bit," he said. "But if I did, it wasn't much. Just promise me that if you go to the hairdressers', you will let Daoud and Fuad wait for you. Perhaps when you have sold off most of the companies and stock you inherited, the risks will be less for you, and you can drop your guard a bit."

He kissed her and petted her like a pet or a child and she agreed to do as he asked. Mirella cuddled up to him. She was delighted with herself. Her plan was working well so far. It would be relatively easy to slip out of the salon through the rear door and come back that way to pick up her bodyguards on her return. Planning this little escapade amused her and she could hardly wait to get on with it. She kissed him tenderly on his cheek, rubbed her cheek up and down against his, and when she caught herself making love to him she stopped abruptly. That was not their kind of loving.

They had a delightful morning and luncheon together and were well pleased with the suite they took for Brindley. As they were walking down the corridor to the beauty salon in the Hilton, something Rashid had said to her flashed through her mind.

"Rashid," she asked, "what did you mean about the Jews controlling Arab money secretly? What has that to do with me and my inheritance?"

"This time I can claim bad timing because it is. Here we are."

He opened the door for her, bent his head down to her hand and kissed it, murmured, "See you at home later," and was gone.

In short order Mirella was sitting in the back of the taxi that she had picked up in front of the Hilton, feeling very smug with herself. It had been safe to do that because she had left

Daoud and Fuad drinking hot sweet mint tea, seated on a pair of chairs in front of the beauty salon, which was nowhere near the entrance of the hotel.

There had been a back door to the salon, just as she had hoped there would be, and when she had explained her plan of escape and return to the manicurist, she got almost more help than she'd hoped for. The salon staff loved the intrigue, but Mirella was quite sure they did not believe she was planning a surprise, preferring their own version of a clandestine liaison with a lover. Whatever they believed they assured Mirella that if her bodyguards outside became restless, there would be no problem. They would cover for her with any number of reasons why she was taking so long—a mud pack, a massage, a permanent. . . .

The taxi driver persisted in honking his horn, though the late afternoon traffic toward the remote part of the city was light. They drove through a rough neighborhood famous for little except its filthy junk bazaar and where parts of every vintage vehicle on wheels could be found. Mirella had made the fatal mistake of telling the driver that she liked Arab music, and it came now with enough volume to crack anyone's nerves along with their eardrums. No matter how many times she asked him to lower the volume it just didn't happen. And, like everyone else in Turkey, he was so overwhelmed by her fluency in his language that he shouted a continuous conversation at her over cassette player and horn alike.

She had been stymied for a moment when he asked her what she meant to do in a place like her destination. Convincing him she was looking for a 1926 Alfa Romeo cylinder block was a small triumph for her.

As they came closer to the area, Mirella began to worry about finding the smarmy young merchant she had met when Rashid took her there. She *had* to find him, though, because it was behind the façade of that man's shop, with its greasy motors, rusted radiators, dented hubcaps, worn pistons, and dirty brake pads, that there lay hidden, under the floor, in his cellar-cave, some of the finest Turkish and Greek antiquities—and all very secretly for sale. It was there that she had seen the Apollo she wanted to buy for Rashid.

Mirella was thrilled to be on her own. Her skill at the language would make the transaction an easy one. Moreover, she had been brought there initially by Rashid. The look on the merchant's face, and the manner in which Rashid had spoken to him, reassured her now that the last thing he would dare to do was to cheat Rashid. Hence, he would certainly not cheat her, especially since she would make it known that her purchase was to be a gift for Rashid.

At last they were there. The taxi driver deposited her beside a crowd of men in the middle of the bazaar. He insisted on being paid, even though he agreed to wait for her, and of course the moment he had the bank notes in his hand, he drove off and left her standing in a cloud of dust. She coughed and spluttered and tried to drive the dust away by waving her hand in front of her face. She fumed with rage at the man.

She looked around. The men, even the place, seemed far more sinister than they had when she had been there before. She felt slightly apprehensive, but she shrugged off her fears and pushed through the crowd of men, who appeared to be friendly enough until she began asking where she might find the young merchant she was seeking. She was directed deeper and deeper into the crowd. The men became more bold. They pushed and jostled her, some even leered in her face. A kind of horror seized her as a dozen taunting men began to close a gap between her and a crumbling building. One reached out and touched her, muttering in a low harsh voice. Another joined him. Alone and in the sun-deserted shadow, the fetid crowd of men pressing in upon her, Mirella began to panic. For a moment she controlled herself by trying to reason with the men who pawed her now, whose putrid breaths she smelled. Their blank stares brought back her panic. She stood against the wall, silent and trembling, and showed her fear. It made the men yet bolder. One of them reached out and slid grimy fingers through her hair, then turned to the others and said, "When we are done with her, I want the hair."

They laughed and egged him on. He did it again, only this time he pulled her hair. Mirella wanted to scream. Her mouth opened, but there was nothing, not a sound. She was terrified, and the crowd laughed. Someone grabbed her handbag from her shoulder, while another man yanked up her skirt with a long stick. She vainly tried to stop him. One of the younger of the men, emboldened by desire, stepped right up to her and tore open the voluminous Miyake jacket she was clutching close against her chest, exposing the low-necked thin silk blouse that showed off her breasts so provocatively. He stepped back into the crowd. What they saw silenced them, even distracted them from rummaging through her purse. They suddenly became ominously silent and together closed in upon her.

But as she shrank within herself before their menacing hands and livid eyes, she sensed, before she saw, the three men who were fighting their way through the tight mesh of bodies. It was Adam Corey accompanied by two huge Turks, his servants. He reached her at last and Mirella almost collapsed into his arms. It was over.

The two Turks held the crowd off. She could hear scuffles, some fighting, a great deal of shouting behind her. She was trembling so, she could hardly stand. Adam, his arm around her shoulder, was walking with her tight up against him.

"Try to compose yourself, Mirella," he said softly. "Straighten up, my girl, that's it. Now we must walk slowly and as calmly as possible to the car. We're not out of this yet. It all depends on you. We must show no fear: these people hate cowards or any show of weakness."

Mirella heard a scream behind her. She jumped and began to turn around, but Adam stopped her.

"No, don't look back. Just keep walking another two hundred yards and we'll be in the car."

They walked in silence. She heard footsteps threateningly close behind them, and voices a hundred yards in back of them begin to heckle.

"Don't worry," Adam said. "The men following us are our men, and don't look back."

"Are you sure they are your friends?" asked Mirella, who had managed to regain speech, but in a voice so filled with fear that Adam gave her an extra squeeze of assurance.

"Yes, very sure. Ah, we're almost there. I can see the car."

He felt her body falter against him from sheer relief when the car was in sight, but she pulled herself up almost immediately and Adam smiled to himself. They had made it.

The driver started the car the moment Adam opened the door. As soon as Mirella and Adam and the two Turks were safely inside, he quickly drove away from the marketplace. Still shaking, Mirella turned and looked through the rear window and saw twenty or thirty angry men, ten abreast, running in a cloud of dust they were raising after the black Citroën.

Mirella simply could not stop trembling. She leaned against Adam who was kind and gentle with her, and gradually she calmed down. He had his driver stop at the first café they found on the waterfront a few miles away from the scene. He helped Mirella out of the car and they sat at a small table overlooking the water. There he made her drink a very strong brandy, and then ordered two more for them. They hardly said five words to each other since he saved her, and they said nothing now. They just listened to the water lapping against the pebbles on the shore. They were there like that for about fifteen minutes. Then, as soon as he saw that she had regained her composure, he asked, "Are you recovered?"

"Yes, I am, thanks to you and your friends. I don't know what would have happened had you not appeared. I shudder to think."

"And well you may. What in heaven's name possessed you to do anything so stupid and dangerous as venturing into that bazaar alone? And how did you know about the place anyway? No matter. You should have known better than to do a thing like that."

"Don't shout at me, Adam."

"Don't shout at you? Answer my questions."

Adam's scolding hurt her but she knew she owed the man who had miraculously saved her the story of how she had come to be there. And so she told him. Briefly. And added, "I admit it was unwise for me to go off alone and I'm so grateful to you for probably saving my life, but please don't remind me of my idiocy. I'm not a child, so don't scold me like one. It irritates me."

"I irritate you?"

"No, of course you don't. It's just your overbearing concern over a stupid mistake that irritates me. And the fact that I still don't have the statue of Apollo for Rashid after all this irritates me. Oh, let's please just drop it."

Adam, ignoring her irritation, ordered two Turkish coffees for them.

"Rashid?" he asked. "Why was a gift for Rashid so important that you risked your life? Couldn't you have bought him something from a London dealer and sent it? Why is it so important to you that he have the Apollo?"

"You are never going to let this drop, are you?" Tears of frustration welled up in Mirella's eyes. She pounded her fist on the table and the little white coffee cups jumped from their saucers, slopping coffee over the sides of the cups.

"Oh, fuck." Her tenseness drew the oath from her, under

her breath, and she fumbled for the napkin at her place
setting, then clumsily wiped the coffee from the table before it
ran onto her lap. She reached over and did the same for
Adam.

"Because I am leaving him for you," she said. "That's why
it's important. It has to be the Apollo because I chose it to be.
Because it's the finest and most beautiful thing I've seen that I
can buy him, and he deserves it. Finally, if you must know,
because I am leaving a fabulous man who has been nothing
but marvelous to me, and I cannot rush into your arms
without a backward glance. Now will you please drop this
subject?"

Adam moved his chair next to Mirella, who was trying to
drink her coffee, although her hands were still shaking. He
took the cup from her and held it to her lips and she took a
few sips. With his finger Adam wiped away the tears at the
corners of her eyes and put the cup down.

"I love you," he said very softly. "More I think than you
will ever believe. I know the statue you want, I know the
dealer. I'll see that it's delivered either before midnight tonight
or tomorrow morning. You'll find this hard to believe, but
the reason I was in the bazaar was because I had just come
from that dealer. I had just purchased the Apollo, Mirella."

Slowly and simultaneously they rose from their chairs and
he took her in his arms. They kissed, and then renewed their
kiss. Mirella felt as if her heart were going to burst with joy.
They smiled and sat down again, he holding both her hands in
his.

"Do you mind losing the statue?" she asked.

"For any reason but this one I would," he said, smiling.

"I must pay you, I must give you a check," she said, feeling
inside the purse that had been retrieved for her by one of
Adam's bodyguards. He stopped her.

"Later, not now," he said. "Now I want to talk seriously to
you. I will wait for you to come to me at my house on the
Bosporus, as I have been waiting ever since the last time we
were together in New York. I will continue to wait, for as
long as it takes. But, I don't want you to have any illusions or
guilt feelings about deceiving or leaving Rashid. I've known
Rashid for a very long time. I've watched him captivate
women before. He is a master at the art. You must be careful,
very careful, because romance, sex, eroticism up to the doors
of depravity—even through the doors of depravity—can

become an enchantment. I'm sure you know that as well as I do. But with depravity the touch of evil slithers in. Sometimes the touch of evil can feel exciting, can even be exciting, but Rashid goes beyond the touch, way beyond it."

Adam's behavior and warning about Rashid came as both an embarrassment and a shock to Mirella. Her anger mounted and she was about to stop him, when he spoke again.

"Now you're furious with me because I'm telling you something you would rather we both ignored. Calm down, because I insist that you listen to what I have to say. Don't be foolish. We can both face the reality of your flirtation with Rashid. I can see signs in Rashid's behavior that always appear when he has total submission from his women. And once he has submission, then comes ruthless abandonment. But only after he gets what he wants. I'm telling you this, Mirella, because I think you should open your eyes and ask yourself what Rashid really wants from you. Protect yourself. That you must do."

Mirella pulled her hands from his and, nearly speechless with rage, she stood up and glared at Adam.

"Now what have I said?" he asked. "What are you all angry and indignant about?"

"Your attack on Rashid, that's what. And your implication that I'm as submissive as a slave, a rag doll. I don't know why you love me when you think me such a fool. Take me back to the hotel."

Seeing that his words meant nothing to her, Adam coldly took her by the arm and led her to the waiting car. He none too gently pushed her into the backseat of the Citroën *Traction-avant*, and she fell into the seat and rubbed her ankle where she had hit it on the unfamiliar running board of the venerable car.

Adam watched her rubbing her ankle and pouting. She sat in the corner of the seat, as far away as she could get from him. He was furious with her, but that didn't stop him from wanting her. Or thinking how special she was to him . . . and how much more beautiful and desirable he found her every time he saw her. However, there was no softness in his voice when he told her, "I have one more thing to say to you, Mirella. Rake that Rashid is, he has at least brought out the female in you, the very essence of your femininity, which I saw buried beneath that cool, intellectual New York façade. Surely now you must face the fact that you've found another part of yourself and can never regress to being the woman you were or to the life that you led before the legacy, before we fell in love. Much as I dislike it, you owe that transformation to Rashid. So stop pouting and face up to the facts of life as they are, not as you wish they were."

"Are you quite finished, Adam?"

"Yes."

"Good. I'm going to do us both a great favor and try to forget that you're jealous of Rashid in every way. You probably always have been, so I don't flatter myself that it's just because of me. Otherwise you wouldn't have said so many negative things about him. Jealousy is a vile emotion. Stop trying to warn me about Rashid. Isn't it enough for you that I'm searching for a way to end my relationship with him? Well, it had better be. Not another word about what you think of either one of us, if you don't mind. Oh, and one more thing—stop pressing me to face issues you think I can't see."

They rode in silence back to the hotel. Adam was truly annoyed with her, coldly trying to examine the magnetic pull between Mirella and himself and concluding that it was the magic, romantic, compulsive part of falling in love. He was locked in it, and he had chosen to let their love take its course, and he knew Mirella was doing the same thing. So he sighed and began to plan how to have the Apollo delivered to Rashid's before midnight.

The Citroën drove down the alley of trash cans to the back door of the Hilton hairdressers. Adam helped Mirella out of the car and they stood among the rubbish bins.

"What are we doing here in a stinking alley in back of a hotel? I am ridiculous sometimes, aren't I?" she asked.

"You said it this time, I didn't." And they both began to laugh.

He put his arm around her waist, pulled her to him, and they walked the few steps to the door marked SALON. He slipped his hands under her jacket and his arms around her. They kissed passionately and with a need for each other that was overwhelmingly loving. Mirella ran her fingers through his hair, touched his cheeks with her fingertips, stood up on her toes and kissed his eyes, then kissed his sensuous lips lightly and nibbled at them, while he caressed her naked breasts under the thin silk blouse. She gave him a love bite on his strong square chin, and licked it, feeling the stubble of an afternoon beard on her tongue.

"Is being married to you always going to be full of adventures, shotgun receptions from your butler, saving you from a fate worse than death, making love among the rubbish bins?"

"Adam, was that a proposal of marriage?"

"Well, yes, come to think of it, I guess it was." Then he smiled and kissed Mirella. It was a quick and happy kiss.

"This isn't exactly how I planned it," he said. "Not among the rubbish of Istanbul's tourists, but yes, consider yourself properly asked. You do accept, don't you?" He asked the question with no doubt that she would do anything but accept.

"Yes, oh yes. I want you to know that I have never loved any man as I love you, and you are the only man I ever wanted to marry except for one college boy, when I was very young, in my teens, and didn't know better."

A bin lid was sent clanking by a cat who howled and fled up the alley. It startled them.

"Will you ask me again when I come to you in your Peramabahçe Palace?"

"Yes," he answered and they kissed again.

Adam tried the doorknob while he was kissing her but the door was locked, so he knocked hard on it.

"You had better go," he said reluctantly. "You have an escapade to complete and I have a statue to deliver."

Mirella put her arms around his neck again and they kissed. He lifted her off the stair while they were still kissing and crushed her to him. His need was great to feel her a part of him. When he put her down, the door of the salon had been opened, and standing in it were the manicurist, two hairdressers, one male and one female, eyes agog, mouths open.

While Mirella was having her hair washed she heard the hairdresser say to the manicurist, "And you believed her story about a surprise gift for a friend? You have no romance in your soul, Ingie. That's because you are too busy looking for a husband instead of a lover."

Mirella thought of nothing but Adam from the time he
left her on the doorstep of the salon until she returned
to Rashid. Their mutual love seemed a miracle to her. That
they would marry seemed an even greater miracle. To love
the way Adam and she loved was so transcendent that the
difficulties and longings other lovers might feel while apart
simply did not exist for them. Because of their commitment,
Mirella was able to give and get a lot more love, and she was
in no way ever going to abuse that luxury. So it was no
surprise to Mirella that when she returned to Rashid, Adam,
who was well and truly locked in her heart, simply vanished
from her mind.

Having returned very late with Daoud and Fuad, Mirella
had little time with Rashid before they left for the airport to
meet Brindley. But in the short time they did have, she was
acutely aware of a slightly disgruntled edge to Rashid's
manner, not so much with her as with the servants, and in
two phone calls he had received while they were having a
drink together.

They were more than halfway to the airport when he said,
"Come closer, I want to feel you next to me."

She did and he put his arm around her.

"Kiss me," he ordered.

And she did. The moment their lips touched he slipped the
tip of his tongue between them and forced her mouth open
with nothing more than the passion their kiss generated. He
sighed and smiled at her. Then pulling her toward him,
he murmured in her ear, "I needed that. I want you to do the
most wild and erotic things to me tonight. Will you?"

Once she gave her assent, he whispered in detail some of
those things they had done together, and suggested to her he
had arranged a sexual pleasure for her of which she was still
innocent. He kissed her again.

"I don't know what has happened," he said as they
approached the terminal, "but I have this tremendous feeling,
a need, if you like, to possess you completely tonight. It's

almost like a premonition that it will be our last night of sexual love."

The expression on Rashid's face was frightening. She was taken aback that his intuition should be so acute, and couldn't make up her mind if that was a good or bad thing under the circumstances. He grabbed her wrist in such a tight grip, she was afraid to turn her wrist for fear he would break a bone in it. "But for that I am not yet quite ready," he said, "so I hope the premonition is false."

"Rashid, let go, you're hurting my wrist. Whatever is the matter with you?"

The shadow darkening his mind vanished as suddenly as it had arrived, and Mirella could actually feel control return to his body. He looked at his hand clasping her wrist and slowly released the pressure. Looking into her eyes, he said, "Forgive me, I don't know what came over me. Probably Brindley walking into our life. I did tell you I didn't want to share you with anyone or anything. Say you forgive me."

"There's nothing to forgive. And don't be silly. Brindley is a necessity. I must get through some work with him. You know as well as I do how I've neglected my affairs because I gave myself up to our good times together."

"Mirella, promise me you will sign those documents of sale tomorrow, so you can be done with all that, and we can go on larking about together."

Adam's warnings flashed through Mirella's mind. She suddenly was unable to dismiss his words. Now for the first time she had serious conflicting feelings about Rashid. The attraction she had for the man, the sensational sex they had together were still there. But now there was Adam's warning and Rashid's barely disguised threat. Even the princess's words about him now seemed ominous. Mirella shrugged them off, believing that if she had come to no harm from Rashid by now, she never would. She had good reason to believe that: she recalled the night he sent her home from Oda-Lala's. She did, though, make up her mind to take Adam's advice. She would protect herself the best way she could at the first sign from Rashid that they would part as anything but the best of friends.

Mirella watched the small jet taxi down the runway and turn. Once the motors were cut the driver pulled the car up close to the plane, and when the door dropped open, Mirella stepped out of the car to greet her solicitor, Rashid standing by her side. She was delighted to see Brindley Ribblesdale and his battered briefcase. They walked toward each other the short distance across the tarmac, Rashid following about ten paces behind, and shook hands.

"I say, Mirella," Brindley said, "I am pleased to see you!" He lowered his voice and continued, "We must talk alone as soon as possible."

"No problem."

"I am not so sure about that," he said, again in a lowered voice. He continued in a normal tone as Rashid approached to shake his hand and make him welcome. "It's good to be back in Turkey again. It will be so much easier to get things done here, now that you are in Turkey," he said to Mirella.

The two men greeted each other cordially. They waited for four pieces of luggage filled with paperwork to be packed into the trunk of the Rolls, and then drove into town to settle Brindley at the Hilton. Afterwards, they went to Rashid's home to dine. A fourth guest, a beautiful Turkish girl Mirella had met before, had been invited as Brindley's dinner partner. After dinner the four went to a nightclub.

Rashid had been at his magical best—attentive, charming, handsome, romantic—and set the tone for the evening. Mirella, swept away by the gaiety, thought of Adam only a few times. She hoped that he had managed to have the Apollo delivered for Rashid. She did so much want to give something special to Rashid, because he had restored the freshness to her life, while opening many new doors for her. Even Brindley seemed revitalized by Rashid during the evening.

"Brindley is going to have the lay of his life tonight," said Rashid, laughing, as the car sped away from the Istanbul Hilton. They waved good-bye to the couple, and watched them turn to go into the hotel. Then Mirella and Rashid turned back to each other with knowing smiles.

"And so are you," both said simultaneously, pointing at each other. They burst out laughing.

When they approached the house the gates were closed, as usual, but all the lights on the ground floor were ablaze and that was unusual at two o'clock in the morning. As always, they were driving in a convoy with Daoud and Fuad in the car behind. As they drew up to the gate, the keeper opened it, the backup car pulled in front of the Rolls and asked the keeper what had happened. Fuad ran back to the Rolls and told Rashid all was well, they were just following Miss Wingfield's instructions to leave all the lights on until they arrived home. Rashid displayed irritation.

"What is all this about, Mirella?"

"It's a surprise. You'll see," she said, recognizing the lights as Adam's spectacular signal to her that he had delivered their Apollo. How had he managed to persuade Rashid's servants to do it, since as far as she knew she had no authority whatsoever in Rashid's house? Rashid ruled that house like a king in his palace or a general in his fort. She could hardly believe that the servants would obey instructions given by anyone else.

Rashid was taking no chances. He ordered the second car to go forward with Daoud and Fuad riding the running board and probing the shrubbery with two large, hand-maneuvered chrome spotlights mounted on either side of the old Chevrolet.

Watching the scene as the two cars slowly wound their way up the drive, Mirella was finding the whole thing distastefully melodramatic. That afternoon's ordeal had sated such appetite as she had for melodrama.

"I find this absolutely incredible," he said.

"So do I," she said under her breath.

"I shall be fascinated to hear my servants explain how you won them over to disobey me and take instructions about my house from anyone but me."

Mirella shot him a look. She didn't like his menacing tone, nor the threat in "disobey." It implied punishment, and Mirella found that disturbing. But she was able to smile with some pride when he said, while walking arm in arm with her up the marble stairs to the huge pair of carved wooden doors, "Mirella, you are an endless surprise to me. You're like quicksilver. Just when I think I have you in the palm of my hand, that I know your form, how to contain you, whoops, you slip around, change shape, and I have to begin again to know you. You're a great challenge."

His voice had changed, it was full of fun and charm. He took her by the hand and asked, "Is it sexual? Something disgracefully depraved, I hope? Is it a couple? A pair of lovely boys?"

Mirella was laughing and shaking her head.

"Stop asking," she said. "I'll tell you nothing. Not a hint. In a few minutes you'll find out."

"I'm guessing you have somehow managed to find the

most perfect young man to make love to me, one who will pleasure me while I am fucking you, and respond to even my lewdest demands of him. If that's it, it's not even depraved! Nothing to what is waiting for us up in my bedroom."

Mirella caught the sexual glint in his eyes, tossed her head back laughingly, and teased, "Well, let me put it this way: he is the most beautiful man I have ever seen, and I'll not say another word more."

They were now at the front door and Fuad rushed up from behind them to put the key in the lock.

At that moment the lights went out everywhere in the house, and the two large doors were slowly swung open from the inside. They revealed in the center of the large, handsome oval-shaped hall, poised upon a three-foot pedestal of black volcanic rock, the marble statue of Apollo, brilliant white under an invisible pinhole spotlight. The statue was the only thing lit in a pool of darkness. And it possessed such unearthly beauty that Mirella actually felt her heartbeat quicken and gasped.

The only other light came through the windows and the open door behind them from the moon and the mass of stars sparkling in the night sky. It was by that light that Mirella was able to see Rashid's face. His love of beautiful things always made it glow with pure pleasure that radiated across it. Mirella took Rashid's hand in hers, and said, "I thought it was about time I gave you something for a change. It had to be a thing of beauty *par excellence,* because of your love and appreciation of all that is beautiful. And Rashid, my dear Rashid, here it is, with my love and affection for giving me some of the most fulfilling moments of my life."

He took her in his arms. Rashid's kiss was not given merely in gratitude, nor was it an expression of love for her generosity and thoughtfulness. They kissed now with all the passion and sexual ardor they felt for each other, and Mirella experienced that painful mix of joy, sadness, and helplessness at being bound to one man by desire and to another by love.

Rashid dismissed the bodyguards, ordered his houseman to bring a bottle of champagne and two glasses at once, and then walked around the Apollo slowly several times, absorbing its beauty. He turned on the other lights in the entrance hall and the long, curved staircase and the other objects sprang to life from the darkness. He folded his arms across his chest and did another slow tour of the statue.

Mirella sat down on the Queen Anne sofa against one of the walls and watched Rashid. Not one word had passed between them since their kiss. She was filled with the infinite joy of giving, and leaned back and reveled at the scene before her.

Greatness, with its ability to humble and inspire simultaneously, radiated from the Hellenistic statue, and seemed at that moment to Mirella to find some not unworthy echo in Rashid.

When the houseman returned with the champagne, Rashid motioned to him to place it on a table opposite the Apollo and leave. He stood in front of the statue, arms behind his back, still enthralled by it. The silence in the house was heavy and compelling and held in a hushed embrace this moment when the antique was brought back to the living.

Rashid, still with his back to Mirella, removed his jacket and dropped it on the black marble floor. He viewed his gift from various angles in the hall, leaving his shoes in one place, his shirt in another, slowly divesting his graceful body until he stood naked in front of the god. She joined him and went down on her knees. Slowly she fed his erect penis into her mouth, then made exquisite long and lingering love to it.

Mirella whimpered in her sleep. She whimpered again. She was fighting against waking up, losing the dream, the ecstasy. She felt the heaviness of sleep lighten, she whimpered aloud, and sensed the force of her waking life seep back. At first in her loins, then in her arms, which she used to reach up and wrap around Rashid's neck, then in her legs, which she wrapped around his waist.

The dream was so vivid, the ecstasy of orgasms sublime, and she groaned aloud yet again. It wasn't a dream in which one sees everything in detail, but where one *feels* everything, as if the skin were being flayed from the body. She felt every thrust in and every withdrawal, and her body worked naturally with it, as he penetrated her two most sacred orifices, in and out, again and again, slowly, rhythmically. Only it was no dream. It was the way Rashid chose to wake Mirella up the day after she gave the Apollo to him.

Her eyes fluttered open, and she saw him from her prone position, mounted on top of her. He had been watching her in her half-sleep while he fucked her, and now that she was awake, without changing the pattern of his fucking he smiled at her and said lightly, "It's time you were fully awake ," then pulled her up from the silk and lace pillows on the bed into his arms and kissed her deeply, pulling his lips from hers only when he came in a copious orgasm so intense for him that he called out, and in a passion beyond control slapped her about the breasts and across the face. She fought to scramble out from under him, but it was impossible. As soon as he had filled her with his last drop of semen, his violent outburst subsided, his face grew calm again, and he said, "Hush, shush, it's over, it's all right. I lost control, it was too thrilling for me. I took you the way I wanted you, completely submissive, silent, at my mercy, my victim. You can't imagine how exciting that is for me."

He kissed her gently on the cheek, and when she shied away from him, he said, "No, don't do that, don't be silly."

Then he soothed her with intimate kisses to cover his violence.

One thought kept going through Mirella's mind: Adam's warning about Rashid and what he did to the women in his life. Mirella knew in her heart that she no longer trusted Rashid, that their sexual life together was over. But she also realized that to know something in the heart and to turn it into action are two quite different things. She was intelligent enough to understand as well that she must not leave Rashid and go to Adam until this, her last affair, was resolved. When she walked into Adam's life and assumed the responsibility of such a real and powerful love as theirs was certain to be, she was determined not to do it on the rebound from anyone or anything. They both deserved better than that.

And so she did calm down and agreed to stay in bed with Rashid and have breakfast and to give up going to see Brindley. They decided on a lazy day together, which they both needed after the experience of the Apollo, and the extraordinary sexual scene he had choreographed for them. But she did have conditions—she wanted to talk seriously about some things to him, make telephone calls to a few people, and read the Oujie journal. He accepted them all.

"No wonder I got carried away waking you up with that morning fuck—what bliss! No conditions!" he said.

He saw her face cloud over and he added, "Sorry about that. I surrender, I give in, we will do anything you want, within reason, and you will do one thing for me: sign those papers. Have Brindley bring them around at dinnertime and sign the bloody papers. Get that done and out of your mind, so one burden at least is removed from this interlude in our life."

Mirella tensed slightly. By mentioning yet again that he wanted her to sign the papers, he linked that act with their affair. Fortunately he never waited for her verbal assent. He simply assumed she would obey him and, smiling at her, said, "Come, let's bathe together before we have our breakfast, and let's take that in bed."

They sat opposite each other in the hot water, made satiny smooth with oil of lily of the valley and orange blossoms. A maid knocked and entered with a silver tray on which there were two tall crystal glasses, two-thirds filled with equal amounts of fresh orange juice and cognac, and two dashes each of grenadine and Cointreau, and a chilled bottle of Dom Pérignon. She placed the tray on a table next to the marble bathtub near Rashid, then topped the glasses up with one-third more champagne, and served first Mirella and then Rashid. The lovers bent forward and touched the rims of their glasses, and together toasted one another in the Turkish style.

"Serefe."

"How delicious," Mirella said. "Oh, that's just what I needed."

"Have I ever offered you anything less than delicious? Have I not always given you everything you needed or wanted?" he asked teasingly. "Isn't that why you bestowed such a magnificent gift on me as the Apollo?"

After serving them the maid had gone to Mirella and, without being asked, tied a length of gold lamé around her hair in a glamorous turban, saying, "To save madam's hair," and she had left.

"I suppose I can thank you for this," Mirella said now, touching the turban with her hand. "You spoil and pamper me too much, Rashid. I think you may have ruined me for having to do for myself ever again."

She took another sip of her drink and remarked again how delicious it was and asked what was in it. He told her and then added, "At the Carlton Hotel in Cannes they call it the Pick-me-up, a good name for it, I think, because it always does the job for me."

"I think for me too," she said, "because I feel revitalized."

"And that is the way you look to me, Mirella."

The maid was just coming back into the bathroom with an exotic antique dressing gown of black silk, trimmed with a ten-inch border of thick gold embroidery around the neck, down the front, and along the bottom, as well as around the cuffs of the sleeves. It was a treasure almost worthy of a glass case in the costume museum in Topkapi.

He laughed lightly and happily at the expression of wonder and wide-eyed delight at the robe and ordered the maid to lay it over the chaise and bring Miss Wingfield a mirror.

"Oh, Rashid, it is the most amazing gown. Now I understand the turban."

Mirella looked in the mirror; she could have been one of the odalisques in the courtyard at Oda-Lala's. The cleverly turned and twisted headdress of gold framed and enhanced her face, highlighting her bone structure and her deep violet eyes. Her fair skin shone like flesh-colored marble from the bath oil. She held the mirror in front of herself in one hand, while with the other she caressed her shoulders and fondled her heavy, glowing breasts. She was mesmerized by the woman she saw, the beauty, the erotic being he seemed tirelessly able to realize in her. She loved this image that was Rashid's handiwork.

She put the mirror down and looked at Rashid, who was feasting on her with his eyes.

"You really would like to turn me into something as exotic and remarkable as your sexual slave Humayun, wouldn't you? Do you think I could pass for one of those odalisques in the courtyard?"

"With flags flying, and especially with the adventuring gift you have for the erotic, of course you could pass for one of the odalisques. And, yes, I would like nothing better than to make you my sexual slave, as we both know well enough. Last night should have proved to you that I have by no means abandoned the task of enslaving you."

He teased her with recollection of the ecstasies they shared, of the sexual antics in her to which he had played the ringmaster. But she probed him about Oda-Lala's, reminding him how she still wondered and fantasized about the place and especially his beautiful sexual slave.

"You are a strange girl, you know. You're jealous of my slave Humayun. And well you should be, she is remarkable. You may never do the things for me that she has done. You don't love me. That is to not say that I don't believe there is any erotic act to which you would not give yourself up completely, if you did love me, as she does, without measure, and to the death. But after every sexual encounter we have, I see you wanting to go further, wanting me to push you that much closer to submitting totally to eros in me. Time will reveal which of us will break or try to run."

They both knew that was part of the sexual excitement between them, and even talking about it was exciting. They gave each other knowing smiles and then laughed. It broke the tension.

Mirella wondered if Rashid knew as she did that time had run out for them. That it was over. She hoped so because it would make leaving him so much easier.

They had the most delicious breakfast in bed together, she dressed in the black and gold of her robe and turban, looking like a resurrected kadin from one of the harems, long since silenced; he naked. They breakfasted on prosciutto and melon, then individual rum omelette soufflés, and ate paper-thin slivers of kidney and mushrooms marinated in twenty-year-old Calvados and charcoal-grilled to a turn on the outside, and so soft and tender on the inside they melted in the mouth. For toast they had a kind of very light brioche, called a Sally Lunn, whose name, she playfully tutored Rashid, was either a corruption of *soleil lune*—sun and moon—a type of French breakfast cake, or that of an eighteenth-century bakeress from the English city of Bath. They ate some plain, others with butter, and at the very end of their meal spread butter and a clear, amber quince jelly over the Sally Lunns that very nearly turned them into a confection. The hot Earl Grey tea they drank blended in its delicacy to perfection.

The breakfast trays removed, they sat back among the cushions close to each other, replete with food, and feeling happy with themselves and the world.

"This robe was made for an Armenian princess in the sultan's harem about a hundred years ago," he said, playing with the gold on her robe. "As you can see it has never been worn. The sultan ordered it as a gift in appreciation for her love, but he never gave it to her because she took the sword that was meant for him, right through the heart, when she stepped between him and his assassin, who got the sultan anyway by just pushing hard on the hilt. I have always wondered who I would give it to. No one could possibly look lovelier in it than you do. Oh, by the way, the assassin was hired by the sultan's mother, who preferred another son. It's always wise to remember how cruel a lot we are."

"Is that a warning?" she asked as he put his arm around her shoulder and fixed a fold in her turban that wasn't quite right.

"No, just a reminder that cruelty runs in families. For all I know you could be more cruel to me than I might imagine you capable of. Shall we talk now, or make phone calls?"

23

"Good morning, Brindley, how are you this morning?"

"Very well, Mirella. Are you coming over?"

"No, as a matter of fact I am still in bed, feeling a bit fragile. Rashid and I have decided to take what is left of the day in a leisurely fashion, and laze around the house here together. I want to make some necessary phone calls to the States, and read some of the family journal. And, to be very honest, I feel the need to rest. I know the most pressing thing is for me to sign the papers that will sell off most of the estate's business assets to that Turkish conglomerate. Rashid suggests you bring them over here so I can sign them and get that out of the way, and then you can stay and have a late dinner with us. How does that sound to you?"

Rashid, who was sitting in bed next to her reading the paper, lowered it from in front of his face, leaned to one side and gently pushed the telephone receiver away from her lips and kissed them, while she waited for an answer from Brindley. She playfully pushed him away and gave him a make-believe glare. He chuckled and went back to reading his newspaper.

"It sounds all right, Mirella, but will we be able to have some privacy? I need to talk to you alone."

"I should think so, Brindley," she answered, noting the slight hesitation in his voice.

"You must see to it, Mirella. It's important, and I have noticed it is very difficult to speak to you without Rashid present. Are you alone now?"

"No," she answered, aware that he was insinuating something.

"Is Rashid near you?" he asked, lowering his voice.

"Yes, very definitely," she answered, trying to sound businesslike.

"My case in point. Mirella, I will be there this evening with the papers for you to sign. They are all in order, but if for any reason you decide you need more time to think it over, don't discuss it in front of Rashid. Wait until we are alone. In that way I can make the excuse that one of the documents is missing."

"Why do you think that's necessary?"

"I take it I can talk without being overheard, so I will carry on, unless you stop me. As far as I can see and have been advised, you can sign. You have a better than fair deal. There can be only two reasons not to go forward with the sale: either you have changed your mind and want to open the sale to the world and accept the highest bids, or you don't want to give up the enormous power that you wield as the sole owner.

"Mirella, if I see that's the case, then so will everyone else, and that could be a potentially dangerous thing for you, especially while you are here in Turkey. Since you have delayed the sale, and virtually disappeared, or to be more accurate have made yourself unavailable, a good deal of pressure has been and is being applied to us to complete the sale, some of which has been quite unpalatable pressure, I must add. And so it would be advisable, if you need more time, to use the legal system as an excuse. It's better protection for you. I have no proof that Rashid is at all involved with this, but I do advise that the less he or anyone else knows about your affairs, the better for you."

"Oh, that's very interesting, Brindley. All right, then, bring the maps with you, and maybe we will make some excursions into the countryside. See you tonight. Oh, wait, I'll ask Rashid what time."

Brindley put the telephone down, smiled to himself, and admired Mirella's quickness of mind. She had understood perfectly what he had been insinuating and had taken it in her stride. She had even been shrewd enough to set up a situation where he and she could get away from Rashid for a few days by leaving town if they had to.

He had watched Rashid and Mirella closely the night before and, having no other proof, believed that Rashid, the great lover, was nothing more than madly possessive about Mirella. There was no denying it: he dominated her by charm and sensuality, to which, Brindley wryly reflected, he had not been immune himself. Sensuousness was a force always included in Rashid's calculations.

He was further amused to think that some of Mirella's sexual sparkle had ignited his own sensual nature, and thought she must be a firecracker in bed.

Mirella put the receiver down, and teasingly ruffled the paper Rashid was reading. When he gave her his attention she removed it and said, "Can we talk now?"

"Yes, but I have one important call to make, so let me do that and then I am all yours," said Rashid, affectionately tapping the end of her nose with his finger.

She handed him the telephone and picked up his copy of the *International Herald Tribune*. He completed his dialing and then took the paper from her and dropped it on the floor on his side of the bed and said, putting his arm around her shoulder, "You can read that later. How about paying some attention to me?" and kissed her on the side of her neck.

His dark, lingering look showed a real need for her that was impossible to resist, no matter how momentary it might be or how quickly it could change into some other emotion. She snuggled up close against his naked body under the silk-and-lace top sheet covering them and traced the features of his face with her finger. He followed her touch with the movement of his head until the person he was calling was on the line, and then concentrated on his conversation while Mirella caressed his dark, hairy chest. He threw the sheet off them, and she slid on top of him, straddled him, and sat back. She threw her arms out and had a great big luxurious stretch. Rashid finished his conversation just then and handed her the telephone receiver. She reached out across the bed, just able to replace it in the cradle, and almost toppled off him. He caught her by the waist and held her on top of him while she completed her task.

Rashid began to unbutton a few of the hundreds of tiny gold-embroidered cloth buttons that closed the front of the black silk robe. She had only done up a few of them just below the breasts and she asked, "Weren't we going to talk?"

"We *are*. What makes you think I can't talk with your robe open?"

She began sliding off him and he stopped her and said, "Or with you sitting on top of me, for that matter. Do stay where you are. If you only knew how sensational you look sitting there! It's a joy for me to look at you."

He touched her turban and finished unbuttoning her robe. He opened it just enough to see down the center of her body between her breasts and down to her navel, the hair covering her mound stretched across him. He ran his index finger from under her chin straight down her body as if he were dissecting her.

"Are you comfortable?"

She squirmed just a little under his strange caress and nodded that she was.

"Good," he said, "then let's talk," taking first one of her hands in his and fondling it, raising it to his lips and kissing it, opening it and licking the palm. She felt the flush in her face and her heart racing but fought against giving in to the delight she was experiencing. He reached out and picked up her other hand and now held them both in his.

"I would like to begin, if you don't mind," he said. "About the Apollo. I want you to know you bowled me over with that gift. There has never been a woman in my life who understood or appreciated what beauty means to me and I have had to suffer some of the most embarrassing gifts, no matter how well-meaning the gestures may have been, or how much love was wrapped up in the giving. There is a room in every house I have set aside for ugly gifts from gorgeous ladies."

"Don't you ever clean them out?" she asked with a teasing smile.

"Oh yes, every time I am finished with the lady," he answered—she thought rather ruthlessly.

"So, my dear Mirella, thank you," he said, slipping his hands under her robe, taking her in his arms while she sat astride him, and kissing her with a profound affection.

"And thank you." He opened her robe wider, and held in the palms of his hands first one breast, whose nipple he fed into his mouth, sucked deeply on, and kissed, and then the other.

"And thank you." He arched her back and placed the tip of his tongue in her navel and licked it in a circle several times, then closed her robe over her breasts but left it partially open as it had been before.

She straightened up and asked, "Did you thank them all like this in spite of their ugly gifts?" with a tease and a light girlish laugh to her voice.

"Of course," he answered with a wry smile.

"You are beyond correction," she said and laughed.

"Oh, am I? Well, so are you. I want you to tell me how you

were able to buy the Apollo for me. And I want you to begin at the beginning, with how you managed to get away, dupe Daoud and Fuad, and find the dealer, when you were supposed to be getting your hair dressed? And, Mirella, don't leave anything out. I am going to be fascinated to hear how you persuaded the dealer and Adam Corey to give up that piece. The three of us have been wrangling over it for more than a year."

Mirella saw the laugh go out of his eyes, and that same glint appear that she had seen the night before when he wanted to know how she got his servants to disobey his orders. She didn't like it.

"I don't think I am going to tell you, Rashid."

"And why not?" he asked.

"Because I deceived you, and your bodyguards and your servants, and you will dismiss them for it."

"I may do worse than that," he said, looking not so much angry as determined.

"No, I don't think you will, Rashid, because unless you give me your solemn word right now, not only to do nothing about it, but never even to question or mention it to any of the servants involved, I will walk out of this house and we will never see each other again."

"Are you so sure that will matter enough to me for me to give my word?"

There was a coldness in his voice, and a steady severe look in his eyes, and Mirella was surprised how much his meanness hurt her. It was cruel, deliberate, frightening. She drew the robe closed and pulled herself up a little straighter where she sat. And her New England pride surfaced. She raised her chin a little higher, a tinge of the haughty passed across her face, and she said, "Yes, I am."

"Oh, and what makes you think so?"

"Because you're not through with me yet."

It wasn't until he threw his head back and began to laugh that she realized that in this, the game of cat and mouse he'd begun, the mouse might just be winning. A smile crept out across her face while she watched him laughing at her.

"You're damn right, I'm not," he said as he roughly pulled her robe open again and pulled her by her breasts down on top of him, and kissed her wildly and passionately. She was able to fight him off and resume her position on top of him because he was still laughing at her. She pulled the robe closed and stared at him.

"Stop laughing at me, Rashid."

"I don't think I am laughing at you, Mirella. I think I am laughing at us. You see, I don't think *you* are quite through with me either."

They sat there looking at each other until a silent truce was established between them. He reached out and removed the turban from her head and her hair tumbled down onto her shoulders. He ran his fingers caressingly through it several times and slowly opened her robe and removed it from her. He put his hand around the back of her neck and began to pull her down on top of him. She held back with as much strength as she could muster and said, "Promise me, first promise me, give me your word to do nothing to the servants or Daoud or Fuad."

He kept pulling her down, and they could both feel the sexual charge they were generating between them, their hearts were pounding, their mutual desire quickening. But still she held back, until he said, "I promise, I give you my word."

Mirella stretched her whole body out flat on top of him. She kissed him lightly on the lips and said, "You know, you are not an easy man to buy a gift for."

They smiled at each other and slowly she slid off his body on to the silk sheet and again laughter came between them. She put her robe on again and went to the dressing table, where she brushed her hair and put on the pearl choker and earrings, then insisted that Rashid put on his robe and they sit in what was left of the sun on the bedroom balcony. It was there that she told him everything that had happened on the afternoon she bought him the Apollo. Or, almost everything.

She did leave out some rather essential things. She told Rashid every detail of what had happened up to the point of the row that took place between Adam and her at the café, and explained that by saying, "I shudder to think what would have happened had he not come along and saved me, Rashid. But that did not give him the right, once he saw that I had myself under control to attack me, to call me stupid, and a fool. Well, never mind all that for now. Let me just get on with the story. We had a dreadful row. I have seen that man three times in my life, and two out of the three times we have had terrible rows."

"I had no idea you knew him before Princess Eirene introduced you."

"I don't *know* him. I just *met* the man, was introduced to him in New York by Brindley as the man who uncovered the Oujie journals. And that meeting ended much the same as this one did with him sticking his nose into my affairs and then telling me how stupid I am, because I told him I was interested in the money more than in Turkey and what the inheritance meant."

Rashid began to laugh. "That's my friend Adam. He has a short fuse with anyone uninterested in his adopted country. Let's not get distracted by him. What happened? He was telling you off for being in the bazaar, and . . ."

"And I broke down and began to cry and scream at him, a reaction, I am sure, to the attack on me by those men, but also out of sheer frustration at not having found and bought the Apollo after going through all that. When I told him that, he was appalled that I had risked my life to find it and buy it for you, and that, rather than being grateful for getting out of the bazaar alive, I was trying to think of a way to get back and make my purchase. I guess I was rather hysterical, and I suppose the only way he thought he could quiet me down was to sell it to me. He told me to pull myself together and stop crying. The statue was his, he had just come from the dealer where he had paid for the Apollo. That was why he was in the bazaar."

Rashid was enthralled with her story, furious with her and Fuad and Daoud, and quite shocked that she was that restless with being kept so closely reined in. Was she truly so devious as to go to the lengths she had to get away and do her own thing? But more than shocked, he was angry that she had managed to pull it off, and make a fool of them all. He had promised he would not punish those in his service and he would keep his word. But, he had said nothing about not punishing her, and that he would most certainly do.

"He convinced me that he sold me the Apollo," continued Mirella, "because he was appalled that I should be so obsessed about having that particular piece for your gift. When I explained to him that it had to be the finest object I could find in thanks for your generosity—because, without you, I might never even have come to Turkey—he floored me by saying, 'I will deliver the piece before midnight.' And that's how I bought your Apollo.

"Of course, I accepted it and now find myself in the awkward position of being indebted to a man who thinks me a money-mad, possession-mad, irresponsible fool. He then—still very angry—all but threw me in his car and never spoke to me again until he delivered me into the salon at the hotel through the back door."

"And, of course, it was he and not you who arranged with the servants the placing of the piece—and the lighting—which he could easily do because they know him to be a trusted friend with the run of my house? Switching on the pinhole spotlight I had installed six months ago specially for the Apollo must have given Adam a jolt! He told me I was a fool to install it because he was the one the dealer was finally going to sell the sculpture to.

"Mirella, you have managed to buy what is probably the most beautiful Apollo since the much earlier one at Olympia. It should by rights be in a museum, the Louvre, the Metropolitan, the British Museum, and one day it will be, when I donate it to the country. But until then it's mine and a gift that I will cherish, not least for the story of how you bought it.

"Now, gift and gratitude aside, don't you ever—and I mean *ever*—do anything as stupid and devious as you did yesterday. Not so long as you are with me. I will not tolerate it. And I mean it. Anything you want to do, you discuss with me first."

"Rashid," she said, "you don't own me, you know, I am only your guest."

"Oh, spare me that old line, Mirella. Let's go look at the Apollo again."

He grabbed her by the hand and dragged her after him through the house, ignoring her half-ironic protests about his being the worst kind of male chauvinist. She only stopped when they glimpsed the Apollo from the top of the staircase. They looked at each other. He put his arm around her waist and shook his head back and forth, as if to say "don't be a fool," and they moved slowly down the grand staircase, half entranced by its radiant beauty.

After that they walked together in the garden where the nightingales were singing in the thick, shadowy cypresses.

"Rashid," said Mirella, "I will have to leave you. You do know that, don't you?"

"Yes, I know that."

"And everything will change for us when I do."

"Yes, I know that too."

They came to a stone bench near the lily pond and they sat down and faced each other. He played with her hair, arranged some of the tendrils close to her face, smiled at her, and said, "But not for a few days, not until this interlude has run its course and is resolved. Then we will separate. And, when we come together again, which we both know is inevitable, we'll begin something new, something fresh."

They kissed on that, and walked back to the house together, where he went to his study to make phone calls and Mirella went to her bedroom to make hers.

24

"Rashid, I think this is really crazy. How do you know we'll even find him there?"

"Oh, you will find him there all right. He wouldn't be anywhere else. His servants at the house told me he left at noon today, and that means they will be having a feast before they climb. Mirella, he wouldn't be anywhere else. Now get in the plane."

"Supposing I get there and they've begun the climb?"

"That's not possible. They will start the climb at two o'clock in the morning in order to reach the summit at sunrise. Now listen, Daoud and Fuad will see to it that you find Adam, who will probably be at the airstrip anyway. He doesn't know who's coming. The message I left was that a friend was arriving at about eleven and that the plane would buzz the village as a signal to light up the airstrip. Now, will you please get in the plane? You wanted to see some of the countryside and this is a terrific way for you to begin. You will be perfectly safe with Adam, who may not be too thrilled to see you at first, but once he is over the shock he will like nothing better than taking you over the mountain. I will fly with Brindley to London in the morning. He will get the missing signature you need, I will do what I have to for my business, and we will be in Istanbul tomorrow night or the next night at the latest. We will fly out and pick you up."

The motors were revving up by now and Mirella at last turned to get into the plane.

"Mirella, it's a very good idea," Brindley said. "Adam

Corey will be delighted that you are taking an interest at last in the country, and honestly I prefer you to be out there rather than alone in Istanbul with people coming after you, trying to exploit your position. And to come to London with us would be tiring and foolish for such a short visit. I can't tell you how sorry I am about this stupid oversight."

Mirella smiled at him and said, "Never mind, Brindley, see you in a couple of days," and they shook hands.

Rashid followed her up into the plane. He took the short sable jacket with the Missoni knit sleeves and cowl collar from over her arm and handed it to Daoud, who rushed to put it away. He adjusted the neckline of her very blousy and full, long-sleeved pale mauve silk shirt and caressed her bottom through the dove gray suede Calvin Klein trousers she wore.

"Do you realize this is the first time we have been apart since we met?"

He watched her shake her head, showing it had not gone unnoticed by her, and he knew instinctively that she was nervous about it. He wasn't. He was just relieved he had struck on a method of getting her safely out of the way until he and Brindley returned with that stupid signature. He could not afford one more slipup, and that was why he was accompanying Brindley to London. The consequences of Mirella's delay in completing the sale were now dire indeed. His partners were the sort of men who made offers you could not refuse or play with for too long, and the too-long had run out.

"Rashid, I want to—"

He stopped her from saying another word by covering her mouth with a kiss. Then he put her in her seat and strapped her in, saying, "Don't, I don't want to hear it. Wait until we meet again in two days' time. You talk too much anyway. I may like you better without a slave collar of pearls around your neck, but I love you more when you are wearing it and are my sexual slave, even if it's only a game for you."

Then he kissed her on the mouth again, moved his lips to her ear, and whispered, "The next time I take you, we will spend the night at Oda-Lala's. It will be your punishment, and our farewell." And he was gone.

An hour and forty minutes later, Daoud, looking dreadfully ill, told her to strap herself in, as they were about to buzz the village. The pilot warned her to hold on tight during the landing. It was a bumpy, primitive, and short private airstrip.

Fuad was moaning, and Mirella thought, "Some body-guards."

She looked out the window. It was black, black, black, and she hoped the pilot knew what he was doing because she could feel their descent. They were practically above the village when she saw the lights and he buzzed and banked steeply, climbed fast, and then straightened out. She looked at Daoud and Fuad and felt sorry for them. They didn't have Maxim for a father, or a hangar of biplanes for toys as she had had.

Everything was awfully black again, and then, off to the right in the nothingness below, suddenly, the airfield sprang into view. It looked from inside the plane like a lifeline from nowhere going nowhere.

Mirella barely felt the plane touch the ground, the landing was that smooth, but she felt every bump in the strip after that. They just made it to the end of the field with about ten feet to spare. The Gulfstream turned and taxied back slowly to a row of car headlights cutting across the field, obviously indicating that was where the plane was to stop. There was nothing else in sight.

Mirella unbuckled her seat belt and stood up. She took a mirror from her big, soft leather handbag, looked in it to make sure she looked as good as she might, and thought how wonderful it was going to be to have a couple of days in the country with Adam. He could not be any more surprised about her arrival in the village at the foot of Nemrut Dagi than she was.

Four hours before, when Brindley had arrived at Rashid's, she had been ready and waiting to sign the final documents of sale to the Turkish conglomerate. The talk with Rashid in the garden had made up her mind; she wanted to sell and get on with investigating the rest of the estate. So, when she and Rashid had greeted him, she had enthusiastically asked Rashid to call for some champagne so he could be the witness to her selling one of the largest private holdings in the world. She had hardly been able to believe it when Brindley had told her that she couldn't: there was a small technicality, a signature was missing, it had somehow been overlooked. He had already called London and he would fly out in the morning, get the paper signed, and return at once. She had thought it was a ploy to get her alone, so she had asked Rashid if he would excuse them. But it hadn't been necessary because

Brindley had shown her the empty line where the signature should have been.

Brindley had been so embarrassed, he had simply slumped into a chair, and Mirella had looked dreadfully dejected. It had been Rashid who had come to their rescue. He had had enough of them both vis-à-vis business, and had taken over. He had simply opened the champagne, had poured the three of them glasses, and had said, "You, Mirella, are going to climb a mountain. And Brindley and I are going to fly into London for a day's business, and that is that."

And that *was* that! And here she was waiting for the pilot to cut his engines. Fuad and Daoud struggled out of their chairs and stood waiting, pale and wobbly on their feet, behind her. At last the door opened and the stairs lowered. The pilot went down first and Mirella stood framed in the door opening by the light behind her, and looked out into the inky black night, the airstrip lights having been turned off. One by one the cars parked across the airfield turned their lights out. It seemed to her so quiet, black, lonely, and barren. She watched an old American army jeep from the Second World War, its top down, its headlights aimed straight at her, bump along up to the plane, swerve, and stop at the door.

He sat at the wheel dressed in an old pair of tan corduroy trousers, a white shirt, a red-and-white-checked cotton scarf tied John Wayne style, and a big, baggy, thick-knit navy blue cardigan with a hole in one of its elbows. And he had a big cigar in his mouth that had not been lit.

With him were half a dozen dark, thin, and wispy-looking children: the boys with closely shaved heads, and the girls with hair tied in pigtails and huge, brightly colored silky bows, wearing odd pieces of his clothing—his navy captain's cap, a worn, cracked, and weary-looking leather bombardier's jacket from the Second World War, a white silk scarf. The children were all piled into the backseat of the jeep, quiet, wide-eyed, and staring at her.

He pulled up the handbrake, then slumped slightly over the wheel, took the cigar out of his mouth, and handed it back over his shoulder to the children, who launched into a little skirmish as to who was going to be the keeper of the cigar. Then he straightened up and turned in his seat to face Mirella, who had not moved.

She watched him as he ran his fingers through his hair, then slowly rubbed his chin and looked at her pensively. He raised his foot up and casually placed it on the running board.

Mirella was taken by his rugged, handsome good looks and warmed as always by them. Finally their eyes met. He leaned on the wheel and then using it for leverage he swung, almost leaped, out of the seat and onto the field.

She walked down two of the stairs, stopped, and said, "Hello." It was all she could find to say.

Adam looked up and saw Daoud and Fuad waiting to follow her down from the plane. He put his hands on her waist and swung her off the step onto the field.

"Hello."

It wasn't cold but there was a slight chill in the air, and a light breeze. It rippled the silk of her blouse and showed off her breasts and their erect nipples. She saw them stir a hungry look in his eyes.

"Unfortunately," he said, "we have rather a large audience." He looked up, greeted Daoud and Fuad, and asked Daoud to throw down Mirella's jacket.

"I feel a bit awkward," she said, "intruding on you like this. It's not what you think, not what I had planned. This was Rashid's idea."

"Here, give me your arm," he said, helping her on with the sable-and-knit jacket.

She let the handbag slip from her shoulder onto the ground and gave him her other arm. He closed the bottom button at her waist, and adjusted it, letting his hands linger for a second on her hips. Then he fussed with the cowl around her neck, and quickly caressed her shoulders under the sable as he took his hands away.

"What had you planned?"

"Not to see you until I was ready to come to you for the rest of my life."

"And you're not quite ready."

"No. I've been single, independent, and alone my whole life. It's difficult for me to give that up, but it gets easier every time I see you."

"I can wait." And then the awkwardness evaporated and they both smiled. He bent down and picked up her bag and slipped it on her shoulder and said, "You look good enough to eat," then turned around and called to Fuad and Daoud, "Well, what are you waiting for, you two? We have a party to go to and a climb to make. Come on."

For the first time since she had met the two bodyguards, they produced huge, open, broad smiles, and hurried to Adam and slapped him on the back and shook hands with him, in spite of their pallor and queasiness. He greeted the pilot, who handed Adam an envelope, and announced that it was from Mr. Lala Mustafa, and was to be read at once. Adam did so under the jeep's headlights, Mirella watching. Suddenly everyone around the jeep and the plane seemed to be terribly happy; there was laughter and talking. Adam put his arm around Mirella's shoulder and walked her to the jeep, sat her down in the passenger's seat, and said, "I am going to give you the best time in your life. *Now* you will first begin to see the real Turkey, and the real Turkish people. We're going to a party."

Then he leaned across her and tooted the horn three times, signaling for the cars waiting in a line across the airfield to come and assist them. He quickly introduced the children to Mirella and left her with them while he went back to talk to the men who were removing the luggage, which consisted of a small Louis Vuitton duffel bag of Mirella's, six cases of Tuborg *bira* (beer), six cases of Turkish red wine, *kirmizi sarap* from Tekirdag, six cases of white *beyaz sarap* from the vineyards around Izmir, eighteen cases of Coke and Pepsi, a twenty-pound bag of coffee beans, a twenty-pound bag of tea, a small box, marked "For Adam Corey only," containing six ounces of cocaine, a bar of opium, and one pound of hashish, and twenty huge, round aluminum baking trays of Turkish sweets, all variations on the theme of baklava—paper-thin layers of phyllo pastry with ground nuts piled one upon the other and dripping in honey. All this was Rashid's contribution to the party.

The cavalcade of cars roared to the end of the runway and took a dirt track that skirted around the base of the mountain for about two miles, and then suddenly they were in the village. If it was a poor village—which it was, and very poor indeed—one would have never known it this night.

It was called Sari and was typical of the eastern provinces, whose harsh winters make for dire poverty. The peasants of this village, like so many others in the area, buried their houses halfway into the hillside. They had dug themselves dwelling places in the rock—one room, sometimes two. The façades were of stone pierced with small windows, wooden shutters, and doors as protection against the cold. They were weathered and worn gray and rough from the wind, the rain, the sand, and stones. Some of the houses extended out from the hill as much as ten feet, and had roofs of slate, or corrugated metal, held down with large stones. A few of the overhanging roofs were made of clay poured onto laths and thatched with straw.

Mirella saw the small houses, strung out one after another like so many beads on a string, against the hill. Their doors and shutters open, they twinkled in dim light from within. She thought them to be about twenty in number. In front there was a crude, deep terrace that followed the contour of the land, and set out on it was one low dining table approximately two hundred feet long. It was laden with food, wine, plates, glasses, candles in holders with glass chimneys, kerosene lamps of all sizes, shapes, and styles. The people sitting at the table on kilims, or cushions spread over the ground, were mostly men, from Sari, the host village, and the surrounding villages, some Turkish archaeologists, local dignitaries, army captains, local policemen.

The narrower terrace running parallel and below the dining terrace had a dozen open pits covered in hot coals scattered over the area, where whole roast lambs and baby goats and a calf were roasting. Row upon row of pigeons, chickens, and other local birds, pierced ten to a skewer, all shiny and golden brown, were being turned slowly round and round on crude but well-made spits by women dressed in their best *salvar*, long baggy bloomers in brightly colored prints, and bodices of darker fabric, pretty sleeveless vests, and headscarves.

Other women stood in groups, some constantly making fresh unleavened bread, and serving the table with it in relays, while others stood around and gossiped, laughed, and waited for their turn to help. Most of them wore shawls over their heads and, although the wearing of the veil was banished with Ataturk, in this part of Turkey they still drew a corner of it up over the lower part of their faces when a man passed them.

Adam helped Mirella out of the jeep and they walked together through the party, skirting the bonfires burning around the village for warmth and light. The women made the token gesture of covering their faces when Adam and Mirella passed them, but dropped it quickly and greeted him. Children followed them around as if he were the Pied Piper, and the man clasped his hand and spoke to him but never looked Mirella in the eye.

Some seats were found at the table for the new arrivals and they all sat down and began drinking and eating. Many of the villagers knew Daoud and Fuad and made the most of their arrival. Adam explained that in this part of Turkey the two were still known as heroes of the wrestling ring and they would be treated as such, bodyguards or not. This was going to give Mirella and him a chance to get rid of them for a while and go up the mountain alone.

And then they started drinking *Raki,* the eighty-seven-proof national alcoholic drink made from distilled grapes with aniseed, diluted in the glass with water. Mirella knew it was sure to blow her head off if she didn't defuse it with tidbits from the groaning platters of hot or cold hors d'oeuvres called *meze.*

For the Turkish people hospitality is a way of life and Mirella's enthusiasm for the food and Raki was all that was needed. The platters of rice, the tureens of hot soup, the mountains of fried eggplant, and bowls of thick yogurt, the small forests of delectable fresh salads, the meat and the birds, were all offered along with the sheep's eyes, the calves' brains, and the bulls' testicles.

"Now you know they really like you," said Adam as he speared a piece of the fried testicle and fed it to her, and ate a piece himself.

That brought on another wave of drinking and new dishes to be tasted. A human circle had started to form around Mirella and Adam soon after they learned she was fluent in their language and grew more dense as the evening wore on. He whispered not to tell that she had Turkish blood in her, or the questions would never stop. As it was, they wanted to know everything about her, but would never ask directly, since she was a woman and with Adam. And so they asked him to ask her and then listened to him phrase the question properly. If satisfied they nodded their approval and waited for her answers, if not they made him rephrase his question. It was all very amusing to Mirella on two counts. First, because she understood their questions but protocol would not allow her to answer directly. And then because Adam's Turkish, though good, was somewhat fractured, and hers was perfect, none of which made any difference to the procedure.

The questions were such curious ones. It was difficult to answer without laughing, which she would of course not do, and the sequence in which they were asked was very odd. How far had she come in the plane? Could her husband speak Turkish too? Was she an archaeologist like Adam? Could she ride a horse? How much did a gallon of gas cost in the U.S.A.? Drive a car? Did she live with her mother since she didn't have a television? Why hadn't she come to the mountain before? How long had it been since she had lost her husband? How much did a gallon of gas for an airplane cost? Both she and Adam were rescued from the questions when the violins, the tambourine, the *saz*, a sort of mandolin, and two singers with *kasic*—miniature cymbals, played something like a castanet, tied to their fingers—cleared a place in the center of the table, sat down, and began to perform.

The party would go on all night and through the next day for those who wanted to stay on. But not for those who wanted to make the climb. They drifted into the open houses and lay down on kilims covering the floors of beaten earth, and were covered with goat and sheep skins to keep them warm while they slept before their ascent.

Exactly at 2 A.M. Mirella, Adam, and half a dozen other people, including Fuad and Daoud, were awakened by women and served small cups of hot, sweet coffee. One of them dragged in a large cardboard box and emptied it onto the floor. Adam pulled off Mirella's boots and selected a pair of sturdy climbing shoes for her. They didn't fit. He tried another, and another, and had success.

"Do you have a scarf, or a warm hat? If not, we can fix you up with one."

He provided her with an old wide-brimmed Herbert Johnson brown felt. She looked if anything more beautiful and wore it with great panache, and struck a pose that set the women tittering. He swung her duffel bag over his shoulder, took her by the hand, and off they went.

The night was still crisp and clear, only now they could see the stars and a sliver-thin crescent moon they had missed before. Adam told her it would get colder as they climbed and how shrewd she was to be wearing the fur jacket, but when the sun was up she would roast on the mountain. She patted the duffel bag, indicating she had something cooler, and he squeezed her hand, as if to say, "Clever girl."

Waiting for them in the jeep were the two old friends with whom Adam always made the first climb of the season, and Adam's three dogs. They were handsome, gentle-looking beasts, somewhat smaller than sheep dogs, short-haired, with outsized jaws and powerful chests. Tan in coloring and dark brown on their ears and their muzzles, they looked not unlike the English mastiff. When Mirella made the comparison, snorts and laughter from the two men, Aslan and Demir, greeted it. They assured her the famed *kurt kopegi* were the cunningest wolf killer-dogs in the world.

"Sorry about this," interrupted Adam, "but you get to ride

with Aslan and the dogs in the backseat. I need Demir to ride shotgun, so to speak, to spot the large rocks and fallen boulders in the road while I concentrate on the driving. I always take the lead jeep. About the only advantage is that we create the dust, and there will be plenty of it. Otherwise prepare yourself for a rough ride up the mountain. It's the first of the season and we have to see what the winter wind, rain, ice, and snow have done to the road."

The two men leaped out of the jeep; the dogs, panting with excitement over their master's return, plunged over the sides at his command and jumped up and down, barking and slobbering for his attention. Adam patted them hard, pulled on their ears, bent down and boxed playfully with them for a minute or two, and then held them back with the help of Aslan and Demir while he settled Mirella in the back of the jeep, a dog next to her, and then Aslan, another dog stretched out happily under their feet.

The third dog bolted into the front seat and was ordered to the floor by Demir, who took his place. Adam changed his cardigan for a bombardier's jacket, tied his white silk scarf around his neck, put his captain's cap on, and slid into the driver's seat. He started the motor, switched on the head-lights, and then turned around in his seat and gave a huge Havana cigar each to Aslan and Demir. He caught the smile on Mirella's lips and asked, "Happy?"

"Very." Thinking to herself, he's not just Adam Corey, he's all the heroes I grew up with. I'm going to marry Adam Corey, and Clark Gable, and Dick Tracy, Errol Flynn, and Earnest Hemingway, and Terry and the Pirates. Is it possible I am Carole Lombard, or maybe even Ingrid Bergman? Is he my Indiana Jones, and am I going to the Temple of Doom, or are we just the Raiders of the Lost Ark? And she began to laugh.

"Oh, very," she repeated. "I think I'm Carole Lombard or maybe Ingrid Bergman."

He threw his head back and joined in her laughter. He flipped open the top of his Zippo lighter, struck it, reached out, and brought the flame close to her face. "You forgot Garbo and Gardner. It's going to be wonderful ending my days with the movie goddesses of my youth."

He held the flame to his cigar and she studied his handsome face while he turned the cigar slowly, lighting it evenly, and never taking his eyes from her. Demir demanded a light and that broke the spell between them. Three giggling women rushed up to the jeep and handed a bottle of Napoleon brandy to Demir and one to Aslan, while another busied herself with a blanket made of wild wolfskins, with which she covered Mirella's legs, tucking it around her hips. A clean white cotton cloth filled with hard biscuits, cookies, some goat cheese, and bread was tied into a bundle and slipped over Mirella's wrist.

Adam turned back in his seat, calling over his shoulder to Mirella, "Hang on to the rod on the side of the jeep there and the one on the back of my seat when the ride gets really rough, Mirella, and if that doesn't work there is always Aslan. Well, we're off."

He changed gears, sounded the horn three times as a signal to the others that he was ready to move, and was about to release the brake when a woman rushed up with a pillow for Mirella's bottom. That started a commotion in the backseat with the dogs, who were just about settled down. Finally they were on their way.

The revelers waved good-bye to the people in the four jeeps, two Land Rovers, an old Mercedes camper, and one old Studebaker that moved like a Sherman tank every time it shifted gears. Everyone was in high spirits as the convoy rolled off to cover the thirty-two-mile climb north to within two hundred fifty yards of the summit. All were looking forward to the stiff fifteen-minute climb thay had to make on foot from the terrace of the two-hundred-foot-high burial mound topping the cone-shaped pinnacle of Nemrut Dagi. And, of course, the reward was watching the sun rise over one of the great wonders of the world.

25

Getting up Nemrut Dagi in the jeep was difficult enough, but the stiff climb on foot for the last two hundred fifty yards up the mountainside to the peak was truly grueling. Mirella thought she would never make it. All that kept her going as her fellow climbers, one by one, surrendered to exhaustion was Adam and his promise that it was worth all the sweat and panting.

At last they were there, just as the sky began to turn from

night black to dawn gray. Revealed by the faint light were thirty-five-foot tall decapitated statues of Olympian gods seated on thrones, their once-lofty heads set upright on the ground and arranged around huge cones of small rocks. Their triumphant daily appearance dated back to fifty years before Christ was born.

It was still freezing cold and Mirella was hot and perspiring profusely from her exertions. Panting and exhausted, she sat on a boulder and tried to catch her breath and make her heart calm down. But to be calm was difficult while the statues, brooding over the ruins, their enormous heads weighing tons, strewn all around the terraces like so many balls of fluff, were coming to life in the light of the slowly rising sun.

Adam, just as much out of breath as Mirella, sat down next to her and stopped her from removing her hat. "No, it's too cold. Keep it on. Here, let me help you."

He removed the red-and-white-checked cotton scarf he wore around his neck and used it as a handkerchief, dabbing the beads of perspiration from her face and neck. Aslan, Demir, and the three dogs arrived on the summit and came to them. The two men slumped down onto the ground, their backs against the boulders where Mirella and Adam sat. No one spoke. Silently they produced the bottles of brandy from inside their jackets, pulled the corks, took deep swallows, and passed the bottles up to their companions.

It was light enough now for them to switch off their flashlights. They saw the outlines of several other people as they arrived and sank to the ground about a hundred yards from them. Adam ordered the dogs, who had been scrambling around nearby, to come to him and sit. They did immediately, then lay down and became very still and quiet. Mirella slipped down off the boulder and Adam had her hoist herself up and sit between his legs. He slipped his arms around her waist and pulled her to him, encompassing her. It felt good to be there, with his warmth against her back, his thighs and legs pushed against hers, to be cuddled on top of the world. She relaxed against him, the back of her head resting on his shoulder, and they waited for the sun to rise just a little further.

The gray turned to a pearly color, and then over the edge of the mountain a streak of yellow appeared and rose higher in the sky by inches, at the same time rolling across the stony ground before them. The sunlight climbed up the giant heads and colossal headless throned figures, until everything was radiant in the yellow light of day. The sky turned blue and was slashed in pink and yellow. The two colors, reflections of the sun, danced together across the summit and turned the stones to flesh, until for a moment Mirella thought she heard them call out. The cry was eerie, and soon changed into a howl that made her cringe in Adam's arms, and spurred the dogs to sit up, nervous and on guard. The sun was rising so fast now that one minute it was a nearly complete disc climbing over the edge of the summit, and the next it was a ball of fire that turned the dawn into day, and changed the flesh-colored giant gods and kings back to stone idols, their cry and howl becoming again no more than the wind.

The stupendous spectacle more than compensated for the discomfort of the ascent and the extremes of heat and cold Mirella endured on the mountain that morning. By nine o'clock it had been so hot on the barren sanctuary, she had changed her trousers for a thin cotton wraparound Ralph Lauren skirt, and her silk shirt for a big, loose Miyake white cotton top she had packed in the duffel bag Adam had lugged up the mountain for her. Mirella had the luxury of seeing King Antiochus of Commagene's incomparable tomb sanctuary with Adam and only four other people, all of them passionately interested in the site.

Now she sat with the dogs around her, resting under a large white cotton umbrella wedged between two boulders that had been found in the primitive hut used by archaeologists and other guests who wanted to sleep overnight at the peak. Adam had disappeared with two of the people, a French and a German archaeologist, having advised her to try to take a nap, but that was impossible.

They took an alfresco meal of wine, cheese, fruit, delicious *dolma*—vine leaves stuffed with rice and herbs that had been cooked in oil—and the bread and biscuits that had been tied in a bundle that Mirella had never relinquished on the difficult climb. Then all sat around and listened to Aslan and Demir tell tales about Nasreddin Hoca, the fourteenth-century sage and humorist, whose so-called sayings and doings left them all laughing until tears had to be wiped away from eyes made red from brandy and wine.

It was two in the afternoon when Daoud, Fuad, and some of the climbers finally reached the peak and joined them. A half hour later Mirella found herself edging down Nemrut

Dagi with Adam and the three dogs. He flung her duffel bag into the jeep, untied the arms of the leather jacket he had tied around his waist, threw that in as well, and looked around. Except for a few climbers struggling high above them there was no one in sight. He walked over to Mirella, who was leaning against the jeep panting for breath.

"At last," he said. "Alone at last."

He took her in his arms, wiped the beads of sweat from her face with the palm of his hand, and pushed the hair off her forehead, tilted her head back, and slowly lowered his lips to hers. He grazed them ever so gently back and forth, back and forth, until he felt her breathing normally and her body grow calm and relaxed in his arms. Then he put his lips to hers and pressed a kiss upon her that revived and nourished her. Their lips parted and their tongues seemed to probe each other's very heart, until Mirella thought she was floating as on a magic carpet somewhere beyond the mountain on which they stood.

Adam again took the checked handkerchief from his pocket and wiped her face and neck with it, unbuttoned her blouse and opened it sufficiently to put his hand under it. He dabbed her chest and shoulders, then licked the moisture from between her breasts, put his handkerchief away, and raised her naked breasts in the large open palms of his hands, and, absorbing their weight, he joggled them lightly and ran his fingers over the nipples in a circle half a dozen times.

"I have wanted to do this ever since you stepped off that plane yesterday," he said in a voice hungry with lust. "I love your breasts, the feel of them in my hands. Very often I dream of them in my mouth; I fantasize about the length of your nipples and the nectar I'll suck from them."

Mirella's chest flushed pink and she closed her eyes and came, contracting her vaginal muscles all the more to sense the excitement of the warm rush his hands and his words filled her with. Adam buttoned her blouse and took her in his arms again.

"Come on," he said. "Let's go before someone catches us. I am going to take you down off this mountain and show you the plain below."

He put her in the front seat, then reached down under the backseat and pulled out a large bowl and dropped it on the ground. The dogs ran to it, sat, and waited while Adam unhooked a large container strapped to the side of the jeep and filled their bowl with water. He soaked his handkerchief and handed it to Mirella, who squeezed it out over her face, then tied it over her hair to cool her off. They drank hot sweet mint tea from a large thermos under the driver's seat, and once they were refreshed, they packed up and took off down the arid and treeless mountain through the oppressive heat.

Adam tried to distract Mirella from her obvious fear of the descent with legends of Nemrut Dagi. The way she clung on for dear life until her knuckles were white, and closed her eyes at every turn, trying not to look over the edge of the dirt road, gave her away. When, around a blind curve, they were confronted by an abandoned vintage Land Rover with a damaged axle and had to inch their way past it, he stopped talking, using all his concentration to avoid getting them killed, Mirella distracted herself by reviewing what she had heard about the party and Adam from Aslan.

It appeared that Adam Corey was the best known and loved Westerner in eastern Turkey. The party he gave was only one of many ways that he repaid the poor peasants from the Anatolian plain as far as the borders of Russia, Iraq, and Iran for their archaeological help and support. The eastern Turks were desperately poor but proud, and so it was always with the greatest subtlety that he helped them.

Sari had electricity, piped-in water from a distant well, and an airfield thanks to Adam, who claimed he needed them for his work. Every item of food for the party was deliberately overbought, so that the village was fed in time of need from the leftover provisions. The jeeps were left there in the care of Aslan and Demir, with the pretense that they were needed to keep a check on the airfield. He had assured Mirella eastern Turkey was in these ways Adam Corey's kingdom.

And when Mirella and Adam were off the mountain and speeding across the countryside through the sparse villages, the waves and smiles of aristocratically boned and milky-brown-skinned men and women confirmed Aslan's words. Adam continuously surprised her with statements like, "Turn around; look back. Do you see those two hills? Well, you, Mirella, own those two hills and everything to the right as far as you can see."

They were driving toward the Mediterranean and were not far from the Syrian border. The hillsides were ablaze with wild flowers, the sun was clouded over, and the temperature had dropped and was perfect for a hot but comfortable spring day. They were heading toward the Euphrates and a town on its left bank called Birecik. Adam took side roads lined with fruit orchards in full bloom—apples, peaches, plums—and they passed groves of pistachio and hazel trees laden with blossoms, and he would say things like, "And those are yours, and those are yours. We are driving through areas that were the most interesting neo-Hittite states before they fell in 717 B.C. Now look at the odometer. Everything we ride through for the next three miles still belongs to you, Mirella—has belonged to your family for five, six hundred years so far as we know."

Adam drove off the secondary road they were traveling on, and onto a dirt track, then left that, and cut across the fields. He stopped the jeep abruptly, and they looked from the edge of a steep hill down into a green and fertile valley whose long grassy hills were dotted with thousands of red poppies and sparsely covered with scented pines and silvery olive trees. Flowing through this paradise hidden in such an arid and harsh landscape was the Euphrates, blue and fresh in the afternoon light as it wound its way in search of the sea.

"And this is mine?" she asked.

"And this, too, is yours. Look, over there, to the left. About ten miles from here is where I found the Oujie journals. And look down over there to the right."

Mirella saw hidden in the tall grass and wild flowers, on the bank of the river, the top of a large, low black bedouin tent.

"No, that's not yours, that's mine. I'm one of your land poachers! Come on, let's go down."

He signaled and the dogs jumped out of the jeep and disappeared in the grass. He tooted his horn to announce his arrival to his servants, who, he told her, expected him with guests.

"I never dreamed that you would be my guest. You can't begin to know how happy it makes me that you're here," he said, leaning over and kissing her with great tenderness.

He cleared his throat, as if trying to cover up the emotion he knew was in his voice, then put the jeep in gear and drove very slowly halfway down the hill through the tall grass and wild flowers. Here they left the jeep and walked hand in hand down the slope together toward the tent. Mirella slipped and slid for a short distance down the steep incline. Adam, never letting go of her hand, went down with her, and they disappeared in the long grass.

"You can trust me to be clumsy in paradise," Mirella said. She felt embarrassed and nervous, not so much because she slipped, but because she wanted to be special and perfect for Adam . . . because she didn't want anything to go wrong for them this time . . . because she loved him so much, with a kind of love that was new to her and so frightening that it made her tremble and become awkward. Her feelings had nothing to do with insecurity. Quite the contrary: she had never felt so secure in her life. It had to do with love, real and masterful love. Love that makes you want to follow, climb mountains. Love that makes you feel humble.

Mirella's wraparound skirt had flown open and she lay among the wild flowers and tall grasses, naked to just above her navel.

"Are you all right?" Adam asked, smiling at her, and at the same time stopping her from closing her skirt.

She nodded and he leaned over her and untied the cords that closed it on her hip. He caressed her now exposed and naked belly and her hips, ran his hands down her thigh and then caressed her mound and the black pubic hair that covered it. He ran his fingers up and down the slit between her legs lovingly, while he bent down and kissed her passionately on the belly, moving his head from side to side. Mirella closed her eyes and sighed and wriggled under his kiss, his hands. Then he closed the skirt and tied it.

"If we hurry," he said, as he rose and helped her to her feet, "we can have a swim in the river and then dry off on the grass in the sun."

They were greeted by Turhan, who, he explained to Mirella, was his houseman and had been with him ever since Adam was eighteen years old, and had traveled everywhere with him.

"Oh, but you've met," Adam teased her. "He was one of the men who saved you the other day in the bazaar."

Then he introduced her to Muhsine, a very pretty Turkish girl dressed in a salvar. It did not go unnoticed by Mirella that the girl's clothes were of much finer quality than the other women she had seen. When Adam explained that Muhsine belonged to the household on the Bosporus she deduced that this was one of the women whom Adam kept for work and his own personal pleasure as well. He confirmed it when he told her that she need never be bashful in front of Muhsine or Turhan because they were his own very personal servants who took care of his every need, and from now on would serve her as well.

They walked straight down to the riverbank after Adam ordered Turhan to place a kilim on the slope of the hill facing the sun, and tossed him a small packet, saying, "You know what I like."

They stood on the bank, Adam with his arm around Mirella, and watched the water flowing by below, listened to the birds singing, and were mesmerized by the tranquility of the place. A flock of birds on the other side of the river flew past them downstream.

"Look, Mirella," Adam said, "there are the bald ibis. Although they're practically extinct, you see them often here because they nest only in Morocco or Birecik. They return to the Euphrates in the middle of February every year."

They watched them disappear from view. Adam turned and faced Mirella. She caressed his cheek with her hand and then stepped back from him and bent down to untie and take off her shoes. He followed suit and was much quicker than she was. He stood up and untied her skirt just as she was straightening up and slid it from around her. Next he raised her blouse over her head and she stood before him naked and beautiful. She reached out and stripped him of his shirt while he loosened and slipped out of his trousers. Then they walked into each other's arms.

His body scent and the feel of his flesh pressed against hers inflamed her. She could feel her lust all but crying out for him. They kissed deeply and passionately and he picked her up and carried her in his arms down several stairs that had been cut into the riverbank, and to the river's edge, while she busied herself with kissing his neck and chest, biting his nipples.

When they came out of the water Muhsine was waiting on the bank for them with handwoven robes made of soft, fluffy cotton. Adam took Mirella by the hand and hurried her along up the slope of the hill, Muhsine following behind. They found several antique kilims still bright in color, woven in bold geometric patterns, lying on the grass where the embankment leveled out in a natural terrace. Two large, soft pillows, covered in tan linen and embroidered all over with small pomegranates the color of fresh raspberries, were laid on them. A bowl filled with fresh fruit and a large rock of agate hollowed out and holding a crystal decanter in the shape of a claret bottle waited for them. Turhan stood by bearing a silver tray with two large Baccarat wine glasses and the empty bottle of Château Lafite 1883 he had decanted the wine from, and waited for Adam to check the bottle and look at the cork. He did so quickly, raised an eyebrow in approval, and Turhan placed the tray down and left.

Adam stripped off his wet robe and handed it to Muhsine, who then helped Mirella off with hers. Mirella and Adam sat down close to each other facing the sun. Mirella closed her eyes and let the heat of the afternoon sun graze her skin. It felt good after the cold swim. Adam poured them wine. He held his glass up to the sun and marveled at the color. Mirella found the bouquet admirable. They touched the rim of their glasses together. "To you, to the gods, and to the good life, always and forever," said Adam.

They tasted the wine, and Mirella exclaimed that the wine was more like a nectar that the gods they toasted might drink. Adam drank again.

"Ever since that night we met," he said, "and I fell in love with you, there has never been a thing I have done, a plan I have made, a moment of joy, pain, or ecstasy that I've not shared in my imagination with you. I would dine with old friends and think, 'Mirella would like them.' During nights of erotic ecstasy, I fantasized that you were the woman with me. I would arrange a dinner party and imagine that you would surprise me and arrive as a guest. I order wine for this trip and include the finest, a rare and ancient vintage such as this"— and he held the glass again up to the light—"not because I thought you would be here and that we would drink it together, but because to see it here waiting for you would remind me that you were on your way to me. I'm never unhappy or in despair that we're not together, because I know when it is right, it is right, and we will be. I have been faithful. I've never doubted you. I've waited for you, and have cherished the memory of making love to you. Now you are here, and I am very happy."

They finished their wine, and then lay down together, Mirella's head resting on his chest, his arm under her back and draped over her hip, caressing it, his other arm thrown back above his head. He could sense her heart beating against him. She kissed him on the nipple closest to her mouth and stroked him lovingly.

"Adam, I didn't know there was love like this, that there were men like you. You once said to me that when two people find real love nothing is ever the same. You are so right. Everything I do in my life now, with or without you, leaves me fulfilled in a new and different way. It's your belief in me, your love for me, that allows me to be as you desire me. I love you, Adam."

They stroked and fondled each other until they fell asleep under the waning sun.

26

It was Mirella who woke first and found Muhsine sitting on the grass close to the edge of the carpets watching them. Mirella untangled herself from Adam's arms without waking him and sat up. Muhsine draped a silk embroidered shawl around Mirella's nakedness and whispered something to her, then poured her a glass of wine. The two women talked in whispers, and by the time Adam woke they were in a deep discussion, with Muhsine sitting on her haunches behind Mirella putting the last touches to Mirella's hair. Adam sat up and gently pushed away the large, round silver-backed mirror Mirella was holding up in front of her face. He was obviously delighted with what he saw.

With the help of Muhsine, Mirella had skillfully made up her face and she looked tantalizingly exotic and beautiful. Adam recognized the pair of large gold hoops in Mirella's ears as the pair he had bought Muhsine himself; he remembered the Mayan fertility god around Mirella's neck from New York. The scene delighted him and he kissed Mirella and smiled at Muhsine, and developed an immediate erection.

He poured himself a glass of wine and Muhsine wrapped a huge embroidered shawl around him, then held a mirror for him with a silver straw and long, thin lines of cocaine prepared on it. Afterward she offered it to Mirella, and then went back to finishing off Mirella's hair, but not before she lit a long cigarette laced with the best Lebanese hashish and handed it to Adam.

"You look very, very beautiful, Mirella," Adam said. He sat back down next to her and raised her hand, kissing her fingers. He took one in his mouth and sucked on it. The simple gesture sent a chill of excitement right through her.

"And my hair?" she asked. "Muhsine is a very clever girl, don't you think?"

"Yes, very clever. You have yet to know how clever. And your hair is wonderful, extremely glamorous." He looked up at Muhsine and said, "Poppies, some pretty poppies pinned in her hair. I would like that, Muhsine." She ran out at once to pick some.

It was seven o'clock in the evening and still light and warm. Adam took the hand mirror away from Mirella, stood up, and pulled her up onto her feet, and they walked through the long grass and wild flowers, where they dropped their shawls and reveled in the natural lust their kisses and caresses were generating.

Adam was bending over, picking a bouquet of wild flowers for her, when she leaned over him and caressed his back with her breasts, following each caress with kisses from an open mouth that licked and nibbled as she continued down his back.

"I'm marking you, claiming you for mine, with all my lust and love," she said, in a voice husky with passion, while caressing his handsome round, muscular ass.

Lost in her desire for him she pushed the cheeks apart, the better to see his testicles, and slid her tongue down the furrow. The sight of the large handsome balls hanging in their loose sac spurred her on. She dropped to her knees and continued licking and probing with her tongue until she had filled her mouth full with his testicles, rolled them around with her tongue, and expelled and sucked them in again, and again and again.

She continued lost in the raunchiness of her act until Adam turned and faced her. She cupped his balls, wet and shining with her saliva, in one hand and put the other as much around his stiff pulsating cock as she could, and marveling at the beauty of it, the magnificence of the huge pink knob, she pointed the tip of her tongue and licked the eye of his penis, the very hole that would pour forth his sperm, inserted it as far as she could and moved it round and round. Her lips opened and with her tongue still kissing, her mouth began kissing as well, covering the knob slowly, she licked and sucked, always taking in a little more, until she had him wholly thrust deep in her throat.

The pleasure Adam derived from seeing her as well as

feeling her make love to him with her mouth was intense. Only action could communicate it to her, and so he stopped fondling her breasts and gently pushed her down on her back, turned around, straddled her, and then went down on his knees and with his rampant cock and balls hanging over her mouth and his face between her legs he proceeded to show her.

His tongue, his fingers, his lips, and his mouth devoured her, sucked out orgasms and sensations that left her unable to satisfy her own desire to take the initiative and give him pleasure. And he, fired with uncontrolled lust, wanted to fuck her, fill her every orifice with his cock and mark *her*, fill *her*, with his lust and love for the rest of their life.

He turned around and faced her, took her in his arms and kissed her, filled her mouth with some of the come their sexual passion had created. Each saw in the other's eyes that this was the right time and the right place to seal their love for life.

He laid her back down on the grass, raised her legs high up and wide apart, resting them on his shoulders, and with his fingers he gently separated her silky wet vaginal lips, held them open, and once the head of his cock stretched them wide enough to receive him, he pressed his hands on her waist, lowered his face over hers, and kissed her with tenderness and love, as he thrust forcefully but slowly into her cunt, savoring every morsel of it.

Once inside he rested there for a few seconds, too overcome by the thrill of being inside her, of the tightness of their fit, of feeling the very opening of her cervix with the eye of his cock, her cunt muscles making love to his penis with every minute movement.

Mirella whispered huskily of the pleasure she felt and was unable to stop calling out from the sheer joy of his fucking. He drove them both to a point of erotic madness before they came in a crescendo of the most blissful orgasm either one had ever known. Here was their real beginning.

The tent was a large and fairly low rambling one, whose floor was covered in fine antique silk carpets. In the center was a huge, square four-poster bed, its posts tall tapering narwhal tusks, the cover white ermine, and the pillows encased in embroidered covers from Morocco and Iraq.

Draped casually across the tops of the tusks was an extremely fine mosquito netting of transparent silk, which served as a canopy and curtains and was tied back onto the tusks with large tassels of white wool and silver.

There were half a dozen fine old brass Turkish braziers with finials of the crescent and the star, used to keep the tent warm. Tall, handsome mother-of-pearl and ivory Damascus mirrors on stands were placed around the tent. Trestle tables covered with embroidered cloths were standing against the black cloth walls and served for dining, a desk, a buffet. There were marvelous chairs and Koran stands of ivory from India and trunks inlaid with silver and gold from Iran, and large, fat cushions covered in handwoven brocades from Tashkent scattered everywhere for guests to sit on. It was lit with candles in desert lanterns hanging, standing, or sitting on tables everywhere.

Adam walked Mirella around the room so she could see it all and stopped at one of the tables that had been laid with food for them for the evening. Here they stood for a few minutes in silence feeding each other some of the delicacies laid out for them and drinking wine from each other's glasses.

The atmosphere was overwhelmingly original and erotic, and there was a kind of thrilling creativity and passion about it. Its sensual intimacy seemed doubly powerful because of Adam himself—his rugged Midwestern manliness was a potent contrast.

She wanted to say something about it and he saw it in her eyes.

"No, tell me later," he said, and walked her to the ermine-covered bed, where they found the bright red poppies Muhsine had picked for her hair. The fragile, blood-red poppies against the soft white ermine were another erotic symbol for them to play with. Adam tied a few in her hair, Mirella made a chain of them, which she hung around his neck and arranged on his chest. They lay down across the sensuous fur and enjoyed the sensation of it teasing their skin.

It was here that they made love that grew more free, more erotic with every orgasm they achieved. As if their love and their own natural riggishness were not enough, there were other things to stimulate them. Adam massaged every inch of her body in a perfume he poured from a bottle next to his bed. A rich resonance of floral harmony escaped from the bottle and settled like an invisible mist over Adam and Mirella. At once their emotions were swayed and all the erotica that had disappeared for them after every orgasm was quickly resuscitated.

The subtle and delicate blend of mimosa, iris, and lily, with the rich tone of rose and jasmine and fruity touches of tuberose and spicy angelica and clove, impregnated her skin and clung to her, releasing its spell all through the night.

He whispered, "*Barynia* . . . Barynia. It's Russian for 'Princess' and that's what I'll call you. My Barynia. It suits you because it reminds me of your romantic soul and your golden personality, your erotic depths, when you lose yourself in our reverie."

They used tricks and treats of the harem, some of which she knew about from Rashid, which Adam had been taught and practiced, enjoyed, and performed masterfully. And again and again their lust was pushed to further and further extremes, all the more exhilarating because it was based on a foundation of love.

Mirella and Adam sat on a pair of ivory chairs set on a kilim close to the tent and had their breakfast of bread, honey, and yogurt, fresh fruit and cheese, and hot black coffee, off an Islamic silver tray inlaid with gold, placed on a portable stand of musharabiya. Muhsine had magically reappeared and was serving them. A pair of bald ibis flew past on the other side of the river.

"Is my whole life going to be as wonderful as this?" Mirella asked.

Adam smiled, and said, "Oh, I do hope so, always different, always interesting. I guess it will be up to us now what we do with it," taking note that she had said "my," not "our."

"Adam, I have to tell you something. I've fallen in love with Turkey. I feel like such a fool for having rejected it without a thought. Even now I find it hard to believe that so much of this country belongs to me. I still keep asking myself how it all could have accumulated and stayed hidden."

"It's all far more simple than you think, Mirella. You have only to understand one thing, which with your background and upbringing is almost impossible to fathom. The Ottoman Jew, and Jewish Ottoman money. The wealthy Jewish people today everywhere in the world except in Russia are no longer persecuted on the level they have been since time immemorial. They, their money, their cleverness, their intellectual abilities, and their power are not just tolerated and used as they once were but have become acceptable, even sought after. But, remember, I am talking about Jewish people, not Zionists and Israelis. Although they are Jewish, they are quite a different thing.

"Try to remember that the Jews became Ottoman subjects by their own choice because they received greater tolerance and greater opportunity from the Ottoman government. In the case of your family they used those things admirably and acquired not only great wealth but power as well. But the Ottomans had something called the *surgun,* which was a method of shifting not just individuals but whole populations, because they believed that the interests of the empire would be served better by transporting them from place to place. It was not just for the Jews, by the way, it was a law for all peoples, for the empire. Now, of course, when populations shifted, the most prosperous were the most desirable because they would serve the interests of the new community best. *Voilà,*" he said with a flip of a hand. "The solution: hide the wealth, distribute it to custodians who are loyal, grow richer, more powerful, and maintain a low profile until such time as the policies change, governments have less power, and the world is free. In that way they had a better chance of remaining settled in one place and prospering. And your ancestors were damned clever—they used the women as added protection. An unheard-of thing to do in those days. So, without going into the remarkable and thrilling stories set out in the journals of how they did it and where their treasures and properties were and are, there is your answer. It's safe now, the world is a different place, the rules have changed, and the Oujie inheritance is free to come out of the closet."

Mirella started to laugh. "Oh," she said, "you're wonderful. Do you always do that—simplify everything, to the point of understanding?"

"I certainly do. Life is far less complicated than you think, Mirella."

He stood up and went to her, bent down and kissed her lovingly on the lips, then on the top of her head. She reached up in search of his hand and he gave it to her. The warmth flowed from him like a current through her. Mirella had a moment of realization: she had never known how unhappy she was without love—until she had it. He squeezed her hand reassuringly and went back to his chair.

"Mirella, I'm sending you back to Istanbul with Daoud and Fuad as soon as Turhan returns."

"I had forgotten all about them. They must be frantic looking for me. If Rash—"

"Stop! I took care of everything. They're in Sari and think we've spent the night on the mountain with the other archaeologists; they expect us down this afternoon. I'm afraid I had to trick them. Aslan and Demir helped. When Fuad and Daoud couldn't find us anywhere around the sepulcher, they told them we went down and back to Sari. Of course, after they rested, Daoud and Fuad followed. They had no sooner discovered we were not in Sari than Aslan appeared, saying I sent him down to say they had made a mistake and we were staying the night on the Nemrut Dagi, but that they needn't make the climb again. That was the last thing they wanted to do and so they are happily awaiting our return. I hated to do such a sneaky thing but the alternative of them coming here with us was impossible."

"I think Rashid is coming to Sari for me," she said.

"I would rather he didn't, Mirella. He thanked me in his letter for saving you, and reminded me that if you save a life then you are responsible for that person, and asked me to show you Nemrut Dagi and take care of you until his return. And that I intend to do. But my way, not his."

He reached across the tray and picked her hand up again and played with her fingers.

"We both have things to do, Mirella. I cannot abandon my guests for much longer, and the sooner you return to Istanbul and finish sorting yourself out the better for us all. Agreed?"

"Agreed," she answered.

"Good," he said, looking very happy with himself. "Have you all your things stuffed in that duffel bag of yours? Are you ready to leave? We'll go directly to the airfield from here. Daoud and Fuad will meet us there. And, oh, I'm sending Turhan along with you as well until Rashid returns."

"You're getting just as bad as Rashid. I'll never quite be able to accept all this protective custody. But never mind, I'm too happy to think about that, and yes, I am all ready except my boots. We left them in Sari."

"Turhan will bring them."

"Oh, and I have to return all this lovely jewelry Muhsine lent me so that I would be more tantalizing for you."

"I don't think she will take it back, but I agree you must try."

Mirella stood up and brushed some crumbs from her suede trousers, and as she passed Adam on her way into the tent to look for Muhsine, he reached out and touched the silk of her blouse. She stepped in closer to him and he ran his hands over her breasts.

"I like this blouse," he said. And ran the palm of his hand down the suede of her trousers, stroked her crotch and thighs beneath, then gave her a playful smack on her bottom and told her to hurry back.

Quite happy, he sat looking across the river and listening to the two women inside discuss the return of the jewelry. He made a small wager with himself that Mirella would win, and she did. She came out and sat on Adam's lap, her head resting on his shoulder, just listening to the birds and gazing across the river at the wild flowers and the old, twisted trees. She was not there more than two minutes when they heard the jeep's horn that signaled Turhan's return.

Adam was rocking her gently on his lap. He raised her hand and kissed her fingers one by one.

"Remember when we met at Mishimo's," he said, "and the rest of that wonderful, crazy afternoon when we made love to each other for the first time?" She nodded and he went on. "I knew I loved you then as I would never love any other woman." Mirella kissed him tenderly on his cheek. "The morning before we met for lunch, I had gone out shopping to buy something, a token of my love for you, which because of both our stupidities I never gave you. After we arrived here yesterday, I sent Turhan back to the airfield and had my pilot fly him to Istanbul to bring it back for you. I want you to have it now. I have wanted you to wear it for so long."

They kissed and then sat silently holding each other while Adam kept rocking her gently, until Turhan arrived five minutes later. They greeted him sitting the way they were, and Turhan handed over the parcel.

Mirella knew by the shape of the green velvet box what it was, but the name on it, Harry Winston, did give her a surprise. Her hands were trembling so much, Adam had to open it for her, but not before he made her close her eyes while he slipped the flawless, thirty-two-carat, cushion-cut diamond on the ring finger of her left hand.

He grazed her lips with his, back and forth a few times, and then placed a trembling, passionate, tender kiss upon them. Still holding her hand he turned it over and kissed the palm, righted it again and said, "Now you can open your eyes."

He watched Mirella go visibly pale as she held up her hand to view the ring, and he laughed.

"Well, what do you think?" he asked.

Mirella let out a deep sigh, the color began to come back into her face. The diamond sparkled in the sunlight. She was mesmerized by the jewel.

"I think you must be very wealthy to buy me something like this."

He laughed and, smiling at her, said, "Yes, very."

"And love me very much," she added, tears of joy in her eyes.

"Yes, very much."

27

Mirella wondered how long she could keep this over-whelming love for Adam a secret, and decided that she couldn't keep it to herself for a minute! But that was on the plane coming from eastern Turkey. Now, standing in front of the statue of Apollo in Rashid's front hall, her relationship with Rashid suddenly seemed alive again, and she knew she would have to keep her secret just a little bit longer until she and he separated. It was clear to her there was nothing to do but wait a while and see what happened, and at the same time, search for ways to end the relationship.

As chance would have it, she didn't have long to wait before things did begin to happen, things that snapped her back to some of the realities of her life that the Oujie legacy, Rashid, and falling in love with Adam had made her leave on the back burner.

Mirella was exhausted, she had had hardly any sleep at all for the last forty-eight hours. And all that climbing and lovemaking had quite worn her out. And so, after requesting a pot of Earl Grey tea from the maid, she all but dragged herself up the long, curving staircase to her room, and was mesmerized once again by the gem Adam had placed on her finger. Her eyes kept following it as her hand on the rail kept pulling her up the stairs. The first thing she would do after her bath was to call Deena and tell her about Adam, the ring, and their coming marriage.

Once in the bath the perfume of the oil Adam had massaged into her skin seemed to rise from every pore. She placed the back of her hand under her nose and sniffed, ran her hand and arm back and forth and sniffed deeply again. She closed her eyes and allowed herself the luxury of reliving her night with Adam once more, and made up her mind never to use any other perfume than the one he'd given her.

Mirella drank her tea while in the bath and was more or less revived. She chose a white satin nightgown, whose halter bodice was of ecru-colored lace. Standing in front of the mirror, she adjusted her breasts so that the bare skin between was visible down to her waist and thought of how sweet Muhsine had been when she worked at making Mirella as seductive as possible for Adam. There were lessons there for Mirella that she would never forget: the generosity of real love, which Muhsine, who was obviously an ex-mistress of Adam's, certainly had for him. The lack of malice for the new woman in his life was certainly another. How rewarding it must be to serve someone you loved was the best lesson of all.

She picked up some newspapers, a cablegram, and her address book, and climbed into bed holding them. The first thing she did was open the cable. With it placed carefully on her lap, she began to laugh. Just threw her head back and laughed and laughed. Was this what life was really like? Feast or famine. Reward upon reward draping themselves around her.

"When the gods are good to you, one must tell the other," she thought.

She picked up the telephone and called Roland Culver, at the U.N. She had no idea what she was going to say to Roland and was surprised when after the usual greetings she heard herself tell him, "I'm very touched by your cable of congratulation on my appointment as head of translations and the foreign publications department, Roland. As you know, it's the job I've always wanted, have worked for since my days at Vassar. I proudly accept, but can only do so conditionally, for one year, to see if I can fit it in with the new life-style I seem to be creating. Can we talk further about it when I return in a few days—a week at the latest?" He agreed and they chatted amiably before parting.

Mirella tried Deena's telephone number half a dozen times and it was constantly busy. She called her father and spoke with him. Maxim was Maxim at his very best. They talked about Turkey and how much she liked it. She went into great detail about the sunrise over Nemrut Dagi. They discussed how her feelings had changed about her inheritance, and she gossiped with him, telling the stories she had heard about her great-grandmother and her grandmother. They enjoyed themselves thoroughly. And when she told him about her new position at the U.N., she was quite overwhelmed by the pride in his voice, and the generous praise with which he applauded her. Finally she spoke of Adam, and Maxim, understanding Mirella as he did, knew at once that they would marry, and consented to keep her secret for the time being. When Mirella said, "I'm too happy to talk to Mother, but is she all right?" he answered, "Never mind her, just be happy and leave your mother to me."

She put the telephone down, happier than she had ever remembered being in her whole life. Deena. She dialed the New York number again, and this time it rang.

They talked and talked, about everything that had happened in the last few days and the joy Deena felt for Mirella and her happiness was boundless. The two friends laughed and cried and philosophized on love, and rationalized about their past relationships, good and bad, and made plans and dropped plans and made more plans and dropped those, and then cried with the joy they felt, not the least of which was that they had each other to share such momentous occasions as love, success, and—as Deena had succinctly pointed out— "just plain winning."

"The ring, the ring, you forgot to tell me about the ring," Deena cried, and they began all over again.

Mirella had no sooner put the telephone down than she was on it again, this time to Moses. She tried to contain herself, behave in a much more controlled and adult manner, and she kept getting responses from Moses like, "You don't say. You don't say. Well, that's good. Well, that's bad. Well, that's better. Congratulations"—that was on her new appointment at the U.N.—and when she told him she was going to marry Adam Corey he said, "Well, that's the best news of all."

She was about to call her brother when she caught sight of a photograph on the front page of the *International Herald Tribune*, and suddenly her spirits just plummeted. It was a photograph of Paul Prescott and his very pregnant wife and two children. The caption gave Mirella an overwhelming sense of loss. It announced Paul's transfer to the Paris office of his firm as executive vice-president.

Mirella picked up the paper. She was unable to take her eyes off the nearly grown children, and was transfixed by his pretty wife's belly swollen with child. The loss she felt so acutely was not of Paul, but of the years she had missed with Adam, the children she had never carried. She put her finger over the swollen belly in the picture and took in the smile on Paul's face, and tears came to her eyes when she thought of his deceit, the children he denied her, and the pain of settling for what you can get—in this case, a married man.

The telephone next to her bed rang and jostled Mirella out of her moment of misery. It was Deena. She had forgotten to ask if she could be Mirella's maid of honor. Their laughter at this question overlapped precisely. When Mirella said, "Oh, I'm so happy you called back. You've shaken me out of a moment of real despair. I've just seen the photograph in the *International Trib* of Paul with his family. The biggest thing in the picture is his wife's pregnancy."

"Just think, shmuck. And don't look back," Deena chipped in. "That's my advice to you," and then she hung up.

Mirella took Deena's advice, and that was the end of Paul Prescott.

Her spirits lifted and she went back to the telephone. She rang through to her brother but he wasn't in.

Mirella went out onto the balcony, leaned against the balustrade, and took in deep breaths of the sweet-scented air from the garden below. It was dusk and she listened to the evening song of the birds in the long shadows dappling the lawns.

The lights in Rashid's study were switched on and fretted the lawn with shadows the shape of the French windows. Rashid must have come home. Her immediate reaction was one of delight, followed by surprise that she should miss that beautiful, fascinating cad as much as she did. She hurried into the bedroom and slipped into the satin dressing gown appliquéd in large ecru lace flowers that matched her night-gown. She checked her hair in the mirror and quickly touched up her makeup, all the while questioning why she should call him a cad when he had been nothing but wonderful to her since the very first day she met him. Yet there was always that something she felt he was hiding from her. It was more than the darkest side of his nature, the evil that Adam had warned her about, but she was never quite sure what.

She decided to surprise him, slip out of the house and into the garden and walk in on him through the French doors. She passed a maid on the stairs who giggled when she heard what Mirella planned to do, then went out through the dining room French window very quietly and along the terrace, keeping her back close to the wall of the house. The French windows to his study were open and she could hear him talking on the telephone, and thought to wait until he finished his conversation and then present herself. Her appearance would be a total surprise since he must have been told on his return that she was upstairs asleep.

What she now overheard between Rashid and someone who could only have been a business associate delivered her a severe blow. She caught a brief exchange that seemed to confirm that he had been planning to get his hands on her estate. It focused suddenly her sense that he had always been more interested in possessing that than even her. She realized that Rashid was one of the dubious men who had been exploiting her legacy for so many years, and that this was what Adam hinted at. It was her estate that Rashid *really* wanted!

Mirella's first concern was to get back up to her bedroom without his discovering her presence on the terrace. Once there, she removed her dressing gown and slipped into bed. She pulled the mauve silk sheet over her, sat back among the pillows, and thought about what she had heard.

Strangely enough, its first impact past, this revelation did not upset her greatly and she felt very much in control of the situation. She had after all not signed the papers as yet.

The three discoveries—her appointment, Paul, and now Rashid—instead of devastating Mirella managed to snap her back to herself, not her old self, but a new Mirella included in the old, that successful, powerful woman at the top of her career. At that moment all that seemed to be real and relevant to her was Adam Corey, his words and his actions. Paul and Rashid had certainly left their marks on her, but she could see clearly now that only Adam Corey's love had been truthful and real. What a fool she had been about him at the first!

Her instinct was to call Adam, but she knew she had no way of reaching him until he returned late tomorrow to his house on the Bosporus. And then she decided that was a good thing. She would handle this properly, and on her own.

In spite of Rashid's deceit in keeping it from her that he would become the conglomerate's chairman of the board of directors and the major stockholder, with sixty-two percent of all the shares, and his virtually holding her a prisoner in a golden cage until she signed, she had in all honesty to admit that he had done her no harm. They were not in love with each other and they both knew that. She had not even fantasized once about a permanency to their relationship or pretended it was anything other than it was. And so, sitting there in bed in his house, it was not difficult to accept this news and deal with it on a strictly impersonal basis.

She quietly went over in her mind every detail she could remember about the sale, the advantages and disadvantages. After an hour she had made up her mind she would sign, and never let Rashid know she had overheard his conversation. She would play his game out with him to the very end and decide then if she would tell him she knew his real motives in their affair before she sold off her companies to him.

He entered her room quietly and, when he saw that she was awake, he smiled. The man was a magician, he used his looks and his charisma like the greatest conjurer of all time.

He was just as the world said he was, she thought—a lady-killer. It was as much a part of him as his skin, his flesh, the blood that ran through his veins. Maybe, she realized, she would feel deeply about him always, for being just what he was, and for making her one of his playmates.

Before he even reached the bed and sat down on the edge, his sensuality, his gaiety, his animal lust was changing the atmosphere in the room. He had been carrying a large dress box, a shoe box, and several other smaller boxes and dropped them on the bed.

"Hello there," he said, touching her lips with his fingers, then running one down from under her chin to her waist. He sensed the shiver instigated by his touch go through her and he stood up and took off his jacket, threw it across the end of the bed, and undid his tie with one hand, while throwing the sheet off her with the other, and sat down again.

"You're a surprise. I expected to pick you up in Sari in the morning. Did you have a good time?"

"Marvelous."

"I thought you might."

There was a strange note of insinuation in his voice and she chose to ignore it, but did wonder if he might just know something about her and Adam. She decided to ignore that as well.

"Where is Brindley?" she asked. "Back with you here in Istanbul, I hope, with that document in proper order?"

"Yes, all is done. Brindley's at the Hilton changing. I have to pick him up shortly. Since we never expected you to be here, I have invited him and a couple of foreign ambassadors to dinner and an evening at Oda-Lala's. Don't you ever do what you're told, and stay where you're put? Now you will have to dine alone, because I can't possibly change plans for this evening, and it would be too embarrassing to bring you to Oda's because you will be meeting these ambassadors and their wives at the ball at the Dolmabahçe Palace tomorrow evening."

"I hope you're not going to corrupt my solicitor," she said. "But then, I don't think I have to worry too much about that, since you haven't managed to break me yet." Mirella made an attempt to rise from the bed.

Rashid began to laugh and stopped her with his hands on her shoulders and none too gently pushed her back against the pillows, at the same time pulling the halter apart at the back of her neck. The tiny lace-covered buttons flew out and she held the two strips of lace together at the front of her throat before they fell and exposed her breasts.

"Now, what was that for?" she asked.

"Now, what do you think that was for, Mirella? Because you excite me, turn me on to you. Because I like not only playing erotically with you, but the challenge you present."

He bent down and kissed the hands on her throat and picked them up. He caught the lusty look in her eyes he had managed to instill, and he smiled.

"A lovely, absolutely remarkable jewel," he said, looking at the diamond sparkling on her finger. "I don't remember seeing this before. Something you found on Nemrut Dagi?"

"No, on Harry Winston. You know there are no diamonds on Nemrut Dagi, just ancient stones."

He laughed and watched the lace slipping down off her breasts. "Shall I pursue this or do you wish to remain secretive and devious?"

"Oh, I think secretive and devious, like you. At least until after I complete my sale, and we part."

His answer to this was to bend his head down and to kiss her lips, which he nibbled and sucked gently at, until they gave in and parted, until he had them reciprocating. His mouth moved away to her nipples, which he tortured with his lips and his teeth. He moved back to her mouth, but before he did, he reveled in the sight of her unable to hold back from him. He was so fired by the passion he brought out in her that, quick as whip, he tore open her nightgown from the waist to the hem. Then sitting where he was he bent again and kissed her deeply, passionately, with his mouth searching hers while his fingers found her clitoris and used it to bring her to half a dozen orgasms so powerful she writhed and wriggled as if commanded to do it by them.

He stopped. He held her firmly by the chin and watched her breathing heavily and panting, and angry fire in her eyes.

"I find you irresistible."

"We both know how we find each other, Rashid. And we both know that it's over, or let me at least say the interlude is at its end, the relationship never resolved. You have led me to the most wonderful awakening and I will be grateful to you always, but, Rashid, my friend, now I want love—something we both know you're not interested in."

Mirella saw in Rashid's face that he was momentarily checked by her rebuff. He strongly assured her that she would change her mind once he had her in bed tonight, after his return from Oda-Lala's, and she was swimming in pools of sex with him. He was only pacified when she pretended that might be the case.

"Rashid, I know what you're like when you are set free at Oda's. Not tonight. Have your evening there and let me sleep, I'm exhausted from the climb. Tomorrow, Rashid. Tomorrow I'll have Brindley bring the papers here and I'll sign. We'll go to the ball, and celebrate afterward, the way you really want to, by your pushing me through every erotic door into depravity."

Mirella felt she might never forget his look at that moment of extreme pleasure and the glint of sensuous sexual evil in his eyes.

The next evening Brindley and Rashid were waiting for her in the hall. They were standing and talking in front of the

Apollo with glasses of champagne in their hands. The look on their faces as she started down the stairs told her what she wanted to know. She looked magnificent.

She had taken great care with her cosmetics and her hair, which was worn soft and loose on her shoulders, was wide and full but swept off her face. She wore a strapless Galanos gown, made solidly of white crystal bugle beads, that was narrow and straight. The tips of her white high-heeled sandals showed in the front, but the skirt of the gown tapered off longer in the back into a short train that followed seductively behind her. She wore long white kidskin gloves that covered her arms to halfway between her elbow and her shoulder, and she wore her pearl collar with the bumblebee turned to one side in front, together with all the other priceless pearls Rashid had given her and the necklaces with Oujie seals on their diamond chains, the diamond sunburst pinned over her heart.

The men gallantly toasted her as the most beautiful woman who would attend the ball. She insisted they go into the library at once as she was anxious to sign the documents. This done, their glasses were refilled and Mirella said, "And now I would like to correct you. I am going to be the most beautiful and the wealthiest woman at the ball."

They drank to that and Mirella turned to Rashid and with the most dazzling and sweet smile, slipping her arm through his, she asked, "Are you happy tonight, Rashid?"

"Yes, very," he answered. "Even my ancestors are happy tonight. It's a night when all wrongs have been righted. The beginning of a new era for you, but maybe not only for you, for me too."

She turned to Brindley and said, "Brindley, I know this is hard to believe, but in the process of trying to understand and make sure I did the best I could with all those advisors and experts, would you believe it, I have forgotten how much we sold out for. What was it now?"

The look on Rashid's face was priceless. The shock of her caring so little about the amount showed plainly on him. She thought for a moment she had even provoked him enough to say something. But he didn't. It was fascinating to see him control himself, the anger die away and the suave charm reappear.

"Seven hundred and eighty million dollars."

"My goodness, I bet someone all but pawned his soul to

raise that kind of cash. How sad to want something that much. Well, I hope he thinks it was worth it, whoever *he* is."

Rashid's and Mirella's eyes met, and they looked coldly at each other. The cold, slowly changed to sadness, dissolved into acceptance, and she raised her glass to Rashid, and said with a tremor in her voice, "To friendship and admiration, which is just another kind of love." And then she smiled and made him her friend for life.

28

The Dolmabahçe Palace was all aglitter, and so were the guests at the ball. It had once been the principal residence for the last of the later sultans, and from the moment Mirella saw it she could not but think of the stories she had heard about Roxelana, her great-grandmother, whom she owed so much to for transforming her life with the legacy. Whether it was frivolous or not, she kept feeling the presence of Roxelana so strongly as she walked from the car down the red carpet to the entrance of the palace that she knew it was time to do something about it.

Just steps before the receiving line, Mirella, who was walking between Rashid and Brindley, stopped, adjusted the white silk chiffon cape trimmed in a double row of white fox she was wearing, and said to Rashid, "Please, Rashid, I would like to be announced as Mirella Roxelana Oujie Wingfield, and please don't tell me it's dangerous and to keep a low profile. We both know that's not necessary anymore, don't we?" The look of surprise on Rashid's face soon changed to admiration.

"You are a constant wonder to me, Mirella. Of course, if that's what you wish."

"I do, since I intend to change my name immediately to include my benefactress. And, Rashid, I want you to tell the truth to anyone who asks about who I am and how I happen to be here."

After dinner Rashid claimed her for the first dance and he said, "Well, now you are the most beautiful, the wealthiest, and the most talked-about woman at the ball," and he laughed. He waltzed her around the ballroom and said, "Just look at them. No one can take his eyes off you. There is no turning back for you, Mirella." He pulled her tighter to him.

"And there will be no turning back for you at Oda-Lala's either," he whispered in her ear. "I will master you tonight. I promise I will enslave you sexually to me for the remainder of your life, and mark you, brand you, in the same way I have Humayun."

He felt her stiffen in his arms, and he smiled and said, "Yes, it is exciting, isn't it?"

Adam's words of warning about the evil in Rashid rang loud in her ears. They finished their dance and Mirella managed to catch Brindley's eye while Rashid was preoccupied with talking to several men. He seemed to understand at once that she needed him because he asked Rashid if he could whisk her away for a few minutes to meet some English friends. Alone on the terrace facing the Bosporus, Brindley asked, "Is everything all right, Mirella?"

"Well, not quite, Brindley. I'm afraid I have a few things to confess to you." She put him completely in the picture.

He asked only one question. "Don't you think this would be the opportune moment to make a getaway?"

"Yes, I do."

"Good. There is only one thing to be done—get you to Adam. You will be safe there, and together you can confront Rashid with the excellent news of your coming marriage. Because, you see, Mirella, the chap is really a most honorable fellow. He has only one problem: he is a sexual madman, and I think you have gone just a little too far playing this game with him. Leave it to me."

"Oh, Brindley, you are wonderful."

"Yes, I know. Now come along. I must say one thing for you, Mirella—you do bring the James Bond out in me."

They had started for the ballroom when Mirella stopped Brindley and asked him to wait while she removed her gloves. She opened her evening bag and found the diamond ring Adam had given her and slipped it on her finger.

"It was too big to get my glove over," she explained, "and I have no intention of going back in there without wearing it. Isn't it a beauty, Brindley?"

"You know, Mirella, there is a part of you that likes to live dangerously. You are determined to play this game as far as you can go, aren't you?"

"Yes, but, Brindley, I don't want to get hurt."

"You won't get hurt as long as you don't go back to Oda-Lala's. Rashid will settle for friendship when he sees he has no other option. He likes you too much to lose you. There is a little bit of Jung in me as well as James Bond. You see before you a faintly unusual English gentleman."

They were both laughing when they went back into the ballroom. Brindley found his friend from the British Embassy, and after introducing Mirella to him, he said, "Now, Bunny, you keep dancing with Mirella until I get back. Don't let her out of your arms."

Rashid cut in on Bunny twice and reminded her that they would leave in about an hour's time, and told her that he had thoughts only for the evening ahead. The third time he cut in on Bunny, it was almost as if he sensed some fear in her, because he said, "Whatever you may think, Mirella, about our interlude, you have always to remember one thing—I never expected to feel as deeply for you as I do. We have tonight. Tomorrow I promise I will let you go, and no matter what happens, my feelings will never be less for you than they are now."

He raised her hand to his lips and kissed it while they danced, and Mirella could actually feel herself slipping under his spell. He saw it, too, and he smiled. The lordly Bunny cut back in and they waltzed away.

At last Brindley returned, and he and Mirella danced through the crowded ballroom and onto the terrace. He took her by the hand and they walked quickly through the garden to the quay where several boats were tied up. They found the one belonging to a diplomat from the English legation and Brindley handed the boatman a handwritten note. The next thing she knew the boat was pulling away from the Dolmabahçe Palace, and heading up the Bosporus at top speed, toward the Peramabahçe Palace, Adam's home.

"Brindley," she shouted above the noise of the powerful motor and the sound of the boat cutting and bouncing through the water, "you are the most romantic Englishman I have ever met."

"I don't doubt it," he shouted back. "Otherwise how would I have gone through what I had to to find you, Mirella Roxelana Oujie Wingfield?" He removed his jacket and put it over her shoulders.

The white marble palace shone in the moonlight but was otherwise dark. They tied up alongside the Peramabahçe's dock and rang a bell announcing their arrival. Dim lights were turned on, lighting their way through the garden, and slowly a trail of lighted windows brought the house to life, the servants to the door, and Adam to the top of the two-story flight of stairs. He looked down at Mirella and Brindley, and bade them welcome by saying, "Well, Mirella, it's taken you long enough to get here. But welcome home," and started down the stairs.

Mirella blurted out, "I've been such a fool, about the inheritance, and then about you in New York, and again at the bazaar, and about Rashid. You warned me and warned me, and still I was stupid and a damned fool. It's over now, though. I worked it all out and I've left him. I gave him the only thing he wanted: my companies. Well, that's not quite true. There were two things he wanted, and the other thing he never got. He never succeeded in mastering me. I led him on until he believed I was ready, and it was to be tonight at Oda-Lala's, before we went our separate ways tomorrow. He had been remarkably good to me, so I never quite believed you about him. And then I saw in a glint in his eye the tenth of everything you said about Rashid and women, and I knew I had played his game long enough, almost too long. And so Brindley and I ran away from the ball, and here I am making a fool of myself all over again."

"Thanks, Brindley," Adam said.

The two men shook hands. Adam carefully removed Brindley's jacket from Mirella's shoulders. He put his arm around her.

"Come on," he said. "I think we all need a drink. Mirella, you look ravishing. You must have knocked them out at the ball."

She stopped and said, "A ravishing fool, that's what I've turned out to be. That's how you see me, isn't it?"

"No, Mirella, you're no fool. You just act like a foolish woman sometimes."

"Is that a sexist remark?"

"No, I don't think so. Does it matter if it is?"

"Not a damn. Oh, Adam, I love you, and I am so happy I'm here."

They had a drink in the great white marble hall that was three stories high and whose long staircase led on into a gallery that overlooked the hall. The huge glass windows opposite the staircase faced the Bosporus, now invisible in the empty blackness outside. A large antique Arab fountain played in the middle of the hall, and the palm and date trees, the mimosa, and flowering magnolia trees of great age and size made Mirella think she had indeed run away into an oasis.

The drink calmed them, and Brindley acquainted Adam with all that had gone on at the ball, especially about Mirella insisting she be announced as Mirella Roxelana Oujie Wingfield. Adam, who was sitting next to Mirella, leaned over and kissed her for that.

"Well, you did say it was safe for the Oujies to emerge from the closet, didn't you?"

"Yes, I did."

"So, now that we are out, out we will stay. I may have sold off the companies to Rashid and his associates—Oh, God, it really annoys me that he couldn't have been honest with me and told me that's what he wanted from me."

"That's not Rashid's way. But the game, the chase, the deviousness are all part of the wheeling and dealing. They're the way the businessman in the East likes to work."

"You think I should have figured that out for myself, don't you?"

"I don't think it matters. What matters is that when you did find out, you used your head, not your heart or any twisted emotions, to deal with it. You did what was best for the estate and for you, and I'm sure you made a good deal. Look, Mirella, for what it is worth, I personally think you did very well to sell off the shipping, rail, oil, and gas interests, and the large international construction companies to Rashid and his dummy company. I had no idea Rashid was involved with the purchase, but I will tell you one thing about him I know to be true: He will be the right man to make the most of it for himself and for his country."

"Oh, you have no idea how much better that makes me feel," she said. "You see, I figured with the money from the sale well invested—which I understand is another problem, but never mind—I would be able to do marvelous things with the remainder of the estate. All the land, buildings, museums, antiquities, and archaeological sites I could give in trust to the country as long as it remains a democracy, and on the condition that they are administered by the trustees: me, you—that is, if you consent to be a trustee, Brindley—and several Turkish and American museum directors."

Brindley plumed inwardly like a peacock. Adam had a look of astonishment on his face.

Mirella frowned and said, "Please, if I got it wrong, don't tell me."

"Got it wrong?" Adam explained. "You couldn't have got it more right. I can see that beneath all that glitter beats the heart of a sometimes foolish, stubborn female who in the end gets it all right."

Adam filled their glasses again and suggested that the right thing for Brindley to do was to go back to the ball at once, find Rashid, and tell him where Mirella was and that she would call him in the morning.

Adam, barefooted and wearing only a pair of silk pajamas bottoms, his arm around Mirella, walked with Brindley to the entrance to the garden. He had called for Turhan, whom he ordered to follow Brindley back to the ball, and stay with him until Brindley had safely delivered the message. They were just shaking hands and saying good-bye when the front doorbell rang. It could only be one person—they all knew that. Adam sent Turhan to answer the door, and he returned with Mirella's white fox-trimmed cape over his arm and a note for Adam. It drew a burst of laughter from Adam that caused him to pass it to Mirella.

> *Instead of pistols at dawn, how about inviting me for breakfast at eleven?*
>
> *Rashid*

She was astonished, and she, too, gave in to laughter and passed the note to Brindley, who smiled and said, "The clever bastard. He knew about you two all along. How? How could he have possibly known?"

"Because he is a devious devil. And as you rightly say, a clever bastard, as well. Good night, Brindley." And after seeing him to the garden door, Adam returned to a still-smiling Mirella.

"Come on, let's go to bed and make love. That's all I've been thinking about since you arrived."

In their lovemaking no part of them was left unabsorbed and unused. The lust and love they craved from each other was all encompassing. Mirella confessed to Adam that she had wanted him from the moment he was introduced to her in New York, and she knew that she had felt the touch of a love that would be forever when they met again at Princess Eirene's picnic, and had accepted it within herself under the soft warm rain.

They were lying in his bed, on their sides facing each other, kissing, making love, he moving slowly and luxuriously in and out of her, while their hands explored and caressed and she whispered in a passionate voice, "Your love woke me up to a part of myself that had been anesthetized; that part of myself that craved love and caring, adventure, a husband and a family, the desire to share. I have never felt such a sense of belonging as I do when we are reveling in our lust and passion."

On a warm June morning, Mirella stood in an Yves Saint Laurent long-sleeved white lace gown, its neckline high in the front and low to the waist in the back. It was worn over a flesh-colored body stocking. A hundred yards of the finest silk chiffon, as transparent as window glass, were draped over her shoulders and tied behind, high up on her neck, and trailed down covering her bare back and fell on the church floor into a train twenty-seven feet long. She wore a wide-brimmed, nearly transparent white horsehair hat with a cluster of fresh magnolias on the side of the crown.

The pews of the white clapboard church were all filled to capacity, and it seemed as if the entire little New England town was bursting with people who flew in from all over the world to watch the Boston society wedding of the year.

Mirella listened to her father standing in the pulpit reading the lesson, saw Lili, who was holding back the vapors admirably as she sat between Marcus Weinbaum and Lawrence. She had never seen Lili looking lovelier, and never known her to be more kind and, yes, even loving to Mirella.

Rashid held her arm. It was he who would accompany her down the aisle. She gave his arm a squeeze and smiled at him in gratitude. He had planned the wedding with Lili; it was his gift to Adam and Mirella.

Adam and his best man, Brindley, were standing calmly at the altar waiting for her to walk down the aisle. They were all there . . . the men who loved her, her good friends, her close colleagues . . . all there to share her happiness. Adam, her one real love, might have come late for her, near her middle age, but he *did* come.

Mirella turned around to look at Moses and Muhsine, who

were fussing with her train; at Deena, who was waiting in front of Rashid and Mirella to walk down the aisle and take her place next to Brindley.

Deena turned around and whispered, "You're almost there, Mirr."

Rashid patted Mirella's hand and said, "You may be marrying Adam, but remember, my dear, both of us will have walked down the aisle with you. You have won us both for life."

"I can't imagine how," she whispered.

"By alluring us with your sensuous soul, like Shakespeare's Cleopatra," he whispered back. "Even 'the holy priests bless her when she is riggish.' That's how."

JEALOUSIES

By Justine Harlowe
bestselling author of MEMORY AND DESIRE

There is nothing as strong
as the love between two sisters ...

Nor anything so corrosive
as when that love turns to jealousy.

A glittering novel of the simmering antagonism between two beautiful half-sisters, as different in nature as they are in looks—both in love with the same man. From the Outback of Australia to the couture salons of Paris, journey with Shannon and Kerry Faloon as they sample all that life has to offer and vie for the true love of one man.

JEALOUSIES

Coming in March '86 from Bantam Books.

Now you can read all of these tantalizing books by a world famous
author who has chosen to remain
Anonymous...

☐	25963	WOMAN	$3.50
☐	22658	TWO	$3.50
☐	25049	HER	$2.95
☐	25954	HIM	$3.50
☐	25971	ME	$3.50
☐	25958	THEM	$3.50
☐	25952	US	$3.50

Color Wonderful

JoAnne Nicholson and
Judy Lewis-Crum

A revolutionary new system of finding your best colors,
by the founders of Color 1 Associates.

- How to create an individual color profile and coordinate wardrobe colors with those of your skin, hair, eyes, and lips.

- How to choose makeup, jewelry and accessories that compliment your coloring.

- How to salvage the "wrong" color choices in your closet by using the right color accents.

- How color can be used as a tool in your quest for career or personal success . . .

And much, much more in this lavishly illustrated trade format paperback.

COLOR WONDERFUL

Available wherever Bantam Books are sold or use this handy coupon for ordering: